MY TRUE NATURE
Volume One

The Angel and the Iceberg

MICHAEL JONES

Published in 2019 by FeedARead.com Publishing

A CIP catalogue record for this title is available from the British Library.

About the author

There are at least 15,000 Michael Joneses world-wide with an email account. The author is one of them.
mjmytruenature@gmail.com

Thanks to

Céline, Brigitte, Émilie, Hilary, Ingrid, Janine, Margaret, Marie-Françoise, Nathalie, Paola, Paul, Simon, Sophie, and Rachel.

Saturday 6th November 1976

I'm nineteen now, and I'm useless in love. I fall hopelessly in love with people, and then they leave me. And then it's always the same; after their sudden departure, or when it's all falling apart, or after I can't take any more, I become completely obsessed with my ex-love. Then my sleep disappears. Actually, I can nearly always drop off to sleep, but then wake a few hours later, obsessing. So I write and write and write, and sometimes I draw and paint. I've got notebooks and notebooks full of my writing and pictures.

I began writing my life story when I had just turned sixteen. That's when my first sleeplessness started. I must have looked awful, as a result of lack of sleep and being so upset. I confided in Madame, and she suggested that whenever I couldn't sleep, I should write about my life. So, while everyone else was fast asleep, I began to write my story. And as the nights wore on, I gradually calmed down, and could sleep better and eat properly.

A very bad outbreak of sleeplessness started about nine months ago; when I felt that I couldn't get any lower. I'd get into bed, drink a large glass of rum, followed by four big spoonsful of cough medicine, and then start writing. Then I'd finally fall asleep, only to wake at four o'clock in the morning.

Nowadays, I don't drink rum and cough linctus, but wake at three, with no possibility of going back to sleep again.

And now I'm here, on the edge of the Big Forest. I love it by day. But by night it returns to the creatures who own it, and the weird people who wander around there, doing their strange things. It fills me with terror. I feel a lot of real terror these days. I think that soon I won't be able to control it. And, if I'm honest, I'm beginning to lose control of myself.

And it's so cold and damp in this caravan, even though it's still only November.

And I wish I could lock the door, but She won't let me have a key.

I feel so unloved.

Here is what I wrote when I was sixteen. If I'm found dead in the morning, at least people who read it will understand me a little bit.

o   o   o   o   o   o   o   o   o   o   o   o   o

I was born in Malaya. When my father was a young man, he worked for a rubber company out there. Now he owns several rubber companies, and much more besides, and is a very wealthy man. I have no memory of living in Malaya. I have never seen any photos of my parents together. When I was five, I found a very large sheet of paper, and spent days drawing *Malaya*. I drew rubber trees, and a huge house with a garden and a swimming pool. There was a dog and a cat and, for some reason, a small green snake. My mother and father were standing in front of the house. But it was not my mother who I drew holding me in her arms; it was my father. I kept the paper hidden behind the cupboard in my bedroom. I thought my mother wouldn't find it, because she never cleaned there.

Every evening after tea, my mother told me to go upstairs and keep myself busy for an hour, before she came and washed my face and, put me to bed. On some evenings, I'd give myself a wash and put myself to bed. But in that hour before bedtime, I'd pull the paper out from its hiding place. I'd add a small detail: something I'd been thinking about during the day. Perhaps a parrot in a tree, or a boat in the distance, loaded with rubber welly boots, or tyres, or rubber bands to take to England. Once, after I had just started school, I saw a large box full of rubber bands on my teacher's desk. I told her, 'My daddy made those.'
The teacher asked my mother, 'Does your husband work in a rubber factory?'
Mummy replied, rather aggressively, 'No. But I believe he owns quite a few.'
After that, my mother told me not to talk to anybody in school about my father.

But one day, while I was at school, my mother gave my bedroom a big clean. That evening, when I looked for my picture, it had gone, and I never saw it again. We never talked about it. I knew not to. The picture had taken me hours and hours to complete, but I found that I had memorised every part of it: the people, the animals, the trees and the buildings. As I lay in bed and thought about my lost picture, I imagined different ways that my mother might have reacted, like scenes in a film. In some scenes, she examined the drawing, and smiled at all the little details. Then she carefully rolled it up, and stored it somewhere safe. I knew this was unlikely. In another version, she didn't even look at what was on the paper, but muttered to herself, screwed the paper up and dumped it in the bin. But the reality, I was sure, was that she examined it closely, tore up the paper in a rage, and burnt the pieces on the fire.

That image came into my mind every night before I went to sleep. For a week after that, as soon as I got into bed, I said my usual prayer: 'Dear God, bless me, bless all the babies that cry, bless Mummy, and please bless Daddy in Malaya.' But I added at the end, 'And ask Mummy to come and kiss me goodnight, because I think she has forgotten.'

Antennae

But she hadn't forgotten. I knew that she was downstairs, sitting in a silent rage. Raging at my father, at herself, and at me. How did I know? From the age of three, I had grown a pair of antennae. Around this time, I started to collect snails. I liked the dry ones best. At first they seemed dead, but I discovered that if I licked my finger and gently touched the dry flat surface of their bodies, the snail would slowly move. First a slit would gradually open up, and then the snail would slowly pop out. If you touched his antennae, he would quickly pull them back in again, and he would go back into his shell. Then, no matter how much you stroked him, he wouldn't come out again. But if you gently moved towards him, then he felt safe. His antennae were sensing what was happening. Beetles and all the insects do that. And cats and dogs, and deer, and horses do it. They can sense you. They can sense how you feel, from the way that you move. And babies do it, and little girls like me, who were only three, do it.

I could sense what Mummy was feeling. I had to. If Mummy was baking, then it was safe to go in the kitchen and offer to help, and chat and ask questions. If she was cooking Sunday lunch, and humming or whistling and singing, then it was safe to be with her. But if she was cooking in silence, then it was best to stay away, until I was called. Then we ate in silence. If she came to my bedroom, and tucked me in, and gave me a kiss goodnight, then I knew I had been good. Sometimes, in the evenings, I'd listen outside the kitchen door, and try to decide if it was safe to knock, or just creep silently upstairs.

Sometimes, on freezing nights, there would be a hot water bottle already in my bed. On others, there would be nothing. So I supposed that if there was no hot water bottle, then I must have done something naughty. This was confusing, because I always did my best to be good.

The first thing I remember
But let's go back to when I was three years old. Mummy brought me back from Malaya, and we lived in a small house in Valley Lane. We had a vase that Mummy kept on the mantelpiece. I loved that vase: for its yellowness, and a pattern of blue flowers, with red dots in the middle of each one. One day we had a visitor, whose loud knock on the front door woke me from my afternoon nap. I must have crept into the dining room, because I was on my own, and I saw the vase was on the table, full of flowers. I climbed onto a chair and onto the table, to get a closer look at the flowers. I must have picked the vase up, because it rolled onto the floor and smashed. In my haste to get down and not be found out, I fell off the chair and cracked my chin on the floor.

At least that's the story that my mother told, when anyone asked her how I had got the scar on my chin. But it was what happened in the bathroom that was my first real memory. I was screaming and covered in blood. Mummy was wrapped in a big

8

bath towel, and she rushed with me into the bathroom, to wash my face.

There was a man sitting in the bath. He said, 'What's going on here then?'

I stopped screaming and asked him, 'Are you Daddy?'

But he wasn't Daddy. He was Uncle Eric, and he had come to stay with us for a few days. He was kind, and put me on his knee, while Mummy cooked the dinner and sang.

My first painting

Just after my fourth birthday, we moved away from Valley Lane. It was warm in Uncle Eric's car, and the smell of petrol made me feel sick. But I was careful not to vomit, or cause a fuss. We went to live in a village in Northumberland. There was a very busy road outside our house, with lorries that rushed straight on to Scotland. We had a big back garden. It was very overgrown, with a lawn full of long grass, and flowerbeds full of weeds. There was an old vegetable patch, with a few vegetables here and there, that were either rotten or gone to seed. There was an old greenhouse at the bottom of the garden. My mother warned me that, under no circumstances, was I to go in there.

A high wooden fence separated our garden from our neighbours' back garden. I soon discovered a large hole in the bottom of the fence, next to the greenhouse. If I bent down, almost lying on my side, I could see into our neighbours' garden.

One day, a football came sailing over the fence, and landed in our garden. I pushed it back through the hole, and a boy shouted, 'Thank you!' It was Trevor, and for the rest of the afternoon he kept trying to kick the ball over, so I could pass it back through our hole.

Our neighbours, Mr and Mrs Eades, had three children. Violet and Robin were teenagers who were both away at school. Trevor was their seven year-old, and became my first friend. It seemed to me that the greatest joy in my life was when Trevor came to the hole, and told me all about the new and interesting things that he had discovered that day.

Trevor once told me that a boy from the village had run into the road without looking, and had been run over by a lorry, and killed. The dead boy's mother and father owned the shop where Mummy did her shopping. I didn't like to look at them. They would say 'hello,' and I would be frightened, and they'd laugh at me. I couldn't understand how they could still laugh, when their son had been killed. Then Trevor told me he had made a mistake, and it was the people at the Post Office who had lost their son. He said that when a child died, people said he had been *lost.* This frightened me, because Mummy once told me, when we were in a big shop, 'Stay near me or you might get lost.'

Once, when Uncle Eric came to stay, he brought me a paint set. It was a long thin white metal case, with a lid. Inside there were six small dried blocks of paint, and a thin paintbrush. He showed me how to use them. We spread newspaper on the kitchen table. He filled a jam jar with water and dipped the brush in, then carefully twirled the wet brush around on the blue block. Then he put a blob of dark blue colour in the middle of a sheet of Mummy's best writing paper. He dipped his brush into the water again, and gently spread the dark blue across the page, until it was the faintest of faintest blues; almost like grey. 'That, my dear,' he said in a quiet voice, 'is *watercolour.* Colour with water, water with colour.'
I was mesmerised: by the water, the brush and the colours. It was magic.
'Now Pippa,' he asked me. 'What's your favourite colour? What colour do you like best?'
There was a horse in the field at the end of the village, and I thought his coat to be the most beautiful colour in the world. So without hesitation I replied, 'Brown.'
Uncle Eric looked puzzled, 'Are you sure? Not red, or blue, or green? Or even yellow?'
'No'. I was very definite, 'brown, like Samson in the field. He's a horse.'
All Uncle Eric said was, 'Ah'. He often said *Ah* after I told him something.
He started to mix the colours, very carefully in the lid of the box.

He stopped and asked me, 'Like that? Is that Samson?'

I wasn't impressed. 'No. That looks like Jack the dog.'

He added a bit of white and a tiny bit of yellow. It looked like Samson's poo, and I told him so. He tried again, and again and again, but still I wasn't satisfied.

Finally, he said the words I'd been waiting for: 'Would you like to try?'

I wetted my brush and I twirled, and I mixed again and again. I seemed to produce every kind of brown except Samson's coat. I started to feel very hot, and wanted to cry.

Uncle Eric must have sensed this, because he said, 'I know what we can do. Why not imagine Samson's brother? I should think he would be that shade of brown that you've just made. And maybe he's a bit light brown too, and a bit darker on his tummy. Let me show you.'

But I wouldn't let go of the brush. I was going to paint Samson's brother, George. And I did. I painted a brown blob with four fat legs. But while I was painting, I was thinking of Samson's long black tail. Somehow, I knew how to flick the brush in exactly the right way, to make his tail look like it was moving.

As I did it, I said, 'And there's his tail, and he swishes it like that to keep the flies away.' I was very impressed with my first painting.

And so was Uncle Eric, because he said, 'Gosh'.

We had to clear the table, because lunch was ready. I was too excited to eat; so Mummy scolded Uncle Eric and said, 'Look what you've done. She's over-excited. It's so tiresome.'

I didn't like Mummy to feel that I was *tiresome*. Sometimes if I sang too loudly, or asked lots of questions, I was *tiresome*, and this *got on Mummy's nerves*. It was not good to get on her nerves.

A few days after that, Uncle Eric went away. Just before he left the house, he bent down, looked me straight in the eyes and said, 'Be a good girl for your mummy. Don't get on her nerves.'

I looked at the floor, and whispered that I always tried to be good. And I thanked him for the box of paints. I kept it under my pillow.

Crab apples

This wasn't the first time I had thought about colour. Mummy told me that the first word I said as a baby was *blue*. That was what I called the blanket in my cot. Now I spent as long as I could outside in the back garden, because of all the colours. There was an asphalt path leading to the old greenhouse, and when it rained, a large dip in the path soon became a very satisfying puddle. I used an old spoon to carefully transfer the water from the puddle into the an old grey metal bucket I had found . Then I'd search for as many colourful things as I could find, such as leaves, weeds and dead grass. Then I'd crush them between two stones, and mix them in the bucket.

I told Trevor about my 'paint pot,' so he gave me a half-rotten beetroot. I cut it into small slices with a sliver of broken glass, and was delighted when the water in the bucket turned to a beautiful shade of purple. I filled a jam jar with the purple liquid, and held it up to the sunlight. I thought it was the most beautiful thing in the world. For days afterwards, I'd look at my purple paint, and searched the garden, to see if I could find anything that matched its colour. I showed Trevor, who was very impressed. Every so often I'd find an old carrot or an onion by the hole, and once some rose petals. I'd mash them up and add small amounts of water, then leave the jam jar for Trevor to look at.

There was a large crab apple tree that grew just on the other side of the fence. Several branches leaned over onto our side. I was fascinated by the tiny fruits, and naturally it was their many colours that held me transfixed. On rainy days, I would long to go into the garden, to see how the rain had transformed the apples' colours. One morning, there had been a very light rain, and a spider's web stretched from one branch to another. I can still see it now. Then a large dirt-covered hand grabbed a branch,

12

and give it a shake. I recoiled in terror. The shaking continued, and I could hear a gentle patter, as the tiny fruits fell to the ground.

Then I heard a man say, 'There you are,' followed by, 'Damn, I'll have to get a bigger bucket.'

I didn't know what was more frightening: a dirty hand grabbing the tree and shaking it violently, or a man's voice saying *damn*. But, as usual, my curiosity eventually got the better of my terror. I peered through the hole in the fence, and saw a pair of wellington boots.

Then I sneezed, and the voice said, 'Hello. You must be Trevor's little friend.'

I ran behind the greenhouse. The man leaned a ladder against the fence and peered over. I thought I was well hidden, but he could see me through the glass.

The next day must have been a Sunday, because we went to Mass. As soon as we got home, I went to the hole. Trevor was very excited. He almost shouted, 'Daddy picked our crab apples yesterday, and Mummy put them into a big copper pan, and boiled them with water, and you'll never guess what... it went all light brown; and then she got a big spoon, and scooped up the mess, and put it in one of her stockings! Then she hung up the stocking on a hook on the ceiling, and slowly all the juice dripped out of the stocking and into a pan, and she cooked it, and now it's turned into crab apple jelly!'

Trevor was very impressed by his mother's stocking. I imagined *jelly* to be the wobbly thing that Mummy made on my birthday, to have with blancmange.

I had lots of questions for Trevor, and he was happy to answer. My main interest was the colour of the jelly. I imagined it to be made up of the yellows and reds and pinks and oranges and hints of white and black, that made up the fruits on the tree.

'No, no! That's what I expected too, but it's like a kind of pinky orange jam. And when you hold the jar up to the light, you can see the sun shining through it. Mummy's awfully pleased with it!'

I longed to see this pinky orange jelly.

But Trevor was now describing the pan. 'It's made of copper. Copper is orange.'

'Like an orange you eat?'

'Well, not exactly. It's darker than that, and sometimes parts of it look black.'

I couldn't imagine such a mix of colours. I told Trevor that I'd love to see it.

He thought for a while. 'Perhaps I could ask Mummy if I could bring it to the fence, to show you.'

He asked his Mummy, but she didn't think that would be a good idea.

'My mummy has a huge scar on her tummy'

Trevor told me many things at the hole. He was a lot older than me, so of course I believed everything that he said. A very important conversation we had went something like this.

Trevor: My mummy's got a huge scar right across her tummy. I saw it when we had a bath together.

Me: You have a bath with your mummy?

Trevor: Oh yes. Especially when Daddy goes away. And she lets me sleep in her bed. And I can get in bed with Mummy and Daddy on Sunday mornings. It's my special treat.

Me: Why has your mummy got a big scar on her tummy? Did she fall over?

Trevor: It's where the doctor cut her open, to pull me out.

After colours, my next biggest fascination was *bodies and how they work*. It still is. I pictured a doctor cutting Mummy open with a large knife, and pulling me out by the legs. The image filled me with horror and fascination; as it does now, whenever I think about Caesareans.

In Northumberland, our bath time was always the same. Once a week, Mummy would switch on the electric immersion heater, to heat just enough water for the bath to be filled with two inches of warm water. Then she'd wash me quickly, then dry me and put on my nightdress. Then I'd go to my bedroom,

14

while she had her bath in my water. Once, I asked her if we could have some more hot water, but she said, 'That's out of the question, because we have to save money.'

I couldn't remember ever seeing my mother with no clothes on. I waited until a day when she was baking and singing; and asked her if we could have a bath together.
She didn't say *yes*. She didn't say *no*. She just asked me, 'Whatever for?'
I said, 'If you get in with me, then the water will be nice and warm for both of us. Then we can stay in the bath for longer.'
And, to my surprise, that's what happened. And we had a lot more water than usual.
All the time we were in the bath, I looked very closely at Mummy. She must have sensed it, because she asked me, 'Why are you looking at me?'
All I could say was, 'I love you Mummy. You look lovely.' It was true.
She looked sad and said, 'I used to look quite nice, but I'm afraid I'm going to seed now.'
I could see her tummy very clearly, but not what was below it, under the water.
I asked, 'Where's your scar?'
'What scar?'
'On your tummy, where the doctor cut you open to pull me out'
'The doctor didn't cut me open.'
'Then how did I get out?'
'Where did you get that idea from?'

I absolutely was not going to tell her, so I said, 'I don't know. I think I just thought about it.'
She looked at me for a long time, and it felt like she was trying to look inside my head.
Then she put her hand under the water and said, 'You came out through here.' She was pointing to the dark curly hair between her legs. 'You came out through here.'
I must have looked utterly shocked, because she said, 'Trevor's mummy had a lot of trouble when Trevor was born. He wouldn't

15

come out down there, like he was supposed to. So the doctors cut her open. They have to do that sometimes. But doctors are very clever, and they just stitch you back up again, and after a while all you have left is a big scar.'

I must have looked even more utterly shocked. Not only did she know about Trevor, but she must have known that we had been talking through the hole. Then she said, 'Come here.'
I thought she was going to slap me hard, so I started to panic and cry and shouted, 'No!'
Then it must have been her turn to be shocked, because she said, 'No, no! I'm not going to hit you.' And she pulled me close to her and cuddled me, and I could feel her crying into my hair.

Jenks tidies the garden

One day, Mummy told me that a man called Jenks would be coming to tidy the garden. He worked for Mr and Mrs Eades, and he was going to come to our house once a week. I had seen Jenks through the hole, and he wore brown trousers and smoked a pipe. Once or twice I had seen him spitting and picking his nose. On his first morning with us, I made sure I was in the garden, and I stood hiding by the greenhouse. Mummy told him to do his best with the long grass and the weeds. Jenks began pulling long weeds out of the border. After a short while, he lit his pipe. It was a very cold and wet morning, and as the sun shone, steam began to rise from the long grass. Blue smoke rose from Jenks' pipe, but the smoke that came down his nose was bluey-grey. He made a strange noise in his throat, and spat on the ground. He looked towards the house, and turned his back on me, so I couldn't see exactly what he was doing. I could tell that he was fumbling with his trousers, and then I heard water spattering on the ground, and saw steam rising.
After that, Jenks finished smoking his pipe, then carried on digging. Soon he straightened up, looked over to where I was hiding and said, 'You can come out now. Would you like to help me?'
I was terrified, and stayed where I was. I closed my eyes and imagined that Jenks couldn't see me. But curiosity got the better

of me, so I decided to walk past him, and go into the house. As I passed him I said, 'I was only playing. I didn't see you spitting and doing a wee wee.'

Jenks just laughed, and carried on digging.

William and Connie come back from school

One very cold day, I heard different voices in Trevor's garden. I looked through the hole, and saw a big boy holding a wooden bat. He was telling a big girl to throw the ball at him, so he could hit it. The girl kept throwing the ball too short, so the boy couldn't hit it. He shouted at her, 'You stupid cow! Just throw it properly will you!'

She shouted back, 'Don't call me a stupid cow!' and threw the ball very hard at him.

It hit him on the shoulder, but he just laughed and began chasing the girl round the garden, shouting, 'You stupid cow! You stupid cow!'

She shrieked with laughter, and they both ran indoors. Later, Trevor came to the hole, and explained that Violet and Robin had come back from school for their Christmas holidays. Violet went to a school where there were only girls, while Robin's school had only boys there.

The next day, there was more shouting in the garden. I went to the hole and saw Robin with a bag full of conkers. He began throwing them over the fence into our garden, and shouting, 'These are for you, you ugly old witch!'

I crouched by the hole, as the conkers came sailing over. After a few minutes, the conkers started hitting the greenhouse. Suddenly, I heard glass shattering and Robin shouted, 'Oh fucking hell!' and stopped throwing things. He must have thrown a stone.

It started to rain, so Mummy called me to come indoors. I went into the playroom and sat quietly. Then I took out my tin of marbles, and one by one, put them on the table. As they rolled off the table onto the rug I said, 'This one's for you, you ugly old witch!' If one rolled off the other side of the table, and landed with a clatter onto the hard floor, I'd shout, 'Oh fucking hell!' I tipped all the marbles onto the table, and they rolled in all directions, and each time one fell onto the hard floor I shouted, louder and louder, 'Oh fucking hell! Oh fucking hell!' A marble rolled towards the door, which was open. I saw Mummy standing there. She put her foot on one of the marbles. I didn't look at her face, but she asked me, 'Where did you hear those nasty words?'

Just before it was getting dark, Mummy helped me put on my coat and hat, and told me that we were going out. I supposed we were going to go shopping, but instead of going towards the shop, we walked in the opposite direction. I sensed that it was not a good idea to talk. I knew where we were going and, sure enough, we stopped at Trevor's front door. Mummy took hold of the door knocker and knocked very loudly. There was no answer, so she knocked even harder. She held my hand very tightly.

I heard footsteps, and a voice shouted, 'Coming!'

Mr Eades opened the door, and my mother immediately began telling him in a loud voice, 'You should control your children. Because of them, my daughter has started swearing!'

I looked at the pavement. Mr Eades said, 'Please come in. Let's not hang out our dirty laundry in public.'

My mother said, 'It's linen actually, and my linen is perfectly clean.'

But my mother didn't go in. She stood still, but her hand holding mine was shaking.

Mr Eades said, 'Robin has told me all about the broken glass. He's very sorry, and I'll make him pay for a new pane. He's in high spirits after coming home from school. But what's this about swearing?'

My mother let go of my hand. 'What pane of glass?'

'The one he broke when he was throwing conkers and stones into your garden. He's a very bright boy, but sometimes he doesn't think before he does things.'

My mother said, again in a loud voice, 'Good. But my daughter has heard him swearing, and now she's copying him. It's really too bad.'

Mr Eades coughed and said, 'I agree. I'll have words with him.'
My mother's voice started to rise. 'Words? Words aren't enough.
He needs thrashing! If he were my child, I'd thrash him to within
an inch of his life.'
Mr Eades coughed again. 'Yes, perhaps you would. But let's not
make a scene out here in the street. Will you come inside, Mrs
Dunbar? Please come in and talk to Irene.'
My mother shouted, 'Damn Irene! Damn the lot of you!' She
pulled my hand, and we walked quickly back home.

Later, there was a knock on our front door. I peeked through
the net curtain in the front room, and saw Mr Eades with Robin.
I quickly dropped the curtain, but I knew that they had seen me.
Robin was holding a bunch of flowers. Mr Eades knocked three
times, but my mother stayed in the kitchen. I heard Mr Eades
say, 'She's not answering the door. That's a pity.' Then they
walked away. Robin wasn't holding the flowers anymore.

The next day was Christmas Eve

The next day was Christmas Eve. In the late afternoon, I
stood in the back garden and looked at the sky. It was freezing
cold, and I was wearing two pairs of tights, two cardigans and
my coat. The sky had been a clear light blue in the morning, but
now it was an unusual grey, with a lot of black in it. I looked up,
and it seemed that the grey of our roof and the grey of the sky
were the same colour. I was thinking about Father Christmas
coming down our chimney, and leaving me some presents. I was
thinking about the grey of the sky, and the bright red of Father
Christmas' coat, and his shiny black boots, and the dirty brown
of his sack, and the presents, wrapped in purple and green paper,
and tied with silver and gold ribbons.

Tiny flakes of snow drifted down out of the sky. Suddenly
our dustbin burst into flames. I wasn't at all frightened, and
watched the flames and smoke and sparks rise until the fire died
down. Mummy came out with Robin's bunch of flowers in her
hand. She walked to the fence, and threw them into the Eades'

garden. She saw the smoking dustbin and said, 'I knew I shouldn't have thrown those hot ashes in there.'

She had a laugh in her voice. But it wasn't a happy laugh, and she told me to come indoors when I got too cold.

I stayed outside, and looked at the yellow of the light coming through the kitchen window, as the sky above me faded to darker and darker grey. I imagined Father Christmas landing his sleigh on our roof, and Mummy shouting at him to get his reindeer down from there, and to be careful where he walked with his dirty boots. I saw her grabbing my presents and shouting, 'Damn you!' as she slung them into the street. Larger snowflakes began to fall, and suddenly the whole sky was full of snow. It was no longer floating, but coming down very fast, and sticking to my coat and gloves. As I lifted my face to the sky, flakes went onto my eyelids and onto my tongue, mixed with the snot that was streaming out of my nose.

That night, I didn't feel excited about Christmas anymore. I didn't want to have a special day. I wanted an ordinary day, with no surprises. I was more excited about the snow than I was about Father Christmas. In the middle of the night, I heard my bedroom door open and I felt my bedclothes being pulled back. I screwed my eyes up tight, expecting it to be Father Christmas. But it was Mummy, lifting me up. She put me into her bed, then she got in beside me and went to sleep. She was snoring very loudly. She rolled over towards me and I could feel her body squashing me, so I moved away quickly, to the side of the bed where the sheets are always cold.

I woke up in the morning, but Mummy was still asleep. She had all her clothes on. It had just started to get light, and it was freezing in the room. At the end of the bed I could see one of Mummy's stockings, with lumps in it. They were presents. I carried the stocking over to the window and looked out. The yellow street light was still on, and there was thick snow on the ground. A car drove by, very slowly. A cat was walking in our front garden, up to his tummy in the snow. One by one, I carefully took out the presents from the stocking, trying to be as quiet as possible. I took out a packet of pencils, then a wooden ruler and a big green rubber. Then a wooden box full of coloured pencils, and two packs of writing paper, just like Mummy's. Right at the bottom of the stocking was a paint box. It was twice the size of Uncle Eric's, and had a black lid.

Mummy was still sleeping, so I carefully went back to my bedroom and put my presents under my pillow. I lay in bed, waiting for Mummy to wake up, but it was freezing cold, so I got dressed and looked out of the window again. A few people were walking in the snow, and saying 'Merry Christmas' to each other.

I went to the toilet, and as I was coming out Mummy walked towards me and said, 'Happy Christmas, Pippa. Do you like your presents? We have to go to Mass this morning.'

But we didn't go to Mass, because it was too late. Mummy said, 'We are real sinners now,' and laughed.

I didn't laugh. I didn't want to be a sinner.

Mummy tells Jenks to block up the hole in the fence

A few days after Christmas, all the snow had melted. Jenks came round, as usual, and I heard my mother tell him to block up my hole in the fence. Usually, when my mother told Jenks what to do, he did it straight away. But this time he asked, 'Why is that then, Mrs Dunbar?'

My mother hesitated, then said, 'To stop their cat from coming into our garden.'

Jenks chewed his bottom lip, and I thought he was going to do as he was told. But he didn't.

He said, 'With respect, Mrs Dunbar, I don't believe that Mr and Mrs Eades have a cat. And if they did, it would just climb over the fence. And, as I'm sure you know, it's your little girl's favourite spot in the garden.'

My mother glared at him. I looked at the ground. She said, 'Mr Jenkinson, are you, or are you not, my gardener?'

'From this minute, Mrs Dunbar, I'm not. I'll fetch my tools and be off.'

My mother told me to go indoors, but from the playroom I could hear a lot of banging on the fence. I knew that she was covering up the hole herself. When I knew my mother wasn't looking, I went to the fence. It was blocked by a large plank of wood, so it was impossible for me to see into next doors' garden. I waited for Trevor, but he never came to the fence again.

Will I go away to school?

Not long after that, my mother told me I was going to go to school. We were eating breakfast, and she said we had to go and visit the school that afternoon. I felt surprised, excited and then anxious, all within the space of a few moments.

All I could think to say was, 'Will I be going far away?'

Mummy laughed and said, 'No, you silly girl. I've been guided by Father, and he says you can go to St. John the Baptist school next week.'

I knew where that was. It was the school next to our church, in the town about ten miles away. I knew that Trevor went to the local village school, so I asked why I couldn't go there.

My mother explained, 'You are a Roman Catholic, and Trevor is a non-Catholic. Roman Catholics must go to Roman Catholic schools. It's quite simple.'

Whenever she said, 'It's quite simple,' that meant that there would be no discussion.

Then I realised that this must be a very special moment, because Mummy had mentioned Daddy. So I supposed it would be safe to talk about him. 'Has Daddy said I can go to school?'

My mother looked puzzled, and then annoyed. She said, 'No. Not him. Not your father. I'm talking about Father Daley.'

Father Daley was a large man who wore very bright clothes in church, and spoke in a very strange language. But when he came to our house, he wore black, and had a round white collar instead of a tie, and spoke English. He would sit with Mummy in the kitchen, and pat me on the head and say, 'Be a good girl, and go and play, while I talk to your mother.'

We went on the bus into town. As we reached the school gates, the children were just going into class, after lunchtime play. The school secretary told us to wait outside Mr Grigson's office, because he was busy dealing with some boys. Opposite where we sat, there was a very large crucifix on the wall. All of the crucifixes I had seen before this were high up, so I could only get a glimpse of the man up there on the cross. Now I could see the thorns on Our Lord's head, and a big cut in his side. He was only wearing a small cloth round his middle, and I could see his tummy button very clearly. He had big black nails sticking into his hands and feet. I didn't want to look at Our Lord, but I couldn't stop myself.

I was concentrating so hard on Our Lord, that I didn't hear Mr Grigson approach us.

He shook Mummy's hand and said, 'Grigson. Just been dealing with two boys who've been fighting.'

Then he looked at me. He said, 'Boys will be boys, but I'm sure you'll be a good little girl. What's your name?'

He was wearing a brown suit, and a white shirt that looked dirty. He had a navy blue tie with red stripes, which looked rather interesting. He had large black hairs growing in his nose, and yellow and brown stains on the fingers of one of his hands. I wondered if perhaps he'd been to the toilet and forgotten to wash his hands.

I looked at the floor and didn't say anything.

Mr Grigson took us upstairs, to an empty classroom. The children had left all their clothes on the chairs. All the clothes were grey, and the shoes were all black. Mr Grigson explained that the children were outside in the playground, doing something called P.E.

I whispered to Mummy, 'What's P.E?'

She whispered back, 'Physical Education. Running around outside in the freezing cold.'

Mr Grigson coughed. 'Yes, your mother is quite right. The children are outside in the fresh air.'

Each of the desks had a little hole at the front, with a white china pot in it. While Mummy was talking to Mr Grigson, I couldn't resist putting my finger in one of the pots, to explore what was inside. Mister Grigson asked Mummy, 'And Mr Dunbar? What does he do?'

Mummy replied, 'He works in Malaya. He's in rubber.'

To my horror, I couldn't pull my finger out of the pot, and I could feel liquid. I thought I had sliced the top of my finger off, and that blood was oozing out. I started to cry, and Mummy helped me pull my finger out of the inkwell. It was covered in black ink.

On the way out of the school, Mummy told me to say goodbye to the school secretary. Mummy said to her, 'That man is a buffoon.'

The school secretary said, 'Goodbye, Mrs Dunbar.'

We went to a big shop, to buy my school uniform. A lady showed us all the items of uniform for my school. Everything was grey. Even the boys' shirts were grey. The tights were grey, but the girls' blouses were white.

Mummy said to the lady, 'I imagine that the blouses will turn grey eventually.'

The lady said, 'My twins go to that school. I like them to have bright ribbons in their hair. Each twin has different coloured ribbons, to help the teachers tell them apart. And I give them colourful you-know-whats to wear too.'

I thought of the grey of our slate roof, and the sky before it snowed. We didn't buy any ribbons or colourful knickers.

That night I lay in bed, trying to get warm. I thought about those poor schoolchildren doing P.E. outside, with no clothes on.

The books that tell you all that there is to know

On the Saturday afternoon before I started school, I heard a lot of children's voices shouting from across the road. I looked out of the window and saw a man with dark brown skin pushing a barrow with a big box in it. Children were running after him and shouting, 'Paki! Paki!' He crossed the road, and knocked on our front door. I was hoping that Mummy wouldn't answer, but she did. She saw the children shouting, and invited the brown man in for a cup of tea. He was selling books called *The Encyclopaedia Britannica*. He told Mummy that everything I needed to know about the world was in those books. He said, 'For example, if we look for India, we can read all about my country.' He showed me the page with India on it, and there was a picture of a brown man with a beard and wearing a cloth hat. Just like the man sitting in front of me.

I said, 'Oh look, there's a Paki!'

Mummy looked very cross, but the man just laughed. Mummy told me to go in the other room, but the man said, 'Please, no. I believe that children should ask questions. It is how they learn. A child who asks a question is a child who will remember the answer.'

Mummy let me stay, but I knew to be quiet. She agreed to buy five books, and went to get her purse and the tea.

As soon as Mummy left the room, I couldn't stop myself from asking, 'Have you been to Malaya?'

The brown man said, 'No I haven't been there, but my cousin works there.'

I felt myself suddenly getting very hot in my face, but I had to ask, 'Does he know my Daddy? He lives in Malaya, and makes rubber for tyres, and rubber bands and welly boots.'

The man said, 'Malaya is a very big country. My cousin works for the government.'

This was disappointing, but I asked another question: 'What's a buffoon?'

He opened the first big book. Mummy came into the room with a tray of tea and cake, and her purse. We had just reached a page with a picture of a large monkey with a frightening blue and red face. I studied the picture very carefully, while the man and Mummy talked together. I didn't think that Mr Grigson looked like that, but I could imagine why Mummy should call him an ugly name. He frightened me, and I didn't want to go to his school.

The man got ready to leave. At the front door he said to Mummy, 'Thank you for your kindness. You are a good mother. But please allow your daughter to ask questions.'

They shook hands. Mummy said, 'Those horrible children have gone.'

The man said, 'If only their parents would buy my books, then their children would be better informed.'

Bottles

Even now, I can remember just how cold I always felt. Our house, in that village in Northumberland, was freezing. When I woke up in the morning, there was often ice on the inside of my bedroom windows. It was like frost, or the ice on car windscreens, that men had to scrape off first thing in the morning. My mother insisted that I sleep with at least one small window open, to let in fresh air. A hot water bottle was essential for me on winter nights. Without one I couldn't get warm, and couldn't go to sleep. I was afraid of the dark, so would hide my head under the covers, and curl up in a ball with my hands between my legs, where they would always be warm. I was in the snow once, and my wellington boots had holes in, so my socks were soaked and I couldn't feel my feet. That's how my feet felt in bed.

On the nights that I had a hot water bottle, I would go to sleep instantly. But later in the night I would be woken up by a cold hand touching my feet, as it searched for my hot water bottle. It was my mother opening up the sheets and blankets at the bottom of my bed, and taking the bottle for her to use for herself.

I used to ask myself, 'Why don't we have two hot water bottles?' I supposed we didn't have enough money for another one.

But other bottles were on my mind. Once, when Uncle Eric came to visit, I asked him about the bottles that he always brought with him. He said it was his and Mummy's medicine. They were big bottles, and the medicine was a yellowy brown, that reminded me of wee. I liked looking at the labels. Uncle Eric taught me that one was called *Teachers* and another was *Grants*.

26

But my favourite was the one with a label with a man with a top hat and a stick, called *Johnnie Walker*.

Mummy did most of her shopping in the village, but only bought her medicine in shops in the town. Once we were in the village shop and I saw a small bottle with Johnnie Walker on it. It was behind the counter, above the shopkeeper's head. I pointed at it and said in an excited voice, 'Look Mummy, there's your medicine!'
When we were outside the shop, my mother grabbed me by the coat and shook me. I thought she was going to slap me.
She whispered, 'Don't ever say that again. Do you understand?' I was too frightened to speak. So she asked me again: 'Do you understand?' I didn't understand, but said 'yes,' and never mentioned her medicine to anyone again. Well, not for a long time.

I cry on the first day of school, but love handwriting

On my first day at school, Mummy took me on the bus. There were two other children dressed all in grey on the bus; also going to St John the Baptist school. Mummy explained that the big girl was called Patricia, and would be in charge of looking after me. She was nine. Her younger brother Matthew would also make sure I was all right. He was seven years old. Mummy knew their mother, and the children had promised to look after me just as carefully as if I was their little sister. There were two other children, who were big boys going to another school. Mummy told me that they looked *common*, and she didn't know their mothers, so it was best that I didn't speak to them. Mummy didn't like common people, or the common way that they pronounced their words. Matthew told me that the town was ten miles away, and that on the way we would go past a sweet shop and a donkey standing in a field.

Mummy took me into my class, and my teacher, Miss Woods, showed me where to hang my coat. Then Mummy said goodbye. She crouched down, and I thought she was going to kiss me, but instead she said, 'Be a good girl.' She found a hair on my grey cardigan, and took it off and threw it on the floor.

Miss Woods showed me where to sit, and I began crying. She said, 'Stop making that noise, or you will make Gordon cry.' Sure enough, a small boy in the front row started to cry. I stopped crying and Miss Woods gave me a thick black pencil, and a book with lines in. She told me to copy what she was writing on the blackboard. This was very exciting, so I stopped missing Mummy and wrote a 'g' in my book. To me, it was perfect. Miss Woods came over to see what I had done. She tapped the back of my hand with a ruler and said, 'Philippa, that is very good, but the 'g' does not have a curly tail like a monkey. Copy exactly what you see next time.'

It had been only the slightest of taps, but it felt as if she had hit my hand with a hammer.

After that, I copied exactly what I saw, trying to make my 'g' as perfect as possible. Miss Woods came back and told me my 'g' was the best in the class. She took me out to the front of the class. She showed all the children my book and said, 'Philippa is our new girl. She has never been to school before. She has written a perfect 'g'. Who will be her friend at playtime?'

Lots of the girls put their hands up. Miss Woods said, 'Gordon, you can be Philippa's special friend.'

Somebody said, 'That's not fair,' but Miss Woods took no notice.

Gordon shits himself

Gordon was much smaller than me, and it was very difficult to understand what he said. He scratched himself a lot, and his hands always looked very red. For some reason, he was allowed to wear very bright jumpers in school. My favourite was a cardigan with blue buttons. If I looked at Gordon from a distance, his cardigan looked orangey-yellow, but close up I could see that it was knitted with a special kind of wool, where every line seemed to be made up of different colours. I told Gordon that this was my favourite cardigan in the whole world. He said he would ask his mum if he could wear it every day.

After that, Gordon always tried to be near me. If I went to the toilet at playtime, he would always wait for me outside. He reminded me of the little dog that waited patiently outside the shop, while its owner was inside.

I once heard two teachers in the playground talking about him. One said 'Poor little Gordon. It's such a shame for the family.'

One day, I went to wash my hands in the basins in the cloakroom outside our class. There was an awful smell, and a grown-up was washing something yellow off Gordon's leg. I felt disgusted and fascinated at the same time. I couldn't stop looking at Gordon's diarrhoea. It reminded me of the colour of his cardigan. After that, Gordon didn't come to school for a long time. Miss Woods said he was in hospital, and that we should all pray for him. Then he came back, but looked quite fat. Miss Woods explained that we were not to play roughly with Gordon, in case he fell over. Then one day he didn't come to school. In assembly Mr Grigson said we were to *remember poor Gordon and his family in our prayers.* I missed his cardigan.

Early art

Though I had my paint box at home, I was rarely allowed to use it. One day, Miss Woods told us all to paint a picture of our house. The person sitting next to us was going to be our *partner*. Two partners made *a couple*. With our partner, we had to cover our desks with newspaper. When we had finished doing that, Miss Woods gave each couple a metal tray with six large round blocks of hard paint. She gave each of us a big paintbrush and a large sheet of very thin paper, and a glass jar of water to share. I shared with Bridget, but she didn't know what to do, and looked like she was going to cry. I told her we had to clean the blocks of paint first, because they were absolutely filthy. So Bridget and I dipped our brushes in the water, and began swirling hard on the blocks, to try and clean away all the different layers of dry coloured paint that were on the top of each one. Bridget was very excited about doing this.

Miss Woods was busy dealing with overturned water jars, and children shouting, 'I've finished! What shall I do now?' Bridget and I were completely absorbed in our paint block cleaning. Unfortunately, by the time we had finished cleaning, all the other children had finished their paintings. Miss Woods was very cross with us, because she said that we had nothing to show for a whole lesson's work. She said we had to stay in class at lunchtime play and do our paintings. I said, 'Oh thank you Miss!' and she told me not to be cheeky.

Bridget looked like she was going to cry.

After we had eaten our lunch, Miss Woods told us to go to class and start our paintings. We had to make sure they were finished by the time the good children were ready to come back in from play. Bridget didn't know what to do, so I asked her lots of questions about her house. She told me it was called a *pre-fab*, and it was grey, but her dad had painted their front door bright red, and her mum had just made some lovely curtains, with red and green flowers on them. They had a chimney, and it was lovely and warm when they lit the fire at night. There was no upstairs, because their house was called a *bungalow*.

While Bridget painted her house, (which I noticed was yellow, and with an upstairs), I sat and thought about where I lived. I thought about Uncle Eric, and his blob of blue paint, that he had stretched with water until it was almost grey. I thought about my house and my garden, and about my mother sitting at home.

When Miss Woods came in, she said, 'Good girl Bridget. That's a lovely house… Philippa, what on earth is that?'

I said, 'It's my roof and the sky, just before it snowed, on the day before Christmas.'

Bridget's painting was put on the wall for everyone else to look at.

Twelve years later, (a few weeks ago), I told Madame about this experience. She asked me to try and recreate the painting, exactly as I had painted it. She made me mount it and frame it, and she has it on display next to her desk. She has called it *Study in Grey: Grey is More Than Black and White Combined.*

I love Madame, and I know that she cares a lot about me.

My Colour Dream

Miss Woods tried to be nice to me, but I was frightened of her, because she shouted at children. I was very keen to please her; not because I liked her, but because I remembered her tapping me with the ruler. I did as I was told, and tried to avoid her attention. When I started school, I already knew quite a lot about reading, so Miss Woods said I was a *good reader*, and praised me a lot in front of the other children. One day after school, Mummy came to see Miss Woods, to ask about my progress. Miss Woods told her that I was a very good speller for a child of my age, considering I had only recently started school. She said, 'I imagine you spend a lot of time teaching Philippa at home.'

Mummy smiled and said, 'One does what one can.'

Miss Woods said that she thought my handwriting was beautiful. She said that my drawing was quite remarkable. But I could tell that she didn't like the way I painted, because she didn't mention it to Mummy.

One day, Miss Woods told us to draw our face, and then colour it in with paint. I started to think about the colour of Bridget's eyes. They were blue, but there was black too, and tiny lines of white. And you could see an oblong of white that was a reflection of the window. And her eyelashes were a light orange, like I imagined the copper of Trevor's mother's jam pan. I suppose I must have been sitting quite still, looking at Bridget and thinking about Trevor, because I didn't notice Miss Woods near me, until I felt her tapping me on the shoulder and saying, 'Philippa, are you all right?'

I was all right, but I had forgotten that I was supposed to be doing a painting of my face. I had even forgotten that I was in a classroom in a school, with lots of children making a noise all around me. I had slipped into what I now call *My Colour Dream*. Back then, I had no name for this thing that I do. I become very still, and focus on a colour or movement that fascinates me. Smells and sounds, and anything I touch, become very sharp. This helps me to focus on the colours and textures and

31

movements of whatever it is that I am concentrating on. Then suddenly everything else around me almost disappears. Later in the day, or even days later, when I have the time and the paint and paper, I can bring those sensations back into focus, and recreate everything I want to.

This was a secret activity for me; a private pleasure, not to be shared with anyone. This was the first time that I had allowed myself to slip into my trance while there were other people around me. I imagine I must have looked quite strange. The sheet of paper in front of me was completely blank. Miss Woods said that she was cross with me, and I heard her use the words *dreaming* and *lazy*.

But I did my painting when I got home. It was of Bridget's face. I brought it to school and showed it to Miss Woods. She said, 'It's very good Philippa. In fact it's remarkable.' She didn't put it on the wall with the other children's paintings. One day, I asked Miss Woods where my painting was, and she told me, 'I showed it to Mr Grigson, and he asked to keep it. It's in his office, on the wall.'

This worried me. In my mind I had a list of things I didn't like about Mr Grigson. I added to my list, *He stole my painting of Bridget*.

Food is God's Love, but sometimes it can taste like Hell

I loved lunch at school, and thought that most of the meals were absolutely delicious. I ate as much as I could, and always asked for seconds. A few months after I started school, the cook left to have a baby, and was replaced by someone who once a week made cheese pie. I liked cheese. Actually, that's not quite true, because I only liked cheddar from the village shop, and the smell of Dairylea Cheese made me feel sick.

One day, we had cheese pie for lunch. It looked nice: a beautiful golden yellow colour, with pools of dark brown and a lovely light brown pastry base. I'm sure the cook made it with love in her heart for us little children, on that cold and windy day in March. But I just couldn't eat it. I knew I wouldn't be able to take even one bite. The potatoes and baked beans that were served with it looked lovely too, and I started to eat as much as I could, but the smell of the cheese pie stopped me from putting any more food in my mouth. My mouth began to fill with saliva, and my eyes were filling with water, in that way that they do just before I'm going to be sick.

I thought that if I concentrated on the beautiful yellowness on the top of the pie, then maybe I might be able to eat it. I noticed that someone was tapping me on the shoulder. It was a dinner lady, who was saying, 'Why haven't you eaten your cheese pie? All of the other children are eating their chocolate cake and custard.'

Then I heard another grown-up say to me, 'If you think you are going to have some pudding, then you are quite mistaken, young lady. Eat up your cheese pie.'

I wanted to say something, but couldn't. I could feel myself starting to cry. I was too frightened to turn round, to see who was talking to me. The first voice said, 'It's all right. Just try a little bit.'

But then I heard the second voice say, 'Don't think that your crocodile tears are going to fool me. You can sit here until you've eaten that all up.'

All the other children left the dining hall, but I stayed sitting, looking at my cheese pie. It still looked lovely, but the thought of eating it filled me with disgust. I couldn't help it. I could hear the grown-ups wiping the tables and chairs, and stacking them up. I could hear voices saying, 'Poor love,' and 'She'll have to learn,' and 'That food is perfectly good,' and 'I don't understand; she's usually such a good eater.' But I just sat, and couldn't turn round.

I wanted to say, 'Please, I'm a good girl, but I just can't eat this cheese. I know I don't like it. It's not my fault, but it just makes me feel sick.' But I had become frozen. I couldn't speak, or even move. I couldn't cry. So I just sat. I could hear the children playing outside, and laughing and shouting and screaming. Every so often I heard a grown-up walking towards me, pause, and then walk away again.

Then I heard the sound of loud footsteps. Someone with hard soles on the bottom of their shoes was walking into the room. I knew it was Mr Grigson.

I heard him say, 'Take her and her food to her classroom, and she can eat it there.'

Then he went out again. Then I heard someone with soft soles walk towards me, and they crouched down and I felt them put their arm around my shoulder, and I felt their warm breath in my ear and a lady whispered, 'It's all right love,' and she ate all my cold lunch as fast as she could. I just sat rigid and looked straight ahead. Then the dinner lady put me on her knee and stroked my hair, and I started to cry and I was sick on her.

The next day, I ate all my lunch. A boy on the table next to us was sitting with his coat on and his legs were bare. Bridget whispered, 'That boy did a wee wee in his pants, so he has to wear his coat all day, until his pants and socks dry. And he has to wear big purple PE knickers, so his whatsit doesn't get cold.'

I looked for the kind dinner lady, but she wasn't there.

The day after that, we had lentil soup for lunch. It was a light orangey-yellow colour. I tried to eat it, but there was something about the smell and the texture of the first mouthful that reminded me immediately of Gordon. I tried to focus on the colour, and to block Gordon out of my mind. But I began to see Gordon in the cloakroom, and the grown-up wiping the diarrhoea off his leg. Mr Grigson had told us to remember Gordon in our prayers, but I was trying my best to forget him.

I knew I would soon hear the grown-ups' voices behind me, and that I would be made to sit and look at my soup until I had eaten it all up.

So I stood up, picked up my plate of soup and threw it as hard as I could on the floor. My plate smashed and the soup made a large blob, just like an enormous pile of sick. I just stood and couldn't move.

A dinner lady came over and I heard her say to Bridget, 'What happened?'

I was just about to tell Bridget what my Mummy called mine, but didn't get a chance because the mob of boys started shouting. A small boy was standing on a big boy's shoulders and looking into Mr Grigson's office.

He shouted, 'He's got the cane and he's whacking him... now!'

The boys started cheering and whooping again. A group of girls came over and one of them asked, 'Is William crying?'

'Not yet' replied the small boy, 'but it's only his second whack. I'd say there's another eight to go! I bet the blood from his arse, I mean bottom, will be running down his legs by the time old Grigson's finished with him!'

The girls ran off, screaming.

My legs felt wobbly, and I suddenly needed to do a poo very badly. Bridget went with me to the outside toilets, and stood outside my toilet cubicle. The door wouldn't shut properly, because the lock had been broken off.

Bridget said, 'Kenneth told me that only a cunt would break the lock off a toilet door like that.'

I wasn't sure that I wanted Bridget to be my friend anymore. There was no more toilet paper, so I had to ask her to get some from the next cubicle. There was a big girl in there, and she shouted, 'Oi! Who's using The C Word out there?'

Bridget put on a big girl's voice and said, 'Shut up and pass me some toilet paper under the door. If you don't hurry up and do it, I'll get my brother to tell Old Grigson that you called me a C Word.'

That afternoon it was my turn to take the register to the secretary's office. As I turned the corner into the corridor, I saw the thrashed boy standing, facing the crucifix opposite Mr Grigson's room. I tried to walk past him without making a sound with my feet, but my hands were shaking so much that I dropped the register. As I picked it up, I took a quick look at the boy. I couldn't see any signs of blood on his legs. Maybe he had wiped it off with toilet paper. He just stood perfectly still. I thought of that horrible picture in church of Jesus being whipped, and blood coming out of his wounds. Suddenly I heard a cough from Mr

Grigson's office. I ran with the register, and threw it in the box outside the secretary's office, and ran back along the corridor.

I heard Mr Grigson shout, 'Who's that running along the corridor?'

Back in class, I said a prayer to God, asking Him to please forgive the boy who had been given a thrashing. And I prayed that I would never use The C Word. But, if I did use it by accident, please could God make sure that nobody heard me do it?

Mr Grigson hits me

I became terrified of Mr Grigson. If I couldn't get to sleep, and I would think about him. I pictured him knocking on our front door, and telling Mummy that I hadn't been a good girl. One morning, Miss Woods asked me to take a message to the office. On my way back I heard Mr Grigson's shoes behind me. I felt him put his arm under my tummy and pick me up, while tapping me on the bottom with his free hand. As he did it, he laughed and said, 'Where are you going then?'

I screamed and wet myself, and he put me down very quickly.

I don't remember what Mr Grigson said to me, or what he said to the teachers who rushed to open their classroom doors, to see what was going on. I do remember wearing my coat and a big pair of navy-blue PE knickers for the rest of the day. Whenever anyone asked me what had happened, I said, 'Mister Grigson thrashed me.'

When I got home, I told my mother that Mr Grigson had thrashed me. I said, 'He did it for no reason. I didn't use The C Word. I promise I didn't.'

My mother looked horrified. All she said was, 'This is too much. This is the last straw.'

The next day, she came with me on the bus to school, and went straight to see Father Daley.

Our student teacher

My first year at school wasn't all about beatings and terror. Sometimes it was absolutely fascinating. In the summer term we had a new teacher. She was a student. Unlike Miss Woods, she was very young. She laughed a lot and called us all *flower*. Bridget was worried about this and asked Miss why she said that. Miss said, 'Oh it's all right, I'm from Lancashire. Everyone gets called *flower* in Lancashire.'

Bridget explained that in her house a *flower* was that thing between a girl's legs. Miss called us all *sweetheart* after that.

Miss set up a *Discovery Table*, with all sorts of interesting things on it, that we were allowed to touch. There was a small box with a glass lid, with iron filings inside it. We were allowed to use a small magnet, to move around on the base of the box, to make the filings stand up on end or move. This was truly mesmerising.

Once, Miss showed us how to mix colours properly with paint. She had taken some of the hard round blocks of paint and put each one into a jam jar with water in. The blocks had turned soft, and the jars were now filled with a lovely coloured mush. She explained that if you added lots of water then the paint would be very runny, but a small amount of water would make it very thick. She put a big piece of paper on the floor, and asked us to sit in a circle around it. She asked if there was anyone in the class who would like to paint something, by mixing two colours together.

Charles called out, 'Miss, Pippa's a lovely painter!'

So Miss asked me to paint something. I took a deep breath and made a big blob of blue, and then added some red. I asked Miss for lots of water and *stretched* the paint, using a lovely thick brush. I made the purple darker towards the top of the paper, and lighter as I brushed in layers lower and lower down. I left a gap of white in the shape of a crescent moon, with a much lighter shade of purple all around it.

Charles said, 'That's lovely.'

Miss asked, 'Does anyone else want to say what they think about the painting?'

A boy called Andrew asked, 'Miss, can Pippa show me how to paint a tractor?'

Miss said, 'What do you think about that Pippa?'

I didn't know what to say. Usually Miss Woods told me what to do, and when I had finished, she told me if she thought it was good or not. So I said, 'Well I'd really like to paint a crab apple. But maybe Andrew could paint a big tractor with a farmer riding it, and a big trailer at the back. And perhaps if you didn't mind, you could show everyone how to mix paint in the jars, and I could show everyone how I like to paint apples, and we can cut them out and stick them in the trailer.'

Miss said, 'What a lovely idea! That's more or less what I was going to suggest.'

And that's what we did, and it was one of the most wonderful experiences in my life up to then. When we had finished, Miss put our huge tractor on the wall. I knew it wasn't quite right to have a night sky with a tractor and apples that looked like they were in the daytime, but I was very happy, all the same.

There was more excitement to come. Usually we did PE in the hall, but because it was a sunny day, Miss took us outside into the playground. This was the first time we had done PE outside, so of course we just ran around everywhere. Miss taught us how to stop running when she clapped her hands. Then she did something truly remarkable. She was wearing a long skirt and a pair of strong shoes. She made us sit in a big circle and she stood in the middle, holding a purple cotton bag. As she was explaining what we were going to do next, she emptied the contents of the bag onto the ground. It was a pair of plimsolls and a very short black skirt. She kicked off her shoes, reached under her skirt and pulled off her green tights. Then she buttoned her mini skirt around her waist, quickly pulled down her long skirt, put her plimsolls on and said, 'Da da! I'm ready to do PE with you!'

We all clapped. And so did a group of men who were working at the GPO sorting depot next door, and who had been watching through the fence. One of them whistled and Miss said, 'Clear off. Please.'

They did. We played with large cane hoops for the rest of the lesson.

Miss told us that when she clapped her hands we were to jump in our hoops, and to stand quiet and still for as long as we could. I started to shake, and couldn't get in my hoop. Miss crouched down next to me and asked me what was wrong, and I said that it reminded me of something horrible.

Miss said, 'Well, can you tell me about that horrible thing?'

I couldn't open my mouth.

Bridget tapped Miss on the shoulder and said, 'Excuse me Miss, Pippa's my friend and we saw something really horrible here.'

The other children had begun to be silly, so Miss asked us if we could tell her at lunchtime about this horrible thing.

After we had eaten our lunch, Bridget and I went to our classroom. Miss was there, eating a sandwich and writing on the board at the same time. She stopped writing, but carried on eating her sandwich. It smelled like fish paste. Bridget told Miss all about the boy who was thrashed, and that whenever this was going to happen, the boy had to stand still in a circle for the whole of morning playtime. Miss stopped eating her sandwich and looked very grave.

She said, 'Thank you for telling me about this.' Then she looked at me and said, 'Pippa, don't worry about standing in a hoop. Nobody's going to hurt you in school.'

I looked into her eyes. They were light green with a splash of brown, all surrounded by a black ring. I found it impossible not to stare into them. I said, 'But it's too late Miss. They already have.'

Then Miss Woods came in, and said to our student teacher, 'Why are these children in here? They should be out at play.'

Miss said, 'They've come in to help me do some tidying up. Girls, please go and arrange the books on the shelf.'

I knew that Miss had said something that wasn't true. I looked at Miss Woods. I could see that she knew it wasn't true either.

Uncle Eric comes to stay

During the summer holidays, Uncle Eric came to stay with us. I liked that, because Mummy cooked big meals, and on most mornings Uncle Eric cooked breakfast. He took me to what he called *The Village Green*. All the local children called it *The Field*. There was a playground there. Uncle Eric would sit on the bench and read his newspaper and smoke his cigarettes, while I played on the roundabout or went on the swings. Uncle Eric sometimes pushed me on the swing, and we laughed a lot. He also cleaned the house and did the shopping. Some people in the village thought he was my daddy. I didn't mind that, but sometimes it was difficult to explain to the other children exactly who he was. If I said that he was my uncle, the children might ask, 'Is he your mum's brother, or your dad's brother?'

I didn't know, so I asked Uncle Eric whose brother he was. He frowned, and didn't say anything for a little while. Then he asked, 'What does your mother say?'

I told him that I didn't like to ask Mummy questions like that,

He smiled and said. 'That sounds like a good plan,' and asked me if I wanted to go on the swing again.

Uncle Eric had his own bedroom, but on most mornings I'd see him coming out of Mummy's room. Then he'd say things like, 'Just checking that your mother is all right.' Or, 'I just brought Mummy her cup of tea.' Once he said, 'I've just checked that Mummy's still alive.'

This really shocked me, and I thought about it for a long time afterwards. Bridget's grandpa had died while he was asleep. Bridget told us that he had had a very bad attack in his angina in the night, and he never woke up again. Her granny had screamed the house down. Miss Woods told us to remember Bridget's grandpa in our prayers, and to pray that his soul might go to Heaven quickly. Bridget said we had to pray a lot for him, because he had been in The War and killed lots of Germans. Also he had stopped going to Mass on Sundays, because he thought that Father Daley was *a bit of a ponce*. Miss Woods told Bridget to be quiet and get on with her prayers.

I looked for the word *ponce* in the Encyclopaedia Britannica, but didn't find it.

Once I was drying myself after my bath. Mummy came in, and saw me drying my face on a big towel I had found on the bathroom floor. She said, 'Don't use that towel; especially not to dry your face. Uncle Eric uses that one. He will have dried his bottom on that towel. Use mine instead.'

The Black Babies

After the summer holidays, we had a new teacher. I don't remember her name or her face, but I do remember very clearly that she liked me a lot. Actually she liked all the children. Bridget told me that Miss liked her best of all. To prove it, she said that Miss had invited Bridget to her house for tea. Bridget said she hadn't gone in the end, because her tummy had been very runny. I wanted to hit Bridget for saying that she had been invited to Miss's house. I almost slapped her round the face. I didn't know why I felt like that.

I asked Miss if I could go to her house for tea. She laughed and said, 'Of course not. Teachers aren't allowed to do that.'

I told Bridget about that school rule, and she made me promise not to tell anyone that Miss had broken the rules. She said that if Mr Grigson found out, then he might give Miss the sack. Bridget didn't know what was in the sack. She asked Kenneth, and he told her that there was a whip in the sack, for thrashing people with.

Miss taught us how to make a dolly out of a clothes peg, and how to plait wool to make her hair. She allowed me to sharpen the pencils in a little machine that she kept on her desk. I would feel warm all over with pleasure, as I gripped the two knobs on top that opened up the clasp. I put the blunt pencil in the hole and released the knobs, so that the clasp held the pencil tight. Then I turned the handle and felt the pencil shudder, as the rasp gently cut into it, and the pencil's shavings fell into the little pot underneath. I asked Miss if she thought the pencils liked to be shaved like that.

She said, 'Oh surely, Pippa. No pencil wants to be blunt. Their job is to help us write and draw beautifully.'

That idea pleased me. It still does.

Miss said, 'You are a sweet girl, but please hurry up.'

From time to time, we learned things in school that really worried me. Miss told us that we were all very lucky children, because we all had enough to eat, and that we knew about God. God loved us, because we knew about Him. I wanted to tell Miss that when I went to bed, I didn't feel that I had had enough to eat. I didn't say anything, and just thought about it instead.

Miss said that lots of black children in Africa didn't have enough to eat. That was awful, of course, but even worse was that nobody had told them about God's Love. Miss gave us a round piece of white card each, and told us to colour it in with a black wax crayon. That was the face of our very own Black Baby. If we brought in a penny from home, then Miss would let us stick on some eyes, a nose and a mouth. The more pennies we brought in, then the more bits of card we could have, to make its body and the arms and legs. When our Black Baby was almost finished, then Miss would give us some black wool, to give it some hair.

I asked Mummy if I could have a penny for my Black Baby. She wanted to know what was going to happen to all the money that we were collecting.

I explained that it was to help the poor Black children know about God's Love.

Mummy said, 'Oh, so it'll be for the priests then.'

The next day, all of the children brought in pennies, apart from me and Dennis Stewart. Miss had pinned all of our Black Baby faces on the wall, and the first lesson was all about choosing sticky coloured paper for the eyes, nose and mouth.

Dennis Stewart smelled quite badly, and always had two long pieces of yellow-green snot running from his nose. Our house had a cellar that had the same smell as Dennis. Mummy said that the cellar smelled like that because water was always getting in, and that the smell was caused by *damp*. The older children had made up a song about Dennis and his three big sisters. It was about them being smelly and having snotty noses, and only having stew to eat, because they were poor. The children also invented a game that was called *Stew*. Someone would run after you in the playground, and grab you and shout, 'You're Stew!' Then you had to catch someone else, and make them *Stew*. This made you *free*, so you couldn't be made *Stew* anymore. If at the end of playtime you were still *Stew*, then you would wake up the next morning with a green snotty nose.

I really didn't like this, because I liked Dennis Stewart. He was better than me at lots of things; especially counting and knowing about money, and tying his shoe laces. But no matter how much Miss blew Dennis' nose, there was always more snot to come down his nostrils. On warm days the snot dried up, and looked like two candles. At playtimes, I'd take some paper from the toilet and wipe his nose for him. But the paper was waxy, and usually I only managed to smear the snot over his cheek. I mixed a paint colour once using yellow and green, and called it *Dennis*.

While the other children made their Black Baby faces, Dennis and I sat together and read a book,. Someone asked Miss why we hadn't brought in a penny, and Miss said that she thought our parents had forgotten. After three days, several of the children had almost completed their Black Babies. Dennis's Baby and my Baby were still just black circles. Dennis said he didn't care, because he liked reading with me. But I cared. I cared because there was a Black Baby in Africa who, because of me, wouldn't have enough to eat, and wouldn't know about God's Love.

On our sideboard was a special tin that Mummy put money in, for what she called *a rainy day*. When Mummy was asleep, I took some money from the tin. I hid it, and took it to school the next day. I told Miss that it was for Dennis and me.

Miss said, 'That's a lovely idea, but you must put that ten-shilling note back where you found it.' Miss had an expression on her face that I hadn't seen before. Then she asked me if

Dennis and I would like to paint a big picture to go on the wall, all about God's Love.

I had been in Uncle Eric's car once, and I saw the clouds open up, and rays from the sun come straight through the clouds, and onto the green fields in front of us. The underneath of the clouds became a beautiful yellow-gold-grey colour, and the shafts of light made the fields below shine.
I asked Uncle Eric if that was Heaven, and he agreed that it was. He stopped the car, and Mummy and I looked at the beautiful sunlight, while Uncle Eric did a wee by the side of the road. I tried to paint that sky, to show God's Love shining down on us. I used light blue and grey and a very light yellow, with light and dark green for the fields. I told Dennis all about it, and he painted a huge red picnic cloth, with all his family sitting round it, with huge plates full of food. He said his mum and dad always thanked God for their food before they ate. We told Miss all about it, and she said we were lovely children, and it was the loveliest picture of God's Love she had ever seen.

Her praise for my painting had a very deep effect on me. I loved my teacher and I felt she loved me. From that moment on, all I wanted to do was paint. Since then I have recreated many times the image of what I think of as *God's Love Descending Through the Clouds*.

Mummy comes to school

One morning after My First Confession, Mummy told me that she was coming to school to collect me, and to talk to my teacher. All day I worried that I had done something wrong. Bridget said she wanted to see what my mummy looked like. She asked me lots of questions: about her hair, her eyes, and did her nose look like mine? I didn't understand. Why should we have noses that looked the same?
Bridget shook her head and looked grave. 'Well, Mum says that we all look like her. Except that Kenneth is going to have a big bottom like my dad's. My dad said that Kenneth looks like the milkman.'

I thought Bridget's dad must be a rude man, and must spend a lot of time going to Confession. I was hoping that Bridget wasn't going to ask the next question. But I knew it was coming: 'Do you look a bit like your Dad? What does he look like?'

I wanted to say, 'Yes. Yes I do look like him.' But I knew that it would be a lie, and then I'd have to go to Confession to tell Father Daley. Bridget kept asking me the same question. She knew that something was wrong. I had never seen a photo of Daddy, so once I asked Uncle Eric if he had seen my daddy, and he said he had. I asked him what he looked like and he said, 'The last time I saw him he was wearing brown trousers.'

So I told Bridget that my Daddy wore brown trousers, just to stop her asking me.

At the end of the day, I stayed in class, and Miss laid out all my work on her table.

She said, 'It looks like Mummy's a bit late. I'm going to tell her what a good girl you are, and how much I like having you in my class.'

Then Mummy came in, and apologised for being late. It was pouring with rain, and her umbrella and coat were all wet, and dripping on the floor. Miss asked Mummy if she would like to take her coat off, but Mummy said, 'No. That's fine. I won't stay too long.' Her voice was a bit loud.

Miss showed Mummy my work, and said that I was a very hard worker, and a joy to teach. Mummy looked very pleased, but started coughing, so Miss got her a glass of water.

Mummy's hand was shaking a bit, and she looked very cold. I thought the water was going to spill over the top of her glass. Then Mummy reached in her bag and took out her purse, and gave Miss a ten-shilling note and said, 'I want you to take this. I want to thank you for looking after Pippa. I'm sorry I haven't done it before, but things have been…'

Miss coughed and looked at me. Miss said, 'It's very kind of you, Mrs Dunbar, but I couldn't possibly take it.'

Mummy said, 'But I insist. Spend it on yourself. But whatever you do, don't give it to The Black Babies!' Mummy laughed loudly, but Miss didn't, and her face went red.

Mummy said, 'You're Jewish, aren't you?'

Miss went even redder and said, 'I am, by birth. How do you know?'

Mummy didn't smile. I thought she looked a bit grave. She said, 'It takes one to know one.'

Miss told me to go into the next class, to see if Miss Woods needed any help. Miss Woods had gone home, so I sat outside where we hang our coats, and tried not to listen to what Mummy was saying. But she was talking very loudly, and then I heard her crying.

Miss came out and saw me. She told me to go to the staff room, and ask a grown-up to quickly bring two cups of tea. On the way to the staff room, I met a teacher who taught the older children. She had her coat on.

I said, 'My Mummy is crying, and Miss wants two cups of tea please.'

The teacher held my hand, and walked quickly with me back to my classroom. On the way, she opened Mr Grigson's door and I heard her say, 'Mrs Dunbar's here.'

He said, 'I'll be along shortly.'

The classroom door was wide open, and I heard Miss say, 'It's all right Mrs Dunbar.'

Mummy shouted, 'No, it's not all right! It'll never be all right!'

The other teacher said to me, 'Stay here, there's a good girl,' and went into the classroom and shut the door. I heard Mr Grigson's shoes coming along the corridor. I was very frightened. I jumped up onto a bench and stood very still, so he wouldn't see me. He went into the classroom, but left the door open.

I heard him say, 'Mrs Dunbar, it's time for you to leave now.'

Then Mummy came out and helped me put my coat on. When we reached the school's front door she said, 'Dash! I've forgotten my umbrella.' But she wouldn't go back in and get it. On the way to the bus station we got very wet. As we came into the bus station we saw our bus, and there were people getting on.

Mummy picked me up and started to run. I thought she was going to drop me.

Then she slipped and said, 'Damn! My heel's come off!'

We managed to get on the bus, just as the driver was about to close the door. All the way home, Mummy kept saying things like, 'What a waste of time that was,' and 'All that way just to get soaked, and break the heel of my shoe.'

Sometimes she laughed when she said it, but other times she just said it as she looked out of the window. But I knew not to say anything, and pretended to go to sleep. I hoped that Mummy would put her arm round me and kiss my hair, but she didn't. By the time we got home, it had stopped raining.

We prepare for Our First Holy Communion

In my third year at school, we were told that we had to prepare for our First Holy Communion. Father Daley came to our classroom, and told us that this would be the most important day in our lives. It would show God that we really loved Him. Then we would know God's Love, and even though we might feel hungry, our bodies would be full of God's Love. After that special day, we would be able to line up with the other children and grown-ups during Mass, to take Communion. I was desperate to take Communion, because I always felt hungry. Bridget was not desperate to take Communion. She told me that having to take Communion was hard, because you had to go without breakfast before you went to Mass. This was so that your body would be clean enough to receive the Communion. After that you could have a cooked breakfast, if you were lucky enough. Non-Catholics and young children who didn't take Communion could eat as much breakfast as they liked on a Sunday morning.

Miss told us that a nun would come into class three times a week, to prepare us for Our First Holy Communion. The first lesson with Sister Theresa was called *Catechism*. There were lots of questions, and we had to learn the answers *off by heart*. I can only remember the first question. It was, *Who made you?* And the answer was, *God made me.*

Sister Theresa introduced us to *Sin*. I knew a little bit about Sin already. If you did something naughty, then some children would say, 'Oh! That's a Sin. I'm telling Miss.' Sin was a word I heard about in Mass. We were asked to pray for *Sinners*. I imagined a Sinner to be just like the man who had stood at the bus stop, and smelled of drink and said The F Word.

Sister said that everyone had a *Soul*. The Soul was like a white sheet, inside your chest. When a baby was born, its Soul was not white, but grey. It was grey because Adam and Eve had sinned. They were the first people to have sinned. What they did was so terrible, that it made God not like them. He called them Sinners. Because of this bad thing that they had done, they were vanished from the garden. Their Souls were black, and this meant that they were not allowed to see God anymore. When Eve had a baby, his Soul was not white, but grey. This grey colour was the stain of Original Sin. That was the Sin that his mummy and daddy had done. So now all babies are born with a Soul that has a nasty grey stain on it. But God loves babies. He wants them to know His Love. So he tells priests to use holy water to baptise babies as Roman Catholics, so then their Souls will be white. This is called being in a State of Grace. After you have had Communion, you are in a State of Grace. So if you die then, you will go straight to Heaven.

If a baby dies before it has been baptised as a Roman Catholic, it can't get into Heaven, because its Soul is grey. It goes to a place called Limbo. A baby in Limbo can never go to Heaven. That is why it is so important for The Black Babies to be baptised as Roman Catholics, so they can go to Heaven. Sister told us that she once worked in a hospital, and a baby was dying of pneumonia, which was like a very bad cold. The priest came and used water from the cold tap to baptise the baby, just in case it died. We all wanted to ask if the baby had died and gone to Heaven, or was saved by the holy water from the tap. At playtime, Bridget told me that she was sure that the baby would

church it was dark and cold. We sat in three rows, on the chairs outside the Confessional, and for some reason I was going to be last child to confess. The first person to go in was John McGreevy. I counted, to see how long he was in there for. I could only count up to 60 before I got mixed up, but I think he was in there for 82 seconds. When he came out, some children asked him what sins he had confessed to, and what prayer he had been given to say. Sister hissed at the children, and told them that Penance was between the Sinner and God.

Suddenly, another worry came into my mind; what if Father Daley recognised my voice? He knew Mummy, and he knew my name, and he had seen me when I couldn't eat the lentil soup. I screwed my eyes up tight, and tried not to think about the soup, or about telling Father Daley about my poo in the toilet. I tried to remember if I had ever said anything to him. I could feel myself getting very cold, and needed a wee. My fingers and toes started to feel like they had pins and needles in them.
I looked at Sister, but she was trying to pull a hair out of her chin. I supposed that someone had asked her a difficult question. I wanted to see Bridget, but Sister had separated us, because she thought that we were *trouble together*. Bridget was sitting next to Charles. Bridget didn't look at all worried. She said she was going to confess that she had said 'Shit,' and she was hoping to get three *Our Fathers* for that.

I looked at the paintings in the church. They were very big and horrible. There was one of Jesus carrying a big wooden cross, and falling down and the soldiers were laughing at him. I looked at the colourful windows. One was lovely. The sunlight shining through it made colours on the floor in front of the altar. I thought of Heaven, and I thought of Mummy in the car, and Uncle Eric doing a wee. I looked very closely at the colours on the floor, and felt myself slipping into My Colour Dream. Then I felt Sister tap me on the shoulder, and heard her say, 'It's your turn now. Go and confess.'

All the other children had left the church, and only Sister was with me. I felt very frightened, and thought I wouldn't be able to move. Sister said, 'Go on now,' and held my hand, and led me to the Confessional. The door was open a little bit, and I stopped walking and started to back away: a bit like a dog I saw once, that wouldn't move, so his master had to pull his lead and drag him. Sister took me up to the door and gave me a little push, and shut the door behind me. There was a chair that was made so that you had to kneel down on it, and face the wall. There was a crucifix on the wall and you could see Our Lord quite clearly. There was a little window to the side of me, that had been covered over by a piece of cloth, and I could hear Father Daley on the other side of it, breathing and moving in his chair.

He said, 'Yes?'

I said, 'Bless me Father, this is the first time I have been in here, and I'm very frightened.'

He said, 'What are you frightened of?'

'Lots of things.'

'What sort of things?'

'I have never done a Sin. Sister said I should tell you that I have Bad Thoughts, but I don't know what that means. I'm sorry. I think I'm not very good at being a Sinner.'

Father Daley coughed, but didn't say anything.

So I said, 'My friend said I should tell you that I left a poo in the toilet, but it wasn't my fault. I tried to flush it down, but for some reason it just kept floating to the top of the water. But that's not true. She had done it, not me.'

Father coughed again.

Then I just told him whatever came into my mind next. I hadn't been thinking of it at all. It just came out. I said, 'I don't think my mummy loves me. I think she's going to die. I don't know who my daddy is. If Mummy dies, then I will have to live in our house all on my own. It's very, very cold and I don't know how to light the fire.'

Father Daley said, 'Ah.' Then he said, 'Of course your Mummy loves you. I know she does. And she's not going to die, and you won't be left on your own.'

I said, 'Can I say a *Hail Mary* now?'

He said, 'Yes, of course you can.'

Ursula sleeps with me

I remember exactly when Ursula came to sleep with me. It on the day that Sister first came to talk to us about My First Holy Communion. I had known for a long time that every Roman Catholic child or grown-up had a Guardian Angel. He was sent by God, to look after us. You couldn't see him, but he was always there. This idea fascinated me. It was a comfort too. Once, in Mass, I was feeling very bored, and I almost fell sleep. To keep myself awake I stared very hard at Father Daley, as he stood in front of the altar. I saw a dark shadow moving behind him. I knew it was his Guardian Angel.

One evening not long after that, I was lying in bed, trying to go to sleep. But it was still light, and I could hear other children playing on the other side of the road. Sometimes I would stare at the curtains, and if I didn't blink they would suddenly seem very far away. Then I knew I was about to go to sleep. This time I stared at the curtains, and I saw a girl my age sitting on the chair by the window, where I always left my clothes. She had long and light orangey-brown hair.

I said, 'Excuse me, but if you sit on my clothes, they will get all squashed.'

She said, 'Whoops-a- daisy. Sorry!' and laughed. This was her way of letting me know that she wasn't sorry at all. Then she said, 'I'm a bit cold. Can I get into bed with you and get warm?'

I said, 'I don't see why not.'

Kenneth said this to me in the playground, when I asked him if I could hold his hand. Bridget said that he was always talking about me at home, so that meant that I was his girlfriend. She said that Kenneth liked me a lot, but he didn't want the boys in his class to know, because they might tease him. So that was why he said, *I don't see why not,* when really he wanted to say, *Of course you can.*

I wasn't sure I wanted to be Kenneth's girlfriend, because he had a wart on his hand. Bridget said he got this because he was always forgetting to wash his hands after he had wiped his bottom. I was careful to hold his other hand, with no warts on.

When I woke up in the morning, Ursula was next to me in bed. She was fast asleep and curled up in a ball. I could feel how warm she was. I said, 'Hey, wake up!' and she did and we talked for a long time. She told me that she was my Guardian Angel. Ursula always listened very carefully to what I had to say. But sometimes she would say things like, 'That sounds a bit silly' or 'You mustn't believe everything Bridget says.' I explained to her all about my Daddy in Malaya and about what a Sinner was. All she said was, 'Ah.'
We cuddled each other in the night, and this stopped me from being so afraid of the dark.

My First Holy Communion
Sister Theresa said we should all be very excited about receiving our First Holy Communion. She said it would be on a Saturday, and all our parents had been invited. The boys had to wear a white shirt, a navy blue tie and a red sash. The girls were going to wear a white dress and white shoes. The boys were told not to wear Brylcreem on their hair, because the Bishop was going to bless us. He was going to do this by touching us on the head. Sister said that the Bishop did not want to get his hands all sticky with Brylcreem.
We were told not to eat anything before Mass, but afterwards we would have a special meal in Father Daley's house. Bridget asked if we were going to have jelly and trifle to eat. Sister began to search for a hair on her chin, so Bridget said, 'It's all right Sister, I think it was a silly question.'

The most exciting thing for the children was that their parents, and perhaps all their families, were coming to see them in church. I was not at all excited. Apart from Christopher Higgis, I was the only one whose dad wouldn't be there. Christopher's dad was dead.
Ever since the time when Mummy came to see Miss, I hadn't wanted her to come to school again. I was worried that she might

talk loudly in church, or try and give Mr Grigson a ten-shilling note, or fall over in the street, or break her heel, or talk to herself on the bus on the way home. But Mummy said that of course she was going to come to see me receive my First Holy Communion. She wouldn't miss it for the world.

The day before our First Holy Communion, Sister took us into the church, and told us what would happen in Mass. She showed us how we should line up in the aisle, and then kneel at the altar, and how the Bishop would hold up the chalice and say, *The Body of Christ*, and then you had to say, *Amen*. Then you had to stick out your tongue, and he would put a very thin piece of dry bread called The Host onto it. But, Sister said, under no circumstances was anyone going to chew The Host, because it was Christ's Body. The secret was to close your mouth and The Host would melt on your tongue. This worried Bridget.

At playtime, Bridget shook her head and looked grave. She said she was worried that she might chew Christ's Body. She and Kenneth had been playing 'Priests and Nuns' in their garden. Kenneth had taken the loaf of white sliced bread from the kitchen, and made Bridget cut round circles out of each slice, to make lots of Hosts. He said that he would be Father Daley and Bridget had to be Sister Theresa. Bridget got cross about this, because Kenneth told her she had to pretend to pick hairs from her chin. Whenever Bridget received The Host from Kenneth, she said that the bread got stuck to the top of her mouth and on the back of her teeth, so she had to stick her finger in her mouth to get it off, and then chew The Host.
Then Bridget's dad came home from work, and fancied a sandwich. When he saw all the holes in the bread, he shouted out of the window, 'What the bloody hell's going on?'
Kenneth said that he was showing Bridget how to be a Good Catholic.
Bridget said her dad just laughed and shook his head. He didn't look grave.

In bed that night, Ursula said she was sure my daddy was funny, just like Kenneth and Bridget's. But she didn't think he was the sort of daddy who said *bloody* all the time.

I receive Communion

On the Saturday of First Holy Communion, Mummy gave me a bowl of cornflakes for breakfast and a boiled egg and toast. I was very careful not to spill anything on my white dress. My white shoes were slightly too big, so I had to walk a bit slower than usual, to stop them from rubbing. When I had finished eating, I reminded Mummy that I wasn't supposed to eat before Mass. Then Mummy said that she wasn't feeling very well, and that I'd have to go on the bus on my own.

I cried. This was the first time I had ever cried when Mummy said something to me. I was frightened of going on the bus on my own. So she changed her mind, and said she would take me on the bus, but perhaps she would sit at the back of the church, just in case she had to pop out and get some fresh air.

Mummy was very quiet on the bus. Her face was very pale, and once I thought she was going to be sick. When we got to the church, we were a bit late, because Mass had already started, so Sister Theresa held my hand and took me to the front. I looked round and saw Mummy sitting at the back. She waved at me.

When Mass was finished, all the children had to wait at the front, while everyone else left the church. Then we were taken out onto the lawn by the side of the church, to have our photo taken. The girls sat on chairs in a row, and the boys stood on a long bench behind us. All the parents were standing behind the photographer, looking at us. But I couldn't see Mummy there at all. I imagined she was sitting down behind the group of parents, because she wasn't feeling very well. After the photographer was finished, all the parents came forward to say *hello* to their child, and to take them to Father Daley's house.

But I knew that Mummy wouldn't be there, so I got up and joined the group of children going into Father Daley's house.

There was lots of lovely food to eat, and it had all been made by Father Daley's Housekeeper. I didn't feel hungry; probably because I had had a big breakfast. Bridget said she was starving, and helped me eat my sausage roll and my fish paste sandwiches. I ate half of my trifle, and Charles helped me to finish it. There was so much noise in the room, that nobody noticed that I wasn't eating. Then we all sat down on the floor, and a man came in and did some astonishing magic tricks. He swallowed a ping pong ball, then made it come out of a boy's ear. Then he swallowed it again, and made it come out of a girl's leg. He screwed up a small coloured hankie in his hand, but when he pulled it out again it was so long it just seemed to go on forever!

Then it was time to go home. When we went outside, all the parents were waiting in the playground. Bridget's dad was smoking a cigarette, but when he saw us he quickly threw it on the ground and trod on it. It was still there on Monday morning. I knew Mummy wouldn't be there, so while the other children were meeting their parents, I walked to the bus station. I thought Mummy would be there, waiting for me to take me home on the bus. But she wasn't there either. Then I realised that I didn't have any money for my bus fare, and didn't know what to do. I thought I was going to cry, but didn't. I ran as fast as I could back to school. One of my new shoes came off, and it started to rain a little bit. I didn't have a coat. I looked in the playground, but everyone had gone.

Then I saw the Bishop and Father Daley standing in front of the church. They were smoking cigars and laughing. Then they shook hands, and Father walked towards his house, while the Bishop got in a car and drove off. I ran to Father's house and knocked on his door. His Housekeeper opened the door and called for Father. He was still smoking his cigar, but as soon as he saw me he handed it to his Housekeeper, and bent down and asked me what was the matter.

Father told me to come inside and sit by the front door, while he went into another room and spoke to his Housekeeper. I heard her say, 'Really Father, the woman is just awful!'

Father came out and told me to go and help his Housekeeper to tidy up, and then I could have a biscuit and a glass of lemonade. He put on his hat and coat, and went out of the front door. I helped the Housekeeper for a long time. She told me to look and see if I could find a ping pong ball, because the magic man had dropped one by mistake. That was a very exciting thing to do. I didn't find it, but picked up three sausage rolls and a tube of Smarties from under the table. Then I heard the front door open, and people talking in the hall. They were all men. I didn't hear Mummy's voice.

Father Daley came in and said to me, 'We are looking for your mummy. Did she say where she might go?'

I told him that she hadn't been feeling well, and had said she might go out of the church to get some fresh air.

Then the phone rang, and Father Daley left the room. He had left the door open, and I could see that one of the men in the hall was a policeman. He had taken his hat off.

I heard him say, 'They've found her. She was down by the river. Quite a long way away, in fact. She was singing. Very loudly. In French.'

Father Daley takes us home in his car

In Father Daley's car, Mummy explained that she had been walking by the river, and hadn't realised what the time was. Mummy was in the front and I was in the back. Mummy had got wet in the rain, and the Housekeeper had given Mummy her coat to put on. Father Daley was very quiet in the car. Once he said to me, 'Are you all right back there? Are you enjoying the ride?'

Mummy tutted, and Father Daley said, 'What on earth is going on here?'

When we got home, Mummy couldn't find her key for the front door. She opened up her bag and everything fell out. There were lots of pieces of toilet paper, all twisted up so they looked like fat white sausages. Father Daley asked her, 'What are those?'

Mummy said, 'Don't you know? Your Church calls it Eve's Curse. I've got My Special Visitor today.'

I looked at Father Daley's face. It was very red.

When we went indoors, Mummy told me to go upstairs. She told Father Daley to wait in the hall, because she wanted to tidy the dining room. I was on the stairs and I could hear her moving some bottles. Father Daley looked at me. He didn't shake his head, but he did look grave. I went to my bedroom and hoped that Ursula would be there.

I could hear Mummy and Father Daley talking in the dining room, but I couldn't hear what they were saying. Then Mummy raised her voice and I heard her say, 'Everything was fine until she was three. Then we had to come back to bloody England!'

I hid under the covers, but Ursula didn't come. Then I heard Mummy's voice call out from her bedroom, 'Father, why not come upstairs and hear my confession?'

I heard the front door close.

In the market

I realise that I haven't really mentioned Patricia and Matthew, the older children who looked after me on the bus, on the way to and from school. Their parents knew Mummy, and they lived in a big house on the other side of the road, past the church. Patricia and Matthew were very quiet, and only really spoke to give me instructions, like telling me to hold their hand when we crossed the road. I liked them a lot, because they were always there, and I knew exactly what to expect from them.

Every Wednesday, there was a market in town. On the way to school, we would walk through the stalls, and watch the stallholders getting everything ready. On the way back home, we would see them all packing up. One day on the bus going home, Patricia told me that sometimes in the holidays her mum took her to the market, to see all the stalls. I asked her to describe each and every one in great detail. Patricia and her brother talked for a whole hour, which is how long it took to travel home from school. As they were talking, I went into My Colour Dream. I had never heard Patricia and Matthew say so much. They knew I loved colour, so described all the different colours of the things for sale.

One Wednesday morning, we were walking through the market, and heard lots of shouting at the fish stall. An enormous seagull had landed on the stall and was trying to steal a large fish. The fishmonger was shouting and waving at the seagull, while his wife was screaming in fright. I was fascinated, and stood still to watch, but Patricia tried to pull me away. All day I thought about that huge bird and the fish. I told Miss, and she was very interested, and asked me to stand at the front of the class, and tell all the other children about what I had seen. Usually I never wanted to talk in front of the other children, but I was so excited that Miss had to tell me to stop. The next day, one of the boys said his dad had heard that the seagull had flown high up in the air, but had dropped the fish, and it had landed on a man's car.

A painting competition

A short while after that, Miss told us some very important news. There was going to be art competition, and children in all the schools in the town had been invited to paint a picture. The title of our picture had to be *The Market*. Miss was sure that I would like to paint a picture, and told me I could spend as long as I liked to think about and finish it. All the girls, and just a few of the boys, wanted to do a painting. The girls all chose their favourite stall, and painted a lady standing behind a table. When they had all finished, I was still thinking. I looked in the Ladybird book, *Sea and Estuary Birds*. I stared at a picture of a seagull for a long time. While I was staring, I was remembering exactly what had happened in the market, and imagined what the bird did before and afterwards. I knew I had to do two paintings.

I drew a line across the middle of my piece of paper. At the top of the first half I wrote *What the seagull saw*. I imagined the

66

bird high up, looking down on the market winding along the road. I imagined him seeing everything as a blur, apart from a huge fish. Miss called it a *bird's eye view*. The stalls were lightly-coloured blocks, and you couldn't really tell what each stall was selling. I imagined the seagull not being interested in those stalls. But the fishmonger's stall was very detailed, with a bright blue and white-striped roof, and a large pot of fish on the pavement next to it. I started to use a pencil to draw all the detail of the fish, but I knew it wouldn't look right. I asked Miss if I could use a pen, but she said we didn't have any in our class. I remembered that the older children were allowed to have pens, so Miss sent Bridget and me upstairs to ask for one.

The only time I had been upstairs in school had been on my first visit with Mummy. She had said that Mr Grigson was a *buffoon*. Patricia told me this was another way to say someone was a stupid fool. Bridget said that Kenneth had told her that a good word to describe Mr Grigson was *arsehole*. Bridget swore a lot these days. She said she didn't care, because all you had to do was confess. Then all your sins, like swearing and leaving floaters in the toilet, would be washed away.

Bridget knocked on the door very loudly and marched into the class. Everyone looked at us. Bridget said, 'This is my friend, Pippa, and she needs a pen and a bottle of ink, because she's going to do a painting, and is going to win the competition.'

The teacher said to me, 'So you are the clever girl who has done all the lovely paintings in Mister Grigson's office? Of course you are going to win.'

We came back to class with three pens and a small bottle of black ink. I was so excited, I felt myself shake all over.

I drew the huge fish very carefully. When the ink had dried, I painted over the fish in a bright but watery red. My next painting was a blur of grey and white feathers, and I used the pen to draw the beak with the pale red fish in it. The only bright colour was the seagull's beak, which I painted yellow. I wrote at the bottom *What the seagull did.*

I had spent most of the morning working on my paintings. Miss allowed Bridget to watch me, and talk to me about what I was doing. I let Bridget help me mix the colours, and write her name next to mine at the bottom. Miss said my painting was *extraordinary*. She said she wanted me to show it to Mr Grigson. I started to cry. This was the first time I had ever cried when Miss said something. Miss asked me, 'But Pippa, whatever is the matter?'

I told her I was worried that Mr Grigson might thrash me and steal my painting.

I think that most teachers would have changed their minds at this point, and allowed me not to go to the Head Teacher. But Miss was, I realise now, a very sensitive and wise person. She said, 'I understand, but I want him to see it. I know he will be very pleased. And I want him to tell you that he is pleased. So I will go with you after you've eaten your lunch. And Bridget can come too.'

I didn't think it was such a good idea to let Bridget come with me. During lunchtime I became less worried about Mr Grigson, but more worried that Bridget might call him an *arsehole* to his face.

Miss came to fetch us from the dining hall. She had my painting with her. We walked along the corridor towards Mr Grigson's office. Miss held my painting and Bridget held my hand. Bridget started to swing her arms as were walking along, and Miss told her to be sensible. I think Bridget was trying to show me that she wasn't scared. We reached the big crucifix, and stopped at Mr Grigson's office. The door was closed. I wondered if he had a boy in there, and was about to thrash him. Miss knocked on the door, and we heard Mr Grigson say, 'Come in.'

He was sitting behind his desk. There was a dirty dinner plate in front of him, and he was just finishing smoking a cigarette.

He said to Miss, 'Please sit down Miss Marchant. And who have you brought with you? Ah, it's Bridget and Miss Dunbar.'

He looked at me, but I tried not to look in his eyes. But I could see that his forehead was covered with long lines going from one side to the other. His whole forehead looked like a leathery field that had just been ploughed. I found this quite fascinating. Every time he asked a question, his big bushy eyebrows went up into his lines.

'What shall I call you, eh?' he asked me, 'Philippa or Pippa?'

I was too frightened and fascinated to speak.

Bridget said, 'I call her Pippa. She's scared of you, Mr Grigson. She don't like to ask questions, so I try and ask them for her. We're best friends, you see.'

Mr Grigson smiled at Bridget. I wondered which hand he did the thrashing with.

He said, 'Well, we shall see. What have you come to show me?'

Miss put the painting in my hand and I quickly gave it to Bridget. She put it on Mr Grigson's desk. The corner of the paper got stuck in a dollop of tomato ketchup on his plate.

Miss said, 'Whoops!' and grabbed the paper and wiped it with her hanky.

Mr Grigson said to Bridget, 'Tell me about the pictures.'

Bridget said, 'On the top there is a market and underneath there is a seagull.'

Mr Grigson said, 'Ah.' I saw that his teeth were all yellow. He said, 'Well that's very interesting, but what is happening in the top part of the picture? And why did you divide the painting into two parts? What's happening on top looks very different to what's happening beneath. And I'm keen to find out why you chose to give the seagull a yellow beak.'

Bridget said, 'Don't ask me. I just mixed the paints for Pippa.'

I thought she was about to call Mr Grigson a *stupid arsehole*. So to save her, I began a long and very detailed explanation about how I had imagined myself as the bird, and how hungry I was, and that was why, as soon as I had seen the fish, without thinking, I flew down and pounced on it. And how I was panicking because the fishmonger was yelling and waving his fists, and his wife was screaming, and how my wings were flapping, and I was filled with terror, because I knew that if I didn't get away, then I would be killed. But even though I was terrified, I wasn't going to let go of that fish.

Then I explained how I wanted everyone to look at the yellow beak, so that would be the main thing that they looked at in the painting. I wanted to say, 'And this is my picture, so you can't have it', but stopped myself just in time.

Mr Grigson said, 'My, my. That is quite remarkable. Truly astonishing. I have never seen anything like it from a child so young. And such a detailed explanation. It's extraordinary, don't you think, Miss Marchant?'

My teacher's face was very red, but I didn't know why. Her voice was a bit wobbly. I wondered if she was as scared of Mr Grigson as I was. She said, 'Yes. I agree. These two children are quite exceptional, in their own ways. It's lovely to see how they help each other. I'm very proud of them.'

Mr Grigson said, 'And so you should be Miss Marchant. You are doing a fine job.'

Then he looked at his watch and at the packet of cigarettes on his desk. I knew this meant that it was time for us to go. Miss said, 'Come on girls.'

As we left the room, I heard Mr Grigson cough and strike a match. Bridget held my hand again, and Miss tickled me behind the ear and gave my other hand a squeeze.

A few weeks later, Miss told the class that Bridget and I had won *First Prize for Primary School Art*. We were given a book each called *Pinocchio, the Tale of a Puppet*. Miss told us that she had gone with Mr Grigson and some of the other teachers to the town library, to see our painting hanging on the wall, and to collect our prizes. She said she was very proud of us, and that it had been one of the proudest days of her life. She was especially proud because I was so young, and a lot of the children in the competition had been much older than me.

A boy called out, 'My mummy says that being proud is a Sin.'

Miss didn't say anything about that, but she did say, 'Of course, all the other paintings we painted were lovely, and everyone in class helped, because you were all so well-behaved while the girls were painting. So I think we all deserve a piece of chocolate.'

She had a very big bar of *Galaxy Milk Chocolate*, and there was enough for one piece each and an extra one for Bridget and me. Bridget said, 'I love you Miss.' Miss went red.

Two things happen

One morning, neither Patricia nor Matthew were waiting for me at the bus stop. For the first time, I had to go to school on my own. I felt quite grown up, but a bit frightened about crossing the big road in the town. That day, two things happened.

The first thing was with Dennis Stewart. For some reason, during lunchtime, we were in our classroom on our own. Dennis said, 'Can I show you something?' I knew, I just knew, exactly what he was going to show me. He pulled down his trousers and I saw something sticking up straight between his legs. I was fascinated. He said, 'My sister calls it my stick. Can I see what you've got?' Then a big girl came in and said, 'Oh you dirty things! Stop doing that!' But she laughed, and said she thought that Dennis' thing was funny.

Then something else happened. On the bus going home, the two big boys from the other school came and sat next to me. I was by the window and they squashed right up against me. One of them said, 'Quick, show her your thing.'

The other one said, 'No. Let's see what she's got.'

He grabbed my dress and tried to pull it up. I tried to slap him, but he just laughed and managed to put his hand on my private parts. He squeezed and it hurt. Nobody else on the bus noticed. The bus came to a stop, and the bus conductor started walking up the aisle towards us, so he let go. She asked if we were all right, and one of the boys said something rude to her, so she said, 'Leave her alone. She doesn't want to hear language like that. Go and sit somewhere else.'

The boys just laughed and went to sit up at the back.

At bedtime, I told Ursula all about Dennis Stewart and the horrible boys on the bus. She said that I must go to Confession. I asked her if I had committed a Sin. Ursula said that she wasn't sure, but if Father Daley told me to say three *Hail Marys*, then that would mean that it was quite a bad sin. If I got three *Our Fathers* then they had been extremely bad Sins. I tried to explain to Ursula that it wasn't me who had sinned. It was the boys on the bus who had done horrible things. But Ursula had curled up next to me, and was already fast sleep.

The next day, I told Mummy I had a tummy ache and didn't want to go to school. She asked me if I had eaten breakfast, and I told her yes, I had made myself some Weetabix. She said, 'Well, you can't be very ill then, can you?'
I told her that Patricia and Matthew hadn't been on the bus, and she said that she had found out that they had chickenpox. I said I was frightened of being on the bus on my own, but she said, 'Nonsense, you're nearly eight.'
Patricia and Matthew weren't at the bus stop, but the horrible boys were there. They looked at me in a nasty way, and one of them whispered, 'Shitpants.' The bus came, and I sat near the front. The bus was already full and I had to sit next to a big man who was very smelly. He had a large blob of red jam on his trousers. I thought he was a tramp. He didn't look at me, and kept making a chewing movement with his mouth.

In class, Miss was speaking to us, but her voice sounded very far away, so I couldn't hear her words properly. At playtime, Bridget asked me to play with her, but I started to cry and told her I wanted to go to Confession. After playtime, it was PE in the hall. We had to get changed into our vest and pants, to do Music and Movement. But while all the other children were getting changed, I just stood there and couldn't move. Miss told me to get a move on, but I just stood still. Then she told me not to worry, and held my hand as we walked with the other children towards the hall.

Mrs Stephenson said, 'Of course she can come. That's a very good idea.'

I was quiet again, and could hear more noise in the hall. Mummy was saying, 'I'm all right. I can walk on my own.'
I knew that Mummy was leaving, so I pushed my bedcovers back, and ran downstairs. Mummy had a small suitcase with her, and the policeman was helping her to stay standing up.
Mummy said, 'Goodbye Pippa. I'll be back soon. Be a good girl for Matthew and Patricia's mummy and daddy.'
The policeman helped Mummy bend down to give me a kiss. Her breath smelled of sick I didn't say anything, and then they went out of the front door.

When we got to Matthew and Patricia's house, their father was already at home. The children still had lots of spots, but Mr Stephenson said that they were no longer infectious, so I couldn't catch chickenpox from them. He had a very kind face, and I couldn't stop myself from talking to him. He sat with me in their front room, and asked me what I liked doing in school. I didn't answer that question. I asked him about Mummy, and if the policeman had come to our house because of the boys on the bus, and because I went to Bridget's house. And was Mummy ill because she was worried sick about me?
I was surprised that I could ask questions so easily.

Mr Stephenson explained that Mummy had been ill for a long time. The policeman had asked a doctor to come to the house, and the doctor had said that Mummy needed to have a rest in hospital. He was sure that Mummy thought about me a lot, and wanted to look after me properly, but that wasn't what had made her feel ill. He said it was a good thing that I had gone to Bridget's house. Mr Grigson had phoned the police, to explain that I was late going home from school, and that he was very worried about me. The policeman had gone round to our house, and found Mummy very ill and lying on the floor. If I had gone home straight from school, then the policeman wouldn't have found her.

I thought to myself, 'That's not such a strange thing. I've seen her like that before.' But I knew not to say it.

Mr Stephenson wagged his finger at me and said, 'But you mustn't do that again.'

I said I wouldn't, and started to explain that Bridget had made a mistake, but Mrs Stephenson came in and said it was time for the children to eat something, and then get ready for bed. She gave me a bath and I was allowed to sleep in Patricia's room. She had a big bedroom, and gave me a toy dog to cuddle in bed.

Mrs Stephenson sat on my bed and read us a story. Then we said our prayers together.

She said, 'Dear God, we pray for Pippa's mummy, and hope that she will be better soon.'

That's when I knew that Mummy was really very ill. We had prayed in school for Gordon when he had been very ill. But he never came back to school, so we *remembered him in our prayers*. We never prayed for people who just had a cold or chickenpox or a runny tummy. Those things got better without God's help.

I looked at the curtains, but Ursula wouldn't come.

In the night, I woke up and was frightened. But Ursula was there beside me. She said that God had told her that Mummy would be well soon. She told me that if I was good, then soon Mummy would come home.

I was very quiet and Ursula asked me, 'What are you thinking about?'

But I wouldn't tell her. So she said, 'I know what you're thinking.'

I said, 'No you don't.'

She said 'Yes I do. You're thinking that it's nice here.'

I didn't like Ursula for saying that, but it was true.

The doctor who fixes unhappy people

The next day was Saturday, so there was no school. We had a nice breakfast together. Mr Stephenson had to go to work, but

I thought that maybe the policeman had told everyone what to do. Then I had a terrible thought: what if Mummy wasn't allowed to go to Mass in the hospital? And what if she died suddenly, and wasn't in a State of Grace? Suddenly I saw a huge wave of water coming towards me from the other side of the room, and I remembered that I couldn't swim. So I screamed and screamed, and Mrs Best rushed into the room and picked me up and put me on her knee.

I said, 'I don't want Mummy to die.'

Mrs Best squeezed me and said, 'Poor lamb.'

Uncle Eric had already gone home.

I didn't go to school the next day. Mrs Best said a doctor was going to come and visit me. He arrived just after breakfast. He said, 'My name is Dr Rees, and my job is to make sure you are properly looked after.' He explained that he was going to give me a thorough examination, and that I had to take all my clothes off, except for my knickers. He listened to my chest, and looked in my ears and mouth and in my eyes. He checked my hair.

Then he said, 'Now if you'd just slip you knickers off, I'll take a quick look down there.'

I was outraged. I nearly shouted at him. I grabbed hold of my knickers, so he wouldn't be able to touch them.

Mrs Best said, 'All right now.'

Dr Rees said, 'Of course. I understand. Don't worry. No harm done.'

I was still angry with him and said, 'The nasty boys didn't see anything, you know. But one of them grabbed me very hard.' I think my voice was very loud.

Dr Rees looked very surprised. He asked me, 'What nasty boys?'

'The ones on the bus. I told the policeman.'

The doctor's face stayed very still. 'And what did the policeman say?'

I told him that the policeman had said *Did they now?*

'And what did he say he would do?'

'He didn't say he would do anything. He just took Mummy away. I think if I hadn't said that about the nasty boys, then maybe she would be here, and not having a rest in hospital.'

'Well, Pippa, I can tell you that you did exactly the right thing. It was right that you told grown-ups about that. Your mummy is having a rest because she is ill. She is not ill because you told the policeman about the boys.' He stopped talking, and looked at me. Then he looked at Mrs Best. I knew he was thinking about what to say next, just like Patricia's dad. So I waited.

Dr Rees said, 'Pippa, I'm going to tell you something very important. Your mummy is very unhappy. Because she is unhappy, she drinks lots of that yellow drink in the bottles. It's called *whisky*. Sometimes grown-ups drink too much of it, and it makes them ill. The problem with whisky and those types of drinks is that once you start drinking too much, it's very difficult to stop. So you have to go away to hospital, so that doctors and nurses can help you stop.'

I didn't say anything.

He said, 'Do you understand?' I told him I did. I didn't say anything else, so he said, 'Do you want to ask me any questions, Pippa? Is there something you would like to know?'

I told him that Mummy didn't like me to ask questions.

Then he said something, and I felt like he had slapped me in the face: 'She doesn't like you to ask questions about your daddy?'

I didn't know what to say. I went red and looked down. He waited, and I knew that he wanted me to say something. I just said, 'We don't talk about Daddy.'

'But you'd like to?'

All I could think to say was, 'All I know is that he makes rubber and wears brown trousers.'

I am in a state of collapse

I didn't go to school the next day either. Mrs Best said that I needed to have a rest and, anyway, she needed me to show her where everything was. She asked me, 'How do you feel about not going to school?'

I didn't really understand what she meant. So she gave me a list of words to choose from. I chose *disappointed*. I explained that when I had gone to bed, I thought I was going to go to school, but then I found out I wasn't going, after all. I was disappointed, because I wanted to see Bridget. I knew that she would be worried about me. I wanted to tell her about everything that had happened.

Mrs Best said that I was very good at explaining how I felt. She said that was a very good thing to be able to do. I looked out of the window, at the bus stop. I could see the nasty boys waiting for the bus. The policeman was there. He was talking to them. They looked frightened. When they got off the bus at the end of the day, the policeman was there again. He had two ladies with him. I think they were the boys' mothers.

That evening, Mrs Best asked me to help her lay the table for tea. During the day, we had made a steak and kidney pie. She taught me to sing a new song: *All Things Bright and Beautiful.* I loved it from the moment I heard it. Mr Best came in, and started whistling the tune. My ear started aching, and the whistling sounded very loud. My fingers started feeling itchy, like I had been touching stinging nettles. Mrs Best asked me to get her a spoon from the drawer. I put my hand among the spoons, but the noise of the spoons banging together was too loud. I tried to say, 'My ear hurts', but no sound came out. I wanted to say, 'I think I'm going to be sick', but my mouth started to fill up with saliva. My eyes filled with water, and I had a horrid taste in my mouth. Then I was sick all over the knives and forks and spoons.

Later, another doctor came to see me. He looked in my ears, and explained to Mrs Best that he could see from looking at my eardrums that there was a lot of liquid behind them. And the smell of my breath told him my tonsils were infected. I found it very difficult to open my mouth and say *aaah*, and it hurt a lot when I swallowed. He took my temperature, and said I was very hot.

Mrs Best said that I had been all right yesterday when Dr Rees had examined me. The doctor said he thought I was in a state of collapse. He told Mrs Best, 'We used to see children like this in Berlin, after The War. They had spent all their time surviving, but once they were safe, just collapsed. Of course they were deeply traumatised too.'

Mrs Best said, 'Poor lamb.'

After the doctor left, I just slept. I slipped in and out of dreams. I wanted to wake up, but the dreams were too powerful. I could feel myself sliding from one dream into another. Sometimes I would almost wake up, and feel that I needed to go to the toilet, but my dream wouldn't let me wake up properly. Some dreams were just silly, but one in particular was very frightening. The nasty boys were in my garden, playing with a white cat. The cat could only move the tip of its tail,, and I could see that it was very old. The boys kicked the cat, to try and make it move. They tried to pick it up, so that they could throw it around. An old lady came out of my house and shouted at them, 'Leave it alone! Can't you see it's dying?' The boys just laughed and ran away.

I reached over to see if Ursula was there, but slipped into another dream. I was at school, and there were empty bottles everywhere. They had all been washed and carefully arranged in boxes. The playground was full of them. They were all very shiny in the sunshine.

In the morning I felt terribly thirsty, but it hurt to open my mouth, and I couldn't swallow. One of my eyes was very itchy, and my cheeks felt boiling. My pillow was all wet and smelled, from where I had been dribbling. Mrs Best had to pick me up, to help me go to the toilet. While I was sitting on the toilet doing a wee, she touched my sweaty hair and said, 'You are a very good girl.'

I said, 'Thank you very much' and she laughed.

Ursula came to see me. She didn't say anything, but I could feel her warmth next to me. I wanted to ask her if Guardian Angels ever got ill. Then I slept again, and suddenly woke up knowing that Guardian Angels were real people who had died and gone to Heaven, and had been given a special job of looking after other people who were still alive. I thought of Mummy being ill. I suddenly knew that she drank too much whisky because of her sadness. I suddenly knew what she was sad about. I had that terrible fear about her not being in a State of Grace. I wanted to scream and scream and scream, but it hurt too much. I tried to get out of bed, but fell over, with a loud bump. Mrs Best came running up the stairs, and picked me up.

She said, 'Let's try putting you in Mummy's bed.' As she carried me across the landing, I could hear a phone ringing. Mrs Best said, 'We've had a phone put in.'

Father Daley comes to visit

I liked being in Mummy's bed. Her pillow was very soft. In fact, the whole bed was soft. Being in her bed made me feel calm. I stopped thinking about her and the State of Grace. Mrs Best stayed with me until I went to sleep. When I woke up, it was dark, and Ursula was lying beside me. I tried to speak to her, but my throat was still very sore, and my mouth felt very dry.

Ursula said, 'Don't try to talk to me. Just think it.' But I fell asleep again.

Mrs Best told me that I would have to stay at home for the rest of the week. Then it would be the Easter holidays, so there would be no school for two weeks. I don't think I quite understood what she was saying; I often got mixed up about what weeks and months and years were. I was in Mummy's room, and the window was open. Though it was still quite cold, I felt warm as the sun shone on the bed. The phone rang. It was Father Daley, telling Mrs Best that he was on his way to see me.

Mrs Best said it would be better if Father could see me in my own bedroom. She asked me if I wanted to walk, but just the thought of walking made me feel tired. She said, 'There's still a little way to go before you are completely better.'

I didn't want Father Daley to come. At the time, I couldn't think why, but looking back I think it was because he knew about everything. He didn't know it because he could talk to God, but because of what Mummy had told him downstairs. I knew that Mummy had told him everything: about why she was unhappy, and about the whisky. And I was absolutely sure that she had told him all about me, and all about Daddy. I could feel myself getting very hot. Ursula came. She gave me a kiss. It was the first time she had ever done that.

Then Father Daley came in. He was dressed all in black, except for his white collar. He was holding something. I thought it might be a present from Mummy, but it was just his big Bible.

He sat on my bed, and straight away said, 'I've seen your Mummy, and she asked me to give you a present.'

I looked at his Bible and he laughed, 'No not that. It's in the car. I'll go and get it.'

I wanted to say, 'You've seen Mummy!' but realised I couldn't say anything. My throat was really starting to hurt, and my ears felt all stuffed up, and I couldn't hear properly.

Father brought me a tin. It was pink and white and it said *Quality Street* on the lid. I knew it had sweets inside. Father said, 'Mummy thought you would like the colours of the sweet wrappers. She said you could ask the doctor if you might eat a sweet after you've had your medicine. She's sorry that you're ill, and wants you to get better as soon as you can. She says she's getting better, and hopes to see you soon.'

I felt myself getting hotter. Then Father said, 'You'll be going to a new school after Easter. In the village. It's not a good idea for you to go so far on the bus.' And he talked some more; about how he was sorry that I wouldn't be going to a Catholic school, and that I must remain a Good Child of Christ. I could still go to Mass on Sundays. Perhaps I would see some of my old friends there.

I could feel myself getting even hotter. Father's mouth was moving, and I could just about hear him ask, 'Will you miss your friends? Is it Bridget you will miss the most? And I expect that you'll miss your nice teacher? It's for the best. Let's say a little prayer together.'

The last thing I remember him saying was, 'I will ask the children to remember you in their prayers.' Then I looked at the curtains. They were speeding towards me, and then suddenly they were rushing far away. I saw Ursula sitting on the windowsill, and I screamed out, 'Save me Ursula! I'm going to die!'

I don't remember anything else about what happened in the house. Later, Mrs Stephenson told me that I suddenly started shouting and making strange noises, and my eyes were wide open. I went blue, and Father Daley yelled, and Mr Best came rushing in. I was turning grey, and he thought I was choking. But I had swallowed my tongue and couldn't breathe. Mr Best put his fingers in my mouth, to try and pull my tongue out of the way, but he said that I slowly began to bite his fingers, and I wouldn't open my mouth. Then he knew exactly what was happening and he shouted, 'She's having a fit. Put her on her side!' As soon as he did that, my tongue flopped out and I could breathe again. But I went very stiff and was still making funny noises. Mrs Best dialled 999, and asked for an ambulance to come. Then she rang Mrs Stephenson, to find out if Dr Stephenson could come and help.
Father Daley had started crying and said, 'Please Lord, don't let her die.'

I don't remember being in an ambulance at all. Everything about that event is very vague in my memory. Apparently, my temperature had risen very rapidly, and this had made me have a fit. Mrs Stephenson came to see me in hospital the next day, and brought Patricia and Matthew with her. Dr Stephenson worked in the hospital, but he was a bit too busy to see me. It was Patricia's birthday, and her Granny and Grandad had come to stay with them. But Patricia was so upset when she heard that I had been taken to hospital, that she had insisted on coming to visit me.
Patricia said, 'I have brought you a present. Well actually we all have. Daddy found it in a big bookshop. He thought I might like it, but then he saw a picture on one of the pages, so he bought it for you, instead.' She handed me a parcel, wrapped in white wrapping paper. Matthew had drawn all over the paper. There was a big heart, and a tank. Patricia told me that their mum had

told Matthew off for drawing the tank. Matthew didn't say anything. His face was very red. He had burst into tears when he saw me for the first time. I was fast asleep when they came in, and he made so much noise that he woke me up.

Inside the paper was the most beautiful book I had ever seen in my whole life. It was *The Flower Fairies of the Trees* by Cicely Mary Barker. Matthew said, 'Have a look at the pages, and see if you see anything special.' I tried to turn the pages, but my fingers were shaky. So Matthew helped me. He showed me a page. It was *The Alder Fairy*. 'Daddy says she looks just like you; your hair, your arms and legs. Everything!'

And she did. There I was, with my short, dark curly hair, swinging on a branch. But I had seen another picture that was much more fascinating. I was looking at *The Willow Fairy*. It was Bridget. In that moment my interest, my fascination, my passion for trees began.

I started to feel hot again, and Mrs Stephenson looked alarmed and told Patricia to go and find a nurse. She said, 'There, there,' and gave me a kiss on my forehead.

I whispered to her, 'Is Mummy in this hospital?'

Mrs Stephenson said, 'No, I'm afraid not. Mummy's in another one.'

I didn't say anything. Mrs Stephenson said, 'It's in London. It's a very, very good hospital.'

I didn't know where London was. Patricia came with a nurse. I reached out my hand and Patricia held it very tight. I pulled her towards me, and whispered to her. Patricia started crying. Not loudly like her brother, but a long stream of tears ran down each cheek. Mrs Stephenson asked her what I had said. Then she started crying too.

What I had wanted to say was, 'I don't want to die'. But what came out was 'Thank you for loving me.'

Mr Shepherd

I didn't die. But the thought of dying was worse than anything I had ever experienced. I was allowed to go home, but it took me several more days to get fully better. Matthew lent me some of his favourite jigsaw puzzles. They were quite difficult, so Mrs Best helped me. My favourite was called *The British Isles*, and had all the big towns on it. Mrs Best explained that Mummy was in a special hospital near London. Sometimes I had to remind myself that Mummy had gone away. It wasn't that I didn't want her to come back; it was just that I knew I was being looked after very well, and didn't want it to stop.

The tin of sweets and the Flower Fairies book became my favourite objects. I took them to bed with me and spent hours looking closely at the fairies in the book. It made me want to go outside and look at as many trees as I could. I was disappointed to find that there was no Crab Apple Fairy in my book. So I invented my own. Mrs Best helped me get my paints out, and to cover the dining room table with newspaper. I found that in a few minutes I had recreated exactly the same colour as I had done for my original crab apples. It was the same yellow-golden-pink colour. I imagined my little fairy with a cloak of the same colours, reaching up to pick an apple from a cluster of three. Her hair and the shine on her cheeks were made up of the same colour.

I wasn't interested in painting the fairy herself; I was trying to make an impression of her movement, as she reached upwards. It was a kind of coloured blur. I got a huge amount of pleasure from thinking about that blur, and how to create it. I tried to make the apples as apple-like as I could.

Mrs Best looked very pleased, and sat down to watch me. She said, 'I'm so pleased to see you up and about again. The colour in your cheeks reminds me a little bit of one of your apples.'

Then I had to stop, because I was feeling tired. Mrs Best said I wasn't to worry about clearing up.

I sat and looked at my painting. I wanted to give it to Bridget. Mrs Best sat in Mummy's armchair and said, 'Come and sit on my knee.' She asked me if I would like to say a prayer with her. She began, 'We are thankful for Pippa and her painting. Thank you for giving her the gift of using colour. We are thankful because she is feeling so much better.'

I was a bit surprised, because she had made up her own prayer. I was quiet for a while, and thought about what to say. I prayed, 'Thank you as well. But I wish I could ask questions.' Then I said to Mrs Best, 'Is that all right?'

She laughed and said, 'Of course it is. And you've just asked me a question!'

A few days later, there was a phone call. Mrs Best said a man called Mr Shepherd was going to visit. They had spoken on the phone for a long time, and he was going to come and introduce himself. Something about Mrs Best's voice made me think that she wasn't pleased about Mr Shepherd coming.

Mr Shepherd arrived the next afternoon. He had driven a long way in his car. As soon as Mrs Best let him in, he said, 'Would you mind most awfully if I use your lavatory?'

I had no idea what he was talking about. He went upstairs and I heard him going to the toilet.

We went into the front room. It was nice and warm in there, but Mr Shepherd kept his coat on. Mrs Best asked him if he would like a cup of tea, but he said, 'No thank you.'

He sat on the settee, and I sat on a small chair in front of him. Mrs Best didn't come back in.

Mr Shepherd coughed and said, 'I hear you have been unwell. I'm sorry to hear about that. Are you feeling better now?'

I looked at the floor, and didn't say anything.

He said, 'I've seen your mother. I saw her yesterday, in fact. She's feeling much better now.'

That was a real surprise. I wanted to ask lots of questions, but the only thing I could say was, 'Ah.'

He carried on: 'Yes. She's so much better, but wants to stay near London. She says it will be better for her. She wants you to move there, to be with her.' He didn't stop to see my reaction. If he had looked, he would have seen me go red and my eyes filling with tears.

He carried on again: 'Yes. And we have found a new house for you both. It's jolly nice, with a big garden, and there's a Roman Catholic school not very far…'

But I was crying loudly now, so he had to stop talking. He took off his coat and opened the door and called, 'Mrs Best, do come in. Perhaps we should have that cup of tea after all.'

I didn't say anything. I was incapable of saying anything. But I felt that I hated Mr Shepherd. I knew it was a Sin to hate, but he deserved it. I sat on my little chair and thought, 'He's seen Mummy, and she's better.' Then I stopped hating him, and stopped crying too.

Mr Shepherd started talking again, but I couldn't pay attention to what he was saying. I felt very thirsty, and wanted to get up and leave the room. But my legs wouldn't move. I wanted to say, 'Excuse me Mrs Best, but I feel very hot,' but I couldn't.

I heard Mr Shepherd ask me if I wanted to speak to Mummy on the phone one day.

I wondered if I looked around, towards the windows, I would see the curtains moving away from me and then rushing towards me again. But I couldn't turn my head. Mrs Best picked me up, and as we left the room I heard Mr Shepherd say, 'Never mind. It will all be fine in the end.'

Goodbye Northumberland

I didn't want to move to a new house near London. I had been trying to get used to the idea of going to the village school. Ursula had convinced me that it would be fun. I thought of it as a way of escaping from going on the bus. I couldn't get used to the idea of not being able to see Bridget in school. I even asked Ursula if I could call her Bridget. Ursula said she would think about it. I think that meant *No*, because she never mentioned it again.

A few days after Mr Shepherd's visit, Mrs Best brought a big suitcase into my room, and said that we had to pack all my belongings, ready to take to my new house in the morning. The new place was called *Rayners Park*. I told Mrs Best that I didn't understand what was going to happen. She sighed. Mrs Best was nearly always cheerful. But sometimes she made a big sigh. Then she would say things like, 'Life can be difficult sometimes.

I'm going to try and explain it to you.' Mrs Best thought that most difficulties in life were caused by grown-ups making the wrong decisions. So when she sighed, I knew that she thought that my move to Rayner's Park was a wrong decision. She didn't say that, but I could feel that she was unhappy about me going. I don't know why, but in a small way, this made me feel better. But the biggest part of me was filled with sadness. I decided to tell Mrs Best how I felt.

I said, 'Mrs Best, you have been very kind to me. Before you came, I was very lonely and frightened. I was always cold and hungry. Thank you for looking after me. I promise you that I shall never forget you. When I am grown-up and have lots of money, I will find you and Mr Best, and buy you a nice big house, next door to mine.'

Mrs Best had small tears in her eyes and said, 'God bless you my dear. I'm happy. I'm happy that Mr Best and I have been able to look after you properly. We will never forget you. How could we? You are such a sweet girl. But I know that you are very strong inside. So you keep being a strong girl. But you must tell people if something happens that you don't like. That's just as important as telling them about things that you do like. Will you remember that?'

I said I would, and gave Mrs Best a kiss.

It didn't take long to pack my suitcase. I didn't have many belongings. I asked Mrs Best if she would look after my paintings for me. She said that she would roll them up carefully, and put them on the lorry that was going to take all Mummy's things. Mrs Best said that I would be leaving early the next morning.

In bed that night, I tried to explain to Ursula how I was feeling inside. But I really didn't know. When you are eight, you really only have the words *happy* and *sad* to explain your feelings. So I tried to picture what was happening inside of me. My life felt like a jam jar full of clean water. There were lots of strong colours dripping into the water, one drop at a time. All the people I had known in my short life were in those drops.

Mummy was in a very big drop of green. Miss was there, and Bridget, and Mrs Best, shining very brightly. Father Daley was in there too, as a drop of purple. Then the nasty boys came in two very dark drops, like ink, which made the water turn very dark and quite ugly-looking.

Ursula said, 'Ah', and was quiet for a long time. Then she said, 'I'm sure if you hold that jar up to the sunlight, it will look like a very unusual and interesting colour.'

I had been thinking exactly the same thing. Ursula promised she would come with me to Rayners Park. That made me feel a lot better.

The next day, after breakfast, Uncle Eric came in a taxi. Inside myself, I wanted to scream and shout at him. But he smiled at me, and said how much better I looked, and how pleased he was to see me again. So I stopped wanting to hurt him. He said that Mr and Mrs Best had done an excellent job of looking after me. Mrs Best looked very sad, so I tried to make everybody laugh. I said, 'Would you mind most awfully if I used the lavatory?'

It worked, because Mrs Best smiled and Uncle Eric laughed. I went upstairs to the toilet, then looked in my bedroom for the last time. The sun was shining through the window. In the street a big dog was doing an enormous poo on the pavement. The dog's owner was standing, waiting for it to finish.

As I came downstairs, Uncle Eric gave Mrs Best an envelope and said, 'This is from Mrs Dunbar. She's very grateful to you, for all that you and Mr Best have done for her daughter.'

Mrs Best hesitated, then took the envelope and said, 'Thank you Mr Baxter. Please thank Mrs Dunbar, and tell her how much we have enjoyed looking after Pippa. It was a real pleasure.'

Then she bent down and gave me a hug and a kiss, then we got in the taxi that was waiting outside.

I think any other child would have asked lots of questions; about the journey, and about where they were going to live. But I felt as if I was completely blocked up. Of course, I wanted to ask if Mummy would be in our new house, but I couldn't ask, in case the answer was *no*. Uncle Eric must have sensed this, because he explained everything in a way that I would understand. We were going to go on a big train to London, and then take a small train to Rayners Park. It would be very late by the time we got there, but Mummy would be waiting for us. Mummy was feeling much better, but still needed lots of peace and quiet.

I began to feel excited, but thought that I shouldn't be happy, because I would never see Bridget again, or Mrs Best, or Patricia and Matthew.

On the train

I had never been on a train before. It was very exciting. We were in a compartment with three other people: an old lady, a man, and a big girl who was wearing school uniform, with a very short grey skirt and no tights. She sat opposite me, and smiled at me every time she caught me looking at her. But when Uncle Eric looked at her and smiled, she went red and looked away. She kept crossing and uncrossing her legs. I wasn't allowed to do that, because grown-ups said that I had to sit nicely, with my legs together.

The man asked Uncle Eric if we were going to London. Uncle Eric said that we were, then carried on looking at his newspaper. The man took out his pipe and asked Uncle Eric if he minded if he smoked it.

Uncle Eric said, 'Actually, I'd rather you didn't, because there are children present.'

The man looked annoyed, and went into the corridor to smoke. When he came back, he started asking Uncle Eric questions. Did Uncle Eric work in London? Yes, he did. What did he do? Uncle Eric tried to pretend he was reading his paper, but the man kept on at him. So Uncle Eric explained that he was an art critic. Sometimes he wrote for newspapers, but mostly he wrote for magazines. Sometimes he gave people advice about art that they might want to buy.

The man got quite excited, but not in a happy sort of way. 'Oh. So I imagine that rich people coma and ask you what's worth buying as an investment, or to hang in their big houses, as a way of impressing their rich friends.'

Uncle Eric looked out of the window. The man went on: 'And what do you think of so-called *Modern Art*? Is that where all the money is these days? Nobody seems to care much about the Old Masters, or what I call good old-fashioned British artists, like Stubbs or Constable, or even Hogarth.'

Uncle Eric cleared his throat. The girl stopped reading her book, and looked at Uncle Eric with interest. 'Well, how to explain? Art is like music. It's a matter of taste. What one person likes, another person can't stand. Like you and your hatred of Modern Art. So my job is to write about art as I see it. Not everything I see appeals to me. Sometimes a painting or a sculpture makes me feel that I might be sick. But then I think, "Is that what the artist wanted me to feel?" I think that being in a gallery is like being in the theatre; where you might not be enjoying what the actors are saying or doing, but they are so good, that you forget that they are acting, and you believe it is real. You are having an intense emotional reaction to something that is art.'

The man kept trying to interrupt, but Uncle Eric wouldn't let him. 'Take Turner, for example, who I'm sure you'll agree, is one of our greatest painters. His work is what one might call *modern*. Often you have to look closely at the painting's title, and read a little of the background to the painting, before you can work out what he has painted. But his technique, his use of light and colour, is masterful.'

Then he rustled his newspaper and pretended to start to read it. But the man kept on again: 'I suppose you'd say the same about music? All this new jazz, for example: all speed and improvisation, but absolutely no tune or rhythm.'

Uncle Eric shook his newspaper and said, 'I think we've taken this conversation as far as it can go.'

The man took his pipe out, and went into the corridor to have another smoke. The old lady leaned over, and tapped Uncle Eric on the knee. She said, 'I'm awfully sorry. Don't take any notice of my son. He lost his father and older brother in The War. He had a breakdown, and ever since he's been quite hostile to people who he doesn't agree with. People like yourself, for example, with new ideas. It's not an excuse for bad behaviour, but it does help to explain it.'

I looked out of the window for a while. It was fascinating to see the backs of houses as we went through towns, and then the fields with cows and sheep and horses in. Then I noticed that I could see the big girl's reflection in the window. She had taken her navy blue school hat off, and had put it on her knees, so she could rest her book on it. She had long dark brown hair in a long plait, which had that kind of shine to it that you see on conkers, as they peep out of their shells. Her blazer was navy blue, and she was wearing a very clean white blouse and a navy tie with gold diagonal stripes. I was surprised that she had chosen a light-grey skirt, but she looked lovely in it. Then I noticed that she was looking at me, and she smiled when she saw that I had seen her.

I tapped Uncle Eric on the arm, and tried to whisper, 'Excuse me Uncle Eric, but I need to go to the toilet.' But my voice came out a bit louder than I had hoped, and the girl smiled again. I could feel myself going red.

He said, 'Oh. Well then…' in a way that made me know that he wasn't sure what to do.

The girl spoke for the first time. She said, 'Excuse me, sir, would you like me to take her?'

Uncle Eric looked very surprised, but said, 'Well, that's very kind of you indeed. What a splendid idea.' He reached in his pocket and offered her some money and said, 'When you've finished, why not pop along to the buffet car, and buy yourselves some chocolate?'

The girl looked very embarrassed, but pleased at the same time.

The train was going very fast, and I almost fell over, so the big girl held my hand. Her hand was very warm. She said her name was Yvonne, and I told her I was Pippa.

She said, 'I have a friend in school called Pippa. She's a very fast runner and can speak French very well.'

I said, 'Well I don't run very much, but I love painting.'

She said, 'That's lovely. So do I.'

We found the toilet, and Yvonne pushed the door open. I had imagined a huge room with a bath in it. This toilet was tiny, so Yvonne had to help me squeeze past her. The train was rocking from side to side, and I was a bit frightened, in case I fell over.

Yvonne was laughing and said, 'Here, let me help you.' She helped me get on the toilet, and held my hand while I did my wee, then helped me wash my hands. Then she said, 'It's my turn, I need to go now.'

I didn't want to wait for her outside, in case the man with the pipe was there. Yvonne told me that she didn't mind if I stayed with her. I tried not to look, but I could see that Yvonne had some hair in her private place. I said, 'My mummy's got hair there too.'

Yvonne smiled and said, 'Well yes, I'm sure she has. All ladies have it.'

I was astonished. 'But you're a girl!'

'Well I'm a grown-up girl. I'm nearly sixteen. All ladies and grown-up girls have hair there. And we have these too.' She pointed to her breasts. 'Your mummy must have those.'

I had to think about that. 'Actually her chest is quite small. But those things, I think they are called *teats*, well they are quite dark and quite large.'

Yvonne laughed and said, 'Nipples. They're called nipples. We use our breasts and nipples for feeding babies.'

It was very noisy in the toilet, and difficult to have a conversation without shouting. I said, 'I suppose that's why you call them *nibbles*, because that's what the baby does when he's feeding.'

Yvonne shouted, 'Nipples! Not nibbles!'

There was a loud knock on the door, and a man shouted, 'Is everything all right in there? There are other people who want to use the lavatory, you know!' It was the man from our compartment. I was frightened. Yvonne laughed.

I couldn't resist telling her, 'When Mummy's cold, you can see her ripples stick right out. Once when she and Uncle Eric were in the bath together, I heard him shout, "Watch where you point those things, or you'll have someone's eye out!" They both laughed so much when he said that.'

97

Yvonne said, 'Goodness.'

A group of young men were standing at the entrance to the buffet car. They were drinking beer from tins. One of them whistled at Yvonne and shouted, 'Lovely legs darling!'

Yvonne laughed and said, 'Thank you very much.'

I told Yvonne I thought they were buffoons. She said, 'I think they're soldiers.'

Yvonne bought a KitKat, and we stood and shared it together. Back in the carriage, Uncle Eric was pleased to see us and said, 'Mission accomplished?'

Yvonne smiled and went red, and gave Uncle Eric his change. The old lady was asleep. The man hadn't come back, so I asked Uncle Eric if I could sit next to Yvonne.

He said I could, until the man wanted his place back.

Yvonne said she wanted to finish reading her book, because she had just come to a good bit. I sat quietly and looked out of the window. I could feel myself falling asleep.

The man must have come back, and sat next to Uncle Eric. I heard him say to Uncle Eric, 'Sorry about being so hostile earlier. It's my nerves. Can we start again? I'm actually interested in art, but am a bit ignorant, as I'm sure you've gathered.'

Uncle Eric laughed and said, 'Yes, of course. And I'm rather interested in your point of view.'

I didn't pay attention to anything else, but felt myself snuggling up to Yvonne. I woke up shortly afterwards, and felt Yvonne's arm around me. She smelled a little bit of sweat. Uncle Eric was saying, 'Take Pippa for example. She's very young, but already quite an extraordinary artist. Her feel for colour and light is very strong, and typical of some of our most accomplished painters. It's pure instinct really. She doesn't realise what she's doing, of course, but her paintings are already highly abstract. Not like a child's painting at all. She's not really interested in drawing or technique, but I'm sure that will come. I'm hoping that she'll meet my aunt soon. She's a well-known watercolour artist and illustrator, and I'm sure that she and Pippa will get on well.'

The man asked, 'And this talent, this gift, where does it come from?'

Uncle Eric said something that kept me wide awake for the rest of the journey: 'Oh, from her father and his relatives. They all love art in some way or another. Her mother's talents lie elsewhere.'

Our new house

It was late evening when we arrived at our new house. Mummy was sitting in the kitchen, drinking a cup of tea. She said, 'Hello. It's very late, but let's all have a cup of tea.' She was looking at the space between Uncle Eric and me, so I couldn't tell which one of us she was talking to.

Uncle Eric patted me on the head and said, 'Well go on, say *hello* to your mother then. Don't be shy.' He gave me a very slight push, and I found myself walking towards Mummy. I wanted to give her a hug and a kiss, but she said, 'Come and sit down. I've made us a cake.'

So I sat down opposite her, but knew that I shouldn't talk about the past.

I was dying for a wee, and said, 'Mummy, I need to go to the toilet.'

Mummy put her cup down so quickly that I thought she had broken the saucer. She stood up and said, 'Of course you do. What am I thinking about? Here, let me take you upstairs and show you our new house. I've made your bedroom nice for you, and I've even been doing the gardening. You will be going to your new school in a few days' time, so we must get you a new uniform and some new clothes; so we'll be very busy.'

The words were rushing out of her mouth. She held my hand as we walked upstairs, and I could feel her hand trembling a little bit.

My bedroom was nice. My window looked out onto the street in front of our house. There was no front garden, but a paved area, with a big dark stain in the middle of it. I supposed it was from some oil, that had leaked from a car that had been parked there. There was a low wall, that I thought would be nice to walk along the top of, and right in the corner was a tree stump with small branches growing up out of it. Across the road, right opposite our house, was a dark alleyway. I thought it would be nice to spend time looking out of that window. Then a man walked by with a dog, and let it do a wee at the entrance to the alley.

But it was the curtains in my room that caught my attention. They were white, with a light blue repeated pattern of a small yacht on the sea. Mummy was standing behind me as I looked out of the window. As I ran my fingers over the curtains, she said, 'I made those curtains for you. I thought you would like them.'

I didn't know what to say. I just kept feeling one of the curtains. I was thinking about the puddle on the path in the garden of our old house. One very cold morning, the puddle was covered in ice. The ice was clear, but looked black. I pressed the ice with my shoe. It moved, but wouldn't break. As I pressed, I could see the water making bubbles, and spreading out under the ice, as if it was trying to escape. I pressed harder and harder, and suddenly the ice shattered, and dirty brown water spurted out all over my shoe, making the foot of my tights wet. I had expected the ice to break, but the dirty cold water gave me a fright. For the rest of the day I walked around with a cold wet foot; too scared to tell Mummy what I had done.

I heard Mummy ask, 'Well, do you like them?'

I nodded. I wanted to say, 'Of course I do! Why did you choose boats? And why that colour?' But I didn't say anything. I couldn't.

She said, 'I saw a hedgehog in the garden last night.'

Uncle Eric didn't stay very long. Before he left, he took me into the garden. We walked through the French windows, onto the stone terrace, and down the steps onto the lawn. Uncle Eric lit a cigarette, and talked about the daffodils that were all dying in one of the borders.

He said, 'They're all finished for this year, but don't worry, they'll come back next Spring.'

At the end of the lawn was a wild patch, that was full of nettles and brambles. I could just see a low wall around a rectangular pit, that was full of old bricks and broken pieces of concrete. I imagined that that was where the hedgehog lived.

We looked at our two trees. One was a cherry that was just coming into blossom. The other was a huge oak. I looked up to the highest branches, and saw Ursula. She waved at me.

I said to Uncle Eric, 'Please Uncle Eric, I want to climb that tree.'

He looked very surprised and said, 'Oh. I thought you had completely lost your tongue. That's a very high tree for a little girl like you to climb.' Then he lit another cigarette. I knew he was thinking about something. 'What about a swing?' he asked, 'Let's see if we can get you a nice rope swing. Would you like that?'

I said, 'Yes please.' Then I surprised myself as I said, 'Uncle Eric please don't go.'

He took his cigarette out of his mouth, and threw it into the daffodils. He squatted down next to me and held both my hands. He asked me, 'Why? Why do you want me to stay?'

'Because I'm frightened. I'm frightened of Mummy.'

He said, 'Ah.'

I thought he wasn't going to say anything else, so I kept talking: 'I know she had a breakdown. Like the man on the train. She has the nerves. It was probably because of The War.'

He said, 'Yes, Mummy has had a kind of breakdown. Yes, her nerves get very… they get very *stretched* sometimes. And I'm sure The War did have something to do with it. But she's getting much better.'

Getting much better? That was not what I wanted him to say. I could hear my voice getting quite loud. 'But *getting much better* is not the same as *she is better*. Mummy is only *getting* better. She's not better yet!'

Uncle Eric didn't reply to that. He just said, 'But I'm coming back. I live in London. That's not so very far away.'

There was something about Uncle Eric that made me want to tell him exactly what I was thinking. Now that I had started saying how I felt, I wasn't going to stop. 'I want Mr and Mrs Best to come and look after me. I wasn't cold with them. I had nice food. They talked to me, and we sang songs, and I had stories at bedtime. I wasn't lonely and on my own, and I was never frightened.'

Uncle Eric said, 'I'm quite sure that you'll like your new school, and will make lots of new friends. And I'm going to introduce you to someone who I know you will like. We really must get you painting again.'

I knew that he was trying to cheer me up, and it was working. I hadn't thought about painting for a long time. I was longing to take a close look at the cherry tree. I looked up at the top of the oak, but Ursula had gone.

That night Mummy made baked beans on toast. She came upstairs and gave me a goodnight kiss. I looked at the curtains, but Ursula didn't come.

My new school

On my first day at my new school, Mummy took me early, before the other children had arrived. As soon as I entered the front door, I knew that I would like this school. We waited outside the office and looked at a very strange painting. It was so real that it looked like a photograph. Jesus was on a cross that was floating in the air. The cross looked like it was made out of cardboard boxes. Jesus had no clothes on, except for a tiny piece of cloth round his Private Place, held on by string.

Mummy said, 'How modern. Just like this school. It's all very modern here.'

I wasn't sure if being *modern* was a good thing or a bad thing, but I liked it.

The head teacher was called Sister Clare, and we met her in her office. I knew immediately that we wouldn't like each other. Mummy sat down in front of Sister Clare's desk, while I stood at Mummy's side. Sister Clare looked me up and down, but didn't speak to me at all. Her clothes were much longer and much blacker that Sister Theresa's at my previous school. Her face was surrounded by stiff white cloth. I didn't like her face, with her small mouth and small ugly glasses. I couldn't imagine her smiling. She had a brief conversation with Mummy, about dinner money, and making sure that I arrived in school on time. She said that she hadn't decided which class I would be in. Then Mummy said goodbye, and Sister Clare asked a big girl to take me to the assembly hall.

I wanted to cry, but the big girl held my hand and said, 'I remember when I was new. I cried when my mummy left me, and all through the first morning. But at lunchtime we had sausage and chips. The cook gave me extra chips, because I was new, and a boy said he wanted to marry me, and I've loved this school ever since!'

I couldn't help smiling when she said that.

In the assembly hall, all of the children were sitting in rows on the floor, facing the stage. I sat at the end of one of the rows. Some children turned round and looked at me, and smiled. Sister Clare stood on the stage. She told everyone that some boys had been putting toilet rolls down the toilet. She said that this was an Extremely Selfish Act, and had to stop. If it continued, then no boys in the school would be allowed to have toilet paper.

She said, 'God is everywhere. He sees everything. He knows who is putting the toilet rolls down the toilet. If you do that, then you are going against God.'

All the teachers sat on chairs round the side of the hall. One of them kept looking at her fingernails while Sister Clare was talking. She had short hair and very round red cheeks, that had lots of tiny holes in them. I looked at her for a long time, and when our eyes met, she smiled at me. I closed my eyes and prayed to God that she would be my teacher. At the end of assembly, all the children left the hall. I didn't know what to do, so I stayed sitting on the floor. Then the teacher with the short hair came over and held out her hand and said, 'Hello Pippa. I'm Miss Dawson. You are going to be in my class. I'm very pleased about that.'

There is such a thing as love at first sight, and I felt it. I felt warm. It was a kind of warmth that started in my tummy and went upwards to my face, and I could feel it in the tips of my ears. Then I felt big tears fall out of my eyes, and run in two long streams down my cheeks. Miss Dawson knelt down next to me and said, 'Goodness! Don't worry; your mummy will be back at the end of school to collect you. And this afternoon we are going to do sewing. I'm sure that you'll love that. And we'll make sure that you have lots of nice friends.' She wiped my eyes with her hanky, and held my hand all the way to class.

I only have a few memories of lessons with Miss Dawson, but I remember, more than anything, that she liked me. And because she liked me, I wanted to be a good girl, and do my best for her in every possible way. I can remember that she taught us how to knit, and I made a scarf and a donkey. I remember standing by Miss Dawson, as she sat at her desk, showing me how to sew the donkey's head on. She asked me what my daddy did and I said, 'I don't know. Mummy says he makes rubber, and has lots of factories in Malaya.'
Miss said, 'That's interesting,' and I knew that she wanted to know lots more. I would have told her if she had asked me, but she didn't. She wore a beautiful ring. It was gold and had three small red stones in it.

One afternoon it was pouring with rain. The sky was so dark that it looked like winter, even though it was late spring. A boy called John Paul stood up, and then fell on the floor and started thrashing around. Some of the children screamed, but Miss Dawson said, 'Everyone be quiet and sit down. I know what to do.'
She told me to get her a wooden ruler, and she forced it sideways between John Paul's teeth. I could hear his teeth biting down hard on the ruler. There was a hissing noise and we could see that John Paul was weeing himself. Miss told a boy to run to the office and say that John Paul was having a fit. None of the children said anything; we were very, very frightened. A nun came running in and told Miss Dawson to phone for an

ambulance. Then she told us we were all very good children, and that John Paul was having a fit, but he would be all right. She took us into the hall, and we all sang hymns with her, while Miss Dawson stayed in class with John Paul.

It was a shock to see John Paul lying on the ground, and making noises like an animal. At home time, all the children from my class were telling their mothers about it. I stood in the playground thinking about whether I should mention it to Mummy or not. Then I noticed that most of the children had gone home, but Mummy hadn't arrived yet. I knew she wasn't going to come, so I walked home. I knocked at the front door. Nobody answered, so I sat on the front step. Then Mummy came round the corner. Her face was red, and she laughed and said that she had gone shopping, and didn't realise that she was late.
I said, 'I'm big enough to walk home on my own from now on.'
Mummy agreed that that might be a good idea.

The attack
If Mummy felt sorry for being late, she didn't say so. She was very cheerful, so I decided not to tell her about John Paul's fit. We had our tea, then she put out two chairs on the terrace. It had stopped raining and the sun had come out, making the large light brown stone slabs on the terrace shine. The rain had knocked all the blossom from the cherry tree, and it was spread out on the bright green grass underneath, like a round pink sheet. I looked intently at the blossom, and felt the sun on my face, and imagined the ripe cherries, and wondered if they would be bright red or red-black, and thought of a time when I had cut my fingertip, and how the blood had been very dark. I could feel myself sliding into My Colour Dream. The colours of the tree and the blossom were becoming very clear to me, and starting to merge together. I held the colours, to stop them from moving, and imagined this as my next painting.

I was swinging my legs, and Mummy said, 'You used to do that when you were little. That's how I knew that you were happy and content, in the time before you could talk.' Mummy's voice sounded as if she was on the other side of the terrace, even though she was sitting right next to me.

She said, 'Are you all right? Are you feeling sleepy? You were a funny little thing; always happy on your own, but happiest when you were with me. We could have left you in your pram for hours. But I didn't want that. Your father would tell me, "Just leave her. If you pick her up all the time, you will spoil her." I fed you myself, until you were quite old. Your father told me to stop doing it, but I didn't listen. You were still feeding from me when you were two and a half years old. I used to love the way your little hand would hold onto my breast.'

She closed her eyes. She had mentioned Daddy twice. She said, still with her eyes shut, 'I was eighteen when I got married. Just ten years older than you are now. Can you imagine that?'

These were the moments I longed for; when Mummy was calm and felt free to mention Daddy.

She smelled my hair and said, 'Come on, let's give that lovely hair of yours a wash.'

I liked it when Mummy offered to wash my hair, because it was a sign that she was happy. Then I could have extra hot water and stay and play in the bath, and Mummy would rub my hair dry, and look me all over, and ask me about any cuts or bruises that she could see.

But over the next few days, Mummy gradually changed. This always happened. I would feel this change in her when I came home from school. She wouldn't turn round to talk to me when I came in the room. And when she finally spoke to me, her voice sounded harsh and grating. We sat in silence while eating our meals, and she sighed deeply. On the following days, if she dropped something, she would shout, 'Oh Damn it. Damn it all!' The next day would be a very angry day, full of rage and terror. On a terrible day like that, she tried to hit me for the first time.

I woke up, and it was a Saturday. I went downstairs, and Mummy was sitting at the kitchen table. She was still wearing her dressing gown. She said, 'I suppose you want some breakfast?'

106

I said, 'Don't worry. I can get it myself.' I went to the cupboard to get the packet of cornflakes, but dropped it and some cornflakes spilled onto the floor. As I was kneeling down, desperately trying to pick the cornflakes up, I heard Mummy's chair scrape backwards, and the sound of her opening the cutlery drawer. I wondered if she was getting a sharp knife to stab me with, but when I looked up she was coming towards me with a wooden spoon. She shouted, 'You minx! You minx!'

I rushed out of the kitchen, and straight up to my bedroom. I waited for her to charge up the stairs, but instead I heard a plate smash against the kitchen wall, and her shouting, 'I never wanted you! You have ruined my life!'

I didn't know what to do. I was too terrified to move, in case I made a noise. I had forgotten to do a wee before I went downstairs, and was bursting. I waited by my bedroom door, listening for a sound that would give me a clue where my mother was, and what she was doing. I opened my door a tiny bit and saw her running up the stairs. I couldn't see a wooden spoon in her hand. She rushed past my room and slammed her bedroom door behind her. I went downstairs as quietly as I could, and went into the garden. I didn't see Mummy for the rest of the morning.

I stayed in the garden, under the oak tree. Finally, I went into the kitchen, and made myself a sandwich with bread and butter and jam, and took it back outside. I needed to do a poo very badly, so went through the back door, into the kitchen. I was being as quiet as possible, but I couldn't hear anything. Then I had a very strange experience. I stood perfectly still in the kitchen, and I could feel myself floating up to the ceiling, so that I was looking down on myself. I could see Pippa looking up at me. Then I shouted, 'Mummy! Are you all right?' But there was no answer. I ran upstairs, and knocked quietly on my mother's bedroom door. The door was locked. For a little while I wondered if she was dead behind that locked door.

I did my poo and sat on the toilet for a long time, listening. Then I went into my bedroom and sat on the bed, hoping that

Ursula would come. I was very hungry and thirsty, but didn't want to open that cupboard in the kitchen again. I thought of Miss Dawson, and decided to tell her all about Mummy trying to hit me.

I go to Mass on Sunday

When I woke up in the morning, I heard Mummy in the toilet and then going downstairs. After a while, I could smell eggs frying, so carefully put my slippers and dressing gown on, went to the toilet, then slowly went down the stairs. Through the bannisters, I could see Mummy in the kitchen. She was listening to the radio. She turned round and looked at me and said, 'What would you like for breakfast, Pippa? I'm frying an egg for myself. Would you like one?' She was smiling. I wanted an egg very badly, but remembered that we had to go to Mass and take Communion.

I said, 'But we have to take Communion.'

Mummy laughed and said, 'We don't have to have Communion today, and anyway, I'm not feeling too special, so I'm not going to Mass.'

This was awful. I was thrown into confusion, and felt panic rising inside me. It began just above my Private Place and ended in my tummy. I wanted to do a poo. I kept very still, but my mind felt like it would burst. Here was the problem that was rushing through my mind:

You must go to Mass on Sunday, unless you are ill.

Mummy says she is *not feeling too special*. But she is smiling and laughing, and cooking a fried egg. This means that she is not ill. Ill people do not smile and laugh and eat eggs.

If we don't go to Mass on Sunday, then we will have committed a Mortal Sin.

If we die, we won't be in a State of Grace, so can't go to Heaven. What shall I do?

I ate my egg, and Mummy gave me some toast and marmalade. The box of cornflakes and a jug of milk were on the table, but I didn't dare touch them. I wanted to ask Mummy if I could go to Mass on my own, but I was too frightened to talk to her. But I didn't want to commit a Cardinal Sin either. Mummy was sitting opposite me, eating a piece of toast and drinking her cup of tea. A fly landed on the jar of marmalade. Mummy saw it, and went to swat it away. She hit the jar of marmalade by mistake and knocked it over. She didn't say *damn*. So I knew it was all right to talk. I didn't look at Mummy. I just said, 'I'm old enough to go to school on my own. I think I'm old enough to go to Mass on my own.'

Mummy looked at me. I put a piece of toast in my mouth, but it tasted dry and horrible, and I wanted to spit it out.

She asked, 'Why do you want to go to Mass?'

I didn't understand why she was asking. Surely she knew about Mortal Sin?

I said, 'Because I want to be in a State of Grace, in case I die.'

Mummy laughed and said, 'Well then, you had better be careful how you cross the road, and make sure you go to Confession before you go to Mass.'

I said I would do both of those things. I didn't understand why she was saying such a serious thing and laughing at the same time. I now know that she was being sarcastic.

I had never been to Mass on my own. Mummy helped me put on my best dress, and brushed my hair. I felt quite grown up. When I arrived at the church I was early, and there were only a few people there. We had two churches. One was big and brown and old, and had been damaged in The War. It was all closed up, but one day, when Father Leighton had enough money, it would be made like new. The church where we had Mass was small and made of wood. I liked it, but Father Leighton said it was *temporary*, and that God wanted to see the old church *restored to its former glory*. I didn't like Father Leighton. He was small, and wore big black glasses that made his eyes look huge. He never smiled at me. Once, a baby started crying during his sermon. Father Leighton stopped talking until the mother took the baby out. Then he started talking again.

Father Leighton heard confessions before Mass. The Confessional Box was at the side of the altar, so if you wanted to go to Confession, you had to sit in the front row of chairs facing the altar. I knew that Father Leighton sometimes took a long time listening to people's Confessions. Once, an old lady was in there for such a long time that I missed my turn. A man sitting next to me in the front row nudged his wife and said, 'I didn't know old Mrs Wilson was such a sinner!'

His wife said, 'Shh!' but I knew that she thought it was funny.

I was always glad when Mummy came with me to Mass, because I still didn't know when was the right time to kneel, or sit down, or stand up. Mummy knew, so I just copied her.

But I thought how awful it would be to sit in the front row on your own, because you might stand up, while everyone behind you was kneeling down. You would look stupid, and people might say 'Shh!' but really be laughing at you.

That morning there were five people sitting in the front row. When they were in the Confessional, I could hear them confessing their sins quietly, and then Father Leighton muttering. I tried to listen to what they were saying, but I couldn't hear any words properly. I was the last one to go in the Confessional Box. Just as I shut the door, the organ started playing. This meant that it would soon be time for Mass to begin.

I said, 'Father Leighton, I haven't sinned, but I want to tell you something.' I tried to say it in a quiet voice, so that nobody outside could hear me.

He said, 'Speak up. I can't hear what you are saying.'

I said, 'I want to tell you that Mummy tried to hit me, and I'm frightened.' '

Father Leighton cleared his throat and said, 'You must have done something naughty. It is right that parents should punish naughtiness. The Confessional is a place for confessing sins, not for telling tales about your parents. Now go and say a Hail Mary, and try and be a good girl.'

When I left the Confessional Box, I could see that the church was full, except for the front row, which was empty. So I had to sit in the front row, all on my own. Once I stood up, but when I looked round, everybody was kneeling. Another time I knelt down when everybody was supposed to stand. Each time I made a mistake I had that horrible feeling just above my Private Place, and could feel my face going very red.

When it was time for Father Leighton to start his sermon, everyone began sitting down and tried to get themselves comfortable. I felt someone tapping me on the shoulder. I turned round, and saw that it was a man who was sitting next to his wife, and had two big girls and a boy with them.
He whispered in my ear, 'Come and sit with us.' I did as I was told.
As I was moving from the front row into the aisle, I could hear Father Leighton just beginning his sermon. He stopped suddenly, looked at me and cleared his throat and said, 'When we are all ready.'
There was an empty space in the row, and there was a bit of confusion and noise, as everybody moved seats so that I could sit next to the man's wife. I imagined that everybody in the church would be looking at me, but I didn't care. The man's wife patted my knee and said, 'Don't worry, you're with us now.'
She smelled of perfume, and her brown hat had a feather in it.

When Mass was finished, the man's wife held my hand. As we were leaving the church, she asked me, 'Why are you here on your own?'
I said, 'Mummy's not feeling too special.'
She said, 'My name is Mrs McCabe, and this is my husband, and these are our children: Peter, Frances and Bernadette. We live near you, so you can walk home with us.'
And that's what we did. Peter went to my school and was in the year above mine. I had seen him in the playground. The girls were much older than him, and went to another school. Both had very long hair.

The girls asked me where I went to school, and I told them it was Blessed Sacrament.

They asked me about my teacher. When I told them it was Miss Dawson, they both clapped their hands and said, 'You lucky thing!' and 'She's the nicest teacher in the world!'

Bernadette said, 'What do you think of The Penguin?'

I didn't know what they were talking about. She explained that this was the nickname that the children had given to Sister Clare. She whispered, 'She's horrible. She has a special stick that she hides in her habit, and uses it to beat boys who use swear words.'

Frances said to her, 'Bernadette, you mustn't say things like that. Have you ever seen The Penguin hit anyone with a stick?'

Bernadette said she hadn't, but she had seen her use a ruler lots of times.

Mrs McCabe said, 'That's quite enough, Bernadette!'

So it was true.

Bernadette kept talking, 'She's called *The Penguin* because last year all the nuns stopped wearing their horrible black habits, and began wearing grey skirts, and nice head coverings, so you can see their hair a bit. They all look really modern. But not Sister Clare. She still likes the old ways of the Church, and still dresses all in black. We think that her and Father Leighton are secretly in love.'

Mrs McCabe got quite cross with Bernadette, and told her to stop frightening me.

When we got to my house, Mrs McCabe took me to our front door, while the rest of the family walked across the road and up the alley. She knocked on the door, but there was no answer.

Mrs McCabe said, 'Perhaps Mummy is having a rest.'

I didn't realise that I was squeezing and un-squeezing Mrs McCabe's hand, until I noticed that she was looking at me and asked, 'Are you all right, Pippa?'

Then Mummy opened the door. She looked very surprised, and said to Mrs McCabe, 'Yes?' and then, 'Is everything all right?' Mummy had a cigarette in her hand. I thought that she didn't sound friendly.

was surrounded by ladies with bikinis on. One of the ladies was pulling the zip down on the man's shirt. He had a very hairy chest. Mummy came out and lit a cigarette, while we looked at the poster together.

She tutted and said, 'What is the world coming to?'

We walked into Peter's road, and Mummy took one last draw on her cigarette and threw it in the gutter.

Mrs McCabe came to the front door, and told us that Peter was very excited, and waiting for me in the garden. She said, 'Gosh, that's a pretty dress. I hope you don't it get filthy. Peter wants you to play in the garden all day.'

I knew that Mummy didn't like me to get dirty. She said, 'Oh, don't worry about that,' but I knew that she didn't mean it.

I looked at Mrs McCabe, and could tell from her face that she didn't believe Mummy either.

I couldn't find Peter in the garden. His garden was as long as ours, but wasn't very neat, and had a tree that was much taller than ours. A lot of trees had been cut down at the bottom of his garden, and were lying in great piles, with branches sticking out everywhere.

Then I heard Peter shout, 'Coo coo!' and saw that he was right at the top of the tree. He climbed down, and said he would show me how to reach the top, just like him. Then he looked at my dress, and looked very disappointed. I didn't want him to feel disappointed, and felt as if I might cry. I had been so excited about seeing him, and now the day was going to be ruined because I had disappointed him.

But if Peter was disappointed, he didn't feel it for more than a minute. There was a rope ladder attached to the first strong branch. He swung on it and told me to push him, and laughed as I spun him round.

Then he grabbed my hand and said, 'Let's go and talk to Mum!'

Peter's mother was in the kitchen. She was reading a book, while the dirty dishes from their breakfast were still on the table. Peter explained the problem of my dress, and then he whispered

117

something in his mum's ear. She smiled and said, 'What a good idea.'

The good idea was that I should wear some of Peter's clothes. I didn't think this was a good idea at all. Mrs McCabe said, 'Just think of it as dressing up. And anyway, nobody else will see you. And what's wrong with wearing trousers? Lots of girls wear them these days.'

I'd never worn trousers before. I knew that some girls and ladies wore them, but they were called *slacks*, and were obviously trousers for girls. Mrs McCabe could see I wasn't impressed, but I knew that it was going to be the only way for me to enjoy myself with Peter. She took me up to Peter's bedroom, and chose a blue polo neck jumper and a pair of green corduroy trousers.

She said, 'You're as tall as Peter. I expect you'll be tall when you grow up. You're a very pretty girl, and now you look like a very pretty girl in boy's clothes.'

She stood behind me as we looked into the mirror. She ran her hands through my hair, and gave both my earlobes a little tug. When Peter saw me, he laughed and said I looked just like him. I suppose I did, except my hair was short and dark and curly, while his was light brown and straight. I put on his wellies, but they were slightly too big.

Peter wanted us to climb the tree straight away. He was so insistent, that I didn't have time to be frightened. He said that he would go first, and all I had to do was to copy where he put his feet and hands. I found it surprisingly easy, until my boot fell off. I watched it fall to the ground, and suddenly realised that I was very high up. I had that strange feeling just above my Private Place. I knew it was fear. Peter was just above me. He laughed.at me, and shouted that he would climb back down and get my boot. Before I could say anything, he was climbing down. He came onto my branch, but had to squeeze himself into me to get past. As he came beside me, I grabbed his arm.

I heard myself say, 'Please don't leave me up here. I'm frightened.'

Then I did something very surprising. I kissed him, on the lips. He was so shocked, I thought he was going to fall off the tree, so I held his arm tighter.

I could feel my face getting very hot. He said, 'Am I your boyfriend now?'

I didn't know what to say. I thought he was going to cry, so I said, 'Yes, you can be my boyfriend,' and we both laughed.

I wasn't frightened anymore. Any thought of climbing down had completely slipped from my mind. We climbed almost to the top of the tree, and Peter helped me to take my other boot off. He said it would be easier to climb down with just my socks on. I looked around and could feel myself going into My Colour Dream. I could see the roof of Peter's house, and right into his sisters' bedroom window. I could see into his neighbour's garden, where a man was mowing the lawn. He was pushing the mower backwards and forwards, backwards and forwards. Behind Peter, on another branch, I saw Ursula. She smiled and waved at me, and then disappeared.

I wanted to tell Peter exactly what I was thinking. I said, 'Peter, I want to paint a picture. In my mind I can see it. I know the colours I'm going to use. It's what I can see from this tree. I'm going to think about you and Ursula while I'm painting.' Then I realised that I had never told anyone about Ursula before. I said, 'She's my Guardian Angel.'

Peter said, 'That's nice. But can we get down now? I need to go to the toilet'

Getting down was not at all easy. I hurt my feet every time I trod on a new branch. Half way down, I thought to myself, 'I should be frightened.' Then I looked down and Peter was just below me, and the ground seemed a long way away. My head felt slightly dizzy, and I had a feeling that I was not entirely inside my body. When I touched the branches, they felt slightly soft, which stopped me from gripping them properly. I heard a ringing in my ears too. I could hear Peter calling to me. He must have been on the ground already, because he shouted, 'Stay there, I'll get my mum.'

By the time Mrs McCabe came to the tree, I had managed to get to the last branch, but was so frightened, I couldn't move. Peter's mum climbed up the ladder and managed to carry me down to the ground. She told me to sit down, and helped me put my head between my knees. Peter came back with a glass of water. I tried to drink it, but could taste metal in my mouth.

I said, 'I wasn't frightened.' Then I was sick.

Peter's mum said, 'I think you've had too much excitement.' She was right.

I felt better after being sick, but didn't want to play outside anymore. I wanted to change back into my dress, but Peter's mum said not to, because I would get my dress dirty during painting. I wanted to say that I had never in my life got paint on my clothes, but realised that that would sound rude.

I quite liked dressing up like Peter, but I was embarrassed when Peter's dad and his sisters came back from swimming.

Peter's dad said, 'Who's that pretty boy?' Peter's mum told him to shush, but I knew she thought it was funny. The girls, I realised, were twins. They weren't identical, but they had Peter's eyes and teeth. They were both wearing slacks, and looked very grown up. During lunch I became quite shy, and went red every time someone talked to me.

Frances asked me about painting. She said that she had been given some paints and a large sketchpad for Christmas, but had never used them. She said that she was no good at painting. Bernadette said that wasn't true, and that really she was just lazy, and spent far too much time thinking about The Beatles and the footballers in West Ham, and reading murder mystery novels by Agatha Christie. I thought that was a rude thing to say, but they were both laughing.

After lunch, we spread newspaper on the kitchen table, and Frances helped me get ready for painting. Her paint set seemed enormous, with more colours than I had seen before. She also had a box with small tubes of paint in it. She had some new brushes too. Peter went back into the garden. I wondered if he had forgotten about being my boyfriend, and for five minutes I just sat and didn't want to paint anything. But then he came back in, and said he wanted to watch what I was doing.

I sat very still, and could feel the moment when I moved towards Peter and kissed him. I felt the greasy surface of the branches, and the smell of the tree's green stain on my hands. I saw the man cutting the grass, and Frances and Bernadette's bedroom window. I saw Ursula, and could taste metal in my mouth. I felt the fear just above my Private Place. Then it all just came out, very fast. The brushes and paint felt beautiful to use, though it was the first time I had used tubes of paint. I should have used just a small amount, but felt greedy and squeezed the tubes hard, and didn't care that I was using them all up. I imagined I was a bird, sitting on a branch just above us. I painted me from slightly above and behind, looking at Peter. Ursula was behind Peter, dressed in white. You couldn't see her face, because she was wearing her straw hat, but you could see her orange-brown curls. Down below, through the branches, you could just make out the man mowing his green lawn.

While I was painting, I wasn't really aware of anything else around me. But when I came out of My Colour Dream, I saw Bernadette and her dad in the room, and they were watching me. Mister McCabe said, 'Can you just explain that bit to me?' He was pointing at Ursula. I had the feeling that he was being polite, and perhaps couldn't make any sense of what I had done.

I said, 'It looks silly' and I thought I was going to cry.

He said, 'No, no. Just tell me about it.'

So I told the whole story about us climbing the tree; though obviously didn't mention the kissing bit.

Peter's dad said, 'I see it now. Once you understand the context, you can absolutely feel it. It reminds one of Turner. Quite remarkable.' Then he asked, 'But why the red? There is so much red.'

I wanted to tell him it was the red of Peter's lips, but couldn't. Then he began to recite a poem

He clasps the crag with crooked hands;

121

Close to the sun in lonely lands,
Ring'd with the azure world, he stands.

Frances finished it:
The wrinkled sea beneath him crawls;
He watches from his mountain walls,
And like a thunderbolt he falls.

Mummy came back, and talked with Peter's mum for a long time. She had been to the hairdresser. Her curly black hair was now straight.

Peter helps me to ask questions

On Monday, Peter told me that our mothers had agreed that every Saturday I could come and play at his house. He was very excited about that. He said that my mummy would be going to see a doctor every Saturday morning, and then have a rest in London in the afternoon. I stopped walking. I wanted to shout, 'And how do you know all about that, and I don't?' But I was just quiet. I was thinking about the time I said to Peter, 'You know lots of things. Lots more than I do.'
He had thought for a while, then told me, 'That's because I'm ten. And I have two big sisters. If I want to know something, I ask them. Or I ask Mum and Dad.'

At that exact moment, I knew that I needed some help. I knew that if you want to know about what's happening in your life, then you have to ask questions. But that was the one thing I couldn't do. In my mind I was like a stream that had become blocked by lots of big pieces of wood; like a huge dam. If I could only move one of these logs out of the way, then a stream of questions would be released.
I said to Peter, 'I can't ask questions. Mummy told me not to.' I explained how she had got cross with me when I was little, for asking her lots of questions.
Peter had an idea: 'Why don't you write your questions down? That's not the same as *asking* them. You can write them to me,

and then I can ask my sisters. And if you like, you can practice asking me questions.'

One of the things I liked about Peter was that I knew that if I told him something, he wouldn't tell anyone else. On the way home from school I told him about Mummy being in a terrible rage and yelling, 'I never wanted you!'
I thought he was going to cry. I began to panic and said, 'No, no, no!' and I held his hand.
He said that he wanted to tell his mum about what I had just told him. I begged him not to. He let go of my hand and shouted at me, 'Well why did you tell me then? I can't keep that a secret!'
Then I realised that I had told him all about it on purpose, so that he would tell his parents. I felt something inside at that moment. It was a new feeling. It was as if my tummy and my heart and everything inside me were moving fast. I wanted to kiss Peter again.

When I went to visit on Saturday, Peter's mum gave me a cuddle, and said I was such a lovely girl, and very special to them. I knew that Peter had told her. He said that this week we would be potholers, and explore the caves at the bottom his garden. He gave me a hard plastic hat to put on, and we spent the morning pretending to be trapped among the piles of branches that had been cut down. Sometimes I was actually quite frightened; not because I believed I was in a cave, but because I had got stuck, and couldn't turn round. Once I started screaming, and Peter was worried, and had to pull me out backwards by my feet. I enjoyed being rescued so much that I kept getting myself stuck on purpose.

By the end of the morning, we were filthy, and my face and hands were covered in scratches. After lunch, Peter's mum asked me if I would like to have a bath. She ran the bath, and the water was a lot deeper than I was used to at home. Then she added some bubble bath. This was the first time I had ever had a bath with bubbles in, and it seemed to me to be a complete luxury. When I got into the water, the whole surface was covered with bubbles. Then I realised that I had forgotten to do a wee. The toilet was next door to the bathroom. I looked for a towel to dry myself, but couldn't find one. I was faced with a choice: wee in the bath (not good) or run into the toilet and make everything wet. I decided to run to the toilet. As I came out, Bernadette came round the corner. She said, 'Mum told me to bring you a towel.'

Looking back, I don't know why I didn't grab the towel off her and hastily cover myself up. Instead, I just stood there with my arms by my sides.
I said, 'I'm sorry. The toilet is all wet. It looks like I've done a wee all over the place.'
She laughed and said, 'Don't worry. Peter is always forgetting his towel. We all know the difference between water and wee!'
Then she smiled at me and gave me the towel.
I lay in the bath, and thought about how lucky Peter was to have sisters. Then I wished Ursula would come. There was a knock on the door. It was Bernadette. She said, 'Mummy wants to know if you would like me to wash your hair.' I did.
While she was drying me she said, 'It's funny. At your age, girls look just like boys. You look lovely. Then it all changes, and nobody could make that mistake ever again.'
I had a very strange feeling inside, as if I was standing on the bank of a huge frozen lake. I couldn't tell, by looking at the ice, whether it would be thick or thin. I just knew that this time the ice would be thick enough to take my weight.
Then I heard myself ask a question: 'Do you give Peter a bath?'
Bernadette laughed. 'Oh yes. Frances and I take turns. He loves me washing his hair. He gets very excited. Sometimes his willy sticks right up.'
Then I asked another question: 'How old are you, Bernadette?'
'I'm sixteen… nearly seventeen actually.'
I said, to myself, 'Mummy was eighteen when she married Daddy.'

When Mummy came back from London, Peter and I went upstairs in his bedroom. His room was above the kitchen. I was painting on the floor, and Peter was helping me. He liked to rinse my brushes. I had begun to paint a cave, high up on a mountain. There was a waterfall coming out of the cave, and crashing far down below.

Mummy's voice was loud. We heard her say, 'Sometimes I just can't control myself. One of the doctors blames it on my experiences during The War. But another one thinks it's my monthly thing. I get this feeling of being blocked. I can feel it coming. My head feels like it's going to split open. It sends me into an uncontrollable rage sometimes. But when the bloods come, it's like a dam bursting. I wish I was a man. Life is so much easier for them.'

There was a long silence.

Peter and I couldn't help listening. He was very still. His mum said, 'It's the opposite for me. I long for my Visitor to come. Then I know I'm not pregnant. I lost a baby two years ago. I don't think I could go through that again.'

Mummy said, 'I lost a baby too. It was my first time being pregnant. I've never really talked about it, but it shook me up terribly.'

I turned the water in the waterfall a shade of red. I thought about Jesus on the cross, and the big gash in his side, and the cruel soldiers laughing at him, while they whipped him. My hand was shaking slightly.

Peter and I didn't talk. I wrote on the back of the paper, *What is The Monthly Thing? Who is The Visitor?*

Peter wrote, *I don't know. Shall I ask my sisters?*

I wrote, *Yes please.*

The Monthly Visitor

That night, I found it impossible to sleep. I was desperate to see Ursula. I talked to her, even though I knew she wasn't there. Here is what was going round and round in my head:

I now know what I am missing. I am missing someone who I can love, and who will love me back. I am missing someone who doesn't care if I get dirty or spill things. I am missing someone who likes to talk to me, and who is interested in what I have to say. I am missing someone who likes my art. I am missing someone to cuddle, and who will cuddle me. I am missing someone who makes me feel safe.

This feels like I don't want Mummy. I do want her, but not as she is now.

Then I thought:

I want The War to be the reason for her problems.

I want The Monthly Thing to be the reason for her problems as well.

If Mummy is ill, or unhappy because of The War, then it is not My Fault. I am not to blame for her being ill and unhappy. I am not to blame for her drinking too much medicine, and having a breakdown. I am not to blame for her nerves being stretched.

But then I feel guilty, because I want Mummy to be ill.

But what if it really is me that is the problem?

And I thought about Bernadette looking at me, and talking to me in the bathroom. I had wanted Bernadette to see all of me; to see me as I really was. I wanted a Mummy who would tell me I was lovely.

But the secret part, the part that I didn't want to think about, was Peter. I had wanted Peter to see me too. I wondered if Bernadette would tell Peter about seeing me. When I thought about that, I could feel my face go red; out of embarrassment, but also from excitement.

And Peter's willy had stuck out. Just like that boy in school when I was six. It stuck out because he was excited.

Then my thoughts would return to the big questions of my life:

What happened in The War?

Why did Mummy leave Malaya and take me with her?

Why does Mummy hate Daddy so much?

Then I would move onto my new preoccupations:

What is The Monthly Thing?

Who is The Visitor?

Peter didn't come to school on Monday. At playtime, I asked a girl in his class if she knew where he was. She said, 'Are

126

you his girlfriend?' I didn't know if she was asking in a nice way or a nasty way, so I didn't say anything. She said she would ask Miss, and tell me at lunchtime. She found out that Peter had a very sore throat, and would be off school for the whole week.

That night, my thoughts about The Visitor and The Monthly Thing started to take over my mind. When I closed my eyes, I saw The Visitor looking at me. He was big, and wore a dark coat and a hat, and smoked a cigarette. I kept turning over in bed, but no matter which way I turned, he was always there, looking at me.

I prayed to God, to make The Visitor go away. I asked God to send Ursula back to me. I asked Him to make Mummy get completely better. And most of all I prayed that Peter would get better, because then he could tell me about The Visitor. As I was praying, Uncle Eric popped into my mind. I remembered that he had promised to introduce me to someone who he thought I would like.

I began to worry that Peter might forget about me when he was ill, and find a new best friend when he came back to school. Then I realised just how important Peter and his family had become to me. I started to feel very shaky, and felt myself crying. I pictured Peter crying in the night, and his mum and dad and his sisters rushing to cuddle him, and arguing quietly among themselves about who would take him into their bed.

Once, in our old house, when I had been crying, Mummy said to me, 'Stop feeling sorry for yourself.'

I thought that I must be feeling sorry for myself now. I tried to stop crying, but kept thinking of Peter. I was becoming very afraid of The Visitor. I put my head under the covers. I thought of Miss Dawson crying in class.

The next day, I held Miss Dawson's hand in the playground. I closed my eyes and thought about how to ask her a question. She asked me, 'Are you all right, Pippa?'

I said, 'No Miss. I am not all right. I want to tell you lots of things. I would like to write you a long, long story, and do lots of drawings. But I don't have an exercise book at home.'

Two boys came running up, and complained that some other boys were pushing them and calling them names. Then it was time for Miss to blow her whistle, and we all had to go into class.

At home time, Miss asked me to stay and talk to her for a few minutes. I thought perhaps I had done something wrong. But she went into her cupboard, and brought out a very big book with a hard cover. It had a picture of the sun and moon on it. Both had faces that were smiling. It looked like the kind of book that somebody had made themselves. The paper was very thick and creamy white.

Miss put the book on her desk and said, 'Come and sit on my lap.' She had her nice ring back on. She said, 'There are just a few weeks left before the summer holidays. When you come back to school, you will be in another teacher's class. And I'm going to live in another part of the country. It's a little town called Appledore, in a county called Kent.'

She could feel me go rigid, but she stroked my hair and said, 'I don't want you or the other children to be upset. I want you to be happy. I want you to be pleased for me, because I am going to be very happy. I've been very lucky to know you… and the other children of course.' She put the notebook in my hands and said, 'I want you to have this nice notebook. Somebody very special made it for me. I want you to fill it full of your writing and drawings and paintings. You can do it at home, and bring it in to show me. But please don't tell the other children; just in case they all want one.'

Then she gave me a squeeze and kissed the top of my head and said, 'Gosh you are getting heavy. My legs have nearly gone to sleep!'

I thought of a river. It was flowing very slowly. I was swimming in the river with Miss Dawson and Peter and his sisters. Bridget had already been in the river, but had floated away. Mummy was sitting on the bank, wearing sunglasses. I hoped that Mummy might jump in the river. Ursula was standing by a weeping willow tree, watching us all. She was holding onto a branch and dipping her toe in the water.

128

On Friday after school, Mummy told me that Peter was feeling much better, and that I could play with him all day on Saturday. She said that she had been having coffee with Julia, Peter's mother, every morning, and that they had been working in their garden together.

At first I was pleased to know this. But later I was worried. What would happen if Mummy got angry, and became nasty with Peter's parents, and stopped me from visiting them? I was thinking about this so much, that I forgot to show Mummy the book that Miss had given me.

That evening, I was sitting in bed, touching the book, and thinking about what to write and draw and paint. Suddenly Mummy came in. I hadn't heard her coming up the stairs. I tried to hide the book under the covers.

Mummy sat on my bed. She said, 'Pippa, I'm feeling much better these days. I'm not going to the doctor on Saturdays anymore. I'm going to see a new doctor, on Fridays. He's Jewish, so doesn't work on a Saturday.' She started to cough, which made her stop talking.

I started to panic; no visit to the doctor on Saturday might mean no playing with Peter.

I suppose she could read from my face what I was thinking: 'No,' she said, 'Don't worry. Julia says that you can still play there at their house.'

I should have been relieved about that, but wasn't. I imagined Mummy staying with us and either causing trouble or telling me not to do things. 'Oh,' she laughed, 'don't worry. I won't be there to spoil your fun. I'll still go to London. The doctors say that doing that will help me feel better. And there's some more news. Peter's parents want you to go on holiday to the seaside with them, for two weeks. I've said that of course you can go. That is, if you'd like to.'

I clapped my hands and tried to give Mummy a hug, but the book under the covers got wedged in my Private Place and I shouted, 'Ow!'

Mummy laughed and said, 'What have you got hidden there?' I slowly pulled out the book. She grabbed it and said, 'Oh, that's lovely! Where did you get it?' Her voice had gone from loud to quiet. I could feel that her happy, light mood was changing.

I had to tell the truth. 'My teacher gave it to me. She's leaving school at the end of term, and she wants me to do some paintings in here.'

Mummy said, to herself, 'Does she now?' Then she asked me, 'What for?'

I answered, very quickly, 'Because she likes my paintings. She thinks they are special.'

That wasn't a lie, but I was not exactly telling the truth. If Mummy noticed that I wasn't being totally honest, she didn't show it. She was quiet, and kept looking at the cover, and opening the pages and running her hands over them. Finally, she said, 'That's a nice idea. And you'll give it to her as a kind of leaving present, I suppose.' Was that a question, or something else? I couldn't tell.

The mood had changed. I thought of myself walking on a patch of the lake where the ice looked thin. One false step and I would be in the filthy, freezing water underneath. Mummy left the room, and took the book with her.

I realised that I had developed a life hidden from my mother. A life I didn't want her to be involved in. There were lots of things I didn't want to tell her. Was I becoming a liar?

The next morning, I could feel that Mummy's mood had changed again. As I came into the kitchen, she was washing up her breakfast things at the sink. My school uniform and clean underwear for the week were on the back of a chair. There was no breakfast laid out on the table for me. Instead there was Miss Dawson's book. I said, 'Thank you for my clothes Mummy.'

Perhaps she hadn't heard me come in the room, because she moved away from the sink, and walked past me, without looking at me. I looked inside the book. On the first page Mummy had written

Dear Miss Dawson

I'm sorry to hear that you will be leaving the school. You have been very kind to Philippa and she has learned a lot from you.

However, if you want to know what is going on in my daughter's life, please come and ask me. Don't give her books to write tales in.

Yours sincerely

Ruth Herman

I got dressed and left the house, without having had breakfast. Peter was sitting on the wall. The first thing I said to him was, 'Mummy is angry with me, and I haven't had any breakfast.'

Peter's face was pale. I think he wasn't quite better yet. He said, 'You can share my banana.' He peeled it and gave it to me.

I said, 'But it's yours!' and tried to give it back to him.

He laughed and said, 'I'll tell my mum we shared it.'

This is what we said to each other. I'm writing it like a play, because to me it was very dramatic:

Me: But that's a lie.

Peter: No it's not. We did share it. But I had the skin. Daddy would call that a *half truth*.

Mum says I'm a sensitive boy. She says the world needs more sensitive boys. Dad says I'm going to be a good actor, or a politician. I thought he said *policeman*. Dad laughed and said that they are not the most sensitive people in the world.

Me: What's a politician?

Peter: Someone who's very polite, I think.

Me: (almost shouting it out) I love you Peter. I missed you so much.

(Peter's face went very red. He looked like a tomato.)

Me: Oh! Please don't be angry. I'm sorry.

Peter: No. I'm not angry. But please don't tell anyone in school. The other children are teasing me all the time. Ruth Kendall asked me if you are my cousin. I said, 'She might be.' Now she's told everybody that you're my cousin.'

Me: But that's not true! It's a lie!

Peter: No it's not. I didn't say you *are* my cousin. I said, 'You might be.' It's a half- truth. I just wish that you could be my cousin. Then when I tell people you are coming on holiday with us, it will stop them from saying, 'Nah nah nah nah nah; she's your girlfriend.' Then I won't get upset, and have to chase them round the playground and punch them.

So I wasn't his girlfriend. I was only like his cousin. I had forgotten that we were going on holiday. I could feel my head getting dizzy. I heard myself ask him a question: 'Can cousins love each other?'

Peter stopped walking and said, 'Yes. I think so. I think it's somewhere in The Bible. One of the Apostles, Doubting Thomas, I think, was in love with his cousin. Another Apostle, maybe Judas, said it was wrong. They were going to start fighting, so Apostle Peter told them to ask Jesus. And they asked Jesus, "Can a man marry his cousin? And Jesus said, "They might do." '

He was smiling while he said it.

So I asked him, 'That's not true, is it?'

He said, 'It might be.'

I heard myself ask another question: 'So would you love me if I was your cousin?'

He said, 'I might do.' And then, 'Stop asking me so many questions!' He was laughing.

Why is it that when you love someone, you sometimes want to hit them?

Peter was walking very slowly, and we were almost at school. The parents were leaving the playground, and all the children were lining up, ready to go into school. Just as we were about to separate to go into our different lines, Peter grabbed me by the shoulder and whispered something in my ear. I could feel the whole of my face tingling as his lips touched my ear. He said, 'I'll tell you after school.'

He was laughing, so I knew that he meant, 'Yes, I do love you.'

In assembly I felt dizzy again. I thought maybe I was having too much excitement. I told Miss about it, and she asked me if I had had any breakfast. I said, 'Peter gave me his banana.'

Miss said, 'So you didn't have any breakfast then.' She took a chair into her cupboard. She came out and said to me, 'Eat and drink what's on the chair, and then come and talk to me.'

There was a chocolate biscuit wrapped in shiny green paper, and a small bottle of milk with a straw stuck in the top. The biscuit tasted of mint. I felt full afterwards; full of chocolate and milk, and full of love for Miss Dawson.

After playtime, while everybody was writing and drawing, Miss gave me the big book and said, 'You can paint in the afternoons, when everyone else is doing craft.' That afternoon, when I opened up the book, I noticed that the page with Mummy's writing in had been cut out. I wondered why Mummy had called herself Ruth *Herman* and not *Dunbar*.

I am good at catching

Mummy was unkind to me for three days. Every morning, Peter brought me a banana and a biscuit. I never asked him again if he loved me, but I knew that he did. On Friday after school, there was nobody at home. After waiting for five minutes, Peter said, 'Let's go to our house. Your mummy will know that we're there.'

When we got to Peter's house, Mummy was in their kitchen, talking to Peter's mum. Mummy said *hello* to me, but I could see that she was upset about something. Mrs McCabe gave us a glass of milk and a sandwich, and told us to play in the garden. We went as far away from the house as possible. Peter looked upset. He said, 'Your Mummy's been crying.'

I said, 'I know. Can you show me how to play cricket?'

Peter looked confused. He said he always got upset if his dad made his mum cry. Then he added very quickly, 'But that only happens sometimes, and he always says *sorry*.'

I didn't know how to explain what I was thinking, so we went to the rope ladder, and Peter pushed me. As I was swinging round and round, I looked up at the top of the tree. There was a big fat pigeon sitting among the leaves.

We climbed a little way up the tree, and sat there. I said, 'Mummy gets upset a lot. I'm used to it. It doesn't seem so horrible anymore. And because I know that her bad moods won't last, I don't get so upset myself.'

Peter said, 'I don't want to play cricket. It will be too noisy.'

So we sat in the tree instead, and talked about all the nice things we would do on holiday together.

The next day, Mummy was cheerful again, and went to London. When I got to Peter's house, a lady who looked just like Mrs McCabe was saying goodbye. She said to me, 'You must be the lovely Pippa.' She even sounded like Peter's mum. In the garden, Peter was playing cricket with another boy. Peter told me that the boy was called Lawrence, and that they were cousins.

Lawrence didn't say *hello*; he just said, 'Girls don't know how to play cricket.'

I sat and watched Peter bowl a tennis ball, while Lawrence tried to hit it as hard as he could with his big wooden bat. Once, he hit the ball so hard that it went over the fence into the street, and we heard it bouncing on a car roof. Lawrence laughed and told Peter to go and get the ball.

While Peter was trying to find the ball, Lawrence didn't say anything to me. He just kept swinging the bat, and looking at me. He swung the bat so close to me that it nearly hit my head. I jumped out of the way, but didn't say anything. I walked towards the house and heard Lawrence say, just quietly enough for me to hear, 'Stupid bitch.'

I went into the kitchen, and asked Mrs McCabe if I could sit with her for a while. She asked me if anything was the matter, but I didn't tell her. She said, 'Lawrence is not really a cousin. He's staying with my sister. She doesn't have children of her own, so from time to time looks after other people's. It's called *fostering*. If Lawrence does or says anything you don't like, just come and tell me.'

I went back outside, just as Lawrence was hitting the ball very hard. It sailed towards me, and I caught it. I think I was as surprised as the boys. Peter shouted to Lawrence, 'You're out! Now it's my turn to bat.'

Lawrence said, 'Give your girlfriend the bat, and let me bowl at her.'

I stood at the wicket, and Lawrence threw the ball at me as hard as he could. It hit me on the shoulder. He laughed, and ran up to me and said in a loud voice, 'Sorry about that.' Then he said, under his breath, 'Silly bitch.'

I gave the bat to Peter. Lawrence bowled the ball at him and Peter hit it hard. Just as the ball was about to fly past me, I jumped, put my left hand out, and caught it. Peter laughed, but Lawrence looked annoyed, and said we should climb the tree.

Lawrence said to me, 'You wait here, while me and Peter climb the tree.'

Peter said, 'Pippa can climb that tree as well as anybody.'

Lawrence said to me, 'Prove it then.'

I was beginning to feel very annoyed. I climbed the rope ladder, and was just hoisting myself onto the first branch when Peter told me to get down. I looked down and saw Lawrence lying on the ground. It was obvious that he was looking up my skirt. He had made his left hand into the shape of a circle, and was pushing the long finger of his right hand in and out of it. I climbed down as quickly as I could. My plan was to go into the house, and ask if I could change into Peter's trousers.

As I walked past the boys, I heard Lawrence say something really disgusting to Peter. The nasty boys on the bus came into my mind. I remembered the look on those boys' faces that seemed to say, 'We can do whatever we want to you. You're just a stupid little girl.'

I walked slowly over to where we had been playing cricket, and picked up the bat. I walked back to the boys, raised the bat, and tried to hit Lawrence as hard as I could. Lawrence lifted his arm to protect his head, and the bat hit him on the hand.

He fell to his knees and shouted, 'You fucking bitch! You've broken my hand!'

Peter tried to take the bat off me, but I was too quick and swung it at Lawrence again. This time Lawrence managed to grab hold of the bat, and tried to pull it from me. He jumped up, and our faces were close to each other, and I could see that he was getting ready to spit in my face. So I closed my eyes and butted him with my forehead, as hard as I could. There was a bang and I fell over.

I heard Mrs McCabe shout from the upstairs window, 'What's going on? Stop fighting at once!' I turned to look at Peter and Lawrence, but everything looked black and red and far away. My forehead and nose hurt, and when I put my hand up to my nose, there was blood there. I walked over to the house, but had to sit down in the middle of the lawn.

I heard Lawrence crying. Peter had run off to get his mum. She ran over and picked me up and said, 'Peter, help Lawrence into the kitchen. I think she's knocked one of his teeth out.'

I sat on a chair at the kitchen table, while Mrs McCabe washed Lawrence's mouth out.

He was wailing, 'She's knocked my teeth out! She started it! I didn't do anything! Ouch! My fingers hurt.'

Peter went over to the sink, to see what was going on.

He came back and told me, 'He's got three teeth missing, and I think you've broken one of his fingers.'

I said, 'I'm not sorry. I'm not saying *sorry*, so nobody had better ask me to. I'll hit him again if he comes near me.' I went over to the sink. Mrs McCabe was about to tell me to go and sit down. But I said to Lawrence, 'You nasty boy. Tell Peter's mum what you did.'

Lawrence said, 'Honest, I didn't do anything. I didn't say anything.'

I said, 'Yes you did. I'm going to tell her what you did, and what you said to me.'

Peter shouted, 'Oh no! Don't do that!' and put his hands over his ears.

Dr Robinson said, 'And this friend of the family? Does she have experience of looking after alcoholics?'

Peter's Dad didn't answer straight away. He said, '*He* actually. Pippa calls him Uncle Eric. I understand he's a very stabilising influence on Mrs Dunbar. That's Pippa's mother. We are still hoping that Pippa will come on holiday with us to the coast soon. We all, including her mother, think it's just what Pippa needs.'

Dr Robinson turned to me and said 'And hopefully it will give mummy a chance to get better.'

It flashed through my mind that it was my bad behaviour that had made Mummy get drunk again. I said, 'If I wasn't so naughty, then she wouldn't have got ill.'

Mrs Robinson said to me, 'Oh no. It's quite the other way round. It's never a child's fault if their mummy or daddy has problems. You must remember that. You are not to blame if your mummy sometimes gets ill.'

I liked Mrs Robinson.

Dr Robinson examined my face. He didn't think my nose was broken. I was feeling wet and uncomfortable. What I really wanted to do was to lie in the bath upstairs. So I said, 'I think I should go home now.'

Mr McCabe got up quickly. He had forgotten all about ringing my house, to find out what was happening. I sat quietly, but I was thinking hard about how to get the grown-ups to allow me to have a bath. I whispered to Mrs Robinson, 'I'm feeling sore, and I think I need a good wash.'

Bernadette heard me and said, 'Why don't you have a bath upstairs?'

Dr Robinson said that this would be a splendid idea, but I was not to be left on my own.

In the bathroom, Bernadette said, 'I think we need to have an extra deep bath today.' She helped me take my clothes off, and to get in the bath. She had put in a lot of bubble bath, and it seemed like there were bubbles everywhere. As I sat in the bath, with the bubbles and lovely deep warm water, I felt strength coming back into my legs and arms, and my nose didn't feel quite so sore. I said how much I hated Father Leighton. Bernadette said the best word to describe him would be *hypocrite*.

I lay back in the warm water. I could feel my arms floating to the surface. I closed my eyes. Bernadette was sitting on a stool, and I knew that she was watching me. I was floating in the sea. It was warm and sunny, and down below me the sea was bright and clear. I could see the light yellow sand at the bottom. Ursula was with me, holding my hand. She wasn't a small girl anymore. She was a teenager, like Bernadette. We sank down into the water. I was surprised to find that if I opened my mouth just a little bit, I could breathe; even though the water was coming into my mouth. We drifted down to the bottom of the water. The sand was hard, and as soon as our feet touched the bottom we pushed ourselves up to the surface. As I looked up, I could see the sun lighting up the water.

I could hear Bernadette saying to me: 'What are you thinking?'
'I'm sinking into the sea.'
'Who is with you?'
'Ursula.'
'Ursula?'
'Yes. She's my friend. We can breathe under water. Ursula is big, like you.'
'What colours can you see?'
'Blues, greens and a lot of yellow. I'd love to know how to swim.'
'I can teach you.'
'I want you to come in the water with us.'
'Not today. When we are on holiday. Today I have my Visitor.'

Suddenly a man was swimming towards us. He had a huge harpoon gun. He had blood coming out of his mouth and nose, rising upwards, like cigarette smoke. He fired the gun, and the harpoon shot towards Ursula. It hit her in the back, and blood started to pour out of her mouth. I couldn't breathe underwater anymore, and could taste Ursula's blood in my mouth. I started thrashing around and knew that I was drowning.

148

Bernadette was holding me by the shoulders. I must have been shouting, because she was saying, 'Shh. Shh. It's all right. It's not real. I'm here. It's a dream. You had a dream.' She sounded frightened.

The door opened. It was Frances. Frances sat with me, while Bernadette went downstairs. I told Frances that The Visitor had killed Ursula. Frances said that she didn't know what I was talking about, so I explained about The Visitor who comes in the night, and makes you bleed.

She said, 'Oh that! That visitor!' and she laughed and went red. I knew she was embarrassed.

Bernadette came back in, and told us that the doctor had gone. My mummy had gone to sleep at our house, so I was going to stay with them for the afternoon. Frances and her dad were going to make lunch.

Frances went out of the bathroom. Bernadette said, 'I've spoken to my Mum on the phone. I asked her if I can tell you about what The Visitor is. Mum said I should, because it's worrying you. Now let me dry you, and I'll tell you all about it.'

She wrapped me in a big white towel and put me on her knee. She explained about something called *periods*.

I could not believe what I was hearing. At the end, she said that today was the last day of her period, but that Frances' was just starting. Bernadette liked her periods, but Frances said that hers hurt her a lot, and she called it her *bloody hell*.

I asked, 'Does Peter know about all this?'

Bernadette said, 'Yes he does, because we are always talking about our periods. And I do believe that is the first question you have ever asked me.'

I could feel my face going red. I was embarrassed, but pleased with myself.

Bernadette dried me. She rubbed me hard, then stopped and held me tight. I felt a warm tingling sensation in my feet. It rose like a wave through my Private Place and tummy, and up into my chest. I was taking deep breaths, and as I breathed out, the wave moved through my face and made my scalp tingle. It was a

149

peculiar but beautiful sensation. Then I made myself three promises: I would never hit anybody again, I would never wet myself again, or faint in public. So far I've managed to keep two of those promises.

Bernadette said, 'I'm going to study to be a doctor when I leave school. I know what you are going to be.'

I said, 'I want to be like you.'

After lunch, Mrs McCabe went to my house and got my teacher's big book, and all afternoon I painted and wrote to Miss Dawson. Peter and Bernadette stayed with me, and they watched me and talked about the holiday. I explained about Ursula, and painted us under the water. Bernadette said that she would teach Peter and me how to swim. She sat close to me, and I could feel her breathing. Once she put her arm around my waist. I had a sensation that the wave was passing through me again. Peter played with his toy soldiers on the floor. He had a small metal cannon. He put a used match in the barrel, and kept firing it, until all the soldiers were knocked down.

Lady Celia Grange-Hoare

In the evening, Mrs McCabe walked home with me. Uncle Eric opened the front door. He had grown a beard and was smoking a pipe. He said that he had given up smoking cigarettes, because they were bad for your lungs. We went into the front room, and Mummy was sitting by the French windows. She was smoking a cigarette. I stood by the door, and she said, 'Come here Pippa.' I went to her and she held my hand. She said, 'I'm sorry I've been a bad mother, and haven't looked after you properly. You're a good girl really.'

I wanted to say, 'I forgive you,' but I didn't say anything.

Uncle Eric explained that I wouldn't be going to school that week, because I had had too much excitement, and needed to have a rest.

I said, 'But it's the last week before the holidays, and my teacher is leaving on Friday, so I won't see her ever again.'

I heard Mummy draw in her breath very sharply. She said, 'Don't argue with adults. That's our decision, and that's final.'

I didn't look at her. I looked at Mrs McCabe. Our eyes met, but I couldn't tell what she was thinking.

Uncle Eric said, 'Let's have a nice cup of tea, shall we?'

After our cup of tea, Mrs McCabe said goodbye. Uncle Eric took me into the garden, and we sat on the bench. I could see Mummy smoking a cigarette, and looking at us. Uncle Eric filled his pipe and lit it. He blew a smoke ring. As it floated away from his mouth, he blew onto it and it broke. I'd never seen that before, and thought of the magician with the ping pong balls.

Uncle Eric said, 'I know about your teacher. I can imagine that you must feel very disappointed. I know about your big painting book too. Mummy and I have talked about your teacher, and how nice she is. So if you are feeling better, then you can go into school on the last day, and say goodbye.'

I wanted to tell Uncle Eric about Peter, and how much I would miss seeing him every day. Uncle Eric said, 'Of course, you can still go on holiday with Peter.'

I said, 'Thank you very much, Uncle Eric.'

He said, 'It's the least we can do for you.' He crossed his legs and smoked his pipe again. He said, 'I want you to listen very carefully, Pippa.'

I didn't want to listen very carefully. When grown-ups said that, they usually had some very bad news to tell you. He said, 'No, no! It's nothing bad. It's something very interesting and exciting. Tomorrow we are going to see my aunt. She's not my real aunt, but I've known her since I was a little boy. Her name is Lady Celia Grange-Hoare. She's a very old lady now, but when she was young, she was one of the most well-known lady painters in the country. She knows all about you, and wants to meet you.'

The next morning, Uncle Eric cooked me a fried egg on toast for breakfast. Mummy sat with us, and was cheerful. She took me to my room and helped me choose my clothes. We decided that I could wear my dark blue blouse and my tartan skirt, with long white socks and my best black shoes. Mummy took me to the long mirror in her room and said, 'You look lovely, as usual. But try not to get dirty. And make sure you say *please* and *thank you*.'

I liked Mummy when she was like this, but I said as little as possible, in case I said the wrong thing.

Uncle Eric drove us in his car. I sat with Mummy in the back. He told us that his aunt was from a wealthy family. She had gone to art school when she was only fourteen, and had been friends with some of the most well-known British artists. Uncle Eric was writing a book about her life and art. He said to Mummy, 'The family used to live up at The Hall. The big house in the park. The park was their front garden. After the First World War, her father sold The Hall and all the land. He made a fortune. He was useless with children, but a very shrewd businessman.'

Mummy said, 'Like someone else we know.'

It took us about fifteen minutes to get to Lady Celia's house. It was in a road with lots of big houses and tall trees. Her house was the smallest, but still much bigger than ours. Mummy said, 'I see she's still got plenty of money then.' I could tell that she was nervous.

The car's tyres made a lovely crunching sound on the gravel in the drive. Uncle Eric rang the doorbell. I heard Mummy take a deep breath and let it out. It sounded like a sigh. Uncle Eric said to her, 'Try and relax. It'll be fine.'

A young lady opened the door. She was wearing white trousers and a bright red blouse. She smiled at us and said, 'I'm Celia's niece, Mary. I look after her and keep her company. Do come in.' She smiled at me and said, 'That's a lovely kilt. Are you Scottish?'

I knew she was trying to make me laugh. It worked.

Lady Celia was in what Mary called *The Drawing Room*. She was sitting by the window. She tried to get out of her chair, but got half-way up, then sat back down with a bump. She laughed and said, 'Wretched legs. Not working so well today. You'll have to greet me sitting down, I'm afraid.'

I could see that she was in pain, but was doing her best not to show it. I liked her straight away. She smiled at me, and I went red and looked at the floor. We all shook hands with her, and Mary brought some chairs for us to sit on. I sat next to Lady Celia. Her hands were very bony and twisted, and covered in big light-brown spots. Her eyes were red and watery, and she had a flap of skin hanging down from her chin, that wobbled every time she laughed. That reminded me of a turkey.

There was a small table in front of Lady Celia, with a glass top. There were several magazines and a book on the table. Lady Celia saw me looking at them. She smiled and said, 'These are just some of Eric's magazines, and a copy of his latest book. He writes about every artist except me!' She laughed, and her flap of skin wobbled. Then she looked at me and said, not laughing this time, 'You look so alike. What a pair of beauties. But your mummy has such beautiful dark brown eyes, and yours are so bright blue. I've always thought that dark hair and blue eyes are such a special combination.'

Uncle Eric said, 'Auntie, I do believe you are talking about yourself. You used to tell me that self-praise is no praise at all.'

Lady Celia laughed and told Uncle Eric not to be such a silly boy. I looked at him, and he was smiling and had gone red. I thought he looked just like a little boy.

Mummy was laughing too.

Mary brought in some coffee for the grown-ups and a small jug of strawberry juice for me. The jug was mainly white, with a black, green, yellow and reddy-orange pattern. They were the sort of colours I would have used together when I was little. It was simple and beautiful and made me smile.

Lady Celia said, 'I see you like the jug. We… Mary and I… thought you would. My friend Clarice made it for me. She was utterly vivacious, and so was her art. I've always found that one's art reflects one's personality; at least when one is young. But as one gets older, one's life experiences and ideas begin to

153

have a strong influence. One just couldn't ignore Clarice, and it's impossible to ignore her art.'

I didn't know what to say. Mummy said, 'Be careful Pippa,' and picked up the jug and poured some juice into my glass. Her hand was very shaky, and she spilled some juice on the table.

Uncle Eric said to Mummy, 'Here Ruth, let me help you.' Mummy pushed his hand away and put the jug down hard on the table. For a moment I thought perhaps either the jug or the table had broken.

Lady Celia said, 'Not to worry. Clarice's work is as tough as old boots; just like she was.' She laughed, but the three of us didn't. Mary came back in with a plate of biscuits. She offered me one, but as I took a bite, it broke and half of it fell on my lap.

Mary said, 'Whoops! They are very crumbly.'

I looked at Mummy. I couldn't tell what she was thinking, but I knew she wasn't happy.

'Tell me my dear,' Lady Celia said to Mummy, 'where do you and your daughter get your beautiful looks from?'

I looked past Mummy's face, out of the window. A cat was sitting, looking with great interest at something in the border.

Mummy said, 'Well, to tell the truth, I don't really know much about my family. Most of them disappeared in The War, apparently. I'm Jewish, you see. My father was an engineer in Germany. One day he was coming out of the synagogue, when some policemen attacked him and killed him in the street. They had brought iron bars with them, especially to hit the Jews with. He had only gone there to unblock the toilet. I was only three at the time. My mother got such a shock. She asked our neighbours to hide me. They were Protestants, and the next day they moved to Lichtenstein. All through their journey, they hid me in a large armchair on the back of a lorry. We stayed in Lichtenstein for a year, and then I travelled with them to England. We lived in Norwich. Then, for some reason, they said I should stay with another family, who lived in a cottage, and they raised me as their own daughter. They were Quakers, so I became a Quaker. But now I'm a Catholic, supposedly.'

154

'Oh,' I added, 'And I was wondering what you were thinking too.'

Mary laughed and said, 'I think that you and I are going to get on very well! Let's go and get lunch ready.'

Why does Lady Celia paint people with no clothes on?

We had a very simple lunch; salad with potatoes and something that I had never eaten before, called *coleslaw*. Mary said she had learned to make it in Switzerland, at something called a *finishing school*. Lady Celia asked me if I had any questions for her. I went red, and said I had lots of questions, but I didn't know how to ask them, and I didn't want to be a chatterbox and upset people.

She said, 'Well, if you don't ask questions, then how are you going to learn anything?'

I sat for a long time and went red again, and felt very uncomfortable in my tummy, and I wanted to leave the room. Mary said, 'Can I ask you a few questions Pippa?'

'Yes.'

'I think I understand you. Did someone once tell you that you ask too many questions?'

'Yes.'

'Was it Mummy?'

'Yes it was.'

'Were you asking about your daddy?'

'Yes I was.'

'And were you frightened of Mummy then?'

'Yes I was.'

'And has that feeling; that feeling of being frightened of your mummy, stayed inside you ever since?'

'Yes it has. There are so many things I want to find out; about all sorts of things. I have a question that is bursting to come out. But I worry that you and Lady Celia might not like me for asking it, and will send me home.'

Lady Celia smiled and said, 'Goodness. And there was I, thinking about having my afternoon nap. But how can I sleep, knowing that you have such a fascinating question to ask?' She was laughing, but I still felt uncomfortable.

I said, 'Peter tells me to write questions on a piece of paper, and then he answers them. But you see, I worry that if I ask something, then grown-ups might find out.'

Mary asked, 'You mean if you say things about Mummy? Then we might tell your Mummy about it?'

'Well yes. And if I ask about other things too. Like private things that perhaps I'm not supposed to know. Things that might be Sins. I was desperate to know who The Monthly Visitor was. It was frightening me. It felt like a huge secret Sin. So Bernadette told me all about it, and I feel so much better for knowing. But I don't want Mummy to know that I know, in case it upsets her. I'm terrified of upsetting her.'

Both of the grown-ups said at the same time, 'I understand.' This made me smile and they smiled too.

I took a deep breath and closed my eyes. All my words came out in a rush: 'So what I really want to know is why have you got all those paintings upstairs of people with no clothes on? And why have you written on the paintings? And why have you spoiled them with such untidy handwriting? And why are there spelling mistakes? Did you paint them when you were a little girl?'

I opened my eyes, and Lady Celia was smiling at me. 'Lots of people have asked me exactly the same questions; though none of them have been as young as you. And I never tell them the answer. What a wise and clever child you are! Eric wants me to tell him all about that, so he can write about it in his book. Well, I am going to tell you first. But please don't worry about talking. I love it. And you will discover that my dear Mary is such a good listener, aren't you Mary?'

Mary's cheeks went a little bit red. I think she was pleased to be praised. She said, 'I do my best.'

I helped Mary clear the table. She told me to go and explore outside in the garden, while she helped Lady Celia into her room. I went to the summer house, and looked at the birds. Mary brought a very large sketch book and some paints and brushes. She said, 'Celia asked me to give these to you, in case you wanted to paint something.'

160

I didn't know what to say. I said, 'Ah.'

We sat very quietly, watching the little birds. They looked like children in the school playground; squabbling and laughing and chasing each other.

Mary said, 'Your Mummy seems very bitter.' I thought that perhaps she meant if you sucked Mummy, she might taste like a lemon. Peter and I had licked each other's arms once. He said I tasted salty.

Mary said, 'Not tasting bitter; but it's a feeling you have inside. It comes from being terribly disappointed. Or it's an anger that you can't talk about, for some reason. I felt like that for a long time after my father was killed in The War. I was upset, because he had been killed. But I was angry with him as well, because he chose to go and join the army. He didn't have to become a soldier, because he already had an important job in London, that was helping us win The War. But he volunteered, and became an officer, and was killed. He wasn't shot, or blown up, or anything like that. The soldier who was driving him fell asleep, and the car crashed down an embankment. My father was killed, but the driver only had scratches and a broken leg.'

'How awful. The War must have been terrible.'

'Yes, and we are still suffering from its after-effects. I know about these feelings, because Celia helped me to understand them. And she knows about feelings, because for a long time she went to a doctor who helped her talk about herself. I think it made her very wise. She once said to me, "It's the things that aren't said that cause most damage. They are like lies that everyone can see." For a long time, I didn't know what she meant, but now I do.'

I saw the cat creeping up on a small squirrel, that was sitting at the base of an enormous oak tree. The lower branches had been cut off. The cat pounced at the squirrel, but the squirrel was too fast and raced up the tree trunk. It climbed in a spiral until it reached the first big branch. Then it sat, looking down at us.

Mary put her arm round my shoulder, and asked me what I was thinking about. I said, 'I'd love to paint the squirrel and the cat.'

Mary squeezed my shoulder and said, 'You are a lamb.'
I wondered if one day I would become bitter.

Mary watched me painting. She said, 'You paint with such energy. I was feeling a bit sleepy, but watching you has made me feel wide awake.' I had painted Peter and myself on the branch of the oak tree. I had imagined the squirrel and the cat looking at us, and wondering what we were talking about.

We went inside, to see if Lady Celia was awake. She was back in the drawing room. She had five framed pictures on the table in front of her. She had turned them face down, so I couldn't see what they were. I had an awful suspicion that one of them would have naked people on it.
Lady Celia wanted to see my painting, and asked me to talk about it. I explained that Mary and I had talked about feeling bitter. She said, 'But I don't see any bitterness in the painting. The colours are bright and gay. It makes one feel happy to look at it. But it's not a relaxing painting. It's so vivid.'
I explained that Peter and I were talking about feeling bitter, but we were happy to be together.
Lady Celia said, 'Of course. Now it makes sense.'

Then she showed me the first picture. It was a black and white photograph of a big girl. We could only see her head and shoulders. I guessed that it was Lady Celia. I was right.
She told me, 'I was fourteen in that photograph. I was such a wild child. I went to school for one day only, but screamed so much that my mother and father educated me at home. Tell me what you see.'
I told her that I saw a beautiful girl, who was not looking straight at the camera. She looked like Bernadette when she was cross about something, and was thinking how best to say it. She looked like she was feeling uncomfortable about having her photo taken. She had a spot on her cheek and another one on her chin. I wondered if she was embarrassed about her spots. And her hair was so thick and dark and long and beautiful.

Lady Celia said, 'Clever girl! You are absolutely right about how I felt. I hated those spots. You see, I was still a girl, and those were my first spots. Mary tells me that these days girls turn into young ladies at a much younger age. A few days later, my father sent me to study art with a lot of grown-ups. Me, who had only ever been to school for one day!

'My mother died when I was eight. My brothers and sisters were all much older than me. Papa didn't know what to do with me. I was like you; I just had to paint and draw all the time. I never learned to write or spell properly, as you have already noticed.'
I looked at my hands in my lap.
She laughed. 'You are not the first person to notice that, but I'll tell you more about that soon.'

She told me that she used to hate wearing clothes, and was always running round outside with next to nothing on. 'Papa used to find me running around naked in the woods, or jumping in the fountain. He was so worried, he said that if I didn't stop stripping off, then he would have to take me to the doctor.'
I could feel myself going red. I couldn't imagine ever doing anything like that, even if I wanted to.
Lady Celia smiled. 'I especially hated the underwear they made us girls wear in those days. Horrible heavy stuff, that made us sweat and itch. Papa got very cross and took me to the doctor. I rubbed myself very hard to make myself very red. The doctor said that I had a terrible rash down there, and should only wear light underwear or nothing at all under my skirts.'
I was shocked. Mary said, 'What do you think about that Pippa?'
I said, 'I'm shocked. Really shocked. Telling lies is a Sin!'
Lady Celia said, 'But I was only fourteen, and still a child. Can you forgive me?'
She made me feel like I was the grown-up, and she was the child.

The next photograph was of one of the most beautiful women I could imagine. She was looking straight at the camera, with her arms by her sides. In one hand she was holding a battered white hat. Her dress was white and quite thick, with a cloth belt with a metal buckle, with a flower tucked into it. I could see a ring on her wedding finger. I wanted to keep that photograph.

I didn't wait to be asked what I thought: 'That's you! I know that's you. You look so lovely. You are lovelier even than Bernadette! You are smiling, but your whole face doesn't look happy. You still have that wave of hair over your left eye, but I think your hair might be shorter. I can just see your pony tail. I think this is the most beautiful person I have ever seen! I wonder what you would have looked like with that old hat on. It makes me think that maybe you didn't care so much about how you looked. And your dress is a bit creased, and it has a smudge on your front. Perhaps you had just had lunch, and you had dropped some soup in your lap.'

Lady Celia looked very pleased, but then she looked grave. 'You are quite right, Pippa. I was nineteen. I had been married for one month, and this photograph was taken in London, the day after we came back from our honeymoon, in Italy. I'm wearing a silver bracelet my husband gave me as a wedding present. I didn't like it.'

The third picture was a drawing of her face. She looked much older, but still lovely. She was looking straight at me. Her nose had changed shape, and her mouth wasn't smiling. Her eyes were very big, and full of sadness. I imagined the artist had spent a lot of time drawing those eyes. Her hair wasn't drawn very much, but I could see that it was shorter than in the photographs. I wondered what had happened to her, to make her feel so sad. She looked like she was just about to cry.

Lady Celia told me that she was twenty-two years old when she drew that picture of herself. 'I remember doing that drawing as if it were yesterday. I can remember exactly how I felt. I was desperately unhappy,, and becoming ill. You see, I realised that my husband, who was twenty years older than me, didn't really care for me very much. I was too wild and untidy for him. He

didn't like me to paint and draw. I felt like a candle that had been blown out. All my brightness and gaiety had been snuffed out. But I'm also showing you this, so that you can see that I was quite good at drawing. It's a very important skill for an artist.'
I thought I was going to cry too. Mary sensed that and said, 'Let's have a drink and a nice piece of cake.'

After a nice cup of tea and a big slice of delicious fruit cake, Lady Celia showed me the fourth picture. It was a painting of a young woman standing up, but resting, by leaning her bottom against a wooden fence. She was wearing a long white tunic, with no collar. Her long skirt was dark blue, but Lady Celia had painted it in such a way to make it look old and worn, and possibly a bit dirty. Her tunic was tied at the waist by a belt, the same colour as her skirt. I wondered if it might have been just a strip of cloth, left over from when the lady had made the skirt. Her brown hair was tied back, but the breeze had blown two long strands slightly away from her face. Behind her was a wooden shelter, with a roof made of straw. It must have been a very hot and sunny day, because everything was bright and brown, as if it had been baked by the sun.
But I was puzzled, because her face seemed unfinished. You could just see her eyes and mouth, and she looked like she might be smiling. The rest of her face was red. It made her look very sunburnt. I couldn't help thinking that she might not have been wearing any underwear.

I told Lady Celia and Mary my thoughts, but didn't mention the underwear.
Lady Celia was pleased with me, because I was absolutely right about her clothes. She had painted this picture of herself on a blistering hot summer day. She had gone for a long walk, and found this shelter. She asked me to look closely at her tunic. Was there anything that I could see there? I had seen something, but didn't want to say. Her chest looked like Mummy's on a cold day. Lady Celia must have thought carefully before she decided to paint her nipples sticking out.

165

She said, 'I was very excited. All day long I was thinking that I'd love to have a baby.'

The last painting had a naked lady and man on it. At first I didn't want to look at it. I wondered if looking at it would be a Sinful Act. They were both standing up, and the man was holding the lady round the waist. He looked like he might be trying to kiss her, but she was pulling away. Behind them was the same shelter from the fourth picture. Lady Celia had obviously paid a lot of attention to painting the man's face, but the lady's face was quite badly painted, I thought, so you couldn't decide what she might be thinking.

But I couldn't help noticing how much care she had taken with the lady's and man's bodies. The Lady had no hair covering her Private Place, so you could see everything. I could feel myself going red when I looked at that. And the man's willy was quite large. I didn't like it at all.

I was so busy looking at the two people, that I almost didn't notice that there was a lot of writing on the bottom part of the painting. The handwriting was so bad that I couldn't read much of it. I saw the words *love* and *envy* and *bodies*.

I didn't say anything. Mary asked me if I was all right, so I said, 'Can I have a glass of water please?'

Lady Celia asked me, 'Are you shocked again?'

I told her I wasn't shocked, but I didn't know how I felt. I was thinking that in school looking at a picture like that would be called being *Very Rude*. It would have been a Sin, like when Lawrence looked up my skirt. At school once, I had been playing at the far end of the playing field. Some boys had found a magazine in the bushes. It had photographs of naked ladies in it. I told Miss Dawson about it, and she said that these were rude photographs, and not at all nice. She said that there was nothing wrong with having no clothes on, but it wasn't at all nice to take photographs of naked people, and then sell them in the shops.

I wanted to explain this to Lady Celia and Mary, but suddenly I felt quite tired, and wanted to be on my own. Actually I wanted to see Bernadette and Peter, and talk to them about everything I

166

had learned today. But then I had a feeling, a sense, an idea, that Lady Celia was showing me these five pictures for a very special reason. I knew that she was a great artist, who was taking her precious time to show a little girl something about Art; something very important. I might not understand now, but it would make sense to me later. I closed my eyes and could see myself as if I was floating just below the ceiling. I was looking down on myself and the two ladies and the five pictures.

Then I knew what that last picture was all about. And I understood Mummy, and why she hated Daddy so much, and didn't want me to talk about him. I saw it all, and all because of five pieces of Art.

Mummy and Uncle Eric came to collect me at five o'clock. I had been sitting in the summer house, but I felt so tired that I could hardly keep my eyes open. I must have fallen asleep, just before Mummy came to get me. I woke up, and she was sitting next to me, and my head was in her lap. She was stroking my hair, and looking at my painting of Peter and myself in the tree. I opened my eyes, but didn't move. Mummy had a sweet smell, and I could smell Uncle Eric's pipe smoke on her too.
She must have noticed that I was awake, because she said, 'Hello Sleepy Head. Are you all right down there?' She laughed quietly and stroked my hair again. She said, 'Goodness, you have been busy! It's a lovely painting. I've been talking to Lady Celia. She has told me all sorts of things about herself. It's very strange, because she reminds me so much of me. She said that her husband was very generous to other people. He was famous for his good works with the poor. But he was not at all generous to Lady Celia. He was much older than she was, and he wanted to keep her just like a little girl. He didn't want her to have children. That upset her terribly. She loved cooking, and especially baking. But her husband was rarely at home to eat with her. He was out doing good works all the time, with the poor people and their children. When Lady Celia made pastry, she used to put cubes of cold butter into the flour. When she squeezed the butter with her fingers, it soon became soft and

lovely to touch. It was a beautiful sensation. But her husband was like a cold slab of butter. No matter how much you tried to warm him up, he remained solid and cold. But she had two children in the end: two boys. She poured all her love into them. She told me that they grew into solid handsome fellows, who love their wives and children, and are kind to them.'

It started to rain. I had been dribbling while I was asleep, and there was a stain on Mummy's nice blue dress.

I have two nightmares

In bed, I talked to Ursula for a long time. She said that when Mummy was a young lady, she had probably been just like Lady Celia. That meant that my Daddy had probably not been very nice to Mummy. I told her that Lady Celia loved her boys, but Mummy didn't like me. Ursula said I was being silly; of course Mummy loved me. Mummy was an alcoholic and was ill; which made her not explain herself very well.

I liked Lady Celia and Mary. It was nice to talk to them, and I had such wonderful paints and paper to use. I wanted to go back to their house the next day, but I was worried that at any minute Mummy might explode. She had told a terrible story about when she was little, and she had talked about Daddy.

Lying there, thinking about those things, I felt that I might explode too. I could hear myself grinding my teeth together, and could feel my blood pumping through my ears and temples. Ursula promised not to leave me in the night.

I had two awful nightmares. In the first one, Mummy was stroking my hair, but I slapped her in the face and called her a bitch, and told her I hated her. This dream moved into another, where I was standing on the bank of a stream. The stream was usually just a trickle, happily running across the stones. But it had been raining very hard, and the stream was full of dark-brown water, that was rushing past. I knew that the water was full of rats, even though I couldn't see them. I was poking the water with a long stick. Suddenly, I fell in the water. I tried frantically to get out, but the bank was high and sheer and slippery, and there was nothing to hold onto. I knew the rats were underneath me, and were swimming towards me.

Mummy came in. She sat on my bed and stroked my hair, and told me that I had been screaming.

I told her, 'I don't want to be on my own.'

She said, 'I'll stay here until you go to sleep again.'

I said, 'I want to get into bed with you.'

She said, 'Wait a minute,' and left the room. She came back and held my hand, and led me into her room. I got into bed beside her. The place next to her was nice and warm. I heard Uncle Eric flushing the toilet. I told Mummy, in a whisper, about my dream about the rats.

She said, 'I dream a lot. Sometimes I have nightmares too.'

I shut my eyes and took a deep breath. I said, 'I'm frightened.'

'What are you frightened of?'

'You.'

'Me?'

Why did she sound so surprised? There was a long pause. She pulled me towards her and cuddled me. I could smell under her arms. It was a slightly sweet, sweaty smell, mixed with her perfume. She asked me, 'Who do you talk to in your bedroom? Is it Ursula?' That was a shock. I tried to keep as still as possible.

I whispered, 'Ursula is my friend.'

'I know. I've known for a long time. Is she nice?'

'Yes. I talk to her, and sometimes she tells me what to do. She's my Guardian Angel.'

'What does she tell you to do?'

'She tells me not to be frightened, and she wants me to talk to you.'

'What about?'

'You know what about.'

'Yes, I suppose I do.'

'I want to ask questions.'

'You can.'

'No I can't. It makes you angry and upset with me, and that's when I get frightened.'

My heart was beating very fast. I wanted to run back to my room, but at the same time I wanted to stay exactly where I was. Mummy said, 'I try to do my best. I really do.' She kept stroking my hair. I must have fallen asleep.

When I woke up, I was back in my own bed.

Lady Celia and CD Thompson

The next day, we arrived at Lady Celia's house in time for coffee. The pictures of her leaning on the gate, and the naked man and woman, were still on the table, along with three other paintings that I hadn't seen yet. I wanted to go into the garden straight away. I didn't want to be in the same room as Mummy, Uncle Eric and a painting of a lady with her Private Place on display, and a man with a very large willy. But Mummy said, 'No Pippa. Please stay.'

I wasn't sure if she was asking me or telling me. She smiled at me and patted the chair next to her. How could I refuse?

I said, 'But Mummy, it's rude.'

Mummy said, 'No it's not. It's Art. And it's perfectly natural to have no clothes on.' She held my hand.

Mary gave Lady Celia a framed painting, and helped her put it on the coffee table. It was another naked lady. She was standing, leaning with her elbow against what looked like a large gravestone. Once again, the lady's body was carefully painted, but this time her Private Place was covered in hair. And once again, her face was painted without much care at all, so I couldn't decide what she was thinking, or feeling inside. I thought that I could have done a better job of painting her face. The gravestone had untidy writing on it, so it was very difficult to understand what she had written. One word was underlined and written in dark ink: *despair.* The background caught my attention; it was mainly a very vivid blue sky, with a small amount of darker blue sea underneath. I focused on those blues, and could imagine exactly how Lady Celia had made them.

Lady Celia was talking to Mummy and Uncle Eric: 'Towards the end of my career, people seemed to be very

170

interested in who I had been friends with at art school. They wanted to write about that, rather than my work. I had been part of a group of young artists who all became very highly regarded. One of them was once called 'the greatest living British artist.' But what people want to know most about these days is my chance meeting with a young man in the Tate Gallery.

'I was furious with my husband. All I wanted from him was to be touched. It had been my obsession. I wanted touch more than anything. When I told my husband I wanted a baby, he said, "Before we bring a poor unfortunate child into this world, you will have to spend less time running around half naked and looking like a Gypsy, and more time in the house, making it fit to live in." I felt like he had slapped me in the face. A few days later, I went into London, and wandered around the Tate Gallery. I was in such a bad mood. All my favourite paintings in the gallery suddenly seemed hideous to me.

'I was all hot and bothered, and felt like crying. I felt trapped in a loveless marriage. I was thinking some very dark thoughts, when a young man approached me and said, "Excuse me. Would you mind if I sit next to you?" I almost told him to go away and leave me alone, but then I looked at his face, and realised that I was looking at a very beautiful man. He started talking to me about the paintings he had just been looking at. He had been to a meeting with his publisher, and had popped into the gallery to seek inspiration for a poem that was forming inside him. He said his name was Charles Thompson. That meant nothing to me at the time. He said that a war was going to start soon. He could feel it. He said that everything we knew and loved would be turned upside down.

'I was quite alarmed by what he was saying. Then he asked me, "And why are you sitting here, all alone, with a face like thunder?"
I felt moved to tell him about my husband. It was very indiscreet to have done that. I said, "All I want is to be touched. I want that more than anything these days." That young man knew exactly

what I was talking about. He told me about his wife, and how they touched each other all the time. They already had three young children, and he imagined more would appear in the future.

'We must have been talking for a very long time, because we heard a loud voice telling us that the gallery was due to close. The young man said, "Good heavens! I must rush or I shall miss my train." He gave me his card. He was the poet CD Thompson. I gave him my card. He stuffed it in his pocket, shook my hand and rushed off. I was left sitting, looking at his card. Then he came back into the room and said, "Oh by the way, I have an idea for my next poem. Thank you so much! I'm looking for an artist to illustrate it, perhaps after the style of William Blake."
A few weeks later I received his poem and a short letter. I blushed bright red when I read it, and hid it from my husband.'

She turned the next painting over. It was another naked lady. She was almost exactly the same as the previous one, but this time the face was much more detailed. At first I thought that she looked happy, but then I wasn't sure. She was still leaning on the stone, but her hand was covering her Private Place (thank goodness). There was a new poem written on the gravestone. This time it was written neatly. It was called *And I Would Touch You*.
Uncle Eric whistled and said, 'Well Auntie, you are a dark horse indeed.'
I thought he was being very rude, but Lady Celia laughed. 'It became one of his best-known and best-loved poems. Nobody has ever seen this painting, apart from Mary and the man who framed it. There is another version, hanging in the Tate Gallery, I believe, but I have some clothes on in that one.' She laughed. Mummy was smiling. Mummy was smiling so much, I could see her teeth. Her cheeks were red.

Lady Celia continued with her story: 'A few years later, Charles came to see me. It was during what people called *The Great War*. He had volunteered to join the army, and was training at a camp nearby. He had walked across the fields to come and visit me. He was completely changed. His lovely golden hair had been practically shaved off, and he had a stubbly moustache. My husband was at home, talking with one of his colleagues, about politics and The Poor. He knew who Charles was, but practically ignored him. So Charles and I had tea in the garden, and talked about Art and his family. His wife, Dorothy, had had two more children.

'I couldn't understand why he would want to go off to the War, and leave his family behind. He told me a story. He said that he and his family lived in a cottage in a valley. He loved to climb the hill above their house, and look at the trees and fields. From time to time, a train would pass along the valley bottom. Across the railway track was a farm. He knew that a large black dog lived there. On the days he couldn't hear the dog barking, he would be content, and feel lazy and unable to write. But then, a few days later, the dog would start barking. Once the barking started, he knew that over the next few days the barking would get louder and louder, until finally he would see the dog crossing the tracks, and coming towards him. He would become filled with dark thoughts, and begin to hate himself and everything around him: the trees, the birds, the plants. He even hated his wife and his children. The warmth from the sun made him feel sweaty and uncomfortable.

'But it was at these times that his best poems would come to him. As the black dog was approaching him, he became filled with a sense of urgency; as if he must work and write as quickly as he could, before the dog finally reached him. On the day the black dog came to him, he despised everything around him. He thought his writing was a waste of time. He felt that all joy and energy had left him; never to return. His wife and children were frightened of him when he was like that, and he despised himself for becoming a brooding, sarcastic presence.

'The black dog was with Charles on the day he volunteered to join the army. He was up on the hill, and saw a train full of soldiers slowly making its way along the valley. He ran into the village, where he met a sergeant who was knocking on doors, looking for men who might want to join up. Charles signed up to join the army. Dorothy fainted when he told her. That was in March 1916. He came to see me three times in August. He was killed the next year, in France. The story goes that a shell exploded near him, and he was killed, instantly. The legend is that his body was completely intact, with not a mark on him. He had been killed by the shock waves from the explosion. I know that wasn't true. Dorothy told me that he had been blown into tiny pieces. He doesn't even have a grave.''

Mummy said, 'Please excuse me,' and went into the garden. We watched her through the window, smoking a cigarette.
Lady Celia said that she needed to leave the room for a short while, and asked Mary to help her. I was left with Uncle Eric. He picked up the painting and examined it. He said, 'This painting will be worth a lot to me. Not for the money it will give; but the story behind it. It's remarkable.'
The poem began
And I would touch you;
Were it not for the skein that binds me to another
And pulls me blindly towards
That dark centre
That pulses and gives heart and body and soul
And Life.

And I would touch you;
Where the mind and the spirit
Mingle and dance and laugh and share

I said, 'Mummy knows the black dog, doesn't she Uncle Eric?'
Uncle Eric didn't say anything. He was looking out of the window, at Mummy. He took his pipe out of his pocket and put it in his mouth. It was empty, but he sucked on it anyway.

At last he said something: 'You are quite right Pippa. She sees that black dog every month. But she doesn't have Art to show for it, once the dog has gone.'

Mummy was leaning against the well. She was smoking another cigarette. I said, 'She has you to look after her. And you touch her, don't you Uncle Eric?'

He said, 'You are a wise little girl. Go outside and give your Mummy's hand a squeeze.'

I did. Mummy squeezed my hand back. She said, 'You really are a lovely girl.'

She said it as if she was noticing me for the first time.

I draw my first nudes

Mary came out to see us in the garden. She said that Lady Celia was feeling a little dizzy, and would need to spend the rest of the day lying down in her room. Lady Celia had asked if Mummy would allow me to stay and do some drawing. Mary was holding a box of pencils. As soon as I saw them, I knew that I had to stay and draw. Mummy agreed. The plan was for me to have lunch with Mary, and then spend the afternoon as I wished.

Mummy asked, 'Did we make her over-excited?' I was wondering the same thing.

Mary explained that sometimes Lady Celia had these dizzy spells, and it was just a part of being very elderly.

I wanted Mummy to stay. I was surprised with myself, because usually I couldn't wait for her to leave me. She gave me a kiss and said, 'Do remember to be a good girl.'

I said, 'Yes Mummy, I will.'

After she and Uncle Eric left, I took my shoes and socks off, because I wanted to walk on the grass with bare feet. Mary sat in the summer house, and watched me walking up and down. I was thinking about Lady Celia being wild and running around with nothing on, and being angry with her husband because he wouldn't touch her. I wondered what it would be like to strip off and run around naked on the grass, and not care if Mary saw what I looked like. Mary called for me to come to her, and as I walked on the path I trod on a sharp stone. She laughed at me. I laughed at myself.

She gave me the box of pencils and said, 'Lady Celia says that the secret to drawing is to find a pencil that feels good.'

Up to that point I had only ever used pencils with *HB* stamped on them, but this box contained so many different types of pencil! I tried them all and thought to myself, 'Surely the right type of pencil for me is the one that I need for a particular type of drawing?'

I asked Mary if she was an artist. She said she liked to draw and paint, because it was in her blood. She particularly enjoyed working with clay. Everybody in her family had had some artistic talent, but she wasn't an artist in the same way as Lady Celia. She said that Lady Celia had told her once that when she was young, she felt she couldn't eat or sleep until she had drawn or painted what was inside or around her. Mary said to me, 'But you are an artist, Pippa, just like her. We all know that.'

I realised I had asked a question and got an answer.

I asked another one: 'Is Uncle Eric an artist?'

'Not in the same sense as his aunt or yourself. He's not really from her family, so the gift wasn't passed to him in the same way as the rest of Lady Celia's relatives. It wasn't in his blood so much. But he understands and loves Art. He's a fine writer.'

I thought about Lady Celia's drawing of her face. Mary took her shoes and stockings off, and sat reading in the sun. I looked at her feet. A pigeon was calling in a tree. A spider was weaving a web in the summer house, above my head. I looked at my feet. Mary got up to go inside the house, to prepare our lunch. When she came back, she looked at what I had done. She said, 'That's a fascinating drawing. But perhaps we had better show it to Lady Celia, and ask her to keep it safe.'

Without thinking I asked, 'Why?'

She said, 'Well, perhaps some people might be a bit surprised to see that you have drawn yourself and a boy and a big girl, all with no clothes on. And you have written a poem about touching them.'

I said, 'I was only copying Lady Celia.'

I wondered if I had sinned, by accident.

As we were talking, the wind suddenly became very strong. The sky was almost completely filled with dark clouds. I could see mauve everywhere, and only a small patch of pure cobalt sky, that was getting smaller and smaller. The wind was so strong that it blew the box of pencils off the table. Mary scrambled to pick them up, while the patch of cobalt completely disappeared.

Mary grabbed me and shouted, 'Quick! Run!'

By the time we had reached the edge of the lawn, we were soaked by tiny hailstones. Mary scooped me up under my arms, so I wouldn't hurt my feet on the path again.

Lady Celia was sitting by the window, watching us.

Our clothes were completely wet through. Even my knickers were wet. My socks and shoes were out in the garden, getting soaked. Mary laughed and said, 'Oh to be in summer, now that England's here.'

We stood in the hallway, and both of us had made wet puddles on the shiny floor.

After lunch, Mummy came with Uncle Eric and another man. She was very surprised to see what I was wearing. Mary had found a piece of white cloth and made me a toga tunic, complete with a red belt made from an old scarf. She had made a garland of laurel leaves, and put it in my hair. The rain had made my hair very curly.

Mummy laughed and said to Uncle Eric, 'Why is it that every time I come to collect my daughter from somebody's house, she's wearing someone else's clothes?'

Then she handed me a piece of paper and said, 'I have a letter from your boyfriend.'

I went bright red and wouldn't look at her. She said, 'Sorry. I'm sorry Pippa. I won't say that again.'

The man said, 'She looks like a young Caravaggio.'

The three of them and Mary talked with Lady Celia, while I went into another room at the front of the house. There were lots more pictures on the walls, and a big brown wooden table. It was so highly polished that I could see myself reflected clearly in its surface. It was like looking in a large brown mirror. Mary had brought in my painting pad, sketchbook, paints and brushes and the box of pencils.

I opened the envelope with Peter's letter in. He had written

Dear Pippa,
Dad has bought us a TV, so we can watch him on it.
He is in a new programme about the police.
I don't like it becaus there is too much talking.
I like the adventures of Robinson Cruesoe better.
Dad says if his programme is a suces then we will have to move to Liverpool.
Please can you wave to me in the mornings?
Love from Peter McCabe
PS I hope your nose and black eyes are better.

My naked drawing was still in my sketchbook, so I painted the sky a very dark grey, with black and a lot of mauve, and just a tine space with some cobalt blue. There was a small space left at the bottom of the tombstone and I wrote in it, *Dear Peter, please don't leave me.* I went to the window and looked out. I felt very angry. I was angry with Peter's father for being on television, and taking the family to Liverpool. Then I felt an awful sadness and started to cry. They were silent tears.

The sun was shining onto the table, and I looked at the reflection of my face. My nose and the skin around my eyes were almost back to normal. I thought of Lady Celia's face in her drawing.
I must have been drawing for an hour or more, because I heard a knock on the door, and realised that my legs and feet felt very cold. The other man came in. He was holding a very large camera.
He said, 'Hello Caravaggio!' I didn't look at him, but carried on drawing. He said, 'My name's Mr Stead. James Stead, but most people call me *Jim*. I've been taking photos of Lady Celia.'

I tried to ignore him. I could hear his camera clicking away. I heard him say, under his breath, 'Good girl, take no notice of me. You keep drawing.'

Then he said, in a much louder voice, 'My camera loves you.' I looked straight at him, and he said, 'Gotcha!'

This made me smile and he said, 'Gotcha again!' and I started to laugh. He reminded me of Peter's father.

I hear noises in the night

I woke up in the night, and felt Ursula poking me. I could hear noises coming from Mummy's bedroom. Mummy was laughing. Ursula said, 'Don't be frightened. Go and see what's going on.'

My bedroom door was slightly open, and I crept as quietly as I could across the landing. There was a thin light shining from under Mummy's bedroom door. Mummy laughed again and said, 'Don't do that, you naughty boy!' Then I heard a slap; a hand on bare flesh.

Uncle Eric laughed and said, 'But you can do that again if you like, you naughty girl!'

Then Mummy said, 'Shh. We're making too much noise. I don't want Pippa to hear us.'

Uncle Eric said, 'I shall miss her. She's a most fascinating child.' Mummy said, 'Well don't go then. Stay here with us.'

He said, 'You know I can't. But you know where I live, and you have my telephone number, so I expect to see you every Saturday.'

Mummy sighed. Uncle Eric said, 'And I would touch you.'

Mummy replied, 'Were it not for the iron band that binds me to another.'

She sighed again, and they didn't say anything more.

I went to the toilet and did a wee, but didn't flush the toilet. As I was passing Mummy's room, the light had been turned off. I heard her say, 'Don't stop. Don't stop.'

I went back to my room and told Ursula that Uncle Eric and Mummy were touching each other.

Ursula asked, 'In a nice way?'

I said, 'I think so. I think they are pretending to be children. They are playing about and slapping and teasing each other, just like Peter and I sometimes do.'

Miss Dawson's last day

The next day, Peter was sitting on my front wall, and I waved to him. He waved back and gave me a very big smile. I put my mouth on the window pane and made a funny face. At Lady Celia's house, I spent the morning talking to Mary, and looking at more of Lady Celia's paintings and drawings. There were a lot of drawings about a lady called Cathy, and a house called *Wuthering Heights*. Mary explained that this was one of the best-loved books for grown-ups, and that Lady Celia's illustrations were just as well-known. She said that when Lady Celia was a young lady, she had been very unhappy and lonely, and she had read *Wuthering Heights* all the time. She began to think that she was just like Cathy in the book. She was able to show exactly how Cathy felt; perhaps because she was suffering in the same way herself. Mary thought this was one of the reasons why so many people liked her illustrations.

I didn't like to think of Lady Celia suffering, though she seemed quite happy now. I thought about Miss Dawson, and how she had cried and taken her ring off, but now she was happy again. I thought of Mumm,y and how she had been so angry and unhappy and dangerous, but now could laugh in the night. And I thought of Lady Celia and her cold husband, and Mary with her feelings of bitterness about her father. And I thought of me; little Pippa, who would soon be on her own again, with just her mummy for company.

I spent the morning and afternoon drawing a lady's face, to give to Miss Dawson. I wrote her a letter.

Dear Miss Dawson
I have been very lucky to have you for a teacher.
I have learned so many things.

Most of all I have learned that you are the lovelyest teacher I have ever met.
Lots of Love from Pippa Dunbar.
PS I wish I could know what your first name is
PPS I really love you and I hope you like my pictures

When I went back to school, Miss kissed me in front of all the other children in class. She said that she and all the children had missed me. I gave her my letter and my big painting book to keep. She read the letter and cried a little bit. She wasn't weeping like the last time, but her eyes became wet, and she blew her nose into her hanky and laughed. She told me her name was Heather, and that her mother had named her after a plant that grows wild in Scotland.

I gave her my drawing of the lady's face. It was a mixture of Miss Dawson, Mary, Mummy, and Lady Celia when she was young. At the bottom of the page was another, smaller painting; of Miss Dawson's hand with the ring on it.

We prepare for the holiday

During the first week of the school holidays, Mummy discovered that my feet had grown again, and that none of my clothes seemed to fit me anymore. She took me to see Peter, and Mummy asked Peter's mother for advice about what I should wear on holiday. Mrs McCabe thought that perhaps I might wear some of Frances and Bernadette's old clothes. The girls thought this was a very funny idea. They brought two big suitcases of clothes out into the garden for me to look at. They laid all the clothes out on the grass, and told Peter and me to choose what we thought might fit me and look nice.

There were a lot of white dresses that used to belong to Frances. Bernadette said that this was because Frances had been the more *ladylike* of the twins. There were hardly any clothes that had belonged to Bernadette. Frances said that this was because Bernadette had been a *tomboy* like me, and had either ruined her clothes, or worn shorts and boys' clothes. Bernadette pretended to get cross with her sister, and explained that she just

181

preferred being outdoors and getting involved in sports, and that this made her *athletic* and not like a boy.

In the end, Mummy decided that she would go into London the next day, to buy my clothes at Selfridges. This was her favourite shop. Peter said that on holiday we would be climbing trees and making dens, and getting very dirty. All day I was worried about what clothes that Mummy might come back with. But I needn't have worried, because I was very pleased with what she had chosen for me. She had been to the girls' department, but she had only seen what she thought was *a lot of frilly nonsense*. She had a long discussion about me with a manager, who suggested that Mummy look in the boys' department. The manager said that a lot of mothers with *tomboyish* daughters did their shopping there. She thought that Selfridges should design a range of clothes for girls who would rather be boys. Mummy had asked her, 'And what exactly are you suggesting? My daughter doesn't want to be a boy; she's athletic.'

At first, Mummy didn't want to look at boys' clothes for me. But she had a pleasant surprise when she saw a huge selection of pairs of shorts, and sensible shirts with short sleeves, that didn't look too *boyish*. The girls made me try all the clothes on, and said that my mother was a genius. I thought I looked like a girl who might be a boy. I was worried that Mummy might have bought me some boys' pants, but when she got home she showed me some nice knickers that she had chosen for me.
She said, 'I've bought you plenty of extra pairs, because I know what you're like.' She was laughing as she said it, so I supposed she was talking about me getting wet a lot, rather than me wetting myself. It was nice to hear her laughing, especially as Uncle Eric had left us that morning.

The only bad thing that Mummy had bought was a bright green bathing costume. I really didn't like it, but didn't dare say so. We went to the local shops, and bought a pair of blue and white striped dungaree shorts, and a pair of black wellington boots. Then, for a really special treat, we went to the shoe shop, and Mummy let me choose a pair of Clarks brown sandals. They looked just like Peter's; though I didn't tell Mummy that.

I remember this as being a very special week. Mummy was looking after me on her own, and hadn't lost her temper once. On the evening before we were due to go away, Mummy remembered that she had to put all my clothes into a suitcase. All our cases were up in the loft. To get into the loft, Mummy had to find a ladder, push the end of it up against the trapdoor, climb up with a torch, and find an empty case. All this proved to be a bit too much for her. I was waiting down at the bottom of the ladder and heard her saying to herself, 'Damn this wretched holiday! Why did I agree to it in the first place?'
But when she came down the ladder with the suitcase, she was smiling.
She said, 'Mummy's getting a bit over-tired. Let's finish all this in the morning.'

I asked Ursula if she would come with me on holiday. She said that she needed a nice holiday too, and asked me if she could wear some of my nice clothes, because she was fed up with always wearing a white dress. I asked her if that made her a tomboy.
She said, 'Don't be stupid.' She had never said that before.
She said she might like to run around naked, like Lady Celia.
I said, 'It's a good thing that Peter can't see you.'
She thought that this was very funny, and laughed so much that I thought she might wake Mummy.

The journey to Norfolk
One thing that really surprised me about Peter's family was the amount of farting they did. To them, it was like a kind of sport. It began as soon as we had said goodbye to Mummy.
The last thing Mummy said was, 'Be a good girl and try not to hit anyone with a wooden cricket bat.'
I looked down, but Mr McCabe said, 'Your Mummy is telling a joke!'

He wound up the window and said to his wife, 'She must be getting better; that's the first funny thing I've heard her say.'

Then someone farted loudly, and everyone laughed. Everyone except me. Mummy had told me never to make that noise in public, because it was *unladylike*.

We were going to stay in a bungalow in the woods, outside a small town in Norfolk, near the sea. All the way there, people were farting. Mr McCabe had to stop the car because he was laughing so much. He said he couldn't drive properly, because people were farting all the time. Mrs McCabe said it wasn't funny anymore, and she would fine everyone a penny every time they did it.

Frances said, 'That's not fair; it's dad who keeps doing it!'

The house belonged to Mr McCabe's brother, who was also an actor. He had been in a film called *Help!* with The Beatles. Bernadette and Frances were very excited, because the film was going to be shown at the cinema in the town near our bungalow. Mr McCabe said that acting was in his family's blood. He imagined that at least one of his children would continue the family tradition, by becoming an actor.

Frances said that she wanted to be a crime writer or a lawyer.

Bernadette said she was going to be a doctor.

Peter farted.

Mrs McCabe suggested that Bernadette become a doctor that helped children who were rude, and who needed to go to the toilet.

Bernadette asked her mum what was in her family's blood. Mrs McCabe said that mainly they had worked in shops, and sometimes owned them. She was the only one who had become an actress, but she had stopped acting when she had got married and had her three lovely children.

Mr McCabe said, 'Before we got married, we used to be in a theatre company, and go on tour together. The actors and the actresses lived in separate houses. In Oxford, I think it was, your mum was staying with a very strict landlady. She wouldn't allow

184

any man visitors, so I couldn't see your mum in the evenings. Your mum had a washing line on the balcony outside her room. If she hung socks on the line, that meant *The landlady is in, so stay away.* If she hung out her knickers...'

Mrs McCabe said, 'Geoffrey!' This stopped him telling the rest of the story, but they were both laughing.

Bernadette told me that they had all heard that story so many times before, but they never found out what happened in the end, because their mum always stops him.

Bernadette asked me, 'What's in your family's blood, Pippa? What have people in your family done?'

I said, 'I'm not really sure.'

Mrs McCabe said, 'Goodness, is that a cow in that field?'

There was no cow in the field. I said to Bernadette, 'I think people in my mummy's family were good at being Jewish, before they were all killed. And my daddy's family are good at owning several rubber plantations in Malaya.'

Peter said, 'I feel sick.'

Frances said, 'Mummy.... My tummy hurts...' She sounded just like a little girl.

Mrs McCabe asked her, 'Have you brought anything for it?'

Frances said, 'No. I forgot.'

Bernadette said, 'I've brought lots. I'm always prepared.'

Peter said, 'You've brought lots of what?' I was thinking the same thing.

We stopped in a lay-by and Peter was sick. Bernadette and Frances went into the bushes together. It started to rain heavily.

The bungalow in the woods

By the time we arrived at the bungalow, it had just stopped raining. We had to park the car by the gate, at the bottom of the drive, because the track leading to the house was too muddy, and the car might get stuck. By the time we had unpacked the car and put all our things in front of the house, we were covered in mud. Everyone was laughing, except for Frances. She looked very pale, and stayed in the car. The bungalow was made of wood and had a thatched roof. It smelt old, and had a wooden veranda at the front and at the back. Peter said that foxes sometimes lived under the veranda, and he had seen mice living in the roof. He kept shouting and jumping about. Mrs McCabe told me that Peter always did that when he came to the bungalow. He just couldn't contain his excitement; just like a caged animal that has been set free.

Peter showed me all the rooms. There were three bedrooms, a kitchen and a living room. I whispered to Peter, 'Where's the toilet and the bathroom?'

'Oh,' he said, 'there isn't one. I wee in the woods, and sometimes do a poo there too. Otherwise we go in that shed out there.' He pointed to the back of the house. 'And we wash in a bowl of water when we wake up, and before we go to sleep.'

I thought that Peter was teasing me; but he wasn't. Each bedroom had a large china bowl with a big jug in it. You had to fill the jug with water and tip it in the bowl, so you could wash your face and hands.

We went to look at the shed. It was dark inside, and all I could see was a large metal can with a lid on it. Peter opened the lid, and I could just see a pool of bright blue liquid, with brown blobs and pieces of wet newspaper floating in it. The strong smell reminded me of disinfectant, mixed with the brown paint used for painting garden fences.

Peter said, 'It looks like nobody's used it for a long time. Maybe my uncle came here and forgot to empty it.'

I wondered if The Beatles had been with him, and done a poo in there too. I was about to ask Peter why there were pieces of newspaper floating in the filthy liquid, but saw some cut up strips of old newspaper hanging on a nail next to the can. I was beginning to enjoy asking questions, so asked Peter, 'What's the matter with Frances?'

He said, 'It's her monthly thing. She gets like that sometimes. She gets these awful pains in her tummy, so Mum gives her a hot water bottle to hold, and an aspirin to take the pain away.'

We ran around in the woods. I kept thinking I might tread on some poo, or see Mr McCabe doing a wee. Peter took me to a place he said was right in the middle of the woods. We ran along a path that someone had made through tall green bracken. In an open space near a huge pine tree, we found a water pump with a handle. It looked very old, but someone had painted it green. Peter asked me to help him pull the handle up and down. We must have done it about twenty times before we heard a gurgle, and water started to rush out of the pump's spout. It sounded like it was being sick. I looked at the water, then up at the tree, then at Peter. I took a deep breath and closed my eyes. I felt my tummy getting warm, and my hands trembled very slightly. I was very excited. I felt thrilled. I called this feeling *The Thrill*.

Who will I sleep with?

When we went back inside the house, Frances was lying on the floor in the living room. She was clutching her tummy and moaning. Mrs McCabe was heating water for a hot water bottle. I was a bit frightened. It stopped me from asking where I could do a wee, where I should wash my hands afterwards, and about where I was going to sleep. There were two bedrooms that had single beds in, and one with a double bed, like the one in Mummy's bedroom. I supposed the one with the double bed was for Mr and Mrs McCabe. I thought that Peter and I were going to sleep in the same room.

We went to look for Bernadette. She was sitting on the veranda, talking to her dad. I took a very deep breath and closed my eyes, and pretended that Mr McCabe wasn't there.
'Excuse me Bernadette', I said, 'can I ask you something?'
Mr McCabe said, 'That sounds ominous,' and asked Peter to take him to see the water pump.
I asked Bernadette about how I was going to go to the toilet. I told her I didn't really like the shed, because it was dark and smelly, and a bit frightening. She said that she felt the same. She explained that I could do a wee in the bushes, or if I needed to do a poo, then I could take a small spade or stick, to dig a hole in the ground somewhere private in the woods.
All my questions came tumbling out. 'But what if you need to go in the middle of the night?'

187

'Well, then we do something a bit different. You can wake me up, and I can go with you, if you like.'

'But where will you be sleeping?'

'With you.'

'But I was thinking that I might sleep with Peter.' This was the nearest I had got to telling an adult that I didn't agree with a decision.

Bernadette explained: 'Mum and Dad talked with your Mummy about this. She doesn't want you and Peter to sleep in the same room. She was very definite about it.'

'But why not?'

'Well, she thinks it's better if boys and girls don't sleep together. So Peter is going to sleep with Frances and you are going to sleep with me.'

'But Frances is a girl.'

'But she's Peter's sister.'

I thought I should have stopped asking questions then, but there was something about Bernadette that made me want to keep asking about this subject. I wanted to sit on Bernadette's knee. I moved closer to her. She said, 'Come and sit on my knee.' I was feeling the same as when I was with Miss Dawson.

Bernadette said, 'Ask me another question.'

'What's wrong with Frances?'

'She has her Period. She always gets these terrible pains until it's almost finished. But sometimes she gets them for no reason, in the middle of the month. There might be some blood, or there might be none. She's been to the doctor, but he says he can't do anything to help her. Maybe it'll settle down and become more regular as she gets older.'

'But do you get those awful pains too?'

'No. I'm very lucky. I just feel a bit uncomfortable. Ask me another question.'

'Well, really I'm very happy to sleep with you, but will we go to bed at the same time?'

'I don't suppose so. Why?'

'Well, will I be in that bedroom on my own then? I think I could be frightened.'

Yes. Did you want to sleep with Peter until I come in?'
'That would be nice.'
'But your Mummy doesn't want you to.' I knew that Bernadette
was trying to get me to ask *why not?* And I knew she wanted to
tell me.
'Why not?'
'Your mummy says that boys and girls should sleep in separate
rooms, because you might be tempted to do things.'
'Did she mean perhaps we might be silly, and start hitting each
other with pillows, or talking all night and not going to sleep?'
'Yes, perhaps that's what she meant.'
I knew it wasn't, but didn't say anything. I thought of Ursula.
She might know the answer.

I asked Bernadette about Frances again: 'Is Frances able to
eat something?'
'Frances loves to eat fish and chips. When she has her Period,
Mum and Dad are always extra kind to her. So Dad has said that
we can have fish and chips tonight.'
I was very excited about that.
'But I'll tell you a very nice thing. Your Mummy has given my
Dad a lot of money. She says we're all to have special treats, like
eating in the café, going to the cinema and having ice cream.'
I was very surprised. Mummy was always telling me how poor
we were, and that was why we had to save water and electricity
and heating.
I said, 'I love you, Bernadette.'
She said, 'Oh... and I love you too, Pippa.'
I've mentioned before that I sometimes felt myself floating up to
the ceiling. This time I felt myself standing on the edge of the
veranda, looking at myself on Bernadette's knee. I was feeling
The Thrill. I was picturing my next painting.

Fish and chips

Mr McCabe, Peter and I went in the car to the fish and chip
shop in the town. I had walked past such places with Mummy,
but had never been inside one. Peter was very surprised when I
told him that. I was beginning to realise that there were lots of

189

things I'd never done before. Peter took me to the front of the big metal and glass cabinet, to look at the adults cooking the fish and chips. I was fascinated by the pieces of cod being dipped in the creamy white batter, and then being lowered into the sizzling fat; the bubbling and spitting chips; the smell of vinegar; the pickled eggs in huge jars; the shiny pink saveloys: the fried sausages in golden batter waiting in the hot cabinets on top of the fryer, and the way that the staff wearing white coats used metal scoops to shovel the chips into sheets of newspaper. I breathed in all the smells and the steam, and the heat.

I was beginning to feel hot. I went back to Mr McCabe, and he held my hand. We hadn't touched each other before. Peter stayed at the front, watching the chips. Every so often he would turn round and smile with excitement at us.

Back at the house, the table was laid, and everyone was very hungry. Peter started eating straight away, but his mum coughed at him.
He said, 'Sorry Mum,' and quickly put his knife and fork down. We hadn't said *Grace*. I put the palms of my hands together and closed my eyes. I was expecting everyone to chant *Bless us oh Lord for these Thy Gifts which we are about to receive from Thy Bounty Amen.* Peter held my hand. For a brief moment I thought it was very nice of him to do that, but then I became embarrassed because his family were watching us. Then I noticed that everyone was holding hands with each other.
Mrs McCabe said, 'Who would like to say Grace?'
Bernadette said, 'Thank you for these lovely fish and chips, and thank you to Pippa's mummy for letting Pippa come on holiday with us.'
Everyone said 'Amen'.

Frances smiled at me, so I went red. I was hoping her fish and chips would make her Period feel better. My fish had quite a few small bones in it, so Mr McCabe helped me take them all out. Peter spilled some tomato ketchup on the tablecloth, but nobody got cross with him.

190

Bernadette told a very rude story. She told us that one evening last summer it was very hot in the chip shop, so the lady serving the fish and chips was only wearing a black lace bra under her white coat.

Mrs McCabe said, 'Bernadette, that's enough.'

But she kept going: 'But Mum, it was Dad who told me, and he said that because of that, the queue for chips that night went out of the door and halfway down the street.'

Mrs McCabe said, 'You can't believe everything your father tells you. He's an actor, after all.'

Our first night in the bungalow

It was still light when Mrs McCabe told Peter and me that it was time to get ready for bed. Bernadette offered to help us get ready. I only washed my hands and face, but Bernadette said that didn't matter, because I could swim in the sea the next day. I went into Peter's room, and we sat up in bed together, while Bernadette read us a story. It was a big picture book of *Treasure Island*. Peter enjoyed looking at the picture of Blind Pew, but I had to turn away, because he looked so frightening. When Bernadette had finished, she told us to say *goodnight* to each other. She gave Peter a kiss and tucked him in. I wanted to give him a kiss as well. I think he wanted one too.

Bernadette took me to my room, and tucked me in. She asked me if I had had a nice day. I told her it had been the best day of my life. She laughed.

I heard Peter shouting 'Night night, Pippa!' and then I think I must have fallen asleep straight away.

I woke up in the darkness, and felt someone in bed with me, holding me round my middle. At first I thought it was Ursula, but realised it was Bernadette.

I kept as still as I could, but needed to go to the toilet. I tried to pretend to myself that I was asleep and dreaming, but the need to wee became urgent. I had to push Bernadette very hard to make her wake up. We whispered together, and decided we would both have to go to the outside toilet.

The whole house was completely dark. We felt our way along the corridor. We could hear snoring coming from the grown-ups' bedroom. Bernadette knew where the switch for the outside light was. She switched it on, and I could see the toilet down the path.

She pointed to the dirt in front of the toilet and whispered, 'Let's wee just there.'

I was bursting, so did as I was told. As we were squatting side by side, Bernadette let out an enormous fart. I had an idea that she had done it on purpose. We couldn't stop laughing. Mrs McCabe came to the door. She was wearing a very thin and very short petticoat. She looked a bit surprised when she saw us, and said, 'Oh, it's you two. I thought it was the foxes.'

That made us laugh even more. When we had finished, we passed by the kitchen. Mrs McCabe was sitting on a chair, drinking a glass of water. I could see all of her legs. She said, 'Night night, you two.'

Bernadette put her arms around her mum, and kissed her on the side of her face.

In bed, we were both wide awake. I asked Bernadette why her mum only wore a short petticoat in bed, and not a long nightie like my mother.

She said, 'Oh, we don't really bother with things like that. Frances is the only one who doesn't really like people seeing her body. She's my twin sister and we love each other, of course, but she doesn't talk to me very much these days. She spends most of her time reading crime novels. I think she's a bit obsessed with Agatha Christie at the moment. Mum says she's like you: very sensitive and a deep thinker.'

I thought about how once, in my first school, our class were getting changed for PE. We had to take off all our clothes, except for our vests and pants. Bridget had no knickers on. I think she must have got herself dressed before she came to school. She started to walk around the class with nothing on. The nun who was helping us get changed told Bridget to *hide her shame*, and not to be so *immodest*.

192

I thought about Lady Celia running around naked when she was a girl.

Once, when I was at Peter's house, Bernadette was coming out of the bath, just as I was going towards the toilet. She was only holding a small towel to cover her front.

Her mum came out of the bedroom and laughed and said, 'Go and get a bigger towel. I'm sure Pippa doesn't want to see your lovely naked bottom!'

She gave it a playful smack. It sounded just like when Mummy had slapped Uncle Eric in bed.

We don't go to the beach

The next day, we didn't go to the beach. At breakfast Mr and Mrs McCabe explained that Frances was still feeling terrible pains in her tummy. Peter said it wasn't fair that just because Frances was ill we all had to stay at home.

Frances said, 'It's not my fault. I don't care if you all go to the beach. I can stay here on my own.'

Peter said to her, 'You're probably just pretending. I bet you're not really ill!'

Frances shouted, 'Shut up, you little brat!'

Mr and Mrs McCabe looked at each other. Mrs McCabe said, 'Please! Let's not talk to each other like this. It's not anyone's fault. What must Pippa think of us, shouting at each other at the table?'

I said, 'I'm used to being shouted at. Mummy shouts at me a lot. Some doctors say it's because of what happened to her in The War, but I wonder if it's her Period that makes her yell at me.'

I had been trying to eat my bacon and eggs, but suddenly it all looked cold and horrible on my plate

Nobody said anything for a while. Peter said, 'Sorry Frances.'

Frances said, 'That's all right,' and started to cry.

Mrs McCabe said to her, 'Come here, love,' but Frances ran out of the room. Bernadette went after her.

Mr McCabe said, 'Let's all have a nice day at home. Shall I get the bath ready, darling?'

Mrs McCabe said, 'That's a good idea. Then we can all calm down.'

Nobody wanted to eat anything else. Mrs McCabe said this was a terrible shame, as it had taken such a long time to make breakfast, and she hated wasting food. I offered to help her clear away the dishes, but she said. 'Why don't we have some more tea, and I'll make some toast?' I turned round to talk to Peter, but he had left the room.

Mr McCabe said it was best to let him be on his own for a while. He said that Peter was a good boy, but sometimes found it difficult to cope with being disappointed.

Then he started to sing *Don't put your daughter on the stage Mrs Worthington*. I was very surprised. I was even more surprised when he grabbed his wife and started dancing with her. She gave him a shove and said, 'Geoffrey, this is neither the time nor place for being silly.' But she was laughing.

It wasn't very often that I was on my own with both Peter's parents. It made me feel slightly uncomfortable. I now know that this feeling is called being *self-conscious*. I suspected they were going to ask me a question.

Mr McCabe said, 'We're all very glad that you've come on holiday with us. I'm sorry if it's been a bit of a muddle so far. That can happen when your normal routine changes. When I'm acting, and we start rehearsals for a new play or series, everyone starts arguing with each other, until we settle down. And sometimes it's hard to make plans when you go on holiday with teenage girls.'

Then he asked the question. 'Is there anything that you would like to do today, Pippa?'

I didn't know what to say. I must have looked very strange; sitting there with a frown on my face, and not able to say anything.

Mr McCabe said, 'Are you all right, Pippa?'

I said, 'Well, you asked me a very difficult question. At school, I just do as I'm told. At home, I do what Mummy tells me. When I'm on my own, I just do whatever I like, as long as I'm quiet. Usually I paint and write stories. When I'm with Peter, I like to do what he wants. So it's hard for me to choose what I might like to do.'

Mrs McCabe looked very serious and said, 'Well, on this holiday we would like to know what *you* would like to do, so you can enjoy yourself as much as possible. I imagine you would like to paint and draw. But would you like to read some books, and play with Peter, and go to the seaside, and go to the cinema?'

I suddenly felt a bit overwhelmed, as if Mrs McCabe had opened a big box, and shown me lots of presents inside, all for me, but I couldn't choose which one to look at first.

I said, 'Sometimes I feel over-excited, and I get very hot and bothered, and need to be quiet.' I didn't know why I said that. I began to feel as if my head was a bit light, and that it wasn't me who was talking.

I said, 'I look at things for a long time. Things that interest me, and that I might like to paint. But sometimes I find things… new things usually… I find them very exciting, and I have to keep very still, so I can feel them properly.'

Mrs McCabe smiled and said, 'We know. We see you do it all the time. We call it *drinking in*. We say, "There's Pippa, drinking something in." Lots of artists do it: writers do it a lot, and actors too. The person who writes Geoff's TV series spends all his time watching people, and thinking about how they talk to each other. Geoff does it too. It's how he knows how to act like the people he is portraying.'

I said, 'I thought it was just me. I thought I was a bit strange.'

We were quiet together. Then I said, 'I'd like to do all those things, and I'd like to learn how to wash myself properly in that bowl in our bedroom. And I mustn't forget to go to Mass on Sunday.'

The grown-ups both laughed.

Mrs McCabe said, 'That's easy. Bernadette will show you how to have a wash. She's always in the bath, or washing her hair. But we're not going to Mass on Sunday. We're going to a church to worship God, but it's not quite the same as Mass.'

I started to panic, but Mrs McCabe was ready for that.

195

'We've talked about this with Mummy, and she doesn't mind at all. She thinks it's a very good idea to try something different.'
She must have guessed what I was going to say next because she said: 'And it isn't a Sin. All of us want to try going to a new church; to see what it might be like.'

Mr McCabe said, 'Come on, let's have our tea and toast and see if we can find Peter. I'll do the washing up later.'
I suddenly felt a rush of warmth rising from my feet, all the way to the top of my head. It wasn't like The Thrill; it was like a wave.
I said, 'I love you, Mr and Mrs McCabe. I wish you could be my Uncle and Auntie.'
Really, I wanted them to be my mum and dad. But I thought about Mummy, sitting in the kitchen all on her own, without me, and I knew that I shouldn't be thinking about leaving her. I nearly started to cry, but stopped myself, just in time.
Mrs McCabe took my hand and put me on her knee. Mr McCabe went outside.
She said, 'That's funny, because we... Geoff and I... we have been thinking the same thing as you. I talked to your mummy about it. Mummy and I are very good friends now, and talk to each other a lot, as I'm sure you know. The girls really want you as their sister, but that's not possible, so they want you as a cousin instead. Peter says he wants to marry you.' She laughed, but I went red. 'So you can call us Auntie Julia and Uncle Geoff. But don't call him *Geoffrey*, because that's his stage name, and I only call him that when I'm cross with him, or telling him off.'
I felt the wave rising inside me again. I kissed Auntie Julia on the cheek and said, 'Thank you Mrs... I mean *Auntie*. I feel much better now.'
She said, 'So do I,' and started to cry a little bit. Her crying sounded like Miss Dawson, when I gave her my letter and the book of paintings.
She said, 'You are such a sweet thing. You make us all feel so *emotional*. I sometimes wonder if that will be your job in life.'

Uncle Geoff came back in, and held my hand, and we went to find Peter. I knew exactly where he would be. As we walked down to the pump, Uncle Geoff said, 'It's my job to make sure that he's sorry for upsetting his sister, and to tell him to try not to do it again.' I wondered what would happen.

Peter had collected a great heap of sticks and branches, and was sorting them into two piles.

He said, 'I'm collecting wood for the fire.' He seemed to have forgotten about all the upset he had caused.

Uncle Geoff said, 'That's good Peter, but first we have to talk about what happened at breakfast.'

Peter went red and looked at me. I knew he was feeling embarrassed, because he was going to get told off in front of me. I went behind the pine tree, and pretended I was collecting sticks.

I heard him crying. His dad said, 'It's all right . But next time try and be kind to your sister. She can't help it.'

Peter said he was sorry, and his dad told him to go and apologise to his sister.

While Peter was gone, Uncle Geoff explained that we were going to collect wood to build a big fire; to heat water, so that we could all have a bath. I imagined us all sitting in a giant bathtub, with no clothes on. Uncle Geoff could see I looked confused and said, 'We take turns. Frances will be first because it's her special time, and then we will find a way for each of you to have a bath after her. That's if you'd like to have one, of course.'

I liked the idea very much.

Uncle Geoff and I carried our sticks and branches to the back of the house. I looked for the wet patches where Bernadette and I had done our wee in the night, but they had dried up. It was beginning to be a very hot day. I could hear music and singing coming from the house. I went inside, and saw Peter sitting with Frances on her bed. There was a small portable record player on the floor, and Bernadette was sorting through a stack of records. The record that was being played was *Can't Buy Me Love* by The Beatles, and the three of them were singing along. I didn't know the words, so stood watching them. I was very happy to have such nice cousins.

Auntie Julia, Peter and I prepared the fire. Uncle Geoff found the big grey tin bath and sat in it with his clothes on. He could just about fit in it if he squashed his knees up to his chest. His daughters were much shorter than he was, so there would be enough space for them to stretch out, and plenty of room for Peter and I. There was a large circle full of grey and black wood ash by the side of the path, near the outside toilet. Uncle Geoff had put two big logs in the middle of it, and filled the space between them with sticks, small branches and pine cones. We filled two very large black metal pans with water, and rested these on the logs. Auntie Julia told us that she would light the twigs and branches, and then keep feeding in small sticks, until the fire heated the water.
I had thought that Auntie Julia would get the lunch ready, and that Uncle Geoff would stay outside with the fire. But for the rest of the morning he stayed away from the fire, and did everything else: washing up, cooking and laying the table outside. Auntie Julia didn't go into the house once.

Frances and Bernadette had been playing records and singing along to them. I peeped through the bedroom window, and they were playing a song called *The Twist* and doing the funniest dance I had ever seen. When I went to tell Frances her bath was ready, they were singing *I Want to Hold Your Hand* as loudly as they could. I had the feeling that Frances was feeling much better.

Frances has a bath
The tub was placed in the full sunshine, in a space round the back of the house, just around the corner from the fire. Auntie Julia put on two very big gloves, and lifted the pans from the fire, while Peter and I used a large blue enamel jug to pour the water into the bath. By the time we had got the water ready, it was nearly lunchtime, and there was only enough time for Frances to have a bath. I came round the corner with one last jug

of hot water, but Frances was already sitting in the bath. I said, 'Whoops! Sorry,' and started to walk away.

Frances said, 'Don't go. Stay and talk to me.'

She had her knees pressed up to her chin, and was looking straight in front of her. Her long wavy hair was tied back in a ponytail, but the end had got slightly wet. I imagined her hair untied, with the ends dark and dripping. She had a habit of putting her fingers up to her temples and pulling her fingers back and up through her hair, like a comb. She would pause with her hands just behind her ears. Then she would flick her hair back and shake her head at the same time, letting her hair settle around her shoulders. I loved seeing her do that. It reminded me of a horse I used to love to stand and watch. I would wait for the horse to flick her head. Her mane would fly around her neck and she would stamp her hooves, and her whole body would shake. It gave me a thrill just to think about it.

Sometimes I would stand in front of the mirror at home and try and do the same as Frances, but my hair was too short.

Frances said, 'What are you thinking about, Pippa?'

I gave a bit of a start. I suppose I must have been drinking her in. 'I'm thinking about the colours in your hair in the sunlight, and how pale and lovely your skin is. And I wonder what I will look like when I grow up.'

She smiled at me and said, 'Bernadette takes after the women in my dad's family; the McCabes. They are quite tall and dark, and well-developed. They don't have much trouble with their Periods and have small families. The McCabes have lots of twins though. I take after my mother: light brown hair, skinny and with an under-developed bust. Her family, the Hendersons, have difficult Periods and big families. That's because they're Catholics.'

I was really confused. I knew this was an important conversation, so I put aside my fear of questions and asked, 'My mummy is a Jewish Alcoholic. Is that why she gets into a rage at me just before her Period, and has only one child? And what is an *under-developed beast*?'

Frances laughed and said, 'Bust! It means I don't have much on top.'

She could see I was looking at her closely. 'And,' she said, smiling, 'we all think that you're going to be a very famous artist, like Lady Celia. I know that one day you're going to paint me with no clothes on, because you're looking at me in that funny way of yours. I don't mind if you do, but you must promise me that you won't sell that painting for thousands of pounds. Or hang it in some art gallery somewhere, so that everyone could see how flat I am.'

Skinny and *under-developed* and *flat* sounded such horrible words to describe what I could see in front of me. I said, 'I think you look lovely.'

Frances looked pleased. 'Thank you Pippa. Mum and Dad don't like me saying horrible things about how I look. Dad says I look like my mum. He once said we are like *perfect Pre-Raphaelites*. Mum told him not to be so silly; and that anyway, she thought she looked more like a Rubens or a Renoir these days. I had no idea what that meant. I asked my art teacher, but she got quite cross with me. She said that I shouldn't be thinking about nudes. So I went to the public library and found a painting called *Hylas and the Nymphs*. It's by a painter called John Williams Waterhouse. I loved it. I suppose I do look a bit like one of the nymphs. But Mum is not at all chubby, like the Rubens or Renoir women. I don't like people looking at me, but my sister couldn't care less. She has no shame.'

There was that word again: *shame*. It sounded frightening, like the word *Sin*. I told Frances about Bridget running around naked in front of the nun. I asked her if it was shameful and a Sin to be naked in front of other people.

Frances realised that she had made a mistake: 'Oh no. I was only joking about Bernadette. She has always liked to run around with nothing on. And she likes to sing and dance about; just like Dad. I prefer to be covered up and keep myself to myself; more like Mum and Peter, I suppose.

She splashed water on her face. 'And I'm fed up with hearing about Sin and Shame.'

t was like she was talking to herself now. 'Mum and Dad are fed up too. And we don't like Father Leighton always preaching about Sin, and trying to make us feel guilty about not giving enough money to repair the old church. I agree with Dad. He says you have to think for yourself, and discover what you believe to be right and wrong. And we should try and do the right thing because it's right, and not because we are terrified of doing something wrong, or committing a Sin. At school the nuns don't want us to talk about periods, or how babies are made. You mustn't mention it: as if it's something sinful and disgusting. I really don't want to be a Catholic anymore.'

She sounded quite angry. I wondered if she was bitter. I felt a shiver pass through me. Uncle Eric had felt that shiver once and said, 'Someone's walking over my grave.' I had told him that was a horrible thing to say, but he thought it was funny.

Frances undid her pony tail, and shook her hair loose. She had soft light-brown hair under her arms. I felt a thrill. We heard her mum call, 'Hurry up Frances! Lunch will soon be ready.'
Frances asked me to go and get her a towel. I didn't want to leave her. I couldn't find a towel in her bedroom, so got mine; the one Mummy had given me from home.
Frances stood up in the bath. She saw me looking away. She said, 'I don't mind you looking at me. It's not a Sin, you know.'
I thought she was teasing me. I must have frowned or blushed, because she said, 'I'm sorry. I suppose I'm still a bit angry with the Catholics.'
That made me feel better about looking at her, though her being angry with the Catholics had made me feel very uncomfortable inside. Frances had a long red and purple line just above and to the right of her Private Place. She rubbed her finger backwards and forwards along it. For a moment I wondered if this was another Private Place; except that this one had no soft orangey-brown hair on it. Perhaps a second Private place appeared when you had your Period? Nothing I learned about girls' bodies could possibly surprise me anymore.
She noticed me looking closely at her. 'That's my appendix scar. I woke up one morning, two years ago, with a dreadful pain just

201

there. I had terrible diarrhoea. Mum phoned the doctor, and he told her to take me to hospital straight away. Something called my *appendix* had become poisoned. It looks like a little worm. The doctors operated on me and cut it out. I was in hospital for a week.'

I looked at the water in the bathtub. I had expected it to be bright red. It was milky-grey from the soap. There might have been just the slightest hint of pink in it, but I wasn't sure. I asked Frances, 'Where's all your blood?'

'Oh, there's only a small amount today. I wish I had regular periods, like Bernadette. I never know when mine is going to start or finish.'

I asked her, 'Does your tummy feel better now?'

She said it did. She said she was lucky to have a mum and dad who understood her problems. She said, 'It's strange. When my body changed, I went all thin, and have stayed like that ever since. Mum says I'm *willowy*. But Bernadette became round. Mum used to say that Bernadette had *burgeoning curves*. She's stayed curvy ever since, just like the McCabes.

I need to have a rest

We ate our lunch sitting at a table under an apple tree. Uncle Geoff asked me if I was having a nice time. I said that I was having the most wonderful time of my life. Everyone looked very pleased with me for saying that. I was very happy. And *happy* really was the best word to use to describe how I felt. But despite feeling happy, I could feel myself getting over-heated.

I had been in the car once, with Mummy and Uncle Eric. We stopped at a garage to get some petrol. A lady near us lifted up the bonnet of her car and there was lots of steam coming out of it. She unscrewed the radiator cap, and an enormous spout of boiling water shot in the air. The lady screamed and started to cry. Her husband rushed out of the garage and shouted, 'Never do that again. You could have been badly scalded!'

The lady shouted back, 'Of course I won't do it again! What do you think I am; stupid or something?' She stopped crying and they both laughed.

Mummy said to Uncle Eric, 'Was that engine over-heated?'

Uncle Eric laughed and said, 'It looks like the driver was too.' They both laughed at that.

I was sitting on a wooden bench, in between Bernadette and Peter. I told Bernadette that I was feeling over-heated. I was hoping she'd say, 'Never mind, come and lie down with me on my bed, and we can talk about what's bothering you.'

But Peter said, 'Oh. I was hoping we could heat some more water, and play in the woods, and build a shelter.'

Auntie Julia said that really everyone should have a quiet afternoon, and have a nice soak in the bath. This idea appealed to me a lot.

She asked me what I would like to do, but I couldn't say it. I didn't want to disappoint Peter, so I just sat with a puzzled look on my face.

Auntie Julia said, 'You have a think about it, and you can tell me later. Why don't you two play together for a short while, and then have a nice bath? It would be such a shame for you to be nice and clean, and then get filthy again. Or would you like to do some painting?'

Peter said 'She's always painting.'

His mum said, 'Pippa needs to paint. It's very important to her, and it helps her to express herself.'

Bernadette said to Peter, 'Why don't you and Pippa have a bath together?'

Peter's face went bright red. Bernadette said, 'I'm sorry Peter, it was just a joke.'

Peter said to her, 'It was a very silly joke.'

I didn't think it was silly. I thought it was a lovely idea, but I didn't dare say so. Peter said, 'Please may I leave the table?' He took his dirty dishes indoors and stomped off to the pump.

Mr McCabe said, 'What's got into him?'

Frances said, 'He's jealous of Bernadette.'

Mr McCabe said, 'Ah.'

I said, 'I know what I'd like to do. I'd like to play with Peter, then have a bath, and then be on my own to paint.'

Mrs McCabe said, 'Well done. But you mustn't try to please Peter, just because he makes you feel guilty. You must do what you want to do.'

I had forgotten that Peter was still my boyfriend.

I took my plate into the kitchen, and put it in the sink. Someone had put a dirty jam jar on the draining board. It still had some tiny bits of blackcurrant jam in it. I filled it with water and put the lid on. I put it in my bedroom and went to find Peter.

Peter was busy collecting more wood for the fire. He had taken off his shirt and draped it over the pump. I took mine off too. I asked him if I could help him. He said, 'If you like.' He sounded a bit grumpy.

We collected lots of pine cones and twigs. I was feeling very hot, so leaned my back against the pine tree. Peter came and stood next to me. I rubbed my back up and down against the prickly bark.

I said, 'I'm an itchy bear having a scratch.'

Peter copied me. He said, 'You look just like me.'

I said, 'You look just like me.'

We both said, at the same time, 'We both look like each other!'

Peter said, 'We said the same thing at the same time. Now we have to say, *Finger to finger, thumb to thumb; make a wish and true it will come.*'

We touched our little fingers and thumbs together. I closed my eyes. I wished that Peter would be my friend forever.

Then Peter grabbed my hand and whispered, 'Look!' A baby rabbit was crouching about six feet in front of us. It was perfectly still, apart from its nose, which quivered every few seconds.

We stood as still as we could. Neither of us wanted the rabbit to run away. I was very happy to have this excuse to hold Peter's hand. I loved holding Peter's hand. I loved it when he took my hand. I loved it when I put my hand in his, as we were walking along the street, and he gave me a special smile. Why was holding someone's hand such a nice thing to do? Why did I want to hold Mummy's hand, but she rarely took mine to hold? Why was it so strange when I held Uncle Geoff's hand for the first time? Sometimes in PE lessons, Miss would tell the children to hold hands. Some boys would make a terrible fuss if they had to hold a girl's hand. Bridget once told me that if you hold hands with a boy, that means you are girlfriend-boyfriend, and in love. Her brother Kenneth liked to hold my hand. I loved to hold Miss Dawson's hand in the playground, and I loved her touching me. I thought that it would be terrible if Peter didn't like me anymore. I was his cousin now. I talked to him every day. I shared everything with him.

In my head I could hear The Beatles singing *I wanna hold your hand*...

Then Peter did a very loud fart, and the baby rabbit got frightened and ran away. I shook my hand free from Peter's and shouted at him, 'What did you do that for? Now you've scared him away!'

Peter said, 'I couldn't help it. It was an accident.'

But I knew he had done it on purpose, because he was laughing. I didn't want to hold his hand anymore. I shouted, 'That was stupid!'

He shouted back, 'You're the stupid one!' and ran into the woods.

I stood still. I was shaking a little bit, so took some deep breaths and counted to a hundred. Suddenly I felt very frightened,, and ran after Peter. I stopped at a fork in the path. I didn't know which way to go. The path to the left was small and looked like nobody had walked on it for a long time. The path to the right was muddy and had footprints on it. I took that path.

I shouted, 'Peter! Peter! Where are you?' but there was no answer.

I ran further on, but the path stopped between some small trees. Suddenly a big black bird flew up. I screamed and screamed and screamed. In front of me, lying stretched out, was a big dead rabbit. It had no eyes.

I heard Uncle Geoff calling my name and running towards me. When he found me, I was still screaming, and hitting the sides of my head with the palms of my hands.

Peter ran up to us. He said, 'I only went to do a poo. I didn't run away from her!' He was very upset.

Uncle Geoff put his arms around me and said, 'There, there. It's all right.'

I said, 'It's not all right.' I knew that God was punishing me for liking Peter too much.

Uncle Geoff picked me up and carried me into the house. I had stopped crying, but was still shaking. He put me on Peter's bed. Auntie Julia and Peter came in the room, and Uncle Geoff went out. Bernadette and Frances were standing by the door. Auntie Julia said, 'You and Peter are going to sleep in the same room from now on. It'll be good for you both. And I'm getting a nice bath ready for both of you. You're still children, after all.'

After our bath, I sat in my new bedroom. Bernadette and Frances were talking in the room next door. My window was open, and I could hear Peter and his dad playing cards. We had a table with a mirror on it. A sunbeam full of dust stretched across the room, onto the table. I held my jam jar up in the sunbeam. The water was pink, with tiny red pieces suspended in it. I looked in the mirror. There I was, with my black hair and thick black eyebrows, and bright blue eyes, and my freckles running across my nose in both directions under my eyes. I smiled, and my teeth looked big and white and strong. My two front teeth had grown slightly in opposite directions, which had made a gap between them. I pushed my hair behind one of my ears. My arm was in the sunlight, and I noticed it was covered in tiny light hairs. I looked at my chest, and thought how much I looked like Peter. I looked at my belly button. Mine was an *inny* and his was an *outy*. I thought about Lady Celia, and how she must have spent a long time looking in the mirror when she drew her self-portrait. Then I sat down and painted my self-portrait.

We finally go to the seaside

I think everybody in the family was afraid of having too much excitement. After supper, Auntie Julia said she felt like going to the sea. Bernadette and Frances said they loved walking on the beach as the sun was going down.

We drove to the beach, at a place called Bacton. The sky was clear, and the wind was blowing in strongly from the sea. We could see the waves far away. Uncle Geoff said the tide was coming in very quickly. Groups of little black and white birds were flying together, and landing on the sand. They would peck for a few minutes, and then fly away again. As they did it, they kept up a constant chatter, with a loud *peep-peeping* sound. Peter and his dad were down on the beach, busy throwing stones into the sea. I put my arm through Bernadette's.

Frances was holding on to her mother's arm, and trying to shelter from the wind. She kissed her mum on the cheek and said, 'I feel better now. I'm sorry if I was horrible, and spoiled everyone's fun.'

Auntie Julia said, 'It's all right. We all had a lovely day, in the end. I used to feel just like you, but it's much easier for me now.'

Frances said, 'So will I have to have three children before I feel better?'

Auntie Julia laughed and said, 'Only if you want to.'

The four of us walked along the beach, and sat on a strange wooden structure that stretched out towards the sea. Bernadette said it was called a *groyne*, and that it had been built there to stop the sea from washing all the sand off the beach. We sat quietly, and watched Peter and his dad in the distance. We could hear them shouting and laughing. Frances was talking to her mother.

Bernadette asked me, 'What are you thinking about?'

'I was thinking about Mummy being on her own at home.'

'Do you worry about her?'

'Well, I imagine her sitting at the table in the kitchen.'

'Perhaps she has gone up to London.'

'Yes. Perhaps she has gone to visit Uncle Eric. I think I'm spoiling your holiday.'

'Not at all. We love you being with us. We all love you.'

'But I was screaming and shouting.'

'We don't mind. We're a dramatic family. We're always having dramas. Is Ursula having a nice holiday with you?' I wasn't expecting her to mention Ursula.

She laughed at the surprised look on my face. 'Everybody knows about Ursula. You talk to her all the time. She's in all your paintings.'

'How do you know about her?'

'Peter told us. He says Ursula has light orange hair, so that's why there's always a tiny bit of orange in all your paintings. Peter showed us your paintings once; when you first came to play with him. I couldn't understand what they were about. He explained what was happening in them, and what you were thinking about and your feelings as you painted. Then it all made perfect sense.'

I liked the idea that Peter had shown his sisters my paintings.

Bernadette told me about their cousin Frank. He used to have an imaginary friend. He called him Claudius. Claudius was a soldier who wasn't very good at fighting in battles. He was the clumsiest soldier in the world, and was always having accidents. He was given the job of looking after the General's clothes. Once Claudius hadn't tied one of his own sandals up properly and it fell off just as a battle was going to start. While everyone else was busy fighting each other, he was looking for his sandal. He was always getting told off by the General for being no good, but he always managed somehow to stop the General from getting captured.

She said, 'When Frances and I were little, we used to beg Frank tell us stories about Claudius. We used to laugh our heads off.'

'What does your cousin Frank do now? Is he a children's story writer?'

'Oh no. He loved electricity, so he works as an electrician. He's married. We helped to make his wedding cake.'

'Does he still talk to Claudius?'

208

Frances teaches me to swim

The next day was hot, so we went to the beach. For me, the seaside had always been a legendary place, that other children went to, but not me. I wanted to do everything. I was like the dog that we had seen the night before; running up to the waves and screaming and shouting, and running away when even the smallest ripple came near my feet. The whole family found this very funny. Frances had decided that she was going to *introduce me to swimming*. She said that learning to swim was like learning to play the violin, or driving. You can't pick up a violin and start to play beautiful music, or get in a car and drive off immediately. She said that I had to understand that the sea was like fire. It is never your friend, and in one split second it can become your enemy. She said I had to always make sure that I never *got out of my depth*; that my feet must always be able to touch the bottom.

Frances' face was very grave when she said those things to me. I watched Peter and Bernadette swimming. It looked as if they had always been doing it. I tried to copy Peter, but felt myself sink, and became frightened as soon as my face went underwater. Frances held me up and taught me how to float on my back and front, and how to open my eyes underwater. I did my best to please her, and she praised me if I got something right. I especially liked it when I managed to copy what she was doing and when she said, 'Good girl, well done.'

Bernadette and Peter were throwing a ball to each other, while my new aunt and uncle sat on the sand, watching us all. When we finally came out of the sea, Uncle Geoff asked Frances, 'And how's your first pupil?'
I was delighted when she said, 'Oh she's a natural swimmer. She's going to be much better than I am.'
When Auntie Julia asked me, 'And how's your teacher?' I told her, 'Oh she's wonderful.'
It felt like I had just been in the sea with Miss Dawson.

I was wearing my new bright green bathing costume. I really didn't like the colour, so wanted to take it off as soon as possible. I had been watching how children from other families got changed. The younger children, under about six or seven, just stripped off, and their parents rubbed them down with towels. Older children wrapped a towel round themselves and did an elaborate dance, as they tried to get their wet costumes off, then dry themselves and put dry clothes on, without anyone seeing their bodies. I just pulled my costume off and started drying myself.

Auntie Julia offered to help me, but Frances said, 'It's all right, I'll do it.' She wrapped me in my towel and sat behind me, while I rested against her, between her legs. I closed my eyes.

Sometimes we used to ask our teachers or the nuns what Heaven was like. They might say 'It's being continually in the presence of God'; or 'being in a state of eternal knowledge and perpetual Grace'; or 'living a life of eternal happiness, free from care.' I could never quite picture Heaven. Bridget once said it might be like always having sixpence for pocket money on a Saturday, but no matter how many sweets you bought, there would always be sixpence in your pocket. But if you had asked me then, as I sat on the beach, 'Pippa, what's your idea of Heaven?' I would have told you, 'To be wrapped in a big towel on a sunny beach, and to always have beautiful Frances holding me tight.'

And if you were to ask me now, I'd say the same thing. Except I wouldn't tell you it was Frances that was holding me.

I opened my eyes, and saw that there was a dry stain of Frances' blood on my towel, from where she had dried herself the day before.

Peter has sunburn

When we got home, we could see that Peter had got quite badly sunburnt. His shoulders and nose were particularly red, and he complained that his skin was itchy, and he shouted when anyone accidentally touched his back. My skin had gone light brown. When I took my clothes off, Peter said he could see that I had lighter skin where I had been wearing my bathing costume. His bottom had stayed pink, so he looked like he was wearing a air of pink trunks. Uncle Geoff said that I had *olive skin*, like my mother. He said it made me look French, or Italian. He said that one of the most beautiful sights in the whole world was his wife's white bits.

Auntie Julia said, 'Geoffrey, that's quite enough!' But she looked very pleased, all the same.

Frances and Uncle Geoff drove into town to get more fish and chips, while Peter and I had a wash. Auntie Julia helped Peter, using the jug and big bowl of water in our bedroom. Bernadette took me out onto the veranda, and said she would show me how to have what her mum called a *comprehensive wash*, and what her dad called *a strip wash*. I didn't know what *comprehensive* meant, but knew that I would have to take everything off. Bernadette started telling me what to do. Then she said, 'This is silly,' and went to get her own jug and bowl. So there we were: two girls stripped off, with two bowls of cold water and two flannels, washing ourselves from head to foot.

Bernadette said, 'You won't believe this, Pippa, but once Frances and I went away with our class, to stay at a Youth Hostel in the hills somewhere. There was no hot water in the showers, and we were all sweaty. Frances and I stripped off to have a wash in the sink. Only our tops, mind you; it's not as if we were completely naked or anything. Some of the other girls were shocked, and called us a very rude word.'

Obviously I wanted to know what this rude word was. I knew that Bernadette wanted to tell me. I decided not to ask. Bernadette looked disappointed, so I gave in. 'What did they call you?'

'It's too awful. I can't possibly tell you.'

We should have stopped right there. But I had been taught the basics of swimming, I had learned how to wash myself properly in a bowl of water. I had looked closely at a naked big girl. I felt that I was becoming a big girl myself. I knew the *C word* and the *F word* and I knew *bloody hell*. I knew *bitch* too. I thought that knowing one more rude word wouldn't hurt, and anyway we

213

were going to Church soon, and I could confess that I had heard a new swear word, but hadn't used it myself.

Bernadette said, 'They called us a pair of *lesbians*.'

Bernadette could see that I didn't understand. She should have stopped, but she explained that a lesbian was a lady who loved other ladies.

I said, 'But I love you. And I love Frances as well. And you said you loved me. So are we... that rude word?'

But we heard Peter calling my name, so wrapped our towels around ourselves, to get ourselves ready to go and see him. As usual, her towel was tiny and hid hardly anything. I looked at her curves. I asked her what *burgeoning* meant.

She laughed and said, 'It means *growing*. And I can tell that you've been talking to my sister about growing up!'

That night, just before we went to sleep, Peter's mum brought in a bottle of pink liquid called *Calamine Lotion*. She poured some lotion onto a piece of cotton wool, and rubbed it gently onto Peter's burnt skin. He shouted out that it was cold. In the night, Peter woke me up. He said his back was very itchy. He asked me to switch the light on, to see if I could find the Calamine Lotion. He was jumping up and down, with just his pants on, and whispered that he thought he would to die of itchiness if I didn't rub the lotion on his shoulders. I tipped the lotion onto the cotton wool, just like Auntie Julia. I told Peter to be brave and not to shout out. He stayed very still, and when I had finished he said, 'Thank you. That was lovely. I feel better now.'

Peter asked me why I wasn't itchy like him. I said, 'I'm a Jewish Catholic, and that's why I go brown and look like an Italian.'

He said, 'Don't you want to have some lotion rubbed on you?'

I said 'No thank you.'

He looked disappointed, so I said, 'All right, but just a little bit.'

I was wearing my pyjamas, so had to take my top off. I turned my back on him, and could hear the lotion dripping onto the

214

carpet, as Peter struggled to get the right amount onto the cotton wool.

It was all over his hands. We held each other's hands and squeezed the lotion through our fingers. He rubbed it all over my shoulders, and I did the same to him. I was very Thrilled, and I knew he was too. It was a lovely feeling.

In the morning, our sheets were pink, and there was hardly any lotion left in the bottle. Auntie Julia laughed and said, 'What have you two been up to?'

Ever since that lovely moment, Calamine Lotion has been one of my favourite smells.

I love the sea

Visiting a fish and chip shop for the first time, going to the beach, learning to swim, washing in a bowl; that holiday was a true adventure. I could feel myself growing. I could feel myself growing inside, as I learned how to do new things, and got lots of praise. And I wasn't so frightened of saying what I thought, thanks to Frances and Bernadette and their parents being so nice to me, and treating me like a member of their family. I suppose I was growing in love too. Not just for Peter, but for all of them. My body was growing as well. I was a light sleeper, and it was rare for me to sleep through the night. But on this holiday I often woke with pains in my legs. Auntie Julia said it was probably cramp, but Bernadette wondered if I was having what she called *growing pains*. I was certainly putting on weight.

Once I was sitting on Auntie Julia's lap when she said, 'Gosh! My legs have gone to sleep! You're becoming such a big girl. Soon you'll be too heavy to sit on my lap!'

I loved to sit on adults' knees, so I found that alarming.

We went to the beach every day, and Frances always spent time with me in the sea. She was pleased with my progress, and I was delighted to be able to please her. One day, Peter and I made friends with two boys and a girl from Holland. We invited them to play cricket with us. Frances and Bernadette joined in, but soon became bored. The Dutch girl, who was the same age as me, went to play in the water. I wasn't bored at all. I soon rediscovered that I was very good at throwing and catching a tennis ball.

The boys told me to go behind the wicket, and I loved leaping about to try and catch the ball, and running after it, and throwing it to the boys from quite a long way away.

We had a game of football, and I was put in goal. The Dutch children's father decided to join in the game, and so did Uncle Geoff. I didn't really know how to play football, but knew the goalkeeper had to stop the ball from going in the goal. Whenever the ball came towards me, I dived to get it. More often than not, I caught the ball, or made a spectacular dive in its direction. I just imagined I was a cat or a monkey, and kept jumping around. The sand was soft and hot, and my dives became more spectacular. Whenever I saved the ball, the Dutch boys clapped and shouted, 'Bravo!'

I heard the Dutch dad say to Uncle Geoff, 'Your daughter is very good. She is as good as a boy.'

Uncle Geoff laughed.

I was fascinated by the sea. I loved the sunlight on the water, the constant movement of the waves, and the changing tides. A large shallow stream flowed down the beach, into the sea, and Peter and I spent a long time at its edge. He liked to throw stones, while I stood on a large flat stone and watched the water flowing over my feet. I would slip into My Colour Dream as often as I could, and felt the water flowing through me; through my feet and up my body, towards my fingertips. If I shut my eyes, I could feel the exact sensation of floating on my back in the sea. Sometimes I felt as if Frances was supporting me, with her hands under my back. This made my heart beat fast, and I became thrilled. Sometimes I imagined I was floating out of my depth, out to sea. This should have alarmed me, but it didn't.

We see The Beatles

My next big adventure was to go to the cinema. The girls had been talking about this ever since we arrived on holiday. The McCabe family went to the cinema regularly, so they no longer got excited by the small delights that make up a trip to the cinema. These included looking at the big poster outside; reading the title of the film and the times in big letters and numbers, high up on the front of the cinema; queuing to buy the tickets, and looking at the sweets and ice lollies on sale in the foyer. I needed to go to the toilet, and went to the Ladies'. As I was about to go in, a lady tapped me on the shoulder and said, 'You don't want to go in there, sonny. It's for ladies.'

I said, 'I'm a girl.'

She said, 'Crikey, so you are! But you look just like a little boy to me.' I supposed my clothes did look a bit *boyish*.

The cinema was almost full. There were lots of advertisements before the film started. Most of them were about fizzy drinks and ice cream. There was a short film, with a chimpanzee eating celery and a man's voice explaining why it was a good idea to eat fruit, and clean your teeth every day.

Lots of children were shouting, 'Oooh, oooh, oooh!' and shrieking like monkeys. The last advert was about the local fish and chip shop, and showed photos of the inside.

A boy near the front shouted, 'Look! There's your dad!' and one of his friends shouted even louder, 'No it's not, it's his granny!'

Just before the film started, the music for the National Anthem started playing, and everybody stood up. I wondered if it was going to be like Mass, where you had to know exactly when to stand up and kneel down.

Peter was sitting on my left, and next to me, on my right, was a group of big girls. They kept talking to each other and laughing loudly. A man behind them said, 'Oi shush will you?'

One of the girls turned round and said, 'Shush yerself Mister. It's a free country, ain't it?'

The man said, 'You sound like a bunch of Gippos from London.' I could tell from his voice that he was teasing them.

They started giggling, and one of them said, 'Takes one to know one, don't it?'

The film started, and everyone started clapping. Peter and his family had already seen the film before, and Peter had explained that it was a comedy. I found it quite frightening. I didn't like to see the Indian people chasing The Beatles, and trying to cut Ringo's finger off. I had forgotten to ask which one of the people in the film was Peter's uncle, so decided it must be John. When The Beatles sang, the big girls next to me started singing along.

The man behind them leaned forward and said, 'I paid my money to hear The Beatles. Not to listen to a load of slappers!'

Some more young people next to him joined in the singing, just to be annoying. Some of the things they said to each other were funnier than the film. When The *Beatles* sang *Help!* I could hear the whole McCabe family singing along.

I said to Peter, 'Oi, shush will you?' and he said, 'Shush yourself, you slapper!'

It was getting dark when we left the cinema, and Uncle Geoff and Auntie Julia suggested we look for a café and have something to eat. Most of the cafés were closed, but we found one that was open, and went inside. There were lots of teenagers in there. We recognised the noisy girls who had been sitting next to me, and the man who had been telling them to be quiet. They were chatting and laughing. A big group of teenagers were standing by the jukebox. Frances and Bernadette ordered a huge ice cream with fruit in it, called a *Knickerbocker Glory*.

The man behind the counter said to them, 'Sorry my lovelies, but it's chaos in here tonight. I'll have your order ready in two shakes!'

Uncle Geoff said, 'Isn't this heaven? What a great night out! Thanks to Pippa's mother for paying for it!'

I had forgotten all about Mummy.

The teenagers put *Help!* on the jukebox, and suddenly it seemed like everyone in the café was singing along to the chorus. A waitress brought our order to our table. She apologised for the delay. 'Normally it's quiet in here at this time, apart from a few teenagers, but it's gone mad, thanks to The Beatles. We love them!' She looked closely at Uncle Geoff, 'Excuse me sir, ut didn't I see you on the TV the other night? You look like that olice detective who got into trouble for hitting a suspect.'

Jncle Geoff said, 'That's right. What did you think of it?'

'he lady said, 'I thought it was great, but my husband and my eenage son Lionel got cross, and said it was typical police rutality.'

Jncle Geoff said, 'We rehearsed that fight for a long time. The irector was getting annoyed with us, because we weren't being iolent enough! I think I was a bit too aggressive in the end, ecause my fellow actor said I had left a nasty bruise on his eck!'

'he lady laughed. She went back behind the counter and we saw er pointing at us, and telling her husband all about her onversation with Uncle Geoff.

3ernadette asked her dad, 'Why didn't you tell her that your rother was in the film?'

'Oh no,' laughed Uncle Geoff, 'we don't want a riot in here! After all, he was one of the baddies.'

n the car on the way home, Frances asked her dad if he liked eing recognised by strangers. He said it was fun, as long as they lidn't think he was a real policeman, and expect him to go and rrest someone. He said that when he was on the radio nobody new who he was.

Auntie Julia said, 'Your father is very modest. When he was in *he Navy Lark* and *Round the Horne* we were in a butcher's in Jondon, and the butcher's wife said, 'I'd recognise that voice nywhere!'

3ernadette asked him, 'Do you think more people will stop you n the street when we move to Liverpool?'

Auntie Julia said, 'Shush Bernadette. It's not decided yet.'

3ut the damage had been done.

We sing and dance at home

As soon as we got back to the bungalow, the girls wanted to lance. Auntie Julia said it was way past our bedtime, but the girls didn't take any notice. They brought the record player and heir favourite records into the kitchen. They opened the window o we could hear the music outside. Uncle Geoff said that everyone should have a chance to choose a record, and that he should go first. He chose *The Twist*. To my surprise, he practically pulled Auntie Julia off the veranda, and danced The Twist with her on the grass next to the fire pit. I'd only seen Frances and Bernadette dancing to that record, but I could tell that both her parents were very good dancers. Uncle Geoff grabbed Peter and shouted, 'Come on Peter, I'll show you how to twist!' Bernadette took me by the hand and showed me what to do.

I don't think I had laughed so much in my whole life. I didn't know that dancing, whether copying what other people did, or just throwing yourself around, could be so much fun! I sat with Peter and his parents on the veranda, and watched the girls singing along to The Beatles. I thought of Mummy. I hoped she was in London, having a nice time with Uncle Eric, and not sitting on her own in the kitchen. I tried to imagine her teaching me to swim, or dancing The Twist. Perhaps she would enjoy doing things like that. But I realised the big problem was that I didn't know how to talk to her, and she didn't know how to talk to me. She didn't know me at all.

All this was flashing through my mind, as everyone except me sang along to *Can't Buy Me Love*, *A Hard day's Night* and *Help*.

Auntie Julia asked me if I was having a nice time. I said I was very happy, but was thinking about Mummy. She said 'What are you thinking about Mummy?'

I wanted to tell her that I didn't know how to talk with Mummy, but instead I said, 'I know you are all going to move to Liverpool.'

Aunty Julia said, 'Nothing has been decided yet.'

She didn't deny it.

Peter and I look in a shop window

The next day was rainy, but still quite warm. I had been thinking some more about Mummy, so wrote her a letter. Peter wrote to his granny. I had never written to Mummy before. I told her I was having a lovely time, and that Frances had been

220

teaching me how to swim, and that I had seen a baby rabbit. I did a very quick drawing to go with the letter. I called it, *Twist and Shout.*

It was still raining when we had finished, so Uncle Geoff suggested that we drive into the town, to buy some envelopes and stamps, and to have a look around the shops. He asked the girls to come with us, because he had to make a phone call to his agent.

Frances wanted to help her mum do some cooking, so Bernadette came with us. All my clothes were dirty, so I had to wear some of Peter's. Uncle Geoff parked in the car park in the centre of the town, and told us to come back to meet him in an hour's time.

The three of us went looking for the Post Office, and soon found it, in a small parade of shops. We bought our envelopes and stamps, and posted our letters. There was a second-hand shop next to the Post Office, and we looked in the window. There were toys and old bits of bicycle and old books. Bernadette pointed at a picture in a frame. It was of a blue woman sitting in a strange pose. She had one arm curled behind her head as if she were scratching the back of her neck. Her knee was bent and her other hand was clasping her ankle. I looked very closely at the picture, and it seemed to me that it had been made using pieces of blue paper, that had been cut out. It was signed *H MATISSE 52*. I decided that a child must have made it, when she was the same age as me. This idea began to take hold in my mind, and I started to imagine what I would do with scissors and glue and beautiful blue paper.

Bernadette must have been watching me staring at the picture, because she said, 'I think you like it. You two wait here, because I want to take a quick look inside the shop.' Just before she went in the shop she took out her camera and said, 'Say cheese' and took our photo.

Peter and I looked in the window of the shop next door. It was selling beer and wine.

A man's voice said, 'Hello boys.'

I could see a man reflected in the window. Peter turned round to look at him, but I kept looking at the bottles of beer. The man said to Peter, 'It's a disgrace. This shop used to sell bicycles, but now it sells alcohol. What is the world coming to?'

Peter didn't say anything.

The man asked him, 'Are you here on holiday?'

Peter said he was. Peter held my hand. I could see that he had closed his eyes tight shut.

Then the man said something very strange: 'Boys and men need to keep healthy and strong. That's what we need to do. Not go drinking beer and wine, and wasting our strength. You look like two strong boys. Not like girls. You can't trust girls. Boys have got something big and strong between their legs. Girls have got nothing. All they have is a slit. Girls are ashamed of their slits. There's nothing there; just something useless and ugly. They don't like to be naked. Not like me and my friends. We like to take our clothes off. Why don't you two boys come to the park this evening, and meet my friends?'

Peter didn't say anything. He pulled my hand. I turned to look at the man.

The man looked at me. 'That's funny,' he said, 'at your age, some boys look just like girls, until you see what is between their legs. Let me give you some advice. Never trust a girl who looks like a boy. They're evil.'

Then he walked away quickly , round the corner.

Peter's hand was shaking, and his face had gone almost white. I thought he was going to be sick. Bernadette found us. Peter said, 'A nasty man has just been speaking to us. He said horrible things.'

Bernadette said, 'Quick, where did he go?'

Peter pointed round the corner. Bernadette ran to see if she could see him, but the man had disappeared. She asked us to tell her what the man had said, but Peter wouldn't say anything. Bernadette took us back to the car park, but it was only half past eleven, so we still had half an hour to wait for their dad. Bernadette said that we ought to find a policeman.

Peter shouted 'No!' and started to cry.

A lady walking past us said to Peter, 'Is everything all right here, son?' but he wouldn't answer.

I said to her, 'We've had a terrible shock, and we're looking for a policeman.'

The lady looked at me in a strange way and said, 'What kind of shock?'

Bernadette said, 'A nasty man has just said horrible things to the children. We're waiting for our dad.'

She said, 'Well, there's a policeman right over there.'

Across the street, a policeman was coming out of a shop. The lady went over to him and we saw her pointing at us, and telling him what we had said. The policeman came over to us immediately. He was huge.

Bernadette explained what had happened. The policeman said, 'I can't do anything until your father comes back, so just tell me exactly what happened, and what the man looked like.'

Peter looked at the ground, and wouldn't speak.

Then Uncle Geoff came back, and Bernadette told him the story all over again.

The policeman said we all had to go with him, to the shop where we had met the man.

Peter was crying and his dad said, 'It's all right. You haven't done anything wrong.'

We had to walk along the street with the policeman. People were looking at us. Bernadette held my hand. Her hand was trembling.

The policeman told us to stand exactly where we had seen the man. He went into the beer and wine shop, and came back out again with the shopkeeper. He said that he hadn't seen us talking to anyone. The policeman went into the second-hand shop and the Post Office, but nobody had seen a strange man, or us talking to him.

Bernadette started to cry. I had never seen her cry before. It made me want to cry too, but I forced myself not to. The policeman crouched down to speak to me. His face was very grave.

He looked in my eyes and said, 'Can you tell me what this man looked like?' I nodded.

He stood up slowly and said to Uncle Geoff, 'Well sir, I need to make some important phone calls, and then I'd like to talk to everybody at your house, as soon as possible.'

In the car, Bernadette said that this was all her fault, because if she hadn't left us outside the shop, then none of this would have happened.

Uncle Geoff said, 'It's not your fault, love. It's not anyone's fault, except that man's.'

Peter said he was frightened of the policeman. I didn't say anything.

When we got back to the house, Bernadette started crying again, so Auntie Julia gave her a hug. Frances held Peter's hand. I stood watching everybody.

The policeman arrived about half an hour later. He said his name was Police Constable Cooper. Auntie Julia made us all a drink. I noticed that PC Cooper put three spoonfuls of sugar in his tea. Then he went for a walk with Uncle Geoff. When they came back, Uncle Geoff explained that the policeman wanted to talk to Peter and me separately. He wanted Uncle Geoff to go in one room with Peter, and Auntie Julia to stay with me. He was going to talk to Peter first. I asked Auntie Julia for my sketchpad.

The talk with Peter and Uncle Geoff lasted only a few minutes. PC Cooper told us that Peter was very upset, and couldn't talk about what had happened. Then he asked to speak to Bernadette with her dad, in Bernadette's bedroom. After about twenty minutes, he went with Auntie Julia and me onto the veranda. He asked me to tell him again exactly what had happened.

Then he asked a new question: 'Why did your cousin leave you outside the shop?'

I told him that she had wanted to look at something inside.

'And do you know what that thing was?'

I told him that I didn't.

224

Do you know if she bought anything in the shop?'
didn't.
He didn't ask me any more about that. I told him that I had
started to draw a picture in my sketchbook, all about the nasty
man.
had drawn the man's face. He had a scar over his left eye, and a
long scar on his left cheek. He had a brown mark on his other
cheek. His hair was light brown and short. He was wearing some
brown glasses. Constable Cooper was very interested in the
marks on the man's face. He was interested in the glasses too.He
asked me, 'Are you sure about the colour of the glasses?'
said, 'Oh yes. I've seen that kind of brown before. I think it
might be called *turtle shell*. But the strange thing was, Officer
Cooper, the strange thing was that there was no glass in them. I
can't understand why someone would wear a pair of glasses with
no glass in them.'

PC Cooper asked me if there was anything else I had
noticed. I told him I'd like to draw the rest. I drew his trousers.
They had a very high waistband and were a greeny-brown
colour, and made with a very soft material.
He asked me, 'Anything else?'
Oh yes. He didn't have a belt on. He was wearing those things
to hold your trousers up.'
Braces?'
Yes. Black ones.'
What about a jacket?'
said I'd have to draw the rest.
While I was drawing, PC Cooper spoke to Auntie Julia. He told
her, 'What has happened here is very unfortunate. It's quite
wrong. But in terms of the law, this is not a crime. He has said
some disgusting things, but we can't arrest him for that.'
finished my drawing. It was a bit hurried. I handed the
sketchpad to Auntie Julia. She looked at it closely, then passed it
quickly to PC Cooper, as if she couldn't wait to get rid of it. It
fell on the floor and PC Cooper picked it up. He started looking
at all my drawings and paintings.

225

When he got to the drawing of the man, he frowned and said, 'I think this might change everything. Tell me about what you have drawn.'

'Well he had his trousers open at the front, and I think he had cut them in a special way so, that he could show us... he could show us everything. It was sticking up straight. Suddenly it stopped being very straight, and went very soft. That was when he walked away. And he had a bicycle too. I think he might have parked it round the corner.'

Auntie Julia made a kind of moaning sound. She said she needed to get a glass of water. PC Cooper said to her, 'Wait a moment. This is very important.'

He said to me, 'A bicycle? That's the first time anyone has mentioned a bicycle.'

I thought before I spoke. 'Well I can't be sure, but just before Bernadette took our photo, I saw a man watching us. He had a bicycle. I remember thinking, "Why would a man ride a ladies bicycle?" Then Bernadette said, "Say cheese," so I forgot about him. That's why I've drawn him with his trousers tucked into his socks; to stop his trousers from getting dirty on his bike.'

PC Cooper said he wanted the whole family to come onto the veranda. We all sat down, but he stood up. He said, 'I'm very sorry that all this has happened. The three children have been involved in a shocking incident. But the information Pippa has given me has been extremely useful. It will help us catch the man, so that we can make sure he doesn't do this kind of thing again. I'm going to leave you now, but I hope to come back with a colleague, another police officer, as soon as I can. He will certainly want to speak to the children again, but he will need the young lady's mother to be present. Can that be arranged? Can she be here tomorrow afternoon?'

He said he wanted to have a private word with the adults. He went inside the house with them, while we waited on the veranda. Bernadette started to cry again, and this set Peter off. Frances hugged Bernadette, and I hugged Peter. Mr McCabe came back in and told us that PC Cooper wanted to take away

226

Bernadette's camera and my sketchpad. I asked Bernadette what she had bought in the shop.

She said that PC Cooper had told her that we mustn't talk to each other about what happened, until the other policeman had been to see us. He had made her promise not to say anything.

I kept very quiet. Everyone else was upset, so I knew I had to stay calm. But I couldn't bear the thought that Bernadette had to keep a secret from me. I went into my bedroom. Uncle Geoff and PC Cooper were standing by the front door.

PC Cooper said, 'The important thing is to get the young girl's parents up here. We can't take a witness statement without her. I'm very sorry that this has happened to your family, but we'll catch him. I'm certain of that.'

After they said goodbye to each other, I heard Uncle Geoff and Auntie Julia talking.

She said, 'So Ruth's coming. How're we going to organise that? Do you think she'll go berserk?'

I couldn't hear what my uncle said, but Auntie Julia said to him, 'Well that's what you said the last time.'

Mummy is going to come

I could hear my tummy rumbling, so I knew that I was very hungry. I didn't feel like eating anything. I went into the corridor, just as the grown-ups were leaving their bedroom.

Auntie Julia said, 'Come here sweetheart,' and squeezed me very tight. I told her I was hungry.

She smiled and said, 'Of course you are. We all are. We must eat something straight away.'

I could tell it wasn't a proper smile. She was smiling to try and cheer me up.

I wanted to go for a walk in the woods with Peter, but he was too frightened to go out of the house. Frances said that she would come with me. She put her arm around me, and we walked down to the pump and sat on a big log. I said, 'That man said that girls don't have anything... down there. He said we only have slits, and that they are ugly and useless.'

227

Frances said, 'That man is ill. He doesn't know what he's talking about. When the police catch him, they'll put him in prison.'

I told her some more. 'And he said that girls who look like boys are evil. I was wearing Peter's clothes, so he thought I was a boy. Then I think he saw that I was a girl. His willy was very big and hard, but suddenly it went all soft. Then he walked away round the corner.'

Frances' face went bright red. She said, 'Oh you poor thing!' and held my hand tight.

I said, 'I know I'm upset, but I have to be sensible, and tell everybody what happened, and what the man looked like, otherwise the police won't catch him.'

Frances didn't say anything. She kept squeezing my hand.

'And I'm really bothered that Mummy is going to come. I know I should be happy about that, but I'm worried she will get angry, and behave badly and upset everyone.'

Frances was very quiet. She said, 'Let's go back to the house.' As we walked back she said, 'I think your Mummy will be very sensible.'

That night, Peter said he wanted to sleep in his mum and dad's bed. Bernadette said she wanted to sleep with Frances, and I said I thought I would be all right sleeping on my own.

I wanted to talk to Ursula. She came straight away. She said that she had seen everything that had happened at the shops, but that I had forgotten to mention something: the man had a tooth missing. When he had smiled at Peter, he had a gap in his top teeth.

Ursula said that she was very angry about what the man had said about girls. She said it wasn't true. She said that what girls have is just as nice as what boys have.

I told her I was very worried about Mummy coming. Ursula told me not to worry, because Mummy was always sensible whenever there was a big problem.

I told her she must have forgotten about when Mummy had been very upset because I attacked Lawrence.

228

The door opened, and it was Auntie Julia. She sat on my bed and said, 'Are you talking to Ursula?'

I nodded and looked a bit embarrassed.

'What does Ursula say?'

'She says that what girls have... our Private Places... are just as nice as what boys have.'

'That's true. She's quite right about that. And what else does she say?'

'She says I mustn't worry that Mummy will come here and spoil things for everybody.'

'And she's right about that too. I've just been down to the village, to talk to Mummy on the phone. I was worried that she might be angry, because she might think we haven't looked after you properly. But she said she hoped that everyone is all right. She thanked us all for taking care of you. She's coming tomorrow afternoon in the car, with your Uncle Eric. The policemen are coming too. They want to talk to you again, but with your mummy there.'

As she was talking, she was smoothing my hair with one of her hands. She said, 'You really are a lovely girl.'

I said, 'And you are a lovely auntie.' She started crying.

I said, 'Will Peter be all right ?'

She sniffed and blew her nose on her hanky. She wiped her eyes with her wrists and said, 'Oh yes. I'm sure he will be fine. He doesn't want to sleep in our bed anymore. He says he wants to come and look after you. This whole episode at the shops is just too awful. But we'll all be fine. I know that everything will be all right.'

The Society of Friends

The police were coming in the afternoon; even though it was a Sunday. Uncle Geoff thought it would be a nice idea if we all had breakfast together, before we went to church. Then, if we could find a café open, maybe we could go out to lunch. We had to be back at the house for two o'clock, when Mummy and Uncle Eric were due to arrive. The girls said that they hadn't slept very well, because Bernadette was still very upset. Frances kept telling her that these things can happen to anyone, and that we had just been in the wrong place at the wrong time.

I had forgotten all about going to the new church. I hadn't had time to worry about committing a Mortal Sin, and dying with a blackened soul. In the car, Auntie Julia explained that we were going to a place called The Friends Meeting House, and that The Friends did things very differently to the Catholics. She hoped that this new adventure would take our minds off what had happened yesterday.

Peter said he was feeling better. His dad said, 'I thought so, because I do believe you have just passed wind.'

Everyone laughed, except Bernadette.

The Friends' Meeting House was not like a church at all. From the outside it looked like a big house that had got mixed up with a small school. A man at the front door said, 'Welcome, I'm Derek,' and shook our hands. We went into a large room with a shiny wooden floor, with about 20 chairs arranged in a circle. Derek said that there might be just a few Friends today, because lots of people were away on holiday. He explained that they usually had separate activities for the children, but that today we were very welcome to join in the worship.

A young lady with a baby was already sitting on a chair, next to two old ladies and an old man. They all smiled at us, but didn't say anything. I sat next to the lady with the baby. Derek explained that they always sat in the circle, and waited for what he called *God's Still Small Voice* to speak through us. I didn't want to say anything. I hoped that if I kept still, then God wouldn't choose me.

The old man stood up. He said, 'I feel old sometimes, and I think about the end of my life. On some days I feel ready to meet the Lord, but on other days I cling to the thought that this life, here and now, is all that matters.'

He sat down. There was a long silence. I looked straight ahead of me, and saw Ursula. She was sitting on a chair by the wall, and was waving at me. She gestured with her arms for me to stand up nd say something. I shut my eyes, and when I opened them gain, she had gone. I looked at the baby, but he had gone to leep. I looked at his mother. She said, 'I'm so tired at the moment. Simon keeps me awake during most nights. He's lucky, ecause he can sleep during the day, but I have so many things to lo.'

Auntie Julia walked across the circle and picked up the sleeping baby, and took him back to her seat.

The young lady said, 'Thank you.'

Nobody said anything. Peter and I looked at each other. I think he was doing his best to stop God's Still Small Voice from oming out of his mouth. Bernadette looked very tired. Frances ooked as if she was going to say something, but changed her mind. Uncle Geoff looked worried about something, and Auntie Julia was holding the baby and smiling. The old people sat very till. The young lady kept closing her eyes, then opening them uddenly.

I stood up. I said, 'Sometimes I say things, but it feels like it's omeone else who's talking. I'm not sure if this is God who is alking today, but it sounds like me. I was just thinking about what that old man... I mean that gentleman over there... was aying. I'm only eight... well nearly nine, actually... I didn't want to get older either. I know my mummy isn't able to look fter me properly. It's not her fault. Sometimes I wanted to be a iny baby, back inside her tummy. I was frightened about all orts of things. I was especially frightened about periods. But my new cousins have helped me a lot, and I'm learning all sorts of nteresting things; like how to swim, and how to have a wash rom top to bottom, with just a bowl of water and a flannel.

'I still do worry about getting older. What will I look like? Will my breasts be small, with big nipples, like Mummy's? And will I be thin like Frances, or have burgeoning curves, like Bernadette? And what will my periods be like? I used to think hat I really didn't want to feel like Frances every month. But now I know Frances; and love her, so I want to be just like her. And I'd just have to put up with suffering a bit. I've seen

Frances' appendix scar. What if I get ill like that? And I lov
Bernadette too, of course. And will I still love painting, or will
get bored with it? What will happen to Mummy? And I'r
finding out that when you get older, you are really just a mixtur
of your mummy and daddy.'

I sat down. I thought that what I had just said had been a
jumbled up, and probably didn't make sense to anyone else bu
me. But I was pleased to have spoken.

Frances was smiling, but Bernadette was giggling quietly behin
her hand.

The young lady said, 'Well that's very interesting. What's you
name?' I said I was Pippa. 'Pippa, that's such a lovely name.
had exactly the same thoughts as you when I was a girl. Perhap
I was a bit older then you are now, because ladies used to wea
clothes that covered them a bit more, so perhaps that's wh
children didn't think about ladies' bodies so much. And w
didn't talk about periods either. These days girls have a lot mor
on display. I'm not saying that's a bad thing. I'd have loved t
have worn a mini skirt when I was younger.'

Frances said, 'Well, you still can. What's stopping you?'

Auntie Julia said, 'Really Frances!'

Frances said, 'But I can say what I like, can't I? It's God's Stil
Voice that's talking. Why should a lady have to cover herself up
just because she's had a baby?'

The young lady said, 'I'm sure my husband would agree! This i
the most interesting meeting I've ever been to. I feel wide awak
now!'

In the café

Afterwards, everyone in the family said how interesting th
Friends' Meeting House had been. Uncle Geoff said that all th
Friends had told him how much they had enjoyed listening t
me. He said that he never quite knew what I was going to sa
next, but it always fascinating. He said that sometimes I talked a
if I was painting: I was inspired by what I was thinking, and b
what was going on around me. He wondered if that was what th
Friends meant when they talked about *God's Still Small Voice*

232

He said, 'Perhaps His Still Small Voice works through you when you are painting.'

Peter laughed and said that sometimes my paintings were like *Pippa's Big Loud Voice*. Auntie Julia said that I had cheered everyone up, and given everyone food for thought. Bernadette said, 'I haven't had my Communion today, and all this talk about food is making me hungry.'

Everyone laughed. It was the first time I had heard anyone make jokes about being a Catholic.

We went in the café. There was only a teenage boy and girl sitting by the window, drinking coffee. Mr McCabe ordered egg and chips for everyone in the family. He said he was going to cook a nice roast dinner, for everyone to eat in the evening. The café owner brought our food over. When we had all finished, he came to collect the dirty dishes. He said, 'You're all a bit quiet today. Not like the other night, when we had half the town in here! But did you hear what happened in the park last night?'

He moved towards Mr McCabe, and tried to speak quietly, so that nobody else could hear him.

'My Lionel was there with his girlfriend, Beryl. He said they were sitting on the park bench, having a quiet chat and holding hands, when suddenly all hell broke loose! Lionel said he saw a lady running out of the trees, with two policemen chasing after her. It looked like she was going to get away, but suddenly Lionel heard a police whistle and dozens of coppers appeared from nowhere! Two of them did a rugby tackle on the lady, and Lionel said that there was such a violent struggle, that he thought one of the coppers had got his teeth knocked out!'

The café owner crouched down next to Peter's dad. I think he was trying to make his voice as quiet as possible, but we were all listening as hard as we could. I heard some chairs scraping across the floor. It was the teenagers coming closer, to listen to the story.

When he could see that everyone in the audience was ready, he continued: 'Anyway, there was a terrific fight going on, and Lionel said that Beryl nearly got up and shouted, "Oi, you brutes! Leave that poor lady alone!" But Lionel dragged her back, and just then he saw a copper pull the lady's hair clean off! It was a wig, and it was a bloke dressed up as a woman! Would you believe it! Lionel said he thought that maybe it was one of those strange actor types… begging your pardon sir… who might have been practising to be in a pantomime or something like that. But the man was… pardon my French… using some very ripe language indeed. He was effin' and jeffin' at the cops, and calling them all sorts of foul things, and demanding to see a lawyer, and shouting about how he was innocent, and he was going to take them all to court for assault.'

The café owner paused, so that his words could sink in. Auntie Julia looked very pale, and Bernadette had torn her paper napkin into shreds. Peter was holding onto his dad's arm, and Frances was biting her bottom lip.

I whispered to her, 'What's *effin and jeffin*?'

She whispered back, 'Using the f word.'

One of the teenagers joined in, 'They say he was some kind of pervert… excuse me… criminal, who was hiding in the bushes and spying on…'

The café owner coughed and interrupted him, 'That's enough Wally. There's children here. As I was saying, Lionel and Beryl saw the whole thing. The cops put handcuffs on the woman… I mean man… and had to drag him off, screaming and shouting and kicking.

Bernadette whispered to her mum, 'Do you think it was that horrible man?'

'Oh and there's another thing,' continued the café owner. He was telling a terrible story, but seemed to be enjoying himself, 'Lionel said the coppers have raided the second-hand shop next to the Post Office. He said they've smashed the door down, and are busy searching the place.'

'Yeah,' said the teenager again, 'I bet that's where the dirty pervert… sorry, I mean criminal… got his ladies' clothes from. My friend said he saw some magazines in there once that would make your eyes water and once…'

'Wally! That's enough!' shouted the café owner. He sounded like he was angry with Wally, but I noticed that he was smiling.

Mummy and the detective discuss my pictures

When we arrived back at the bungalow, Mummy and Uncle Eric were sitting on the veranda. Mummy was smoking a cigarette, and Uncle Eric was smoking a small cigar. I walked up to mummy and stood next to her. She said, 'Hello Pippa,' and kissed me on the cheek.

Uncle Eric shook my hand. He said he was smoking cigars now, because he had read that that pipe smoking was even worse for your health than cigarettes. He suggested that Peter and I take him to look around the woods. He was just finishing his cigar when two police cars drove up to the house, and three people got out. It was PC Cooper, a policewoman, and a man wearing a suit. He was holding my sketchbook.

Uncle Eric said, 'That was quick. We'll have to change our plans.' He said he would go into the house with Auntie Julia, and help her make a cup of tea for everyone.

PC Cooper explained that he had come to introduce his colleagues, Detective Constable Montague and WPC Rawlings. They were from Norwich, and would be leading the investigation.

Uncle Geoff said, 'What investigation?'

Mr Montague said, 'We have been conducting an investigation for a number of years, and there has been a major development. We are here to ask some questions. We need to talk to the young girl.' He looked at me and smiled. I smiled back at him. 'And the young gentleman,' he smiled at Peter. Peter went red in the face and looked at his shoes. 'We will need to interview each child separately, with one of their parents present.'

The grown-ups talked to each other, then Uncle Geoff said that they had agreed that Auntie Julia would stay with Peter, while Mummy was going to be with me.

I could feel myself panicking. It felt like I hadn't seen Mummy for a very long time. And now I was going to be sitting in a room with her and two police officers. What worried me most was that I knew that they were going to talk to me about the contents of my sketch book.

We went into my bedroom. I sat on my bed with Mummy, while the police officers sat on chairs, facing us. Mr Montague asked me to describe to him exactly what had happened outside the beer and wine shop. I didn't want to, because Mummy was listening. I looked at my hands in my lap. I squeezed them together tightly, because I could feel them trembling.

Mr Montague leaned forward in his chair. I looked in his eyes. He smiled at me.

He said, 'Pippa, I understand that you might not want to tell me exactly what happened. But it's very important that you do.'

I said, 'But I already told Constable Cooper.'

Mummy said, 'Pippa, please don't be rude. Officer, I think that Pippa is embarrassed, because I'm here. I can leave the room, if that will help.'

Mr Montague said, 'I understand. Thank you for your offer Mrs Dunbar, but no, I must ask you to stay here. It's police procedure that a parent is present when we are interviewing a child, and it's very important that you understand what happened.'

Mr Montague used the word *understand* a lot. His voice was very quiet, and he kept looking in my eyes. I wanted to please him, but I didn't want to talk in front of Mummy.

Mr Montague said he wanted to talk to Constable Rawlings outside for a few minutes. When they left the room, Mummy said, 'Pippa, you must tell them what happened. It doesn't matter what I think. Auntie Julia told me all about it on the telephone, anyway. We have to help the police catch this wicked man, so he doesn't do horrible things to any more children.'

I looked at my hands and whispered, 'I can draw them a picture and write about what happened.'

Mummy said, 'If you can do that, then you can tell them.'

'It's not the same. I'm ashamed to say those things in front of you.'

Ashamed? What have you got to be ashamed about? I hate that word. Why should we be made to feel ashamed? We haven't done anything wrong. We must help the police to catch that man who does the terrible things to children.'

Mummy's voice had started off quietly, but was getting louder and louder. 'Are you worried about talking about seeing the man's willy? Please don't be worried about that. I won't be embarrassed.'

I had never heard her use the word *willy* before. I knew that she must know about them, because she was a grown-up, but it made me feel very uncomfortable. I wouldn't just have to talk about the willy. I knew I would have to say what it looked like too. That made me feel even more uncomfortable; like they were going to take all *my* clothes off, and make *me* stand naked in front of everybody.

Mummy took my hand and pulled me gently towards her. I didn't resist.

She said, 'Come and sit on my lap.' She pulled me up onto her knees, and put her arm around me. I leaned into her body. She smelled of perfume and cigarettes.

The two police officers came back in, and sat down again. Mr Montague said to me, 'Pippa, let's talk about the man outside the Off Licence. Tell us what he looked like.'

I could talk now. I described the man's face and his clothes. I said that I had forgotten to mention his missing tooth.

Mr Montague asked me, 'Can you draw his face again for us? Can you do that for us right now?'

WPC Rawlings had brought her own sketchbook and a pencil. It was an HB pencil, which was my least favourite pencil for drawing.

I told her, 'I don't wish to be rude, but I prefer to draw with better pencils. Please can I use mine?'

She laughed. This made Mummy laugh, and Mr Montague smiled. His teeth were very crooked.

I stayed on Mummy's lap, and drew the horrible man who had shown me his stiff willy. I was very pleased to be so close to

Mummy, and to be doing something that she thought was ver
important. I drew the man smiling, so that everyone could se
that he had a tooth missing.

When I had finished, Mr Montague took my drawing, an
put it on his lap. He asked WPC Rawlings to pass him a bi
brown envelope. He took out my first drawing of the nasty man.
He held up both drawings for Mummy and me to look at. I coul
see the man's willy sticking up. I could feel Mummy stiffenin;
and heard her take a deep breath, then let it out. The man's fac
in both pictures was almost the same, apart from his smile.

Mr Montague said, 'Thank you Pippa. Thank you very muct
We've decided not to ask you any more questions about that ma
now. But I would like to talk about your sketchbook.'

WPC Rawlings passed him the sketchbook. All of the pages ha
been carefully cut out. They had been put back inside the cove
in a strange order.

Mummy held me tight. Mr Montague showed us m
paintings and drawings, one at a time, and talked about each on
'Let's start with this one first. I can see a jar with pink water an
small pieces of red floating in it, in the sunlight. It's quit
beautiful. This next one is called A *bottle of Calamine Lotior*
Here's a baby rabbit, and here's a dead rabbit stretched out, wit
its eyes missing. I wonder why you painted that.'

I wasn't sure if he was talking to himself, or asking me
question. I didn't say anything, so he continued looking at m
pictures.

'Here's a starfish. It's magnificent. It looks so real, and th
colours are so creamy and soft. I wonder, was it still alive whe
you saw it?'

I said that I had poked it, but that it had been dead. I liked hir
telling me that my starfish was *magnificent*. I had spent a lot c
time getting the colours just right.

He carried on, 'And here are several paintings of waves. It'
remarkable how you have captured the light dancing on them a
they break. It makes you want to jump into them.' He laughed

238

but I was getting ready for what I knew was coming. I wanted to jump off Mummy's lap, and run out of the room.

'And you've called this one *Everybody Twist*. I can just make out the figures, but you can feel the movement. It's marvellous. And this one you've called *Sitting on Bernadette's Knee*.'

He stopped turning over the pages and looked at me. I looked back into his eyes. I knew what he was doing. Mummy coughed. Mr Montague started again. He took a long look at the next picture, before he gave it to us to look at. 'And this one is called *Swimming With Frances*. May I ask, Pippa, is that you without a bathing costume on? Were you swimming in the sea with nothing on?'

I put my head down. Mummy said, 'Pippa, tell Mr Montague.'

'No, 'I whispered, 'I had my bathing costume on, but I don't really like the colour. I was in a bit of a hurry when I was painting, so thought it would be easier to paint myself with nothing on.'

'I see. It's a very fine painting, all the same.'

'Now tell me about this one, that you call *Peter is asleep, I can hear his heart beating*.'

I didn't know what to say. I suddenly remembered that Mummy hadn't wanted Peter and me to sleep together, in case we got tempted.

Mummy said, 'Pippa, don't worry. Julia told me that you and Peter have been sleeping in the same bedroom. I'm pleased that you do. Now tell Mr Montague about the picture. I won't mind. I think it's lovely.'

She squeezed my tummy gently. That took me by surprise. I said, 'Well, I like Peter a lot. I'm not a very good sleeper, but he usually goes to sleep straight away. One night he was snoring. He looked just like a very little boy. I wanted to feel his heart beating, so I put my hand under the covers.'

Mr Montague said, 'I see.'

He didn't say *I understand*. He had begun to sound like a teacher who was about to tell me off.

'Now let's look at these drawings and paintings. They are quite different from the others.' His voice had become soft again, but I knew what was coming.

239

'You've called this one *Ursula*. Who's Ursula?'

'She's my Guardian Angel. She's like my best friend really.'

'Your best friend?'

'Yes. All Catholics have a Guardian Angel. She talks to me in the night, but sometimes I see her in the day.'

'But you've drawn her with no clothes on?'

'Yes.'

'Why?'

'I don't know. Usually she wears clothes, but on that night she had nothing on. She said she was very hot.'

He stopped asking me questions, and started talking to Mummy. 'This one looks like your daughter naked, with a penis. And this one shows a boy's head with a girl's naked body. In this next one we see a metal bathtub, with a nude teenage girl sitting in it. Judging from her hair, I'd say it's Frances.'

He pointed at some drawings I had made at the top of the page. 'And here we can see, very clearly, detail of the hair under her arms, and her pubic hair. And this one, called *How to wash in a bowl of water*, shows a girl and a teenager naked, and washing together. I assume that's your daughter and one of the McCabe girls. And this one's called *Auntie Julia in a very short petticoat*. It was a very thin petticoat too, by the look of it, which had left nothing to Pippa's imagination. And another one of a boy and a girl stripped to the waist and holding hands. It's called *We both feel thrilled*. And finally this one, called *Pippa and Peter in the bath*.

Mummy was about to say something, but Mr Montague held up his hand. 'Mrs Dunbar, I need to ask Pippa if she did these pictures, and to explain why.'

Mummy held me tight again. She said, 'I don't see anything wrong with these paintings. They show what she's interested in, and what excited her imagination at the time. It's like she's thinking onto the paper. I had exactly the same preoccupations when I was her age. I imagine that most girls do. There is nothing at all to worry about.'

240

'You are assuming, Mrs Dunbar, that your daughter did them. I must ask my questions again: Pippa, did you do these paintings and drawings?'

'Yes I did.'

'Can you tell me why?'

Mummy said, 'Go on, Pippa. Try and explain. Nobody is cross with you. Are they Mr Montague?'

Mr Montague said, 'Oh no. Of course not. I'm not cross at all. I just need to know more about the pictures, and then I'll explain why I'm asking all these questions.'

I felt that Mummy was defending and protecting me. When I spoke, I tried to imagine that God's Still Small Voice was talking. So I explained how I used to feel very confused and frightened about some things; like The Monthly Visitor, and what happens to you as you grow. I explained that being on holiday with Peter and his sisters had helped me to understand these things a lot more. Now that I understood, I wasn't frightened any more.

I told him how I loved Peter, but I had become frightened, because holding his hand was so thrilling for both of us. I said I thought that God had killed the rabbit, to punish me for feeling thrilled. I explained that Bernadette and I had got up in the night to do a wee, and Auntie Julia was in the kitchen having a drink. I drew her because she looked so lovely, and made me think of Mummy.

I looked at WPC Rawlings. She was busy writing in her notebook, but I could see that she was smiling. Mr Montague looked grave. He said, 'Thank you Pippa. Now I understand. I understand completely.'

My father

Mr Montague moved in his chair, so that he was turned slightly away from me, and towards Mummy. 'Now Mrs Dunbar, I need some information from you. Tell me about your husband, Mr Dunbar.'

241

Uncle Eric and I once saw a cat being threatened by a dog. The dog was barking, so the cat arched its back and its hair stood on end. Uncle Eric said the cat was trying to make itself look as big as possible, to scare the dog away. He said its hair was *bristling*. I could feel Mummy bristling all over.

She said, in a whisper that sounded like a hiss, 'I don't see why I should answer questions about my private life.'

Mr Montague's face didn't look friendly and kind any more. He reminded me of that horrible Head Teacher, Mr Grigson.

'Mrs Dunbar, please cooperate with me. This case is no longer just about a man who exposed himself to children. This is now a murder investigation. Believe me, all my questions are relevant, and your answers will be very important. Now tell me about Mr Dunbar.'

Mummy said, 'Murder? Who has been murdered?'

He took a deep breath. 'Over the past three years, three children... three boys aged between six and eleven... have been murdered in seaside towns in Norfolk. You may have read about it in the papers.'

Mummy said she hadn't. She wasn't bristling anymore. She said, 'I'm sorry, please can you ask me the question again?'

'Your husband. Pippa's father. Tell me about him'

'He... we don't live together. He lives in Malaya. And sometimes in Saudi Arabia, and South Africa.'

'You are divorced?'

'No.'

'Please explain.'

Mummy didn't say anything. Mr Montague looked at her. I was still on Mummy's knee, but I could see her face, in the mirror behind Mr Montague. She turned her head away from him.

'But you live apart?'

'Yes. We have been estranged since Pippa was three years old. He stayed in Malaya, while I returned to England with my daughter.'

'Why?'

'I don't want to talk about that in front of her.'

'Very well. What does your husband do for a living?'

'He owns rubber plantations.'

242

So he is wealthy?'

Mr Montague, Andrew Dunbar.... my husband...Pippa's father, is extremely wealthy. He owns copper mines. He owns factories that make clothes, concrete, shoes and many other things besides. He trades in oil. He owns properties and has financial interests all over the world. His wealth, as you can imagine, makes him a very influential man. But you know that already. He is not the kind of man who likes people to disobey him. And that's why we live apart. He suspected me... he accused me, of something I did not do. Something very serious. He said I had breached his trust. But I hadn't. He told me to leave.'

Mr Montague didn't seem to be surprised at all. I knew he was looking at me.

Tell me about the man who brought you here...Mr Baxter. Is that right?'

You know it is.'

What is your relationship with Mr Baxter?'

Mummy started to cry. Her chest was moving in and out very quickly. I felt her getting very hot, and I could smell her sweating under her arms.

She said, 'Stop it. Please stop it.'

Tell me about Mr Baxter.'

He's my friend.'

Your friend?'

My companion.'

He stays with you in your house?'

Yes. What's wrong with that, for God's sake? Is it a crime?'

Mummy was shouting. Her crying became weeping. She was squeezing me very tightly. I looked in the mirror. Her face was red, and tears were all over her cheeks.

She said, very quietly now, 'I love my daughter. I can't always show it in the same way as other mothers, but I love her very much. I'm not going to let her go. Please don't take her away from me. Don't let her father... and that man Shepherd, take her away from me!'

Mummy couldn't say anything else, because she was crying so much. Her shoulders were moving up and down,, and she was

243

taking deep breaths in huge gulps, and gasping as she let them out.

Uncle Eric opened the door. He looked very angry. He said 'What's going on? What have you done to Ruth?'

Mr Montague was very still. He kept looking at Mummy. She had stopped weeping, and was crying quietly now. She said, 'It's all right Eric. I'm helping the police with their enquiries. It's just a bit painful, that's all. Can you get me a drink of water please?'

Uncle Eric looked at me. He asked Mummy, 'Do you want me to take Pippa?'

Mummy asked me, 'Do you want to stay with me, or go with Uncle Eric?'

I didn't say anything. I couldn't say anything.

Mummy said, 'That means she wants to stay.' She rubbed my hair, and then wiped her nose with the back of her hand. Uncle Eric gave her his hanky. She blew her nose very loudly and then started to weep again. Uncle Eric put his hand on her shoulder and gave it a squeeze. Then he left the room.

Auntie Julia came in, with a glass of water and Mummy's cigarettes. Auntie Julia asked if she could stay. Mr Montague said, 'Yes. Yes, of course.'

Auntie Julia looked at me and said, 'Come and sit on my knee so Mummy can have a cigarette.' I was bursting to do a wee, but didn't want to leave the room, in case I wasn't allowed back in again. There was a knock on the door. It was PC Cooper. He handed Mr Montague a white envelope. Mr Montague opened it and read what was written on a piece of paper.

PC Cooper said, 'Shall I give a reply sir? They are expecting a reply.'

Mr Montague said, 'Tell them I have received the message and will comply. And tell Mr Baxter to come in here.'

There was hardly any room for anyone to move. Mummy sat on my bed, smoking. She had drunk all the water, and was using her glass as an ashtray. Auntie Julia sat next to Mummy with me on her knee. I couldn't see into the mirror anymore. M

244

Montague and WPC Rawlings sat on their chairs, and Uncle Eric stood by the door.

Mr Montague asked Uncle Eric what the time was. He said it was half past three.

Mr Montague said, 'Constable Rawlings, make a note of the time on Mr Baxter's watch, and then stop taking notes. Mrs Dunbar and her daughter are from this moment no longer part of this investigation. However, though I may have finished asking questions now, I'm going to give everyone some information.'

He said to Uncle Eric, 'Mr Baxter, are you satisfied with these arrangements?'

Uncle Eric said, 'Why shouldn't I be? It's not for me to decide.'

Mr Montague looked at Mummy. Mummy looked at Uncle Eric. Auntie Julia looked at Uncle Eric. WPC Rawlings looked at Uncle Eric. Uncle Eric tried not to look at anybody.

Mummy said, 'Eric, what's going on?'

He said, 'I have no idea what's going on.'

Mr Montague said to him, 'Really Mr Baxter, I thought you could do better than that. But I'll leave you to explain yourself to Mrs Dunbar, after we have left.'

I was very confused.

Mr Montague started talking to Mummy again. 'Mrs Dunbar, some adults would say that your daughter's pictures are innocent. I would agree, entirely. But let's look at them from the point of view of someone who doesn't know your daughter. Or perhaps someone who has never brought up children, so doesn't understand about the everyday events and behaviour of children in families. There is a lot of nudity and very intimate detail in these pictures. Some people would be shocked and appalled by that.

'You may not be worried about these pictures, Mrs Dunbar, but there is a concern for us. We have a man in custody. One day, this man will be tried in court. He will have a lawyer defending him. That lawyer's job will be to make the jury feel doubtful that his client is guilty. If they doubt his guilt, then he must be set free. So the lawyer will do everything he can to destroy the prosecution's case. That usually involves attacking the Police. We are always ready for that. But he will also try to destroy our witnesses. And when I say *destroy*, I mean it in all senses of the word.

'Let's imagine that your daughter is a witness. The lawyer will explain to the jury that Pippa has an imaginary friend, that she believes is real. Sometimes she imagines her friend naked. He will show the jury these pictures. Some members of the jury might be shocked. They might think that the pictures are obscene. He will tell the jury that Pippa comes from a broken home and is being brought up by her alcoholic mother.'

Mummy said, 'I used to drink, but I've stopped now. I'm having treatment. And how did you find out?' Her voice was very quiet. She sounded a bit like me, when I thought I was going to be told off.

'I'm a detective. In a case as serious as this, we need to know everything.'

Mummy sighed. I was hoping that she would still feel strong enough to protect me.

Mr Montague carried on explaining. 'The lawyer will say that your daughter was on holiday with friends of yours. He will describe their lifestyle as *Bohemian*. After all, they don't care if their son and teenager daughters walk around in the nude, or that eight and nine year-old children of the opposite sex share a bath together, and sleep in the same bedroom. He might suggest that the McCabe family are *immoral*. He might say that they have been a bad influence on your daughter's impressionable young mind. All this could give ammunition to the defence. It could discredit the prosecution's case.'

I thought Mummy was going to say something. I wanted her to get cross with this man. But she stayed quiet, while he kept on talking to her.

'I have no doubt that your daughter is telling the truth. No doubt whatsoever. But a jury might be made to doubt it. Some members of the jury might think that she is a child who is not

246

clear about the difference between fantasy and reality. They might think that she is obsessed with… with sex.'

He paused for a short while. I didn't know what *sex* was.

He continued: 'Witnesses can suffer terribly, if they appear in court and their evidence is not believed. It can destroy children's and women's confidence. I don't want that to happen to either of you.'

Mummy said, 'So if I understand you Mr Montague, you want to use Pippa's drawings to help you identify this man, but we won't appear as witnesses in court.'

Mr Montague and the WPC stood up. He said, 'That's a very good way of putting it, Mrs Dunbar.' He put my drawings of the nasty man into the brown envelope. He smiled at us and put his hand out for Mummy to shake. She took it.

He said to her,' I want to thank you for everything that you have done. The children have had a horrible experience. But I believe that what happened to them has helped us catch this man, and has stopped him from doing more terrible things.'

Mummy let go of his hand and said, 'My daughter is very strong. And I have no doubt, that with time, she will think of this incident in the same way as you do.'

Mr Montague smiled at Mummy, and then he smiled at me. He thanked Mummy again, and asked her what her plans were for the rest of the holiday.

She said, 'We haven't decided yet.'

Mr Montague said, 'I'd like you to stay in the area for a few days, in case we need to meet again.'

Then he did a very strange thing. I was still sitting on Auntie Julie's lap. He crouched down, so that his face was almost at the same level as mine. He looked at Auntie Julia, then he looked at me.

He said to me, 'Pippa, I think your pictures are extraordinary. I particularly love the starfish. I'm sure that one day your pictures will be worth a lot of money.' He put the sketchbook in my hands. 'But please, don't show what's written in this book to anyone else. Keep your pictures safe. Keep them very safe.'

WPC Rawlings smiled at me.

I whispered to Mummy that I was bursting to do a wee.

She said, 'Off you go then. Why don't you go and see what Peter is doing?'

She said to Uncle Eric, 'I just need to have a private word with Mr Montague, if you wouldn't mind?'

Uncle Eric said, 'Of course not. I'll just pop into the village again to get some lemonade, and possibly some beer and cigars for later.'

I took the sketchbook with me. As I was just about to leave the room, Mummy said, 'Come here Pippa.' She put her hands on my shoulders, and gave me a big kiss on each cheek. She said, 'You are a very good girl.'

I said, 'And you are a very good Mummy,' and ran out of the room.

I didn't look for Peter. I went to find Frances. She was sitting on a tree stump, reading a book.

She said, 'You've been talking to a real detective. It's just like these Agatha Christie books I've been reading.'

I asked her to come with me down to the pump. I opened my sketchbook and looked for the starfish. There was the white envelope. I said, 'I'm frightened. I'm sure I was the only one who saw Mr Montague hide it there. He looked at me, then looked down at his hands. I'm sure that he wanted me to see what he was doing.'

On the front of the envelope was typed *For Attention of DC Montague. Open Immediately... URGENT*

There was a very thin piece of paper inside. The message written on it was in capital letters. It said

MR ERIC BAXTER & MR BRIAN SHEPHERD, BOTH REPRESENTATIVES OF MR ANDREW DUNBAR, HAVE BEEN IN CONTACT WITH THE CHIEF CONSTABLE. THE CHIEF CONSTABLE INSTRUCTS YOU THAT MRS DUNBAR AND HER DAUGHTER ARE TO STOP BEING PART OF THIS INVESTIGATION IMMEDIATELY.

Frances read the note again. 'Mr Eric Baxter...
representative of Mr Andrew Dunbar. You are Pippa Dunbar. Is
Andrew Dunbar your father?'

I looked around, to check that nobody could see us. I told
Frances that yes, Andrew Dunbar was my father.

'Then this note is saying that Eric Baxter is working for your
father. Uncle Eric has told your father about the nasty man, and
about the police coming to see us. Your father doesn't want you
or your mummy to talk to the police. Uncle Eric is a spy for your
father!'

She screwed up the paper. 'I imagine that the detective gave you
this paper, so that you will know that Uncle Eric is spying on
you and your mummy. He probably tells your father everything
that happens to you, and about what your mummy is doing. And
your father is powerful enough to tell a chief constable what to
do.'

I told Frances that I felt a terrible pain in my tummy. I said I
had always thought that Uncle Eric was our friend, and that he
was there to help Mummy when she was in trouble. Sometimes I
imagined that one day he might even come to live with us
forever. And all the time he was telling my daddy all about us!
Sometimes I wondered if my daddy was actually a real person. I
had never even seen a photo of him. But now he felt very real
indeed. And Daddy was using someone to make friends with us,
so he could find out all about what we were doing.

I asked Frances, 'Why doesn't Daddy just come and see us
instead?'

Frances asked me, 'Do you think your Mummy knows? Do you
think you should show her this message? Is that why the
detective gave it to you?'

I said, 'Frances, have you got any toilet paper? I think I need to
do a big poo. Very soon. Now!'

Frances didn't have any toilet paper. I ran round the back of the
big pine tree. I found a stick and scraped a hole in the ground. I
did a huge poo into the hole. I took the piece of paper and wiped
my bottom with it. Then I covered up the hole. The paper had
been so thin that my finger had gone through it. When I had

249

finished, Frances took me indoors, and I washed my hands. Sh
promised to keep my sketchbook safely hidden.

Mummy tucks me in

As soon as the police left, Mummy and Auntie Julia cooke
us a nice dinner. Uncle Geoff had been preparing all th
vegetables and cooking the meat while the police were visitin;
He said, 'I couldn't think of anything else to do.'

During dinner, nobody talked about the police. Uncle Geoff tol
us some stories about famous actors he knew, or had worke
with. Mummy said that she was very impressed, and thought w
might get a television. She said that there were lots of unsuitabl
programmes, like wrestling and boxing, but there were som
nice programmes for children.

Uncle Eric came back, when we had just finished our fir:
course. He said he had been to the town, to make a phone cal
but there had been a queue of people waiting to use the telephon
box, which was why it had taken him so long to get back.

Mummy asked him, 'Who were you calling?'

Uncle Eric told her it was someone who wanted to talk to hir
about a book he was writing.

Mummy said, 'That's interesting.' But she didn't sound at a
interested.

Uncle Eric didn't look at her. He said, 'I've brought some bee
and lemonade... and a few cigars for the men later on.' H
winked at Uncle Geoff.

Uncle Geoff didn't laugh, or even smile.

Mummy asked Uncle Eric, 'Have you talked to Brian Shepher
recently?'

Uncle Eric didn't answer straight away. He scratched the back c
his head and said, 'Let's change the subject shall we? Thes
good people are getting awfully bored.'

Uncle Geoff said, 'Actually, this is all rather interesting.'

Auntie Julia said, 'Not now Geoffrey, please.'

Mummy said, 'Doesn't it seem strange to you that one minut
we were going full speed ahead with lots of questions, then
letter gets handed to a detective, and all of a sudden we are no

part of the investigation anymore? He stops asking me questions; just like that.' She clicked her fingers.

Uncle Eric looked at me. I looked at Frances. Frances looked at Bernadette and Bernadette shrugged, as if to say, *Don't ask me what's going on!*

Mummy was not going to let Uncle Eric get away with telling lies. She said, 'Eric, after you and Pippa left the room, I asked Mr Montague to explain his strange behaviour. He said he couldn't possibly comment.'

She looked straight at Uncle Eric and said, 'But he told me that you might be able help me.'

Uncle Eric said, 'Well he was wrong. I can't help you.'

Mummy said,

'No, not anymore. You can't help us anymore.'

After dinner, Mummy wanted to wash up, but Auntie Julia said the girls would do it. I went for a walk with Mummy down to the pump. I showed her where we had seen the baby rabbit. She said, 'God doesn't punish people. Some people say He does, but I don't believe them. He wants us to live a good life, and to try to make the right decisions. Sometimes we make wrong decisions, but we can't always know what's right and wrong.'

I said, 'Yes Mummy. I think like that too.' I wanted to walk somewhere else, because we were standing near the place where I had done my poo, and I was worried that she might tread there, and find the paper.

Mummy said that she wanted to help me get ready for bed. In the bedroom, she told me that when she was a little girl, she used to wash in a bowl just like mine. And she used to go to the toilet in a shed, just like the one we had been using.

I asked her, 'And did you use newspaper that hung on a nail?'

She said that they did.

Then she told me that when she was little, during The War, she had lived in a village not too far away from where we were now, just outside Norwich. She had lived with a couple called Mr and Mrs Keeping. They didn't have any children of their own. Mr Keeping couldn't see very well, so couldn't become a soldier. That was just as well, because they were from a religious group called The Quakers, who didn't believe in going to war. They lived in a small house, and sometimes the children in school used to tease Mummy, because she was German. Then her teacher told them that Mummy's family had all been killed by German soldiers, and after that the children were kind to her.

Mummy said, 'Children can seem to be quite cruel sometimes, but they don't really understand things in the same way that adults do. If you explain things to them, then they will usually stop being nasty.'

I got into bed, and Mummy knelt down and tucked me in. She looked in my eyes, and pushed my hair away from my forehead. She asked, 'Do you say your prayers?'

I hadn't said my prayers for a long time. I said, 'Well, not really, but I talk to Ursula instead. She knows what God is thinking, so I suppose that's the same thing.'

Mummy smiled at me. She said, 'Tomorrow I'm taking you to meet Mr and Mrs Keeping, the people who were like my mummy and daddy in The War, and while I was growing up. I haven't seen them for a very long time. Uncle Eric has to go and see someone in Norwich, so he'll drop us off in Mr and Mrs Keepings' village, and we can spend the day with them. I'm very excited about it, and I'm sure you'll like them.'

'But won't the police want to talk to me?'

'No, not anymore. I've talked to Julia, and she agrees that everyone should have a quiet day, and try and get back to normal. I think that the police still want to talk to Bernadette about something, but that doesn't really concern us.'

I said, 'Yes Mummy. It will be very nice.'

She kissed me on the forehead, and said, 'You're a very good girl. I'm going to go now, and stay with Uncle Eric in the hotel in the town. We have some important things to talk about. You have a nice sleep, and I'll see you early in the morning.'

She was just about to leave the room when she said, 'Oh I almost forgot! What clothes would you like to wear tomorrow?'

After Mummy left, I was just falling asleep, when Auntie Julia came in with Peter. She had given him a wash in the kitchen, and he was wearing his pyjamas. She gave me a kiss on the cheek, and then tucked Peter into his bed.

A wasp on my arm

In the morning, we had a big breakfast, then Mummy and Uncle Eric came to collect me in the car. It felt very strange to be sitting in the back of Uncle Eric's car and driving out of the gate, instead of being with Peter and his family. I was wearing my blue and white striped dungaree shorts, and a clean white blouse with short sleeves. My legs and arms looked very brown. Mummy sat in the back with me. She didn't speak to Uncle Eric. We drove into Mummy's old village, and she began to point at all the houses, and to tell me how much they had changed. She hadn't been there since she had got married. I thought she would have been very excited, but she seemed a bit sad.

Uncle Eric dropped us at a small shop next to a pub. He stayed in the car, and said he had to go and meet someone in Norwich. Mummy said, 'Give my regards to Brian Shepherd.'
Uncle Eric ignored her. He said to me, 'Goodbye Pippa.' I ignored him, and he drove off.
We went into the shop, and Mummy bought a lot of food, to give Mr and Mrs Keeping. The shopkeeper gave us two boxes to put it all in, but they were too heavy for us to carry. Mummy asked if someone might be able to deliver the box to *Gable Cottage*. He said, 'I'll get my son George to pop it over in the van, as soon as he gets back from his deliveries.'
Mummy asked him, 'Is there a taxi service here?'
The man smiled. 'That's my son George.'

Mummy held my hand as we walked along the village street. She was very quiet now.
The house we were looking for had a small white gate, and a path that led up to the front door. Mummy knocked, but there was no answer. We went round the side of the house, but there was no answer there either. There was nobody in the house.

I asked Mummy if her stepmother and stepfather had forgotten that we were coming.

She smiled and said, 'Oh I don't have their phone number, so I couldn't tell them. I thought it would be a nice surprise if we just turned up. Let's go and sit in the back garden.'

The garden was full of flowers and fruit bushes. We sat on a wooden bench at the top of the garden, under a pear tree. A wasp landed on my arm. I shuddered, and was about to hit it, but Mummy said, 'Leave it, Pippa. If you hit it, then it will probably sting you. If you don't touch it, then it will probably fly away. It likes you because you are so sweet.'

I kept as still as I could. The wasp walked around on my arm for a few seconds. I could see its bottom moving up and down. Then it flew away.

Mummy said, 'You see. I was right.'

The wasp landed on her hand. She jumped up and shouted, 'Oh no! There's a wasp. Quick, kill it!'

She laughed, and I realised it was a joke.

I said, 'Mummy, that's not funny!' But it was.

I felt quite sleepy, even though it was well before lunchtime. Mummy told me to lie down and put my head in her lap. We stayed like that, with her stroking my hair.

Mummy said, 'I'm going to take you home to Rayners Park tomorrow.'

I said, 'I'm glad.'

We were quiet again. I could hear a tractor in the distance.

Mummy said, 'Uncle Eric's not coming back.'

I said, 'I know.'

She was quiet again. Then she asked me, 'How do you feel about that?'

It was my turn to be quiet. Mummy gave my arm a little poke. She said, 'Hello. Is there anybody in there?'

I said, 'Shall I tell the truth?'

'I should hope you always do.'

'Well, I like Uncle Eric a lot. He's always been good to me.' I wanted to say, 'He has always made sure that I was properly

oked after, when you were ill,' but decided not to. It seemed to
e that I still had to be very careful what I said. So instead I
id, 'I wonder if he was finding out all about us, then telling Mr
hepherd, who then told Daddy.'

Mummy didn't seem surprised that I said that. She asked me,
What made you think like that?'

was quiet again. Mummy said, 'Let me guess. You read the
ote that Mr Montague put in your sketchbook.'

didn't know what to say. Mummy said, 'So it's true then. I saw
im slip it in there. He might be very good at discovering other
eople's secrets, but he's useless at keeping his own!'

he laughed to herself, quietly. 'Your father found out about us
eing involved with the police. Eric told him. I'm sure your
ther didn't want to have my name, or his daughter's name,
ppear in the newspapers, or even on television. So he got
hepherd to contact Mr Montague's boss, and told him to stop
sking us questions. Am I right? Is that what was in the note?'

didn't say anything, so Mummy said, 'So it was true then!'

still didn't say anything.

Mummy seemed to be enjoying herself. 'Don't worry, Pippa, I
ade Uncle Eric confess. I thought he was my friend, but really
e was working for your father. I felt very cross with him, and
our father. But really they are both trying to make sure that you
re properly looked after. Now I don't feel cross. I feel
isappointed.'

We were both quiet and still. Mummy stroked my hair
gain. Bees were buzzing, as they gathered pollen from the
owers all around us. Somewhere nearby, two pigeons were
ooing to each other.

Mummy asked, 'What did you do with the note?' I didn't say
nything.

Have you still got it?'

kept my eyes closed. 'Please don't be cross with me, Mummy'
wanted this peaceful moment to last as long as possible.

I won't be cross.'

It's buried in the woods.'

Can we go and find it?'

I took a deep breath. 'I did a poo in the woods, and wiped my bottom with the paper.'

Mummy laughed out loud. 'You're joking! Tell the truth. What did you do with it?'

'That is the truth!' I was annoyed that she wasn't taking me seriously.

Mummy laughed again. 'Well, I really can't think of a better way to dispose of it. How funny!'

We waited for an hour, but Mr and Mrs Keeping didn't come back to the house. Mummy was disappointed, but said that it would be lovely if she could take me there for a proper visit one day soon. She wrote a note for them, and put it through the letter box. The man in the shop told us he would make sure that he gave Mr and Mrs Keeping the boxes, as soon he saw them next. We went to the pub, and ate something called *Ploughman's Lunch.* Then George drove us to the hotel where Mummy and Uncle Eric had been staying.

The man at the desk said, 'Good afternoon Mrs Baxter. We've put fresh linen on your bed, as you requested.'

We went up to her room. There was a nice big bed in it. Mummy asked me if I'd like to sleep in it with her that night.

I said that I'd love to. This wasn't exactly true. Really I wanted to sleep with Peter, but I didn't like to think of Mummy sleeping on her own. It already felt like the holiday with Peter's family was over, while Mummy and I were beginning a new life together.

What happened to the nasty man?

We went for a walk in the town. I showed Mummy where we had been to the cinema. Mummy saw a bookshop across the street, and we looked in the window. She took me inside. Some of the books were new, but most of them were second-hand. The whole shop had an old smell about it. Mummy asked the man behind the counter if he had any copies of *Alice's Adventures in Wonderland*.

'Oh yes,' he replied. 'We always have plenty of those in stock.' He found five copies, and put them on the counter.

Mummy said, 'Pippa, have a look at these, and tell me which one you like best.'

I had heard of the story, but never had a copy of my own. I felt myself freezing up. I couldn't make a choice. The man picked one up and said, 'This edition was a favourite of mine when I was a little boy. It has the original illustrations.'

Mummy said, 'Good. Let's have that one. It was my favourite too. In fact, it's still my favourite book.'

While Mummy was paying, I looked out of the shop window. It had started to rain, and people were walking by with their coats on and their umbrellas up. I realised that we were near the place where we had spoken to the policeman. I had forgotten all about the nasty man and everything that had happened afterwards. I suddenly felt frightened, and turned to look for Mummy. She wasn't at the counter. I screamed, 'Mummy!' She came out from behind a bookshelf. I wasn't crying, but I was shaking.

Mummy crouched down in front of me. She said, 'It's all right. Mummy's here.'

The shopkeeper asked, 'Is everything all right?'

Mummy said, 'I'm sorry. I think she panicked because she couldn't see me. '

The man said, 'I'm not surprised. A lot of parents are keeping a very close eye on their children now.'

Mummy said, 'Whatever do you mean?'

He told us the whole story. The police had arrested a man in the park. He had been dressed up as a lady. They had been given a tip-off that he would be lurking there; waiting to molest children who might be playing on their own. The police found his van. In the back were ropes and sacks and tape; probably for tying up children. There were lots of different sets of men's and lady's clothes, and several pairs of glasses. The police thought he used these to disguise himself. They found a lady's bicycle in the van too. Apparently the man would park outside a town, then cycle around, looking for children to talk to. Then he'd invite them to the park and see if he could kidnap them.

The man could see that I was getting upset by the story. He said to Mummy, 'I'm sorry, but everyone's talking about it.'

Mummy said, 'Well we haven't heard it. Do go on, but please be careful not to say anything awful.'

The man said he would try his best. I held Mummy's hand tightly.

Apparently, the kidnapper had been to the town before. He knew the owner of the second-hand shop next to the post office, and used to buy his disguises there, and nasty magazines and photos to look at. A nice girl had gone into the shop, and asked to buy a painting that was in the shop window. The man wouldn't sell it to her. The police thought that was very suspicious. They discovered this was his signal to other nasty men. If the painting was in the window, then he had horrible magazines and pictures for them to buy. If it wasn't there, it meant that there was nothing for sale.

Then the kidnapper exposed himself to some children in the street. He'd given himself away though, before he did that. He told the children that the Off Licence used to be a bike shop. That's how the police knew he'd been to the town before. And a girl took a photograph of him by accident, when she was taking a photo of the children. The police took her camera, and developed the photos. And there he was, in the background; probably going to put his bike round the corner, so that he could make a quick getaway. Then he must have taken his glasses off, so that nobody would recognise him. Then he probably dressed up as a woman and went cycling round looking for more children to try and lure into the park.

I whispered to Mummy, 'Bernadette was going to buy that picture for me. I thought that was why she went in there.'

Mummy told me to shush; not in a nasty way, but to calm me down.

The man continued: 'Well, it turns out the man in the park confessed to everything. He's been charged with the kidnapping and murder of three children from different towns on the Norfolk

Coast.   Everyone in the town is in shock. To think that those poor innocent children near our Post Office could have been…'

Mummy said, 'Thank you. I think we've heard enough.'

Just before we left the shop, Mummy said, 'By the way, how do you know all that?'

The shopkeeper said, 'Oh that's easy. PC Cooper is my brother-in-law.'

We both went to bed very early. Mummy began to read me the story of Alice. She said she was delighted that I liked the same book that she had done, when she was my age. I felt exhausted.

We say goodbye

In the morning, we had a huge breakfast in the hotel dining room. Afterwards, Mummy packed her bag, and we took a taxi to Peter's bungalow.

Mummy told Auntie Julia and Uncle Geoff all about what the man in the bookshop had said. Uncle Geoff said that PC Cooper had just been to see them, and had told them the same story. Auntie Julia told Mummy how sorry she was about everything that had happened.

Mummy said that it was all just an accident, and she didn't blame anybody. She said that it must have been an awful experience for the children, but, in a strange way, she now felt so much closer to me.

Mummy said that she was going to have to get a taxi to the station, so that we could catch the train home.

Auntie Julia asked her: 'Is Eric not taking you home then?'

Mummy told me to go and pack all my things, while she talked a bit more with the grown-ups.

Peter and the girls had already packed my suitcase for me. Bernadette and Frances took turns to give me a big hug. Peter was very quiet.

I thought I was going to cry. I told Frances that I didn't want to go back home, and only have Ursula as a friend, and sit upstairs

259

being frightened of Mummy, and not knowing what was going on.

Frances said, 'You must ask questions. Your mummy is much better now. And you can always write to us.'

I said, 'You're going to live in Liverpool, aren't you?'

Frances said, 'Yes we are.'

Uncle Geoff drove us to the station.

On the train, I told Mummy about a dream I had had in the night. I was by the sea, and standing by a big stream. The banks of the stream were made of mud and sand. The water in the stream was rushing out into the sea. The water was clear, and I could see the bottom. I knew that the water would come rushing back again; probably in the night. The sand and the mud looked perfect, like desert sand dunes I had once seen in a photograph. A little bird had been walking on the muddy sand, and had left little footprints. I wanted to climb down to the bottom of the stream. But I knew that if I took just one step forwards, I would sink deep into the mud.

Mummy said, 'Dreams are very important. I've been going to two doctors. One tells me to keep taking my tablets. The other one talks to me about my dreams. I often dream about water.' She looked out of the window. 'And it usually means that I need to get up and do a wee.'

I looked at her reflection in the window. She was smiling to herself. The man opposite us coughed, and rustled his newspaper.

Mummy gave me a kiss and said, 'You must paint that dream when we get home.'

o   o   o   o   o   o   o   o   o   o   o   o   o

Sunday 7th November 1976

I'm freezing. My feet are already like blocks of ice. I'm going to have to put some socks on.

Last night I had a nightmare. I was an assassin. My job was to kill whoever I was told to kill. I went outside the caravan, to think about the best way of murdering someone. A stagecoach me rushing towards me. It was being pulled by three wild white horses, that were bearing down on me. I realised that the river had trained them to destroy everything in their path.

What I really crave now is some warmth. What I need, more than anything, is to lie beside someone who loves me, and to get nice and warm. The only problem is that I don't know anyone who loves me anymore.

I have read somewhere that children between the age of eight and puberty are not very emotional. Then at puberty they enter an emotional storm. Well, that may be true for lots of children, or perhaps just for boys, but it certainly wasn't true for me. I could feel myself becoming more and more intense.

o   o   o   o   o   o   o   o   o   o   o   o

The holiday with Peter's family had made me feel very tired. When we got back home, I felt like I had been asleep for two weeks, and everything that had happened had been a series of dreams. Mummy seemed quite different. She began to ask me questions. One of her first questions when we got home was 'What would you like to do tomorrow?'
She was very surprised and pleased when I answered, 'Nothing special, really. I'd just like to stay at home with you.'

It took me a while to get used to this new Mummy. Before the holidays, I'd always treated her like a dangerous snake, which might pounce on me at any moment, or if I made a wrong move. But now, now I'm sixteen, I think it was me who had changed, as much as her. I discovered that I could ask her questions. Not big questions about my father and Uncle Eric, or why Mummy became ill. I knew I'd have to wait to find out about those things. The first question I asked her was, 'Can I sit on your lap?'
She smiled and said, 'Of course you can, Pippa.'
When I was on Mummy's knee I said to her, 'I'm going to look after you, Mummy.'

She laughed quietly and said, 'We have to look after each other now.'

I decided to have no more secrets from Mummy. I wondered if it was the secretive side of me that had driven Mummy away from me. So whenever I was sitting on her knee, or while we were eating, or while she was giving me a bath, or putting me to bed, I'd tell her about things. I'd tell her about what I'd like to paint and draw, or about a story I was thinking of writing. I'd carry on talking to her until she said something like, 'Gosh, you are a chatterbox!' or 'My! You have got a lot to say for yourself!' That meant that she wanted me to be quiet.

I knew that Peter and his family had come home, because one afternoon Auntie Julia rang up. She didn't ask Mummy if I wanted to come round and play. Afterwards Mummy explained that they would only be staying at home for a few days. Then they were driving up to a place called Chester; to look at a house that they might live in, and to arrange for the children to go to new schools.

Mummy asked me, 'What do you think about that? I imagine you'll be very sad?'

I had been thinking about this a lot, but still didn't know how to put it into words. I had spent so much time with Peter, and had just got to know his sisters. I suppose I should have felt angry, or terribly sad. Perhaps I did feel those things. But I wasn't going to allow myself to get upset, because this might spoil my new life with Mummy. So on some days I just pretended to myself that it wasn't going to happen, and at other times I told myself that I really wouldn't mind very much.

Mummy takes me to London

Mummy still had to go to her doctor's appointments in London. She said that talking to the doctor helped her to feel better. He had told her that the time had come for him to meet me. So on Friday we were going to go on the train into London and then on the Underground, to a place called Camden Town. I was excited, because I had never been to London with Mummy

262

ınd we would be meeting her special doctor. Our appointment vas at half past nine, so we had to get up early to catch a train. The train was full of people going to work, so we had to stand ıp. A man said to Mummy, 'Excuse me madam, would you like ɔ have my seat?'

Mummy said she would, and the man looked a bit disappointed.

I had only been in an underground train once before, when Uncle Eric brought me to Rayners Park for the first time. We were going to take two underground trains today. When the first train came in, the doors opened right in front of us. Mummy said, 'We're not going in there. It's full of smokers.'

We rushed along the platform, to try to get into the next carriage. Passengers were pushing each other, as they tried to get off, while at the same time people were trying to squeeze inside. There was no chance that we were going to get on that train.

A man in a uniform next to us was shouting, 'Move right down inside the cars!' Then he shouted, 'Mind the doors!' At the same time, a young lady rushed from the passage behind us, and tried to jump into the train. A man inside the train pushed the other passengers with his back, to make a space for her, and at the same time pulled her inside. She had just enough space for herself, but she couldn't get her basket inside. The doors slid together and her arm holding the basket was trapped. She was yelling as she dropped her basket onto the platform.

A man behind us muttered, 'Stupid bitch,' as the doors swished open again. The young lady sprang out of the train, and bumped into me. I would have fallen over backwards, but there were so many people all around me. The doors closed again and the train moved forwards, into the tunnel.

While all of this was happening, more and more people were pouring in from the passage behind us. The uniformed man was shouting at them to stand back, while the young lady tried to pick up her things. Mummy let go of my hand and bent down to help her.

263

The young lady said to Mummy, 'I'm fine, thanks. That was my own stupid fault.' She wasn't upset; she was laughing. A man tried to squeeze past me, and his suitcase hit me on the back of my legs, and I fell forward, right on top of the young lady.

She shouted at the man, 'Hey! Take care will you, otherwise we'll all get crushed to death!'

I suddenly felt terrified. Mummy held my hand tightly, and tried to get up. She staggered, and said to me in a very hoarse voice, 'We must get out. I can't breathe!'

The man in the uniform stepped forward, and took Mummy under the arm.

I shouted at him, 'Please help us! My mummy can't breathe!'

The young lady grabbed my hand.

The man shouted, 'Make way! Make way!' and pulled Mummy along the corridor, back towards the escalator.

The young lady said to me, 'Don't worry. He's just going to take her outside, to get some fresh air. I'll come with you.'

We reached the bottom of the escalator, but Mummy sank to her knees.

The young lady pushed the man in the uniform out of the way, and told him to make sure we had enough space, among the hordes of people swarming off the escalator.

The man said to her, 'Who do you think you are? Don't tell me what to do. You're the one who caused the problem in the first place.'

She said, 'I'm a nurse. So are you going to help or not? Why don't you do something useful? Go and get a chair and a glass of water.'

He did as he was told. The young lady leant against the wall, and put her arms around Mummy's chest.

She said in Mummy's ear, 'It's all right. I've got you. Just lean on me. As long as I hold onto you, you won't fall.'

The man came back with a chair and a glass of water, while another man in uniform started to tell people who were crowding round to move out of the way. The young lady helped Mummy to sit down.

An old lady said, 'That happens to our Connie. She's just found out she's in the family way again. She's always fainting.'

The new man in the uniform said, 'My wife's got a bun in the oven too. Can't stop eating. This place is awful for pregnant ladies. We have at least one to sort out every morning. Harry loves it, don't you mate?'

Harry looked embarrassed and said, 'It's all in a day's work. That's all it is.'

Mummy had a drink and took a few deep breaths, then said she felt able to stand up. We walked outside the station with the young lady, and sat together on a bench.

She said her name was Muriel. She said, 'I'm a nurse. It's my day off. I don't know why I jumped on the train like that, because I'm in no hurry to go anywhere.' She told Mummy to lean forward and take some deep breaths. She put her hand on Mummy's back and rubbed her gently.

While Mummy was bending forward, I whispered to Muriel, 'If you're a nurse, then you must know what's wrong with Mummy. People were saying she might be *in the family way* or have *a bun in the oven*. And what does *pregnant* mean? Mummy's a Jewish Catholic.'

Muriel said, 'Oh. I didn't think you could be Jewish and a Catholic at the same time. I'd have thought that being one was enough, but surely not both.'

Mummy sat up as Muriel was saying that. It made her laugh, so I knew that she wasn't going to die.

Muriel asked Mummy if she had enough money to pay for a taxi to where we were going.

Mummy told me to find her purse in her bag, and give it Muriel.

Muriel took a quick look in the purse and said, 'Crikey. There's enough cash in here for a taxi ride to Scotland!'

Mummy said, 'I'm going to the doctor, and that's to pay his fees.'

Muriel gave Mummy a funny look and said, 'I see.'

Mummy looked shocked, and I thought she was going to be cross with Muriel about something. But she smiled and said, 'No. You don't see. I'm not pregnant. At least I don't think I am.' Muriel's cheeks went bright red. Mummy added, 'And he's not that kind of doctor.'

Muriel took her hat off, and it fell onto the pavement. She tried to pick it up, but somehow managed to knock her basket off the bench. She had shiny fair hair in a long plait. Wisps of hair were falling into her face, and she kept brushing them back using her knuckles. Her cheeks were big and round, like Miss Dawson's. When she spoke, she had a slight lisp. When she said the words *taxi* and *nurse* they sounded like *taxthi* and *nurth* instead, and the pink tip of her tongue stuck out between her teeth as she spoke. I was captivated by her.

Mummy asked Muriel, 'Would you be a lamb, and get us a taxi? Tell the driver we want to go to Camden Town.'
Muriel did as she was told. She went over to the road, and stuck her arm out. A black taxi pulled over immediately. Muriel waved to us. Mummy stood up slowly. I tried to help her by putting my arm through hers, but she said, 'Thank you darling. I'm fine now. But please bring Muriel's basket and her hat. And try not to drop them.' We laughed.
Mummy and I got in the taxi. Mummy looked at Muriel. I thought she was going to say *goodbye* and *thank you.* But she didn't say anything. Both of them just looked at each other.
The taxi driver said, 'Are we ready?'
Then Mummy did the strangest thing. She reached out her hand to Muriel. Muriel held it. She looked Mummy in the eyes, and Mummy pulled her into the taxi.
Mummy said, 'Would you like to come with us?'
Muriel's cheeks went red and she said, 'Yes please.'

On the way to Camden Town, Muriel took the grips out of her hair, and tried to rearrange them, so that her hair wouldn't go into her eyes. She dropped the grips on the floor, and I spent five minutes trying to find them all.

nd that was how we met Muriel.

I meet Mummy's doctor

We were half an hour late for our appointment. We stopped
utside a large white house with two enormous pillars. There
ere several gold plates on the wall, by the front door. Mummy
ing the bell next to one that said, *Dr Maximilian Gold*. We
aited for a few minutes, and Mummy was just about to ring
gain, when a lady opened the door. She said, 'Ruth, how are
ou? Goodness, you do look pale. Are you all right ?'
/e stood at the bottom of the stairs, and Mummy explained
hat had happened. Then she said, 'And this is my daughter,
ippa, and this is Muriel, who is going to spend the day with us.'
he lady said to me, 'I'm Mrs Parker. Goodness, of course you
·e your mother's daughter. You look just like two peas in a pod.
ome upstairs.'
/e went into a lift that took us to the top floor. I looked at
luriel. She wasn't wearing her hat. She could see I was looking
: her bare head. She said, 'Oh no! I've left my hat in the taxi!'
lummy pulled the hat out from behind her back and said, 'Here.
can see that being with you is always going to be an adventure.'
luriel's cheeks went red again. She looked at Mummy, and they
oth smiled at each other.

Dr Gold was waiting for us at the top of the stairs. He spoke
· me straight away. He crouched down and shook my hand and
iid, 'Pippa, how lovely to meet you.' He looked straight into
·y eyes and waited, still holding my hand.
said, 'I like your name.'
le smiled and said, 'You must call me *Max*.

Max explained that usually Mummy spoke to him for fifty
inutes, and then the next person came in. But this morning he
ad only two people to see, and that was Mummy and me.
lummy went in first, and Muriel and I sat outside the door. We
·ere in a square hallway that had two other doors. There was a
icture on each wall. The first was a big photograph of a
eautiful white flower. Muriel said it looked like an orchid.

267

The next was a strange blue painting of a man and lady hugging each other. The man was wearing a pair of underpants, but the lady had nothing on. The man was talking to another lady dressed in blue. She looked very cross, and was holding a baby.

I once heard a lady at the bus stop say, 'I was so surprised what the doctor said, that it almost took my breath away.' I thought this was just an exaggeration. But when I looked at the other two paintings I felt I almost couldn't breathe. I had to sit down. One was of a naked boy pushing a big heavy door, and the other was of two girls in a garden, holding paper lanterns.
Muriel asked me if I was all right. All I could say was, 'Oh.'
She held my hand and said, 'What is it? What is it, Pippa?'
It sounded like she was a long way away.

Mummy came out after her talk with Max, and saw Muriel and I sitting together, looking at the pictures. She said to me, 'I thought you'd like those.'
Muriel said, 'Pippa's been in a funny trance. I was starting to get worried.'
Mummy told her that it was quite normal for me to behave like that, when I had something beautiful in front of me. I said, 'I have never seen such beautiful paintings.'

I talk to Max

Mummy told me that it was time for me to come and talk to Max. She said to Muriel, 'I'm really sorry, but we'll be exactly 50 minutes. Will you wait for us? It won't be too boring for you?'
Muriel said, 'Oh no. I've got nothing else to do, really. But I would like a drink. I'm awfully thirsty, and a bit hungry. Perhaps I'll just go out, and see if I can find a café, or something like that.'
Mummy looked alarmed. She said, 'Well, I can't stop you, but you will promise me that you'll come back?'
Muriel said, 'Of course. Of course I will.'
They looked into each other's eyes. Muriel's cheeks went red again.

Mummy and I went into Max's room. There was a desk and some very comfortable chairs. I sat next to Mummy, and Max sat in front of us. He looked at his watch and said, 'Goodness! It's time to have a drink and a biscuit. I'll ask Mrs Parker if she can bring something in.'

And that's all he said. Mummy and I sat there and he just looked at us. I thought perhaps he was a Friend, and he was waiting for me to talk in God's Still Small Voice.

Mrs Parker brought in some coffee for the grown-ups and a lemon drink for me. There was a biscuit for each of us. Max asked me if I'd like a biscuit, but I said *no thank you* and told him I was worried about making a mess.

Max asked, 'Worried about making a mess?'

'Yes. I don't want to upset Mummy.'

'Upset Mummy?'

'Yes. I know she's not well sometimes, and I want to be good, so I can help her.'

'What is it like, trying to be good all the time?'

That was a small question that I knew would need a long answer, and it wasn't what I wanted to talk about. I said, 'I shall have to think about that.'

Max smiled and said, 'Try not to think. Just say whatever comes into your mind.'

'Well, what's in my mind is the painting outside of the boy with no clothes on. Why have you got it there? The policeman told me that some people would be upset at the pictures I have painted of me and my friends with no clothes on. But you're a doctor, and you've got one.'

'What do you think?'

'About what?'

'What does the painting make you feel?'

'I like it. I like the colours, and the boy looks very nice. I'd like to talk to him. But I don't understand. Why is he leaning against the door?'

'He's supposed to be pushing it, to try and open it, because it's locked.'

269

'Well, the artist hasn't taken much trouble about that. He's only leaning on it. If he wants to get in, then he needs to make a bit more effort.'

'Tell me more about that... *more effort*.'

'Well if a door won't open, then you have to give it a really hard shove, because maybe it's just stuck. I tried to open a door once when I thought it was stuck. I leaned forwards with my shoulder and pushed with all my strength. He looks like he's just leaning on it.'

'Maybe he doesn't really want to get in.'

That didn't make sense. So I talked about something else. 'I don't understand why the boy hasn't got any clothes on.'

'You think he's a boy?'

'Yes I do.'

'Why are you so sure?'

I had completely forgotten that Mummy was sitting next to me. She was sitting very still.

'Well, I suppose he could be a boy who looks like a girl. Or it could be a girl who looks like a boy, but...'

'Yes?'

'He looks just like Peter.'

Max ignored that and said, 'Tell me about the locked door. Have you ever been in front of a locked door?'

He could see I was shocked. Once, when I was little, I touched an electric wire that was sticking out of the wall. The shock was so strong, it threw me across the room. Now I felt the same shock, but I couldn't understand why. I said to Mummy, 'It was your bedroom door. You had said horrible things to me, and I woke up in the morning, and there was no answer from behind your door. I thought you were very ill, or perhaps dead. I phoned Uncle Eric. You had gone out all night, and got drunk.'

Mummy began to cry. I said, 'Oh Mummy please don't cry. I didn't mean to upset you, please don't cry!'

I stood by her chair and tried to put my arms round her. She grabbed me and pulled me onto her lap and held me tight. She said, 'I was ill. I was very ill. I won't ever do that again. I promise.'

We didn't say anything else until Max said, 'We'll have to finish in five minutes.'

In the café

When we left Max's room, Muriel wasn't in the hall. Mrs Parker was waiting with a big diary.

Mummy asked her, 'Have you seen that girl… that young lady who we came in with?'

Mrs Parker smiled and said, 'Oh yes. She went out to buy a sandwich, but discovered that she'd left her bag behind. She asked me to tell you to meet her in the café down the road. She's beautiful, isn't she? But quite scatty!'

Mummy held my hand all the way along the street. I wanted to tell her I was sorry for making her cry, but she was too busy looking for the café. We saw Muriel inside a dirty-looking café, sitting by the window, reading a newspaper.She said, 'I've already eaten a sandwich and a piece of cake. I was starving!'

Mummy said, 'I've just been crying my eyes out. I haven't been a good mother, but I'm doing my best. Sometimes it's not easy to be me.'

Muriel said, 'Oh I can imagine.' Her cheeks went red. 'Sorry, I don't mean that it's easy to imagine you as a bad mother. But I was thinking about you not being easy. No, no… not about you being difficult. I don't mean that. What do I mean? I think I'll just be quiet.'

Mummy looked at Muriel, and Muriel looked at Mummy. Mummy said, 'No, please tell me what you mean.'

Muriel looked at her empty plate. She started to cry. Mummy reached over and held her hand.

The waiter said, 'Would you like to order now? Or shall I come back in a few minutes' time?'

When Muriel stopped crying, Mummy ordered some lunch. There wasn't very much on the menu, because it was what Mummy called *a working men's café*. Muriel said she liked these types of *greasy spoon* cafés. I looked at our spoons very carefully but they seemed quite clean. All the customers seemed

271

to be eating bacon, fried eggs, baked beans and chips. I loved egg, beans and chips, so Mummy ordered some for the three of us.

So there we were, in a café in London, planning how to spend the afternoon, with a pretty young lady that we knew nothing about. If Mummy thought this was odd, she didn't show it. I thought it was very strange. Mummy talked about the paintings in Max's hallway. She said that they were only copies and asked me if I would like to go to see the original paintings. I wondered if this was a joke, and a sign that she was getting better. But it wasn't a joke. She told us that they were hanging in a place called The Tate Gallery, and that she had been to see them several times. I said I'd love to go. Then Mummy asked Muriel some questions about herself.

Muriel said that she was twenty-six, and not married. She wasn't married, because she didn't want to settle down with a man, and have children. She'd had lots of different jobs since she had left school. She had worked in a small hotel by the seaside; starting off as a cleaner, and working her way up to be assistant manager. Unfortunately, the manager had wanted to marry Muriel, but when she told him that she wasn't interested, he said she had to leave. She had worked on a farm, but one day the farmer tried to kiss her, and his wife found out, so Muriel had to leave. Then she worked in a pub, in a shop, and as a bus conductor. She ended up leaving every job she had ever had, because some man always wanted to kiss her, or marry her, or sometimes both. Now she was working as a nurse in a big hospital in London. She said it was very hard work, with lots of horrible things to do. But she said she enjoyed it, and she had somewhere to live. It was called a nurses' home.

Then Muriel said something that Mummy found very funny: 'We're all girls and women living together, so I hope I'll be quite safe there.'

Mummy asked Muriel about her parents. Muriel coughed and called the waiter over, and asked him for another cup of tea. Muriel said to Mummy, 'That's all about me, now what about ou? I know you're called Ruth, but that's all. What does ippa's father, your husband, do?'

Mummy coughed and said, 'I'll just ask the waiter to get me a cup of tea shall I?'

They looked at each other and smiled. Both of them had red cheeks. Muriel said, 'Is it just me, or is it hot in here?'

Mummy smiled and said, 'It's you, my dear. It's you.' They both took their coats off.

Love Locked Out

We took a taxi from the café to the Tate Gallery. This was the very first time I had been in an art gallery. As soon as I saw the huge front of the building and the steps, I became very excited. I realised that, if I wasn't careful, I would get over-excited and spoil the afternoon.

Mummy said, 'This is where Lady Celia met her poet friend.' There was a very slight tremble in her voice. When she said that, I knew that something important was going to happen. I didn't know quite what, but I had a feeling it would be something to do with love.

Mummy knew exactly where to go. I had to make a tremendous effort not to look at all the paintings that covered every wall. Mummy said, 'Here it is!'

And there he was. It was Peter. The colours were different from the ones on the picture in Max's hallway. They seemed to me to be more *real*. The boy looked real. I wanted him to turn around, so that I could see his face and talk to him. I wanted to step into the painting and hold his hand, and help him to push the door open. I went into My Colour Dream. Mummy and Muriel left me standing in front of the painting, and sat down on a bench with an old lady.

The painting of the naked boy was called *Love Locked Out*, and was by a famous lady painter from America, called Anna Lea Merritt. She had been a Quaker, and her husband had died a few months after they got married. She was terribly upset, and this painting shows Love, in the form of Cupid, pushing against

273

a door, but being unable to get to the other side. Cupid is usuall shown as a naked boy, and this explained why Mrs Lea Merri had spent so much time making a ten-year-old boy stand f hours with nothing on, pretending he was trying to push a do open. No wonder he looked so tired and bored.

I knew all this, because I could hear the old lady tellin Mummy and Muriel all about the painting. She said, 'It make one think. In Anna Lea Merritt's day, it was all right to ask child to strip off, and stand for hours while you painted hir Then they could put his naked bottom in a gallery, for everyor to look at. But nowadays we wouldn't like children to do th sort of thing, but it's all right for us to use men, and especial women, instead.'

Mummy said, 'That's a very interesting point. I imagine he g quite cold as well.'

The old lady said, 'My daddy brought me here when I was little girl. I remember asking him, "Daddy, why are there s many paintings of ladies with nothing on?"

He said, "Because men like to look at naked ladies. We thin they are lovely."

But this was only the first of lots of questions:

Do ladies like to look at men with no clothes on? Do ladies lik to look at ladies with no clothes on? Do men like to look at me with no clothes on?

To each question he said, "Of course they do." '

Muriel tapped me on the shoulder. She said that Mumm wanted me to come over and meet this interesting lady. The ol lady said, 'Hello my dear. Your mummy tells me that you a very interested in painting.' She had very watery red eyes, an her teeth were very yellow. She had hairs growing out of h chin. She kept hold of my hand.

I said, 'I love painting.'

I wanted to pull my hand away, but I thought that would be rud She said to me, 'It's the story of the pictures that interests n most. Who was the artist? What was their story? What were the

274

eeling when they painted this picture? What were they trying to ell us? What did they want us to think and feel?'

said, 'When I paint a picture, most people don't know what it s. When I tell them, they're quite surprised. Mummy's very ind. She buys me lots of paints and paper and brushes.'

he lady smiled her yellow smile. 'You are lucky to have such a ice mummy.'

he said to Mummy, 'I arranged for this this bench to be put ere.'

Mummy looked surprised, 'You told the managers to put it ere?'

Not exactly *told* them. Let's just say I *suggested* it.'

But why this picture? It's not the most well-known work in the allery.'

My dear, I'm a very generous benefactor of this gallery. My amily has been associated with The Tate before it was even uilt. Some rather special people come to look at this painting. Like yourselves, I imagine.'

looked at Mummy. She was smiling. I looked at Muriel. She ooked puzzled.

Mummy said, 'You mean patients of Doctor Gold.'

he old lady smiled. 'That's right. Max is one of the most ighly-skilled psychoanalysts in the country. And I've no doubt e's the most expensive.' She looked Mummy up and down. She ontinued, 'All sorts of wealthy and well-known people go to see im. He's a typical Jew, of course: talented and shrewd. Such a hame that Hitler decided to kill six million of the Jews in The War. Europe is much worse off since they were exterminated, lon't you think?'

Mummy gasped. She wasn't smiling anymore. She said, 'Yes, vell, it's been a pleasure talking to you, but we really must go now.'

he old lady said, 'Oh, I'm sorry, I hope I haven't offended you y suggesting that you are one of Max's patients? Many people vould want to keep that a secret.'

Mummy said, 'Oh no. Not at all. I know I'm very lucky to see im. It's just that I'm Jewish. But I'm not at all talented, or hrewd. I'm quite ordinary, really. And Hitler killed my mother and father, and every single member of my family. My father was beaten to death, in broad daylight, in the street, and we think my mother was shot, but she might have starved to death in an awful camp. Some of my aunts and uncles and their families went up the chimney in a puff of smoke, or some just disappeared. All Jewish people are different. Thank you for telling us about the painting, and for installing the bench. Goodbye.'

Mummy took my hand, and we walked round the corner. Muriel said, 'I don't think she meant to be rude.'
Mummy was cross. 'That's not the point. In fact, that makes it worse. Why do people hate Jews so much?'
Muriel didn't say anything. I saw her touch Mummy's hand.
Muriel said, 'My parents were killed in The War as well. My dad was a sailor, and drowned when his ship was sunk. My mother was killed when a bomb hit our house. My granny was looking after me at her house, up the road, because my mum was expecting twins, and needed a rest.'
Mummy squeezed Muriel's hand. I thought Muriel was going to cry, but she stopped herself.
Mummy said, 'Shall we have a cup of tea?'
Muriel said, 'Good idea.'

I was worried that we would be going to have our cup of tea somewhere outside the gallery, and that our visit would end. How did Muriel know what I was thinking? She said, 'Oh, but will we have time to take Pippa to see the other painting?'
Mummy said she'd like to take us to the tea room, at the other end of the building. On the way there, we saw a young man drawing. He was sitting on a small stool, and had a very large sketchbook resting on his knees. In front of him was a large stone thing. As we were walking past, I caught a quick glimpse of what he was doing. Then I did something I hadn't done for a long time. I was holding Mummy's hand, and I stopped walking. This made her stop. She said, 'What is it? What is it, Pippa?'
I said, 'Please can I stay here for a little while?'
Mummy sighed. I said, 'It's all right. It doesn't matter.'

276

Mummy looked at me. She looked at the young man. She looked at the stone thing. She said, 'This is going to take a long time, isn't it?'

The young man looked up. He smiled at me. He said, 'Do you want to ask a question?'

Mummy said to him, 'My daughter is full of questions. I'm afraid she'll take up a lot of your time.' To me she said, 'Come on Pippa. Leave this gentleman to get on with his work.'

I didn't move. Mummy said, 'Come on Pippa.'

Still I didn't move.

Muriel crouched down beside me and said, 'What are the questions you want to ask?'

I said, 'Well, to start with, I want to know why he is only drawing a very small part of the... that thing. And what is he trying to tell us in his drawing, and what does he want us to think and feel, and what is his story?'

The young man laughed. He said, 'I'd love to tell you, but it would take me at least an hour to explain! Why don't you come back tomorrow afternoon with your mother and big sister? Then we will have more time to talk.'

Mummy said, 'You really are a charming young man. Will you really be here tomorrow? You see, it's a long journey for us to come here, and I don't want to set up an expectation in Pippa's mind, and then find that she's disappointed. She's very... well I'm not sure how to describe her.'

He smiled and said, 'Would you call her *intense*?'

'Oh yes, but in an entirely positive way. Artists love her.'

'Yes. I can imagine that they do. I was exactly the same as a child. I'll definitely be here. I've only just begun. I'm going to be making my own sculptures, and this is the start of the process. I love Henry Moore's work.'

Mummy held out her hand. 'By the way, my name's Ruth Dunbar. And you are?'

'McCusker. Matthew McCusker.'

'*The* Matthew McCusker?'

'Yes indeed, the only one!'

'I had no idea.'

277

'Most people don't. I try to keep my photograph out of the papers.'

Mummy said to me, 'Come here, Pippa.' I thought she was going to tell me off. She must have seen the expression on my face because she said, 'No, no, no.' She crouched down in front of me and took my hands in hers. She said in a very quiet voice, 'I'm not cross. Not at all. It's just that this gentleman is very busy. I know what you're like. You'll stand next to him for hours, and he won't get anything done. We can come back tomorrow, if you like. After all, we haven't seen *Carnation, Lily, Lily, Rose* yet. That's the second painting on Max's wall.'
She whispered something in my ear. I said, 'Sorry Mummy. I didn't know.'
Mummy was still crouching down, and said to the young man, 'Well, if you are here tomorrow afternoon, we will look out for you. But be prepared to be pestered by Pippa!'
The young man said to me, 'Are you an artist?' I felt my face going red, and I looked at my shoes. He persisted, 'Do you have a sketchbook?' I couldn't speak. He said, 'Well if you have one, bring it, and some of your favourite pencils. I'll arrange for the gallery to provide you with a stool.' Then he started drawing again and ignored me.

Mummy straightened herself up, and I thought she was going to fall over. Muriel grabbed her by the elbow and said, 'Whoops.'
Mummy laughed and said, 'Ladies of my age shouldn't get up too quickly.'
She took my hand, and we walked towards the tea room. Muriel didn't let go of Mummy's arm.
On the way, Mummy and I went to the toilet together. She had whispered in my ear that she had been bursting to do a wee. Muriel said she would order drinks for us, and a piece of cake each. When we went into the tea room, Muriel was sitting at a table. There was no tea or cakes. Muriel's cheeks were red. She said to Mummy, 'I'm afraid it's very expensive in here. I haven't got enough money to pay for us all.'

278

Mummy said, 'Don't be silly, I'll pay.' She gave Muriel a ten-shilling note and said, 'I'm still feeling a little light headed. Would you mind going with Pippa to choose something nice to eat?'

As we stood by the counter, I felt like I had known Muriel all my life. I wanted to hold her hand.

While we ate our tea, I asked Mummy if we could really come back the next day. She said, 'It'll be a great pleasure. I don't know why I didn't think of bringing you here before.' I knew why not.

Mummy felt much better after she had drunk her tea and eaten her cake, but she said she felt hot, and that it was very stuffy in the gallery, and we would have to go home soon.

Muriel said, 'Goodness! I don't even know where you both live!'

Mummy said, 'And I don't know where you live either!'

Muriel said that the nurses' home where she was living was near Kings Cross. She seemed a bit embarrassed to admit that.

Mummy was quiet. Muriel kept looking at Mummy's face, as if she was waiting for her to say something.

Mummy said, 'You are remarkable.'

Muriel's cheeks went red again. She said, 'Thank you, Ruth.'

Mummy said, 'How old do you think I am?'

Muriel smiled: 'I wouldn't like to say. But I'd guess that you are just the other side of thirty.'

Mummy looked pleased. She said, 'Muriel, it's going to be very hard to say goodbye to you.'

Muriel's cheeks went the reddest I had seen them all day. She looked at her plate. She started to cry. She didn't make a noise, but two enormous tears rolled down her cheeks. Mummy held my hand under the table. I couldn't be certain, but I think she put her other hand in Muriel's.

Mummy said to Muriel, 'I take tablets, that are meant to stop me from getting what the doctor calls *over-emotional*. They don't seem to be working very well at this moment.'

Muriel sniffed, and laughed at the same time. 'Maybe I need some of those. I have a friend who's always telling me that my feelings are too close to the surface.'

'Well he doesn't know what he's talking about.'

Muriel frowned and said, 'Not *he*. She's a she. There's no *he* in my life.'

The two of them stopped talking for a while. Muriel blew her nose and smiled at me. Mummy said, 'I feel a little unwell. have to get Pippa home. It seems so far away. I don't want to make any more mistakes.'

Muriel said, 'Do you want me to come with you to Liverpool Street, and help you get on the train?'

Mummy said, 'Yes. Yes please. That would be very kind, but as long as we aren't taking you out of your way.'

Muriel said, 'It would make me very happy.'

The train home

On the underground, I sat in between Muriel and Mummy. For most of the time, Muriel looked straight ahead of her. When we were a few stops away from Liverpool Street, I said to her 'Thank you for being with us today. It's been very interesting.'

Muriel said, 'Yes it has, hasn't it?' Then she looked ahead again. Her cheeks didn't seem very pink anymore.

Then I did something strange. I pulled Muriel's arm, and whispered in her ear, 'Have you and Mummy had an argument You don't seem to be friends anymore.'

I looked at Muriel's reflection in the window opposite. The corners of her mouth had gone down.

She said to me, 'Excuse me Pippa, but would you mind awfully if we swapped places?'

We did, and Muriel touched Mummy's arm and said something into her ear. Mummy frowned. I couldn't see their reflection anymore, because a man had got on and sat opposite us. He was watching Mummy and Muriel very closely. His eyes kept darting from one to the other, as each spoke. He looked worried, and then he smiled, and then he looked worried again.

We got off the train, and Mummy asked me to hold her hand. I reached over to Muriel, to see if she would hold my other hand, but she was out of reach, and slightly behind us. The station was very busy, with people pushing and shoving each other and running for trains. Mummy looked at her watch, and said that our train was due to leave in ten minutes, and we had better go and get on it.

Muriel said, 'Well, I had better say goodbye then.'

Mummy's grabbed Muriel's arm, so that she had to turn and look in Mummy's face. Mummy's words came out very loud and very fast. 'Do you have to go to work tomorrow?'

Muriel looked a bit surprised. 'Why?'

Mummy blushed.

Muriel said, 'Why Ruth? Why do you want to know?'

Mummy said, 'No. It's silly.'

Muriel wasn't smiling anymore. She said, 'You must tell me. Hurry up. Please. I could walk away now, and never see either of you again. I don't know why, but right now that seems to me to be the saddest thought in the whole world. I don't think I could bear it.'

Mummy almost shouted, 'Please come and stay with us tonight. Please say you will!'

Muriel held Mummy by the shoulders, and whispered something in Mummy's ear. Mummy pushed her away and said, 'Quick, go and get a ticket!'

Muriel turned to go, but Mummy grabbed her hand, 'No. Don't get a ticket. I don't want to lose you. If an inspector comes, I'll be delighted to pay your fine.'

All three of us ran for our train.

The train was full, and we had to stand up. Muriel said in a loud voice, 'Would anyone be so kind as to give up their seats for us? We are both expecting.'

Three men immediately stood up. When we were sitting down, Muriel nudged me and whispered, 'That works every time. I can't tell you how many babies I've had!'

She was sitting next to me, and Mummy sat opposite us. A man next to Mummy was doing the crossword in his copy of The

Times. Muriel leaned forward and tapped Mummy on her knee
Muriel put her hand by the side of her mouth and whispere
something.

Mummy laughed and said, 'Don't worry; you can wear a pair o
mine.'

Muriel's mouth was smiling, but I thought her eyes looked sad
Mummy's eyes were shining.

The man said to Mummy, 'When is your baby due?'

Mummy looked startled and said, 'What baby?'

The man chuckled to himself..

I must have fallen asleep, because I felt someone shakin;
my shoulder, and a man's voice saying, 'Come on sleepyhead
it's time you got off the train.' It was Uncle Geoff.

As we were walking out of the station, he explained that he ha
been in London, and had seen us at the station, and got in th
same carriage as us. But he hadn't been able to talk to us
because he had been squashed up against the door, at the far en
of the carriage. Mummy said to him, 'Geoff, this is Muriel. W
are friends.'

Uncle Geoff said that he was delighted to meet Muriel, and tha
we must come round for a cup of tea. He said that Peter and th
girls kept saying that they wanted to see me. The summe
holidays were nearly over, and soon they would be moving t
Chester.

It seemed the most natural thing in the world that Murie
was going to stay in our house. She talked with me, and pai
attention to me until I was tucked up in bed. She even kissed m
goodnight.

I said to her, 'Are you really going to stay here tonight?'

Muriel smiled and kissed me again. She said, 'It looks like it.'

She left the room and went downstairs. Mummy came up to tal
to me. She asked me if I liked Muriel. I said I did. Mummy aske
me why. I was a bit surprised, because she never asked me wha
I thought about anything.

I closed my eyes, and thought for a little while. Mummy aske
me if I was asleep. I said, 'When I am with Muriel, it's like bein;

282

with Bernadette and Frances. I can say anything to Muriel, and I know she will be interested.'

Mummy said, 'Hmm. Not like me then?'

I didn't say anything.

Mummy put her hands under the covers and tickled me. She said, 'You are a funny one, Philippa Dunbar.'

She kissed me goodnight and went downstairs.

I woke in the night, and felt very thirsty. I went quietly down the stairs, and saw a dim light coming from the living room. I could hear voices, talking very quietly. The door was slightly open, and I could just see Muriel and Mummy, sitting side by side. Muriel had her legs tucked up underneath her, and Mummy was sitting upright. Muriel's head was resting on Mummy's shoulder. They were holding hands. I listened as hard as I could to what they were saying.

I didn't know it then, but that day, and that moment, would change my life, forever.

A conversation with Matthew McCusker

The next morning, it took us a long time to get ready to go out. Mummy insisted on cooking us a nice big breakfast, and then running a bath for Muriel. Muriel explained that she could come with us to the Tate Gallery, but after that had to go back to work. She was going to work in the hospital all night.

On the train into London, Muriel remembered that she'd left her hat at our house. Mummy smiled and said, 'Good. I'm glad. That means you'll have to come back and get it.'

We arrived at the gallery, and went straight to see the stone thing. Matthew McCusker was there. He said to me, 'I'm so glad you could make it. I wondered if you might have changed your mind.'

He said to Mummy and Muriel, 'How do you do?' and shook both their hands.

Mummy had brought my large sketch book, my box of pencils and my painting equipment. She had carried it all the way, in two

283

bags. Muriel had offered to carry one of the bags but Mummy said, 'No thank you, my dear. I'm worried that you might drop it or forget it somewhere.'

I thought she was being rude, but she was smiling and her eyes were shining. Muriel's eyes were shining too.

Mummy said that she and Muriel would just have a look at the paintings and sculptures nearby, and that Matthew McCusker was to send me away when he had had enough of me. They didn't go far. They went to sit on a bench, and began talking to each other.

Mr McCusker asked me to look closely at the stone. He said it was called *Recumbent Figure 1938*.

I told him that I wanted to touch it. I wanted to run my hands all over it and feel it.

Mr McCusker said that he was sure that Henry Moore would like me to do exactly that, but there were very strict rules about not touching the exhibits. A man in a black uniform was watching us.

Mr McCusker said, 'I imagine this as a huge block of stone. I think of Henry Moore choosing it. Did he already have a plan for what it would look like, or did it just take shape as he chipped away at it? It's much easier when you have a model in front of you, because you know exactly what they look like, and you can use your sketches of the model as your starting point. But how did this take shape? Look at the surface here. Was that an accident, or did the artist choose to expose that pattern exactly in that spot? Once you have studied that pattern, you can't imagine it anywhere else. And as you look around the sculpture, it seems to move, almost like liquid.'

As he was talking, I could feel myself slipping into My Colour Dream. I could see the stone sticking out of a cliff. I could feel the stone's roughness, and then its smoothness and coldness.

The man in a black uniform came over and said to me, 'Be careful not to touch, young lady!'

r McCusker said to him, 'It's all right . I'll make sure that her
ngers don't come into contact with the stone.'

he man said, 'I'm sure you will, but the rules are the rules, even
r you, Mr McCusker.'

Mr McCusker explained that he was making lots of sketches
' what his sculpture was going to look like. Then he was going
make a mould, and use bronze.

asked him, 'Isn't that expensive? And won't it take a long
ne? And how will you have enough money to live, during all
e time that you are making it?'

r McCusker said, 'Oh, I'm lucky. People buy my work. My
ulpture has been *commissioned*. That means that the person
ho wants to buy it has already paid me some money in advance
r all my materials, and then he will pay me the rest when it's
nished.'

But how will he know if he's going to like it?'

'hat's the exciting part. He doesn't know.'

But what if he puts it in his garden, and his wife and friends
ink it's horrible?'

'hen he will sell it to someone else, who likes it more than he
oes.'

was quiet for a short while. Mr McCusker looked at me. He
dn't seem to be in a hurry to do any drawing. I asked him, 'Do
ou sell lots of pictures?'

'es, lots.'

Are there any hanging here?'

'es. Three.'

Mr McCusker started drawing. He was focusing on a small
art of the stone's surface, where there were some beautiful
apes, like clouds.

said to him, 'I hope you don't think I'm being rude, but you are
vfully slow. I do things very quickly. I see something, and look
it very closely. Then I remember all about it, and when I'm
ady to draw or paint, it all comes out in a rush.'

He didn't say anything. I thought perhaps I'd been rude about h
art. But he smiled at me and said, 'Every artist is differen
Would you like to draw something for me now?'

He watched me as I drew. He said, 'I know exactly what you'
doing. This is Henry Moore's sculpture, as if it were a re
person, isn't it?'

That was true

Mr McCusker asked if he could took more closely at m
sketch. He looked through the sketchbook, at all my drawin;
and watercolours, and then looked at my sketch again. He aske
'Have you met this person before?'

I told him it was my cousin Frances, and that I had seen her in
tin bath, on holiday, and now I was imagining her, as if she we
in front of me. He asked, 'Do you paint many people with i
clothes on?'

'Well yes. It was Lady Celia who got me interested in that.'

'Lady Celia?'

'Yes, Lady Celia Grange-Hoare.'

'You know her?'

So I explained about Uncle Eric, and how he and Mumn
used to be friends, but now he didn't visit us anymore. I told hi
about Mary, and how she was Lady Celia's companion, and ho
Muriel would probably be Mummy's companion.

Mr McCusker said, 'Your Uncle Eric. Is he by any chance Er
Baxter?'

'Yes, Eric Baxter. He writes about art.'

'I know him. He has written a lot about my work.'

'What does he say?'

'It's hard to tell. I think he doesn't like it, but is afraid to say so.

'Why?'

'Because my work is very popular; at the moment anyway. You
Uncle doesn't tend to like art that's *popular*. Funnily enough, h
wants to come and see me soon. He wants to talk about my fora
into the world of sculpture.'

286

I wanted to say to Matthew McCusker, 'That lady you thought was my big sister, is really twenty-six years old. We met her for the first time yesterday. When I was looking at them sitting on the settee in the night, I heard Mummy say, "I love my daughter, but something gets in the way when I try and get near her. Her holiday has been so important for her. I need some help to get back in touch with her. Do you think Pippa's strange?"

Muriel said, "No. Not strange. She's beautiful. Did you see the way that artist reacted to her? They were talking like equals."

Mummy said, "I need to break free. I need to live a life of my own. I need to work, and have a good income. I need to be free of the pills the doctor gives me. I need help to do all that."

There was a long silence.

Muriel asked Mummy, "Do you believe we were meant to meet?"

Mummy said, "After today, I can believe anything." Then one of them started crying. I thought it was Muriel, but then I heard her say to Mummy, "Come here. There, there. It's all right. It's going to be all right " '

I wanted to say all that to Matthew McCusker. I wanted to ask him if he knew what it all meant. But I didn't tell him anything. I knew not to.

The lady in the doorway

Mummy came back and said, 'Come on Pippa; it's time to leave Mr McCusker to get on with his work.'

He gave his card to Mummy and said, 'It's been a huge pleasure.'

He took my hand and said, 'I've really enjoyed myself. I hope you will keep in touch. You have a remarkable talent. You must keep painting and drawing and creating art as often as you can. I don't think I was as talented as you when I was your age.'

He said to Mummy, 'You must make sure that Pippa goes to the right school. One where the teachers appreciate art; and know how to nurture young artists. It's not just about giving her lots of paper and paint, but having teachers who understand your daughter, and who can guide her.'

287

He showed Mummy my drawing of Frances. I felt myself going red, and I wouldn't look at it.

Mr McCusker and I were still sitting on our small seats. Mummy crouched down behind me, so she could get a better view.

She said, 'How extraordinary. It's obviously Frances.'

Muriel bent over beside Mummy. She rested her hand on Mummy's shoulder.

Mr McCusker was still holding my hand and massaging my knuckles. He looked at Muriel. I turned to look at her face. She was smiling. And she kept her hand on Mummy's shoulder.

We walked towards the bus stop. I was in between Mummy and Muriel, and they each held one of my hands. We were passing a parade of shops, when we saw a large figure sitting in an office doorway. It was a lady wearing very dirty clothes. All around her were big cloth bags, full of what looked like rubbish. I thought we were going to walk past her, but Mummy stopped. She reached in her handbag and took out her purse. She took out a two-shilling piece and offered it to the lady. She had a very strong smell; like poo and wee and sweat and dirt all mixed together.

The lady said, 'I don't need money.' She reached in her coat pocket and gave Mummy a ten shilling note. 'But if you want to help me, then take this money, and go in that restaurant across the road, and ask them to give me a meal. They know what I like. And tell them to keep the change.'

Muriel said to her, 'Are you sure they will give it to us?'

The lady said, 'We'll see. I used to go in there, but I think I scare their customers away.' She didn't sound upset or angry. I was hoping she wouldn't smile, because I didn't want to see her teeth.

We crossed the road to the restaurant. I didn't want to go inside, but Mummy said, 'We must help that poor unfortunate lady.'

As soon as the manager saw us, he came over and said, 'One of my staff has been watching you. Every day it's the same. He

288

ood will be ready in a few minutes. Of course we can't have her coming in the restaurant. She knows that.'

Mummy asked him, 'What's wrong with her? Is she a beggar? She sounds very well-educated.'

He said, 'Nobody knows. Some people say she's from a wealthy family, but has become sick in the head. She wanders the streets all day, and collects rubbish from the bins. Every afternoon she settles down there for the night. Maybe it was The War that made her go mad. Someone said that she's a Jew, and her parents were killed in the camps, but she survived. Who knows? London's full of people like her. We call her *The Bag Lady*. Ah, here's her food.'

He handed Mummy a large cardboard plate with food on, and another cardboard plate on top.

We took it back to The Bag Lady. She took the plates without saying *thank you*.

Mummy asked, 'Do you have any family?'

The Bag Lady said, 'No questions.' She took a spoon out of her coat pocket and started eating. We went away, without saying *goodbye*.

Mummy said to Muriel, 'I don't know why, but I think I must be someone who is attracted to unusual people. I just can't walk past them. Why am I like that, Muriel?'

Muriel said, 'I think you know better than I do why that is.'

We walked a little further without talking. Then Muriel asked Mummy, 'Am I unusual?'

Mummy laughed and said, 'Oh yes, very unusual. But in the nicest possible way.'

They were quiet again. Mummy said, 'Do you think I'm unusual?'

Muriel said, 'Oh yes, very unusual. But in the nicest possible way.'

I was in between them, with each one holding one of my hands. As they talked, I could feel them squeezing and un-squeezing my hands. I felt like a human telephone, as they passed messages through me, towards each other.

289

We got on a bus, and sat downstairs, because Mummy didn't want to be with the smokers upstairs. I sat next to the window, and Muriel and Mummy sat next to each other.

Mummy said very quietly to Muriel, 'Muriel, I'm not sure how to say goodbye to you.'

Muriel said, 'Ruth, neither am I. Shall we just shake hands?'

Mummy sounded very serious, 'If we do that, you must know that it will mean so much more than just a handshake.'

Muriel put the palm of her hand to her mouth. I heard her kissing it quietly. She put her hand in Mummy's, and held it there. Somebody rang the bell for the bus to stop.

Muriel jumped up and said, 'Oh no! This is my stop! Bye bye!!' She blew me a kiss and jumped off the bus.

On the train home, Mummy and I sat side by side. She was very quiet, and looked straight ahead. Every so often, she took in a deep breath and sighed. I wondered if I should ask her what she was thinking. I wondered if I dared. I said, 'Thank you for a lovely day.'

Mummy smiled at me, 'Yes, it was quite an adventure, wasn't it?'

Then she was quiet again. After a while she said, 'I imagine that every day with Muriel must be a bit of an adventure. What do you think about her?'

I had been hoping that she would ask me that question. I had been rehearsing my answer: 'Well, I think she would be very easy to fall in love with.'

Mummy sighed. I wasn't sure what that sigh meant.

I wanted us to keep talking about Muriel. I knew exactly what I wanted to say. I put my hand in Mummy's. I closed my eyes and took a deep breath. I said, 'Mummy, I think it would be lovely if she could come and live with us.'

'Do you really think so?'

'Oh yes, I really do think so.'

I thought that would be all I would have to say. But I got a very big surprise, because Mummy asked me, 'Why? Why Pippa? Why do you think that Muriel should come and live with us, in

290

ur house? We hardly know her. We don't know anything about
er family, or what she's really like.'

I kept quiet. I hoped that Mummy would be quiet too. But she
said, 'Tell me Pippa, what are you thinking?'

I said, 'I really don't want to say it, because I'm frightened that
you will be cross with me, or even get angry.'

Mummy squeezed my hand. She said, 'Come and sit on my
knee.'

She put her arm around my shoulder and gave me a squeeze.
'Come on', she said, 'Tell me what you think.'

I whispered in her ear, 'I think she will make you very happy.'

I could feel the heat coming off Mummy's face and neck. They
were both bright red. I thought she was angry with me. I went
stiff, and tried to climb off her knee. She held me tight.

She said, 'I was hoping you'd think something like that, because
Muriel is coming to stay with us next Saturday.'

I sighed. Mummy said, 'So does that little sigh mean that you're
happy with the arrangement?'

When we got home we couldn't find my picture of Frances.
Mummy said, 'I think that Mr McCusker must have kept it, by
accident.'

Hokusai

We had one more week before the beginning of the new
school term. Mummy asked me to try on my school uniform, and
we discovered that nothing seemed to fit me anymore. My
school shoes were too tight, I could only just do up the buttons
on my blouses, and my pinafore dress was very uncomfortable to
wear. Mummy blamed it on all the fresh air I had been breathing,
and all my running around and climbing trees.

We went on the bus to the big shop that sold the uniforms.
The woman in the girls' department said that I could just about
fit into clothes for ten year-olds, but suggested mummy buy
clothes that were for older girls, as I seemed to be growing up
very fast. Afterwards we had lunch in a café, and for dessert
Mummy bought me a delicious ice cream called a *sorbet*. She

291

didn't order one for herself, but told the waiter that she wou
help me. We laughed, because she ate most of mine, and had
order us another one for us to share.

Then she took me to the Post Office, to help me open
Savings Account. She said it was very important for me to lea
how to manage my own money. On the way to the Post Offic
we looked in the window of a large toy shop. I saw a jigsa
puzzle of a painting of a huge blue wave. There were three boa
full of people, all rowing. In the top left-hand corner there w
some strange writing that looked like small beautiful drawings
couldn't take my eyes of that painting. The puzzle cost tw
shillings and sixpence,
Mummy said, 'Come along Pipsqueak.'
That made me laugh, because she'd never called me that before

In the Post Office, Mummy took a half a crown out of h
purse. She put it in my hand and said, 'I want you to rememb
this moment Pippa. It's the start of your savings.'
I said, 'I will Mummy. I will remember it.' But I was thinkir
that the half a crown could buy me the beautiful jigsaw.
The lady behind the counter took out a little grey book, a
wrote my name and address in it. I gave her my half a crow
and she wrote the amount in my book. Then she picked up
rubber stamper and pressed it into a small ink pad then, with
flourish, banged the stamper onto my book.
She said, 'There you are, my dear. What a sensible girl you ar
to start saving. And I hope to see you here very often, puttir
more money into your account.'

Mummy held my hand and said, 'Right my dear, it's time
go home.' I was happy; that's the only way to describe how
felt.
We stopped at the toy shop, and Mummy said, 'I have to go
and buy something for someone very special.' I was confuse
because I didn't think that Muriel would like toys.
Mummy took me to the counter and said to the lady, 'Please ca
I have the jigsaw puzzle with the Japanese painting on it?'

he brought it for us, and Mummy said to me, 'There you are, ippa. It's from me, to say *thank you* for being such a special irl.' My face went red, and I cried. Not loudly. I didn't make a oise, but some big tears came into my eyes, and seemed to pour ke a waterfall onto my cheeks.

Mummy crouched down and said, 'Oh dear. It's just a jigsaw uzzle,' and kissed my cheeks.

he lady said, 'How lovely. Let me get some nice wrapping aper, and wrap it up for you.'

was very thin pink tissue paper, and she tied it with a thin reen ribbon.

he said, 'Don't tell the manager I wrapped it for you, because e're only supposed to do that for children's birthdays.'

he painting was *The Great Wave off Kanagawa* by Katsushika Iokusai.

When we got home, Mummy said she was tired, and wanted lie down upstairs.

asked if I could go with her. I could feel her hesitate, so said, No. It's all right. I'll stay downstairs.'

Mummy shook her head, and said that it would be nice to lie own with me.

he took off her shoes and stockings and lay on her back, and uddled me, then fell asleep almost straight away. I wasn't leepy at all. I lay with Mummy for a while, then crept out of the oom. Mummy had left all my old school clothes on my bed, so took them downstairs. I found Mummy's sewing basket, and ook out my favourite tool of hers; a stitch unpicker. I sat by the indow, and removed all of the name tags from my old clothes. After a while, I heard Mummy calling my name. I ran upstairs, nd her door was open.

he said, 'Come here.' I jumped onto the bed and she gave me a ug. She said, 'I feel better now. What have you been up to?'

That evening, the phone rang. It was Auntie Julia. She told Mummy that they finally had a date for moving. It was next Monday; the day I was to restart school. Mummy invited them to ome over for tea on Sunday.

Nobody had ever been invited for a meal at our house.

I feel Mummy change

We spent the next few days at home. Mummy decided to
clean the house from top to bottom, and tidy the garden. The
house and garden looked clean enough to me, but Mummy said
that visitors needed to come to a clean house. I wanted to explain
that Auntie Julia and her family were friends, and they had been
to our house before. Then I remembered that they had really only
been inside our house when there had been a disaster. I could
feel a disaster building inside Mummy, as she scrubbed the floor
in the bathroom, and took all the pots and pans out from
underneath the sink, and started to wipe inside the cupboard.

Mummy was on her hands and knees with her head in the
cupboard. I offered to help, but she sighed and said, without
turning round, 'The best way you can help is to go out.'
I said, 'Mummy, please stop. Please talk to me.'
Mummy pulled her head out of the cupboard. She had dust on
her nose. She sneezed, and I laughed.
Mummy laughed too. She said, 'Pippa, why am I doing this?'
I said, 'Is it because Muriel is coming?'
She said, 'Yes. Yes it is. I want to make a good impression.'
I wanted to say, 'But you will scare her away if you behave like
this.' But I didn't say anything. It felt like a big balloon was
slowly deflating inside me.
Mummy said, 'You're right. I'm being very silly. Let's have a
cup of tea.'
For the rest of the day, we tidied up the garden.

Ursula came to me just before I was going to sleep. She
said, 'You were a very brave girl for talking to Mummy like
that.'

The day before Muriel came, it poured with rain. Mummy
said that it felt like autumn already. We sat at the kitchen table
and she showed me how to sew on my name tags.
She kept sighing, and said, 'This job is so tiresome.'

294

said, 'But I like it. While I'm doing it, I'm thinking about going back to school, and all the nice things I will do.'

She said, 'And I suppose I'm thinking about all the empty space there will be in my days, while you're at school. And I'm getting my terrible blocked feeling. I can feel a storm brewing in my head. I wish I hadn't invited Peter and his family and Muriel to come.'

heard a sound like an alarm bell going off in my head. I stood up and almost shouted at her, 'You can't mean that, surely. Please don't change your mind. Please!'

Mummy looked shocked. I said, 'Sorry Mummy, I'll go up to my room.'

She stopped looking shocked. She said, 'No. It's me who should say *sorry* to you. Of course Muriel can come, and it will be lovely to see Julia and her family once more. I suppose I'm feeling anxious about all these changes.'

said, 'What changes? There's only one change, isn't there? Peter will be going away. That's the only change, isn't it?'

Mummy didn't say anything. I put my hand on hers. I thought about Frances writhing on the floor in agony. I said, 'Why don't you have a nice warm bath?'

Mummy looked at me. She said, 'Like Frances?'

went red.

Mummy said, 'You have learned a lot, haven't you?' She smiled and squeezed my hand.

suddenly felt very tired, and wanted to cry.

Mummy said, 'What's wrong?'

couldn't put it into words. I said, 'I can't explain.'

Mummy said, 'Try. Please try.'

closed my eyes and pretended that Max was sitting in front of me. 'I've been so frightened of you all my life. I'm scared that if I say the wrong thing, then you will hate me.' Mummy tried to interrupt me, but I wouldn't stop. 'I want you to be different. I love it when you're nice to me. I know you are trying very hard to love me.'

Mummy didn't say anything. I opened my eyes, and she was holding her head in her hands. She said, 'I'm sorry Pippa. I'm getting better.'

I said, 'You won't make Muriel go away, will you?'
She whispered, 'No. I'll do my best not to.'

The Change comes

In the night, I asked Ursula if she thought I should have left Mummy alone. Ursula said she was very proud of me, for having said what I had been thinking and feeling.

In the morning I knocked on Mummy's door. There was no answer. Everything in front of my eyes started to look black.

Then I heard Mummy say, 'Pippa, I feel horrible today. I need to be on my own for a while. Can you make your own breakfast?'

I wanted to shout, *But Muriel is coming this morning!*

But instead I said, 'Yes, all right. Can I make you anything?'

I was cross. I was annoyed. I was… what was I? I was nine years old. I was only a child. I was feeling desperate. I was desperate for Muriel to come and stay with us. But I was sure that Mummy would scream and yell at her, and send her away.

Then there was a very loud knock at the door, and it was Muriel. She said, 'Hello Pippa! I've been looking forward to seeing you all week. But what's the matter?'

I had been trying to make my face look happy, but I must have failed. I said, 'Mummy's not feeling well, and I'm worried she's going to start shouting and you won't want to be with us.'

Muriel frowned. Then she smiled and said, 'Oh, it's that, is it? I've got you a present.'

She was wearing a long blue skirt. I was sure I had seen one like that before. Her hair was very untidy, as usual. Her shoes looked old and a bit dirty. She had on a small black velvet jacket, with a red brooch in the shape of a rose. She was carrying a small case.

She patted it and said, 'I've got the weekend off, and I'm staying here tonight. So I don't care what your mummy says to me. I'm not going anywhere.'

She went straight upstairs. I stood in the hallway. I heard her knock on Mummy's door. There was no answer. Muriel said, 'Ruth, let me in.' Nothing happened. Muriel knocked again. She

296

id, 'Ruth, I've come all this way to be with you. Please don't
rn me away.'
ne door opened. Muriel said, 'Thank you.'

I sat on the step outside the back door. Our neighbour's cat
as sitting on our lawn, in the sunshine. He was licking himself
l over. He turned and looked at me. I thought he was smiling.
uriel found me. She said, 'Listen Pippa. Mummy's very
nxious and is becoming very upset.'
said, 'I know. It's always like that.'
ne said, 'Yes, your mummy did warn me. I want to try and
ake her feel a little bit better. Would you mind if I spend time
ith her, on my own? It might be for a few hours. What would
ou like to do? I don't want you to feel that you've been pushed
ut, or that we don't want you to be here.'
said I didn't mind.
uriel asked me, 'Are you really sure you don't mind?'
held on to her arm. I said, 'I really am sure that I don't mind.
m glad that you're here. Please don't leave us.'
ne smiled, then kissed me on both cheeks and on the nose.
Don't be silly. I've been working like a slave all week. I've
een thinking about you all the time. I'm here to have a fun
eekend.'
nen she looked grave. 'You know what's wrong with your
ummy, don't you?'
t's her period.'
'es, that's true, but most of all, your Mummy is desperate for
ve. That's her problem.'
nd are you going to love her?'
'll do my best. Have you had any breakfast?'
old her I hadn't.
Me neither. I'm starving. Let's make some toast, and then I'll
ke something up to Mummy.'

By the time Muriel came downstairs again, I had finished
wing the name tags on all my new clothes. Mummy was
leep. Muriel looked in my eyes and said, 'Mummy told me to
ve you one of these.' She gave me a big kiss, on the lips.

She said that she had done something nice, to help Mummy relax.

I said, 'Can you show me what you did, so I can help Mummy relax when you aren't here?'

Muriel laughed. She swept her hair out of her eyes and said, 'C no. You see, I'm not going anywhere. Mummy's asked me stay and live with you both, and I said of course I would. Wh do you think about that?'

This was the beginning of what I think of as *Our Golden Tin Together*.

Muriel made us lunch, and took some upstairs to Mumm After about an hour, Muriel came down again, and we ma cakes together. We talked as we cooked. Muriel let me lick t bowl. I'm sure she left extra cake mix, just so I could have mo to eat. She asked me all sorts of questions; mainly abo Mummy, and about Peter and his family. When I talked abo the holiday, it seemed like it was something that had happened long time ago. I realised that I missed Peter and his siste Muriel explained that it is good to cry. She said that she cried a the time, and especially when other people cried. She said t doctors at the hospital had told her that she wasn't a very go nurse, because she kept crying all the time. She said that t patients didn't seem to mind. They told her it helped them cheer up.

Later in the afternoon, Muriel ran Mummy a bath. They stay in the bathroom together, and I heard them talking. I was gl that Muriel was a nurse. Afterwards, Mummy came downstai in her dressing gown. Her hair was damp and wet at the end which made the shoulders of her dressing gown wet. She sa she felt much better, and thanked me for being such a good girl.

I went to bed early. Muriel came up to see me. She told n to close my eyes, and put something in my hand. She said, 'Op your eyes, and you can see what my present is.'

It was a pendant in the shape of a star with six points, on a silv chain. She helped me to put it on, and brought me a hand mirr so I could see myself. It was beautiful.

played with it as I fell asleep, listening to Mummy and Muriel
talking and laughing downstairs. Ursula slept with me, and was
still there when I woke up.

I say goodbye to Peter

The next day was Sunday, and it rained all morning.
Mummy said that we might have to light the fire. But in the
afternoon the rain stopped, and the sun shone. I walked in the
garden, and watched the cat from next door trying to catch the
birds. Peter and the girls came out to see me. Bernadette picked
me up and gave me a big hug, and Frances kissed me, and said
how much she had missed me. Peter didn't say anything. The
girls went into the house, and left Peter and me looking at each
other.

I didn't know what to say to him. I said, 'I like your shoes.'

He said, 'That's a very stupid thing to say.'

I said, 'I know. That's why I said it.'

We both laughed, and then started to cry.

Peter said, 'I hate crying. Boys aren't supposed to cry.'

I said, 'That's a very stupid thing to say.'

He said,' I know. That's why I said it. I've got you a present.'

He ran indoors, and came back with something wrapped in pink
tissue paper and tied with a thin green ribbon. The paper had got
torn and I could see the lid of a jigsaw puzzle.

I said, 'Oh Peter, you shouldn't have. Is it all right if I kiss you?'

He said, 'Yes please. Bernadette has something for you too. I'm
a bit embarrassed about it, so please promise me you won't ever
tell anyone at school.'

When we went indoors, Auntie Julia and Mummy and
Muriel were putting the food on the table.

Peter asked me, 'Is Muriel your mummy's sister or cousin, or
something like that?'

I said, 'Something like that.'

After we had eaten, Bernadette gave me a very big brown
envelope, with the words DO NOT BEND stamped on it in big
red letters. It was a big photo of Peter and me sitting in the tin

299

bath together. Peter was splashing me and I was pretending to b cross.

Auntie Julia explained that the police had developed a Bernadette's photographs, but had only needed to use one. P Cooper had brought the spare photos round to the bungalow o the morning before the family left.

Mummy thought the photo was beautiful. For a few moments thought about the nasty man, but didn't say anything.

Muriel was very quiet, and spent most of her time in th kitchen. I wondered if Mummy ever had any brothers and sister She never mentioned any. Muriel was just like how I imagine Mummy's younger sister might have been, except that Mumm was very dark, and Muriel was very fair.

After Peter and his family had left, Muriel said that Mummy wa very lucky to have such nice friends.

Mummy said, 'I've had quite a horrible life in one way o another, but I'm lucky that people seem to rescue me in the end. Muriel and Mummy did the washing up together. Muriel sai 'You've rescued me too, you know.'

In bed, I looked at my two identical jigsaw puzzles. Even now when I look at that painting, I think of the love a mother ca have for her child, and the love a child has for her mother. An I'm reminded of the love that two children can have for eac other: as long as adults allow it. Other people look at tha painting, and see a huge wave about to drown lots of poo unfortunate sailors.

Mummy and Muriel both came to kiss me goodnight. Th next day Mummy took me back to school.

I don't like Mr Harris

My new class teacher was a man. He had been a soldier i The War, and shouted at us a lot. He wanted us to be quiet all th time, and would shout, 'Just dry up will you!' He used to leav the classroom a lot, and chose one of us to stand at th blackboard. If anyone was silly, then we were to write thei initials on the board. The first time he did it, he chose me to b what he called *his eyes and ears*. A new boy called Glenn said, 'He's gone out to have a fag in the toilet.'

Michelle laughed loudly, so I wrote both their initials on the board. They both looked very worried. Just as the door opened; I quickly rubbed their initials off with my hand.

In the playground, Michelle and Glenn asked me why I had rubbed their initials off. I said, 'Well, Mr Harris didn't tell me not to.'

Michelle said that it was a good job that I had done it, otherwise Harris would have probably pulled her knickers down and whacked her bare arse. And if he had done that, then she would have got her brother to come and beat me up. I tried to walk away, but she grabbed me and said, 'I'm only joking; my brother's just a baby.'

Glenn was excellent at drawing, but said he had a problem called *word blindness*. This meant that he couldn't read or write. Mr Harris didn't believe him, and told him he was lazy. I felt sorry for Glenn, because once a week we had a lesson where we all had to take turns to stand up and read out loud from a book. When it was Glenn's turn, he stood up, but no words came out. Mr Harris just sat at his desk and waited for Glenn to say something, but he never did.

At playtime I held Glenn's hand and said, 'If that was me, I'd have burst out crying.'

Glenn said, 'Boys aren't supposed to cry, and anyway, my big brother says I shouldn't give that bastard the pleasure of knowing that I'm angry.'

Whenever it was wet playtime, Glenn and I had drawing competitions. He loved to draw cars and motorbikes, and knights in armour. These were not my favourite subjects, so he always beat me.

Whenever he asked me about what I liked to draw, I didn't want to tell him about my drawings of people with no clothes on. So I'd tell him, 'Oh, Nature, and things like that.'

He had to admit that I was much better at drawing trees than he was.

301

Mr Harris liked to teach art. He would say, 'Today I'm going to show you how to draw a bottle.' Then he'd draw a bottle on the board and say, 'Look where the light is coming from, and see how it casts a shadow, and makes the bottle look like it is real and solid.'

That was very interesting, because although I could already draw things to make them look quite real, I didn't know how I did it.

But Glenn would mutter under his breath, 'He's just copying that from a book. He doesn't know how to draw.' Then Glenn drew a beautiful bottle, that looked nothing like the one we were all supposed to copy from the board.

It was obvious to all of us children that Mr Harris didn't like Glenn. He never praised Glenn for trying hard to learn to read and write, or said how good his drawings were, or how good he was at football. One afternoon, we were learning how to do lino cuts, and printing on cloth. Mr Harris made Glenn and me work together. Mr Harris gave everyone a square piece of thick lino and a sharp knife each. He told us to cut a design into the lino with the knife. I didn't know what my design was going to be. Glenn wanted to do a football, but couldn't cut into his square of lino. Mr Harris came over to see what we were doing. He picked up a ruler and tapped Glenn on the back of the head with it.

He said, 'Come on boy. You've been sitting there for an age, and have nothing to show for it.'

Glenn said, 'My knife is blunt. I can't cut anything.'

Mr Harris tutted and said, 'A bad workman always blames his tools. If you haven't cut something by the time I come back, then you will be staying in every playtime until it's finished.'

To me he said, 'Get a move on Philippa.'

He left the room, and put Michelle in charge of spying on the children. Glenn muttered to me, 'Harris' shit stinks.'

I was a bit surprised, 'Doesn't everyone's?'

Glenn said, 'It's what my big brother says, when someone at his work is being unfair to him.'

I took a ruler and made a very quick design on my tile. My ife was very sharp. Mr Harris came back in, and walked aight over to us. I pushed my tile in front of Glenn. Mr Harris :ked it up and inspected it. He said to Glenn, 'Not only are you 1alf-caste, but now you're drawing Jewish designs. You know 1at is written in The Bible? The Jews killed Jesus. Don't let me : that sort of thing in here again.'

hen I got home, I asked Mummy what a half-caste was, and if : Jews had killed Jesus. The next morning Mummy went to see ster in her office.

Michelle

Michelle was very funny. She reminded me of Bridget. She d me that she was born when her mum and dad were still :nagers, and that's why they looked so young. Her dad had en in the army, and her mum said that this was why they had eded to have something called a *shotgun wedding*.

ichelle loved boys. Once we were having lunch together, and : said to a boy sitting at our table, 'You have beautiful lips.' : said, 'Thanks Michelle,' and carried on eating his mashed tato.

)art from me, Michelle's other best friend was Janice. Michelle d Janice were always talking about boys. They seemed to have lifferent boyfriend every week. On Friday, Michelle would tell boy that she was in love with him, but by Wednesday she)uld have changed her mind, and offered him to Janice. Janice)uld then dump her current boyfriend, in favour of Michelle's ject. Janice's ex-boyfriend would then have a weekend of spair, but by Wednesday he would discover that Michelle was love with him. I found it all very confusing, and so did the ys.

Our new teacher, the one who replaced Mr Harris, was very ce, but she couldn't get us to behave. Then she would lose her mper, and hit the naughty boys on the backs of their legs with a)oden ruler. Her name was Miss Green, and she was often ill. ie day when Miss Green was ill, Sister Carmel was put in arge of our class. She walked with a limp, and usually looked

303

after children when they were ill, or when they had had an accident. She told us that we could choose a partner, and write a story together. Michelle chose me to be her partner. Sister Carmel liked Glenn, and she said she was going to spend the lesson helping him. Glenn didn't like to be helped by Sister Carmel, because she had bad breath.

Michelle began to whisper to me, about boys. She said she had learned a new word from a boy who had watched television programme for grown-ups. The word was *sexy*. I had never heard that word before. She said that it was a word that had just been invented, and that it meant *being rude*. She said that once she had seen a boy's thingy, and that had been a very *sexy* thing to do. Michelle didn't think you had to go to Confession to tell the priest about *being sexy*, because the priest wouldn't know what you were talking about, because it was new word. So he wouldn't know what prayers to make you say for penance

As a joke once, Michelle and Janice had told Vincent Collins that if he wanted to, he could come to Janice's house and watch Michelle and Janice having a bath together. Michelle said that Vincent got very excited, and told her that his thingy was sticking up. Michelle said that getting excited like that was *being sexy*.

I didn't know what to say to Michelle, but I felt my hand trembling. I thought of Peter and me under the tree, when I had felt The Thrill. I thought about us in the tin bath together. hadn't felt The Thrill then. I thought about Peter's willy sticking up when Bernadette gave him a bath. I didn't think that his willy had been sticking up when he was in the tin bath with me, but then again, I had tried very hard not to look.

I told Michelle we had to write something in our book otherwise we would get in trouble from Sister Carmel. I said 'Quick, let's write about a girl who finds a lost puppy.'
We made it up, and wrote it very quickly.

During lunchtime play, I asked Michelle if she would feel sexy if she was in the bath with Janice.

She said, 'Don't be stupid. Boys think girls are sexy, and girls think boys are sexy, but girls just think other girls look nice.'

I wanted to ask her how a girl knew if she was feeling sexy, but decided not to, in case she told me I was stupid again.

That night I thought about what Michelle had told me. Ursula said she had never heard of *sexy* before. She said she would ask the other angels what they thought. I asked Ursula if I should ask Mummy. She said not to, in case Mummy got angry, and went to complain to Sister about it. She had a think, then said, 'Why don't you ask Muriel? She's a nurse, and knows all about bodies.'

Michelle must have sensed that I was just as fascinated about the topic of *being sexy* as she was. She told me that she had once gone into her mum and dad's bedroom in the middle of the afternoon. Her mum and dad were in bed together, and they weren't even tired. Her dad told Michelle to *get lost*. Michelle pretended to go downstairs, but halfway down she crept back up again. She listened outside her parents' bedroom, and she heard her dad say that her mummy was *a sexy thing* and he couldn't keep his hands off her. Later on, Michelle asked her mum what they had been doing, and she went red and told her to mind her own business. Michelle told me that being sexy was private. She asked me if I could ask my mum about it.

Muriel

Muriel came to stay with us every weekend. She said that she still had to work in London for a few months longer, and had already paid her rent at the nurses' home, so needed to stay there. She said it was horrible, with nurses making lots of noise in the night, and during the day, when she was trying to sleep. She said that there was never enough space to have a proper bath, or cook, or even dry your clothes. She said it was like being at boarding school. Mummy tried to persuade Muriel to come and stay with us every night. But Muriel said it would be difficult, because

Rayners Park was quite far away, and sometimes she had to work in the night, so needed to live near the hospital.

Muriel left her dirty clothes at our house at the end of the weekends. Mummy washed them and hung them out to dry, and ironed them, and put them in a draw in her room. Once, Muriel came to our house wearing her nurse's uniform. She said that she had rushed straight from work, to catch the train to come and see us. A man on the underground had put his hand on her bottom. She looked around to see who it was, but all the men were looking straight ahead. She said that if she had seen who it was, she would have slapped his face. She said that lots of men on the train to Rayners Park had offered to give up their seats for her and quite a few men had chatted to her. She said she should wear her uniform more often, because usually men just ignored her and she had to stand up. Mummy laughed, and said she looked lovely in her uniform, and couldn't imagine how anyone could ignore Muriel. I certainly didn't want to ignore her. I had the same feelings for Muriel that I had for Frances and Bernadette.

Muriel stayed with us for three more weekends, and then said that she was finally able to come and live with us. The day before that, Mummy went through The Change again. I came home from school, and she was sitting at the kitchen table smoking a cigarette.
I said, 'Hello Mummy,' but she didn't take any notice of me.
I was just about to leave the room when she said, 'Come here Pippa.'
I didn't want to go to her, and stood by the door. Mummy stubbed her cigarette out in the ashtray and said,' I'm sorry Mummy's feeling wretched again. I've been to see Max, and I'm worn out. Please don't tell Muriel that I was smoking. She really doesn't like it.' I didn't know what to say. I had had a wretched day too.
Mummy said, 'Are you going to stand there being quiet, or are you going to tell me what you're thinking?'
I said, 'I think you are a good girl, Mummy.'
She said, 'I must go and lie down.'

said, 'Why don't you have a nice warm bath?'

She said, 'That's a lovely idea, but I've got so many things to do before Muriel comes.'

I wanted to say, 'Don't be so silly', but Mummy put her hands to her temples and squeezed them very hard, and shouted 'Aaargh! Aaaargh!' and then banged her hands hard on the table.

I jumped back in terror. Mummy looked at me. Her face was white with red blotches.

Then she said, 'I'm sorry. I'm sorry. I think a warm bath would be a very good idea. But first I'm going to make your tea. '

I said, 'I'm proud of you Mummy.'

I put lots of water in her bath, and when I came down there was scrambled eggs on toast on the table for me.

○   ○   ○   ○   ○   ○   ○   ○   ○   ○   ○   ○

Monday 8th November 1976

I have just woken up from a nightmare. I was driving a car, on a motorway. The traffic was very slow, and I had to overtake a huge lorry. As I overtook, the driver looked at me and waved. I waved back, and he smiled at me. Suddenly, I saw a young woman in the middle of the road. At first I thought she was a hitch-hiker, so I tried to attract her attention, to ask her to get in my car, because it was against the law to walk on a motorway. But she took no notice of me, and started to walk on the grass, by the side of the road. I could tell from her face and the way that she walked, that there was something wrong with her. Then she took off her shoes and started walking very quickly. I thought to myself, 'She is definitely mentally ill. Thank goodness I didn't invite her into my car.' But then she started screaming, and running as fast as she could. A young man was running after her. He had taken his shirt off, so I could see his powerful chest. He started racing after the young woman. She ran off the side of the road, down a slope, so I couldn't see what they were doing. But then I saw him coming up the slope. He was dragging the young woman along the ground, by her ponytail. She was yelling and screaming for mercy. The man waved and smiled at me. I don't

307

know what was more shocking; the woman screaming, or the man's smile.

Today I asked again if I could have a key to my caravan because I was frightened in the night, and worried that someone might come in during the day, and steal my things. She said that I was being childish for being frightened, and that nobody had ever had anything stolen. I wanted to say, 'Well, in that case why do you lock the house door before you go to bed?' But decided not to. I wanted to ask for an extra blanket, but She told me to do something in the kitchen. I'll have to use my coat as a blanket.

o   o   o   o   o   o   o   o   o   o   o   o   o

Vincent brings rude pictures into school
Mummy went to bed after her bath, but left her door open. I didn't go into her room, but said, 'Goodnight Mummy.' I heard her breathing deeply, so knew she was asleep. I went into my room, and thought about all the awful things that were worrying me. I looked at the curtains, and wished for Ursula to come. She came straight away.
I cried, so she held my hand and said, 'Tell me all about it.' I explained that on Monday Michelle had told me a secret. She said that Vincent had been to the park with his friends, and seen pages of a magazine floating in the stream. They could see that one of the pages had a picture of a lady with no clothes on, so they all got long sticks and fished all the pages out of the water. They put them on the bank to dry. Vincent told Michelle that all the boys were so excited that their willies were sticking up. Michelle asked him how he knew that, and he said that they had all looked at each other's willies.

Michelle said that she was going to tell Vincent to bring the photos into school, for her to look at. I begged her not to, but she took no notice of me. Vincent hid the photos in his school bag, and at lunchtime play he went with Michelle to the bottom of the field, and showed them to her. She said that one was of a lady on e beach, and you could see her Bristols and her bottom. nother photo showed a lady in the snow, building a snowman. e was smiling, but she looked freezing. Michelle said she just ughed, because the ladies looked just like her mum. Vincent t cross and said that they were very rude pictures, and she ouldn't laugh, because they made his willy stick up. Michelle ked Vincent to prove it, so he did.

Michelle had the front page of the magazine hidden in her ck. She said we should go to the toilets together, and she ould show it to me. I didn't want to look, but she said I had to, cause I was a better reader than her, and she couldn't read hat the magazine was called. I went with her to the toilets, and e locked ourselves in a cubicle. She took the paper out of her ck. The magazine was called *Health and Efficiency*, and there as a photo of a lady wearing a bikini.

n Wednesday, Sister came to our classroom, and said she anted to see Vincent in her office. He started to cry. He didn't me back into class. Michelle told us that someone had told ster that Vincent had got rude pictures in his bag. Sister had und them. She had hit Vincent very hard with a ruler, and rung s parents, and they had come to take him home.

Vincent didn't come to school on Thursday. The day after at, we were getting changed for our Music and Movement sson in the hall. Vincent was getting changed next to me, and I w big red marks on his legs. He said that was where Sister had him very hard. Then he showed me his back. It was covered th red and navy blue lines. He said his dad had taken off his lt and beaten him. He said he could hardly sit down because s bottom hurt so much.

thought I was going to be sick. My hands were shaking so uch, I couldn't undo my buttons. Sister was taking our class, cause Miss was ill again. She came over and asked me what as the matter.

e saw Vincent's back and said, 'That serves you right.'

y legs felt wobbly, and I had to sit down. Sister told me to rry up and get changed. I said I couldn't, so she said, 'Hurry

up, or you'll be the first girl in this school to feel my ruler on t
back of your legs.'

Ursula held my hand and said I must tell a grown-up
about this. I said I couldn't, because I didn't want to talk abc
being sexy, and about Vincent's willy sticking up. Ursula said
only needed to talk about Vincent getting beaten, and Sis
threatening to hit me.

I told Ursula that I really couldn't keep my worries in a
longer. I was beginning to feel like Mummy, when she had T
Change. I thought I was going to explode.

Ursula said she would go away, and ask the other angels abc
what they thought I should do. I begged her not to leave me
my own, but she disappeared.

I walked up and down my room. I looked out of the window.
was still light outside. I got out my paints, and put my b
sketchbook on my desk. I closed my eyes and saw a painting
front of me.

Ursula came back, just as I was getting into bed. She sa
that I was a *poor thing*, and that she felt very sorry for Vince
Nobody deserved to be hit with a belt. She said that the ang
had told her that I must tell Mummy and Muriel everything. S
said that the angels knew that Muriel was a nurse, and th
nurses understood these things. If Mummy was upset, then s
could talk to Muriel about it. If she was really, really upset, th
she could go and tell Max.

I kissed Ursula, and told her I loved her, and that I was so luc
that she slept with me and kept me company.

Muriel explains

Muriel arrived the next morning, and brought a suitcase. S
said that inside was almost everything that she owned in t
whole wide world. Mummy started to cook us a spec
breakfast, but one of the eggs she was cracking broke, and lots
pieces of shell went in the frying pan.

310

Mummy said, 'Oh damn!' and said she had to sit down. Muriel put her arm round Mummy and said that we would cook the breakfast for her.

Mummy said, 'You are a lamb.'

Muriel said, 'Baah' and I laughed.

Mummy smiled, and crossed her arms over her tummy.

We were all very quiet during breakfast. Mummy said she couldn't eat anything, so Muriel said she would help Mummy, by eating all her food. She said she was starving, because she hadn't eaten properly for days. Mummy said to Muriel, 'I'm sorry, but I haven't quite got your room ready.'

I closed my eyes. I saw a big wooden door closing, and heard someone on the other side of it sliding a big metal bolt, to shut it tight. Muriel was pushing on the door and shouting, 'Let me in! Ruth, please don't lock me out!'

I don't know how long I had closed my eyes for, but when I opened them Muriel and Mummy were both looking at me, with worried expressions on their faces.

Muriel said, 'Pippa, are you all right?'

I said I was, but I realised I wasn't feeling all right at all. I felt dizzy, and I could feel all my breakfast rising up from my tummy into my mouth. I managed to swallow it back down, but I had the horrible feeling of hot tears in my eyes. I heard myself saying, 'I don't understand. Why does Muriel have to sleep in another room? Why doesn't she sleep with Mummy? It's horrible to be lonely in the night, and have nobody to talk to. It was lovely to sleep in bed with Peter on holiday, and I miss that a lot.'

Mummy said, 'Goodness.'

Muriel said, 'Well, I'm not sure what to say.'

Then I heard myself telling them all about Michelle and Vincent, and the rude pictures in *Health and Efficiency*, and Vincent's back, and Sister threatening to hit me, and I wanted to know all about *being sexy*, because it was really worrying me, and that Ursula had said I should tell them all about it.

It all came out in a rush, just like I was sicking up the words.

Mummy got up quickly and left the room. Muriel got up too. She held me gently by the shoulders, and kissed me on the cheek, and said in my ear, 'You're a very good girl. We love you very much. Don't worry. Everything will be all right, in the end.' She took my hand, and we found Mummy sitting on the bottom step of the stairs. Muriel sat down next to her and I sat on her knee.

Muriel started talking to me, and I shut my eyes very tightly. Muriel's clothes smelled of damp and hospital. She said, ' would love to sleep with Mummy. I feel lonely in the night sometimes, and it's very reassuring to wake up and feel someone next to you; especially if it's someone that you love and can trust. We haven't talked about it yet, but it's what I want to do. What do you think, Ruth?'

I couldn't see Mummy's face. Muriel said, 'Ruth? What do you think?'

Mummy said, 'Yes. I agree. Let's not make a fuss about it. Let's all try and be happy.'

Muriel said, 'So is that a *yes*? A *yes* to you and I sleeping in the same room? And in the same bed?'

Mummy whispered, 'Yes. Yes please.'

Muriel then asked her, 'And what do you think about pictures of ladies with nothing on? The Tate Gallery is full of them.'

Mummy said, 'Well, there's nothing wrong with taking picture of people to show how lovely they are, and so we can see what people look like, but it's not right to put them in magazines, so that people can get all excited about them.'

I said that Miss Dawson had said the same thing to me. Muriel said, 'I think the human body is beautiful. I've seen so many of them recently, so I should know. And what about this thing that people call *being sexy*? Well I'll tell you what I think.' She held me tighter. 'I think it's lovely when grown-ups who love each other can cuddle up and feel nice together. It's the loveliest feeling in the world. It's not rude at all. But it is rude to take photographs of ladies, so that men will get excited about i. That's not nice at all. What do you think Mummy?'

312

Mummy said, 'I agree. I've always thought that. There's nothing wrong with having no clothes on. It's just that some people are a bit shy about it, and you have to respect that.'

Muriel said, 'And as for *Health and Efficiency*, it's not rude at all. I've read it. It's all about people who like to have holidays in the sunshine, and get the sun and fresh air all over their bodies. There are photographs of pretty young ladies, but you can see photos of men as well. And there are photos of older people too, and people of all different shapes and sizes.'

Mummy was a bit surprised. She said, 'Really Muriel, I had no idea you read that sort of thing.'

Muriel laughed, 'Oh I don't mind at all. I love the sun. You should try it sometime.'

Then Mummy and Muriel were very serious. Mummy said, 'If that poor boy was beaten black and blue for looking at a health magazine, then it's too awful to think about.'

Muriel said, 'I wonder what was going through Sister's mind as she looked at the photographs. It's wicked.'

Mummy was quiet. Muriel asked her, 'What are you thinking, Ruth?

Mummy said, 'I feel so sad. Sad and angry.'

Muriel kissed me on the cheek. 'And what do you think Pippa?'

I had been in a kind of dream, where their voices were coming from the distance; like when I was dozing on the train. I said, 'I love you Muriel. I loved you right from the start. I know you love Mummy too. I knew it straight away. Thank you for coming to look after us. I hope you have a nice time living with us.'

Muriel didn't say anything. She sniffed. Mummy took her hanky out of her sleeve and passed it to Muriel. Muriel blew her nose.

Mummy said, 'I'd take Pippa out of that school if I could, but as you know, my hands are tied.'

Muriel didn't respond to that. She said, 'What shall we all do today? I was going to suggest a walk in the park, but who knows what we might find there!'

I said, 'I'd love to do some painting.'

Mummy said, 'I don't think I can go very far in my present condition. Pippa was very kind to me yesterday, but today the floodgates are about to open; I can feel it.'

Muriel squeezed me again. She laughed and said, 'If I don't go to the toilet this minute, then my floodgates will open too!'

We all laughed.

I decided to paint a picture of the cat from next door, and to write Peter a letter, to tell him how much I missed him. I looked at the painting I had done the night before. I couldn't remember anything about actually painting it. There were lots of painted shapes that showed Vincent's bruises, a lady with no clothes on, Sister beating Vincent, and Peter's willy sticking up. There was a bright orange background. I had called the painting, *Jesus loves us all.*

Muriel knocked on my bedroom door and came in. She said that Mummy was in the bath, and afterwards would need to have a lie down. She sat on my bed and asked me all about the painting. I wasn't at all shy about explaining it to her.

I asked Muriel if she wanted to lie down with Mummy.

She said, 'I'm sure there'll be plenty of time for that in the future.'

We go to the park

Muriel said she was bursting to go for a walk. She went to check that Mummy was all right, and then we walked to the park, hand in hand. She was very surprised when I told her that I had never been there before. When she asked me why not, I explained that Mummy had been ill, so hadn't really taken me anywhere. There was a playground in the park, with swings and a roundabout and a see-saw. There were some children there who I recognised from school. They were playing on the swings and invited me to join them. I realised that I hadn't been on a swing since Uncle Eric had taken me to the village playground when I was five years old.

314

One of the children jumped off her swing, and said I could ve a go. I got on and she started to push me. I don't think that e was pushing me particularly hard, but I lost my ncentration and fell off, and banged me knee on the ground. It lly didn't hurt that much, but when I looked at the hole in my hts and saw some blood coming out, I started to cry. Actually was more like wailing.

ie girl looked frightened, and said to Muriel, 'Honest Miss, I dn't push 'er very 'ard.'

uriel said, 'I know; it's all right. Don't worry. Everyone has cidents.'

ie boy on the other swing said, 'What a stupid cry-baby girl.'

ie girl said, 'Shut up you fat shit,' and then she said to Muriel, orry Miss, but us girls 'ave got to stick up for ourselves, don't ?'

uriel said, 'Yeh, but 'e ain't fat is 'e?'

ie girl looked astonished. Then she laughed. 'Nah, but callin' n a skinny shit don't sound right, neiver.' The she said, 'Is you m London?'

uriel laughed and said;, 'Yes I am, actually, and I used to eak just like you when I was your age!'

Muriel took me over to a bench, and waited for me to stop ying. I said, 'I'm sorry for crying. You must think I'm a baby.' ie said, 'Not at all. But perhaps you aren't just crying about ur knee. Are you crying about other hurts?'

iis was true. I suppose I had been holding everything in for a ng time, and it all had to come out somehow. Muriel took ummy's hanky out of her pocket and licked it and dabbed my azed knee. She said, 'It's not very hygienic to mix my snot and it with your blood. I hope your Mummy doesn't want this nky back, because I'm going to keep it forever.'

We went for a walk around the park. It was the loveliest eling; to hold this lady's hand, and have her all to myself. We dn't say anything for a while. Then Muriel asked me what I is thinking about.

aid, 'I'm not hurt anymore.'

315

She sighed and said, 'The hurts we carry inside us c sometimes take a lot longer to heal than the ones on the outside We were quiet again. Then Muriel said, to herself, 'It must very difficult for a mother to look after her child all on her ow

I thought about when we lived in Northumberland, and h the dustbin had caught fire on Christmas Eve, and how Mumi used to get drunk all on her own, and send me to bed with food inside me.

I didn't want to talk about that. Instead I said, 'I don't kno anything about my daddy.'

There was another long silence.

Muriel put her arm round my shoulder and said, 'You can alwa ask your Mummy.'

I said, 'I'm not sure if I want to know any more about him.'

I don't know why I said that. I felt that Muriel was a daddy : me now, but I wasn't quite ready to say that to her.

Television

We had a small black and white television set in the fro room, but we rarely watched it. Mummy wasn't keen on i watching any programmes apart from *Children's Hour*. S particularly didn't like me to watch *The News*. I didn't mi because I wanted to spend as much of my free time as possible the garden, or painting, or writing stories. But Muriel lov watching TV. She especially liked *Top of the Pops*, and wou sing along to all the hits.

Mummy told her that she was an overgrown teenager, a Muriel laughed at her and said, 'I'll take that as a complime then!'

Mummy said, 'I hope you aren't going to become a b influence on my daughter.'

Muriel frowned, so Mummy said quickly, 'Oh no. You know was only teasing. You could never be a bad influence.'

On Sundays, I went to Mass with Mummy, while Mur stayed at home and cooked the lunch. In the afternoon v sometimes watched a film together. If the film was borin

316

Mummy and Muriel would go upstairs and have a rest. One afternoon we saw a wonderful film with Fred Astaire and Ginger Rogers. They were wearing roller skates and dancing round a skating rink. They began to sing a song. Muriel shouted, 'Oh I love this one!' It was called *Let's Call the Whole Thing Off*, and was about the different ways that Fred and Ginger pronounced words. Muriel sang it all the way through. She grabbed me, and started dancing me around the room. Mummy didn't join in with the singing.

Muriel said to her, 'Are you all right Ruth? Shall we stop?'

Mummy smiled, but her eyes looked sad. She said, 'Pippa's father loved that song. It was one of the few he could sing in tune. And he did call the whole thing off.'

Muriel turned down the sound on the TV. She said, 'I'm sorry. I didn't know about the song.'

Mummy reached out to hold Muriel's hand. 'No, no. Carry on. All of those things have got to come out sometime. Can we go for a walk?'

I said, 'Why don't you two have a rest, and I'll watch the rest of the film? I don't mind.'

They looked at each other. I knew that they thought that was a good idea. Muriel said, 'I'd like to go to the park. We can all have a rest later.'

Mummy smiled.

I wasn't sure why, but I knew that we had just shared a very important moment together. I was pleased with myself, and I was pleased with Mummy.

Singing Duets

One of my favourite cartoons was *Tom and Jerry*. Muriel said she loved it too, and told me to call her every time it was on, so we could watch it together. We saw one where Tom the cat is serenading his new cat girlfriend. She is upstairs in the house, and he is in the alley, playing his double bass, and singing up to her. He sings *Is You Is Or Is You Ain't my Baby?* Muriel and I laughed so much, and I was surprised that she knew the words of the song.

317

She told me it was by Louis Jordan, and that she loved jazz, an any music that made her want to get up and dance.

I said I didn't know if Mummy liked to dance or not.

Muriel said, 'Oh well, I can answer that. If Mummy's in the rig mood, she can dance me out of the kitchen. And she can sin too.'

After tea, Mummy was doing the washing up, and Muri had just started the ironing. I was sitting at the table, and Muri winked at me. She began singing, 'All I want is a roo somewhere.'

Mummy looked around and sang, 'Far away from the cold nig air.' She kept singing and stopped washing up. Muriel lifted u her skirt and held it above her knees, and started dancing. Sh jumped on and off the chairs, and at one point I thought she wa going to climb on the table. She grabbed Mummy, and danc with her around the kitchen. When they had both finished, the sat down at the table with me and laughed.

Muriel sniffed her armpit. She said, 'I'm all sweaty.' Mumm said, 'Me too!' I could smell them both.

I sat opposite Muriel and Mummy. Muriel had her hand o top of Mummy's. Muriel said to her, 'You have a lovely voic Can you sing something else?'

Mummy looked serious. 'In the dark days, I'd look for a cinem in London where they were showing *My Fair Lady*. I'd sit the for hours. I must have seen it at least 25 times. I love Audre Hepburn. She suffered in The War, you know. When I came t England as a little girl, I had to learn English very quickly, an soon I had a broad Norfolk accent. When I went to Malaya, m husband told me I had to stop talking like a turnip head, so h paid for me to have lessons, so I could learn to talk posh, ju like Audrey Hepburn in *My Fair Lady*.'

Muriel laughed. 'And I was a little cock sparrow from the Ea End. After my parents were killed, my grandmother sent me t boarding school, where the posh girls teased me for saying *ai* and *wotcha*. I learned to be posh too, just like Eliza Doolittle.'

Mummy tells the truth

Muriel kicked off one of her slippers, and put her bare foot on top of mine. She said to Mummy, 'Please sing us something.'

Mummy said, 'I'm shy. I haven't sung anything for a long time.'

Muriel said, 'Don't worry about me. I'll close my eyes and pretend you are someone else.'

Mummy sang a song in French. I think it was called *La Viande Rose*. When she had finished, Muriel opened her eyes and asked Mummy where she had heard such a beautiful song.

Mummy said to her, 'It's not a happy story.'

I felt Muriel's foot pressing on mine. She said, 'Well tell it anyway.'

'When I lived with my stepmother and stepfather in Norfolk, they often had people to stay with them. People who were *down on their luck*, because of The War. One of them was a French lady. She had a job picking peas for one of the farmers. She used to sing that song a lot. Every time she heard a plane overhead, she'd start screaming. One day she didn't come home from work, and was missing for a few days. She was found dead in one of the canals. It shook me up terribly.'

Muriel's foot was moving up and down on top of mine as Mummy was talking.

'Then, when I met my husband-to-be, Pippa's father, he liked me to sing to him. He especially liked me to sing in French. I never told him that the songs reminded me of a French woman who had gone off her head and killed herself.'

I felt Muriel's hand on my knee. She asked Mummy, 'Why did you get married?' Mummy closed her eyes. Muriel rubbed my knee gently. She didn't look at me; just at Mummy.

Mummy sighed. 'I was seduced, I suppose. Not just physically, but swept away by his charm, and lovely clothes and manners, and his voice and Scottish accent. I was only a child really. I was desperate to get away from that village in Norfolk. I wasn't ungrateful to my step-parents, but no matter how hard I tried to be English, I still felt like a foreigner. I was in the park once and a man tried to... to force himself on me. I managed to push him away. He called me a *dirty German slag*. I didn't even know

who he was, but he must have known all about me. I knew I ha
to get away from the village.

'I was working in a local factory. I was helping in th
accounts department, because I was very good at maths. Andre
was a friend of the owner. They had been at public schoc
together in Scotland. Andrew came to visit the factory one day
and saw me. He started chatting to me, and told me that he wa
looking for staff to work with him abroad, and would I b
interested? He didn't ask any of the other girls in the office, s
obviously I was very flattered. Not long after we met, he phone
me at the office, and invited me to see him in London. I staye
with him in a hotel for a weekend, and then a few weeks later
left my job, and he put me up in a hotel for a month. My step
parents were very upset about that. Later, he told me it had bee
love at first sight, but now I know that he was just bein
charming.

'Then I found out I was pregnant, so Andrew had to marr
me. He said he was ashamed of himself, and he didn't want t
tell his family. He wanted to have a very quiet wedding. Hi
father was furious with him, and insisted on coming to th
wedding. We didn't get married in a Catholic church; just in
registry office. A few weeks later, we left for Malaya. We wer
on a big ship. I started to feel very sick. It wasn't seasicknes
but the sickness you get when you are pregnant. I really thoug
I was going to die. The ship's doctor was very kind, but he sai
that a ship was the worst place in the world if you are expectin
a baby. Then one night I lost the baby. I could see that Andre
was relieved. He tried to hide his feelings, but I knew he wa
glad.

'We stayed in a lovely house on a plantation. Andrew wa
away a lot, looking for new properties to buy. When he cam
home I found I... I didn't like to be... I didn't like to be close t
him anymore. I can't explain why.'
Muriel said, 'I'm sure you can.'
'But I'd rather not. It's too painful.'

uriel said, 'And it's painful if you don't explain it. It's painful
 us. How am I…how are we… going to know what to think?
 e might spend the rest of our lives blaming you.'

's not a question of *blame*.' Mummy's voice rose and got
 uder. Muriel had both her feet on top of mine.

 ummy opened her eyes and turned to look at Muriel. 'It's
 out being honest, and taking responsibility for our mistakes.
 d taking responsibility when we have done the wrong thing on
 rpose. He was a very attractive man. I'm sure he still is. And
 had a lot of money. People were attracted to him.

'Then finally I got pregnant again, and I discovered that
 hough Andrew liked the idea of having children, he didn't like
 e reality. He was shocked by how my body was changing. He
 ggested I move into a small bungalow on the plantation, with
 own swimming pool. He spent more and more time away
 m home, and I spent as much time as I could in the swimming
 ol. I loved being pregnant. For a start, I didn't have any more
 riods, and that was such a relief. But more than anything, I
 ved my little baby growing inside me. I knew my baby would
 a little girl. I just knew it.

'Pippa came out so quickly. There was just me and the
 aid. She was the same age as me, and didn't speak any English
 all, but she showed me exactly what to do. I don't know how
 e knew. Your father tried his best to be a good father, but it
 emed that he lost interest. He had been brought up to believe
 at children should be seen and not heard. He did his best
 ough, and that's the most important thing.

'I became very friendly with the maid. Because she had
 lped me give birth and care for Pippa, some kind of door in my
 art opened for her. I taught her how to speak English, and she
 ught me how to speak Malay and Chinese. She was very
 ever, so she stopped being just a maid, and I put her in charge
 Pippa. She loved her as if she were her own child.'
 en Mummy spoke directly to me. 'Your Father was always
 viting business colleagues, and clients and friends, to come and

321

stay. One of them was quite vulgar. He liked to watch the th
of us in the swimming pool. One night, your father went away
business, and left this man on his own with us. I heard so
awful noises from down by the pool, and when I ran down th
I saw that he was… was… was attacking my friend. So I hit h
I hit him quite hard, but he walked off, laughing. He was dru
My friend was hurt quite badly. She was terribly upset, so I ma
her sleep in my bed, while I went in to sleep with you. My frie
was crying a lot in the night, so I got into bed and tried
comfort her. In the morning she was still upset, so I helped her
have a bath. One of the other maids came in, and saw
together.

'I didn't know it, but the horrible man sent a message
your father, and said all sorts of terrible things about me. He s
that he had discovered me kissing my friend by the pool, a
that's why I had hit him. He said a maid had seen me and r
friend in the bath together as well. That wasn't true. I was sitt
talking to my friend, while she was trying to get clean. Y
father came rushing back from his business trip, and told me
leave. He gave me enough money to get a plane back to Engla
I refused to go. I took you in my arms and locked myself into
little house. I stayed there with you for three weeks. My frie
was sent away in disgrace.

'Your father said he was sorry for being horrible to me,
he insisted that we leave. He sent his lawyer to talk to me.
was a very nice man, and terribly embarrassed. He gave me
sorts of advice about what to ask your father for, financia
speaking. Your father wanted to divorce me, but I refused
reminded him that he was a Catholic, and that the Chu
doesn't allow divorce. So finally we agreed that I should bri
you back to England, and that he would pay for all reasonal
expenses for us. The lawyer made sure that this included medi
fees for us both. Your father wanted to have you sent to
Catholic boarding school, but I said, 'Over my dead body.'
made me agree that you should have, in his words, *A Go
Catholic Education*, and that you should be brought up as

ood Catholic, and not as a Jew. He was very insistent on that. I
ought that was a very small thing to agree to, if it meant that I
uld be together with you.

'When we came back to England, his friend Eric Baxter and
ur father's agent, Mr Shepherd, arranged for us to live in
rious places'.
e took a deep breath and looked at Muriel. 'When we came
ck to England I went mad. I went completely mad.'
uriel squeezed Mummy's hand and said, 'Anyone would have
lt the same as you. How could they not? Don't blame
urself.'
ummy blew her nose. 'I do blame myself. And I know that I
ust take responsibility for it all too. I don't blame Andrew
ymore. He's a good man, and he has helped me in so many
ays, even though he must despair of me and the things I've
ne. But I wonder if he feels any kind of responsibility. I tried
tell him the truth, but it was too late for him. He just wouldn't
sten to me.'

Mummy put both of her hands on the back of her head, and
en banged her elbows hard on the table. She laughed and said,
)w that hurt!' and then her tears came pouring out onto the
ble. They wouldn't stop. Her shoulders were moving up and
)wn, and I thought she was choking.
uriel said to me, 'Quick, let's get her upstairs.'
e helped Mummy climb the stairs, and helped her into their
droom. Muriel told her to lie on the bed. She helped Mummy
ke off her cardigan and told her to get into bed. Then Muriel
eled off her jumper and got in beside Mummy.
said, 'What shall I do? Shall I go downstairs, or out in the
rden?'
ummy had buried her head in her pillow, and was still sobbing
udly. Muriel was stroking her back. Muriel said, 'No. Come in
ith us. We are going to make this better.'
was so glad to be with them both.

When Mummy finally stopped crying, she told me ho
sorry she was for being a bad mother. I stroked the back of h
neck and said that I loved her, and that she had always done h
best. Then she started crying again; but much quieter this tim
Finally, she went to sleep. Muriel gave me a cuddle, and told n
I was the best girl in the world. She held me for a long time, ar
played with my hair. Then she fell asleep too. I was a bit like tl
filling in the middle of a Mummy and Muriel sandwich.

I crept downstairs. We must have left the back door ope
because the cat was sitting on the kitchen floor. He looked at m
and then carried on licking his bottom.

Saturday swimming lessons with Muriel
Muriel told me that she loved swimming, and especial
diving. I was delighted when she asked Mummy if she cou
take me swimming on Saturday mornings. I knew wh
swimming in the sea was like, but had never been to a swimmir
pool before. Muriel tried to persuade Mummy to come with u
At first she refused, but then agreed to sit and watch us. We ha
to take a bus to get to the pool, which was near the centre of tl
big town. I had seen swimming pools on TV, and they wei
always shiny and light and modern. Our pool was in a big, ol
dingy building in Olive Street. Mummy said that it didn't loc
very promising, but I loved everything about it: the chlorir
smell, the children shouting, the way the sound bounced arour
off the walls, the way the sunlight rested on the water and tl
tiles.

Mummy said goodbye to us in the foyer, and Muriel boug
two tickets. I hadn't really thought about getting changed. On tl
way into the changing room, an attendant gave us a grey wi
basket each, to put our clothes in. There was a space at tl
bottom to put your shoes, tights and underwear, and then a lor
piece of metal with a hook on the end for you to hang your oth
clothes on. Each basket had a number on it. When you ge
changed you gave your basket to the attendant, and she hung

p, and gave you a little metal circle with your number on, and a safety pin to clip it onto your costume.

We got changed in a room with a tiled floor, and wooden benches round the outside and down the middle. Women and girls were sitting and standing, getting dressed or undressed. Muriel started to take her clothes off, but I just stood watching her. She said, 'Come on Pippa. Let's get changed.'

I just stood there. An old lady in the corner was sitting completely naked on a bench, drying in between her toes with her towel. A mother was trying very hard to dry her toddler, while he laughed and tried to wriggle away whenever he could. Muriel whispered in my ear, 'It's all right darling; you don't need to be shy.'

I wasn't shy. I was fascinated.

Muriel changed into her costume, and asked me to help her put on her swimming cap. She had so much hair, that she was having a lot of difficulty getting all of it underneath. She went over to help the mother with her toddler. The mother was very pleased, because she said she was freezing cold. She said, 'It's lovely in here, but the water is like ice today.'

And it was. Everybody seemed to be jumping around and shouting and having a lovely time, but I put my foot in the water and wanted to get dressed again, straight away. Muriel said, 'Watch me!' and dived in the water. A young man wearing a yellow shirt and white shorts blew a whistle and shouted at Muriel, 'Oi! No diving in the shallow end!'

I looked up and saw Mummy sitting above the pool, leaning on a railing. She waved at me. A little boy came running by and jumped in the pool. The water splashed all over me and I lost my balance and fell in. The shock of the cold was like nothing I had experienced before. I swallowed some water and was coughing and spluttering. Muriel swam over to me and gave me a kiss and said, 'You are a brave girl. When I was your age, I was terrified of water. Come and swim with me.'

I loved the water and I loved Muriel. I didn't care anymore about being freezing.

I showed Muriel all the things I had learned from Frances and she said she thought that Frances had been an excellent teacher. After about 20 minute I was freezing, so Muriel said was time for her to have a few dives from the diving board, and then we could get out. She showed me how to hold onto the side of the pool, and pull myself along towards the deep end. Up t then, we had been in the shallow end, and I stayed at the dept where the water came up no further than my shoulders. Now, as pulled myself along, I could see that if I let go, then I wouldn be able to put my feet on the bottom. I was out of my dept Muriel swam alongside me and saw that I was looking anxiou. She said, 'Don't worry. I'll never ask you to do anything that you won't be able to manage. I'll look after you.'

We came to a place where the tiles of the bottom of the poo were a darker blue, and suddenly the bottom of the pool slope down sharply. This was the deep end, and I was in it. Murie gave me a kiss and said, 'What a brave girl you are. Wait her and I'll do a few dives.' She helped me to get out and to sit o the edge, with my feet dangling in the water.

The man in the yellow shirt came over to me and said, 'Excus me Miss, can you swim?' I said I couldn't and he said, 'The dee end is only for swimmers. It's very dangerous here if you can swim.'

I said, 'But that's my Mummy's friend, and she told me to sta here. If I move, then she might not find me.'

He said, 'OK, but I'll stay here until she comes over.'

He kept looking at Muriel. She climbed the ladder up to th highest board. A man was there, and he seemed very nervou about jumping off. I didn't want Muriel to be up so high. Sh waved at me, and then at Mummy. The man dived off, but as h hit the water there was a bang and he made a huge splash Muriel was just about to dive, when two young men swan underneath the diving board. The man in yellow blew his whistl and shouted for them to move out of the way. I imagined Murie landing on top of them. By this time, there were quite a fev

326

eople watching Muriel. The young men swam over and stayed
ext to me. One said, 'Look at the arse on that!'
he other young man nudged him, and nodded his head towards
ie. He said, 'Shut up, Jerry.'

Muriel spread her arms out wide and stood on tiptoe. She
ent her knees and then it seemed like she was throwing herself
ɔ in the air. For a second, I thought she had stopped in mid-air.
he bent forward and touched her toes and then straightened up
id formed a perfect point with her body, and pierced the water
ke a spear. There was hardly a splash.
he young man called Jerry said 'Fucking hell. Did you see
at?'
furiel swam over to me and said, 'Oh, I needed that!'
s we walked away, one of the men whistled after us. I had
ard that kind of whistle before. Once Mummy and I had been
alking past a building site. Some builders whistled at Mummy.
ie of them shouted, 'Nice leg's darling, but where's yer
ruppnies?'
ie said, 'Men can be such animals sometimes.'

Before we got changed, we had to have a shower. There
ere three shower heads attached to the wall. There were two
dies under two of the showers. They still had their swimming
stumes on.
uriel peeled her costume off and said, 'Come on Pippa, hurry
and get warm.'
ie pulled me under the shower. I saw both of the ladies looking
Muriel. Muriel explained that if I took my costume off, then I
ɔuld feel much warmer when I got dried, so I took it off. The
dies kept watching us. We wrapped our towels around
rselves and walked as quickly as we could to get our clothes
ɔm the attendant, then sat down in the changing room.

Muriel dried herself off, but I went into My Colour Dream. I
uldn't stop looking at her. I heard her say, 'Come on Pippa, or
u'll get freezing.' I just watched her.

I felt her rubbing my leg and heard her say, 'Come on darli
You're starting to shiver.' She started to rub me down with
towel. I stopped dreaming, and got myself dried and dressed
quickly as I could. When I was finished, Muriel went to do
wee, and I sat on the bench waiting for her.
One of the ladies from the shower said to me, 'Is that your
sister?'
I said, 'She's Mummy's friend.'
The lady said, 'Lucky mummy.'

Mummy was waiting for us in the foyer. She wanted
know why we had taken so long to get changed. Muriel sa
'Your daughter went into a trance, so I had to help her get drie
Mummy smiled and said, 'Oh. I can just imagine what's going
happen now.' She said to Muriel, 'I loved your dive.'
Muriel said, 'I did it for you.'
Mummy said to me, 'You were having such fun. You must co
every Saturday.'
I asked Mummy if she would come in the water with us n
time, and she said, 'We'll see.'

We went to a café, and I had a fried egg, beans and chi
Muriel said she was starving. I was very quiet. I was thinki
about what the young man had said about Muriel's bottom. I w
thinking about her beautiful dive. But most of all I was thinki
about her in the changing room. I had felt thrilled. I knew I h
to paint her.
Mummy said, 'What are you thinking, darling?' Since meeti
Muriel, she had begun calling me *darling*, and I liked it ve
much.
'I'm thinking about painting something.'
Muriel said, 'Something or someone?'
'Someone.'
'Let me guess… someone who was getting changed?'
'Well first of all I want to paint you diving.'
'And then?' I went red, and didn't want to say.
Mummy squeezed my hand and said, 'Well whatever you pai
let's hope that Mr McCusker doesn't steal it!'

328

uriel held my other hand and said, 'Imagine me being turned
to a stone thing, and being stuck on a plinth in the Tate
allery!'

s we were leaving the café, Muriel realised that she had left her
wel and swimming costume in the changing room. We went
ck to the pool. Mummy waited outside, while Muriel and I
ent back into the foyer of the building. The young lifeguard
as selling tickets. He went in to get Muriel's towel and
stume. He handed them to her, then winked at her and said,
here you are.'

e thanked him, and was just about to turn round with me,
hen the young man said to Muriel, 'Excuse me Miss. I loved
ur diving. My name's Maurice. If you'd fancy coming for a
p of tea sometime, you know where to find me.'

uriel smiled at him and said, 'That's very kind of you, but I'm
ready spoken for.'

e said, 'Lucky fellow.'

whispered to Muriel, 'What does that mean; *already spoken
r*?

e whispered back, 'It means that I already have a boyfriend.'

vas shocked. 'But is that true? Have you got a boyfriend?'

Jo. Of course not. But it is true, in a way. I have a very special
iend.'

elt a huge sense of relief.

My nightmares

Muriel had brought excitement to our lives. Knowing that
e was going to live with us forever filled me with love and
armth. These feelings took away some of my horror at the
rrible things that Mummy had told us about. and the awful
ings that had happened to me.

. the Tate Gallery she had described her family being killed in
e most horrific ways. A lady had killed herself by jumping in
e canal. Mummy had been in a park, and a man had forced
mself on her. One of Daddy's friends had attacked Mummy's
aid, and told lies about her. A nasty man showed us his stiff
illy and dressed up like a lady. He had kidnapped children like
s, and then killed them.

329

As I lay in bed at night, I turned these scenes around in my hea
All of this horror became an image of The Nasty Man, hidir
outside our house, and waiting to force himself onto the three
us. When I was little, I found some beautiful shiny conkers, ar
decided to turn them into conker jam. I put them in a jar
water, screwed on the lid, then forgot about them. A couple
months later, I found the jar and opened the lid. There was
awful stink, and the water was bubbling, as if the conkers ha
come alive, and were furious with me for trying to drown them
was horrified. My nightmares were like that; horrific ar
stinking, and they left me with a feeling that I couldn't shake or
no matter how hard I tried.

On top of this fear of The Nasty Man, I couldn't sto
thinking about poor Vincent being beaten for looking at nake
ladies. And I kept wondering about the lady in rags lookir
through rubbish bins and sitting in a doorway, eating off pap
plates. She wasn't a poor beggar. She had more money in h
pocket than Muriel. Perhaps she had had a breakdown? Did sl
drink too much whisky? Would Mummy become like that?
Another general worry was about the young men who had bee
rude about Muriel's bottom. What might they say about Mumn
when they saw her? Might they say something horrible about h
breasts being small, and the way her nipples stuck out when the
were cold? And how might Mummy react if they whistled
her?
And mixed up with all this fear and worry was the memory
Mummy telling the truth about Daddy. She had said that he wa
a good man, even though he had sent both of us away.

My fear and confusion developed into a story that I neve
wrote down, but kept playing over and over in my mind, like
TV programme. In my story, a girl called Fiona went for a wal
in the woods every day. She didn't realise that a Nasty Man wa
following her, until one day he attacked her and forced himse
on her with his stiff willy. Fiona fought and fought and scream
and screamed, until finally a good man heard her. But instead
protecting Fiona, the good man blamed her for being in tl

330

oods on her own. The Nasty Man and the good man were
iends, and The Nasty Man told lies that the good man believed.
iona was banished from her family, and was forced to live in
1e woods, where she was always terrified of being attacked.

I wanted desperately to talk to Muriel. But every day I had
) go to school, and when I came home I would watch Children's
lour, have my tea and do my homework, and then I would feel
) tired, that I had to go to bed straight away. Mummy would
:ad me a story and give me a kiss goodnight, but I didn't feel
1at I could tell her about my worries. I didn't want to be a
urden to her. But, if I'm honest, I still didn't quite trust her
1ough to tell her about my deepest thought and fears. It was no
·onder that I was plagued by nightmares

One night, I had a terrible nightmare and fell out of bed. In
1y dream I was diving off the board with Mummy. Muriel was
wimming underneath us. We both hit the water and just missed
er. Then Muriel took me up to an even higher diving board.
1ummy was in the water below us, and we hit the water with a
uge splash. I couldn't tell if we had hit Mummy or not, but I
new she was under the water somewhere, but I couldn't find
er.

Muriel came in and picked me up. She said, 'Shh. Shh. Try
ot to wake Mummy.' She put me back into bed, and I told her
ll about my dream. She got into bed with me and cuddled me
nd said, 'Goodness, that was an awful dream.'
'hen she asked me if I was worried about anything.
said, 'Not really.'
he said, 'When someone says *not really,* it means that they
:ally are. You can tell me.'
Well, I have been thinking about that man who asked you if
ou'd like to go for a cup of tea.'
1uriel laughed and said, 'Oh him. He's just a nice young man,
vho was being kind.'
You won't leave us, will you?'
)h no. I'm not going anywhere.'

'Are you spoken for?'

'What do you think?'

I knew she was. Mummy had spoken for her.

I was quiet for a while, and Muriel thought I was asleep. Sh got out of bed very carefully. She knelt down and gave me kiss. She whispered, 'I love you, you beautiful child.'

I whispered back, 'Thank you Muriel, but can I ask a mor questions?'

Muriel chuckled and asked me, 'Shall I get back into bed?'

I told her that I would be as quick as I could. I started m questions. 'Why haven't you had a baby?'

'You need a husband for that.'

'Don't you want a husband?'

'No. I used to think I did, but now I don't.'

'So you'll never have a baby?'

'No. I don't think so.'

'Won't that be a shame?'

'Why are you asking me, Pippa? Would like a baby brother sister? Is that why you're asking?'

'No. I'm just trying to understand things. I like the way thing are. We're so much happier since you've been here. I think baby might make things very complicated.'

Muriel laughed. She said, 'I agree. I'm very happy with the wa things are too. And so is Mummy.'

She gave me another kiss and went back to Mummy's bed

We swim, and I learn about tenderness

The following Saturday morning, the three of us went to th swimming pool again. This time we went very early, so we wer the first customers there. Muriel said that if the pool was empty then she could do lots of diving, and she wanted me to see th water in the pool when it was completely still. She said that was one of her favourite sights. Mummy agreed to swim with u All the way to the pool, she kept saying how nervous she wa about going in the water. I told her that I had been frightened first, but now I found it very exciting.

mmy said, 'I'm not frightened of the water. I hate my
mming costume. You've got a new costume that looks nice. I
ow you don't like the colour I chose, but mine is so old and
rible. I don't want people to see me looking like something
m before The War.'

w I had another thing to worry about; what would the young
n say if they saw Mummy's awful swimming costume? I
ndered if I had the courage to suggest that Muriel and
mmy swap costumes.

We were the only people in the changing room. I felt shy
out getting changed in front of Mummy, and I sensed that she
n't want to be naked in front of me, either. Muriel, as usual,
s not at all bothered. Mummy took out her bathing costume. I
ld see why she hated it. It was navy blue and had two hard
s inside, where her breasts had to go. She said to Muriel, 'I
l look a fright. You must promise not to laugh at me.'
ent into the toilet, so I wouldn't see Mummy getting changed.
ile I was in the toilet, I heard Muriel laugh and say, 'You're
ht; it's not the most beautiful costume in the world, but Ruth,
u would look lovely in a sack.'
mmy said, 'Shh. But I'd rather swim naked than wear this
ful thing.'
riel laughed again and said, 'What a lovely thought! We
uld try it sometime. I know just the place. Let me wear your
tume, and you can wear mine.'

The water in the pool was almost still. Muriel dived in and
am up to the deep end. As she swam, she parted the water, and
ecame almost still again behind her.
mmy said, 'Watch me Pippa!' She dived in and chased after
riel. I walked along beside her, by the side of the pool. She
s making powerful strokes as she moved her arms forward
l out, while at the same times stretching her legs out wide, and
n kicking them together. She looked strong, but I couldn't
nk of a word to describe how she moved.

333

I stood still at the place where the bottom of the pool slo
sharply, and the water changed colour. Mummy swam to the
of the pool, then climbed out and dived in again. She sta
under the water until she reached me. She popped up
shouted, 'It's freezing in here, but lovely! Come in and show
what you've learned from Frances and Muriel!'
We heard a small splash, and realised that Muriel had just di
in.

More and more people came into the pool, while Mum
and I swam and splashed about. Muriel spent the whole ti
diving. Her dives looked beautiful, but her swimming costu
looked awful. Her bottom fitted into the costume, but her brea
were squashed together, and I wondered if they might pop
for everyone to see. I looked around, but couldn't see the na
young men. The young lifeguard was watching Muriel v
closely.
After about three quarters of an hour, Mummy said she v
freezing, so the three of us went to get changed. I decided th
wasn't going to be shy anymore, so peeled off my costume
got in the shower. Mummy must have been still feeling s
because she kept her costume on in the shower. When she
out, she wrapped her towel round her and managed to take
costume off without anybody seeing her body.

The young lady with the toddler, who we had met
previous week, was trying to get her little boy undressed. He v
wriggling around, so Mummy offered to hold him, so his mot
could get undressed and put her costume on. The toddler grab
Mummy's towel, and somehow it slipped to the floor. She turn
her back to me, and the little boy laughed and looked at me o
Mummy's shoulder.
Mummy said to me, 'He's so cuddly. You were just the sa
when you were a baby. I carried you everywhere. Your fat
said that you would grow up to be spoiled rotten. He believ
that babies should be left to cry, and not picked up. I could ne
agree to that.'

So there was my mother, standing completely naked in front
me, while holding someone else's baby, and talking about
ddy. She was acting as if these were the most normal things in
e world to do. I looked at Muriel. She was looking at Mummy.
ummy handed the toddler back to his mother, and picked up
r towel from the floor. She sat next to Muriel, who ran her
ngers gently across Mummy's shoulders. Mummy shivered and
niled. She was just like the cat in our garden, when I had found
e exact spot where he liked to be stroked. Then Muriel moved
r hand slowly down Mummy's back. She said to Mummy,
hat mole is getting bigger. You really ought to get it looked
,

uriel took off her swimsuit. She had two bright red circles on
r breasts. She said, 'I'm so glad to be released from that thing.
felt like a straitjacket. Every time my friends hit the water, I
ought they were going to be crushed to pieces. Those hard cups
e lethal! Where did you get it from?'

ummy said, 'I bought it from the Gamages catalogue when I
rst came to England. It was designed for *the lady with a less-
eveloped bust*. I was feeling so terrible, and I thought that
vimming would make me feel better. I never went swimming,
.t started drinking whisky instead.'

The young mother was watching Mummy and Muriel, and
retending that she wasn't listening. Her little boy grabbed at her
vimming costume.

he lady said to him, 'Not now Alex; surely you can't be hungry
ter your huge breakfast?' He grabbed at her again. She pulled
own her costume, and Alex started feeding from one of her
reasts.

he lady said to us, 'I hope you don't mind. I can go somewhere
se if you like.'

ummy tutted and said to her, 'Don't be silly. It's the most
atural thing in the world. We don't mind at all, do we Muriel?
nd Pippa, what do you think?'

was fascinated, but didn't say so; though it must have been
ovious from the way I was staring at her.

Muriel asked her, 'Isn't he a little old for that? And what do your husband think?'

The lady switched Alex to her other breast. 'Oh there are defini advantages for all of us. When we lived in Kenya, I noticed th lots of the African women do it for as long as they possibly ca It's a way of...' She looked towards me. I knew that she w thinking carefully about what words to use, so that I wouldr understand. 'It's a way to help you plan your family.'

She put her breasts back in her costume. Alex burped.

She said to Mummy and Muriel, 'Thank you for helping n again.' Then she blushed bright red and said, 'It's lovely to s two people showing such tenderness. I think that is what missing in the world; we're not allowed to be tender towar each other. I had a friend at boarding school who reminds me you.'

Then she picked up her toddler and rushed out. Mummy's fa was bright red. Muriel said, 'Well, well.' Then she chased aft the mother.

When Muriel came back in, she had a big smile on her face.

Mummy talks about her emotions

We went to Gamages, and Mummy bought me a beautif light blue-grey duffel coat. I was delighted, because she said th I could wear it straight away. Afterwards, we went to the café f lunch. Mummy said that being in the water, and holding bat Alex, and seeing the young mother breastfeeding, had made h feel very *emotional*. It reminded her of when she and her Mal: friend would spend hours in the pool with me. She said that th never bothered to wear swimsuits, and it had been one of t most wonderful experiences in her life. She said to Muriel, ' wasn't just a wonderful physical experience. It was somethir very profound. I often thought about it, when I was in n deepest despair. Thinking of those moments saved me fro going under, if you know what I mean.'

They looked at each other. I think they were feeling somethir very profound.

336

Muriel asked her, 'What's the difference between feeling *emotional* and feeling *upset*?'

Mummy explained that, to her, being *emotional* meant that she could have strong feelings without them becoming overwhelming, and making her feel out of control. She thought that *being upset* was a very powerful feeling that she used to experience a lot, and it was something that she was learning to understand and cope with. If she had too much to do, or if powerful thoughts and memories began to overtake her, then she called this *feeling overwrought*. If she was very worried about something, then this was *anxiety* or *feeling anxious.*

Then she said, 'Thank goodness I don't drink alcohol and have to take tablets anymore. Alcohol made me feel far too emotional and upset, but the tablets made me feel nothing at all. I couldn't have done it without you, Muriel. Thank you.'

Muriel said, 'Or without Max.'

Mummy frowned, then she smiled. 'One could say that I'm a very lucky unlucky person, really. I'm lucky to be alive, but unlucky to have been so unhappily married. But then I'm very lucky that Andrew pays for me to have the best treatment in London. And his money pays for us to live in a nice house.'

Muriel said, 'He doesn't pay for me.'

Mummy frowned. She stayed frowning as they talked. She said to Muriel, 'I understand exactly how you feel, and why you won't allow me to pay for anything for you, but you must stop giving me money; I just don't need it.'

Muriel said, 'Well, if anyone asks about me, then we can say, with all honesty, that I'm just your lodger.'

Mummy was still frowning. I wanted her to smile. She said, 'Let's talk about this at another time. You know that I don't want the subject of money to come between us.'

Muriel didn't smile, but she put her hand on top of Mummy's, and squeezed it. She said, 'You're right, but I think I'd like to find a job soon, all the same.'

They were quiet for a while. Mummy looked out of the window. It was pouring with rain, and people were hurrying by with their umbrellas open. Muriel leaned forward towards me and tapped me on the knee, under the table. I looked in her eye and she winked at me.

She said to Mummy, 'Oh Ruth, I almost forgot. I have somethin for you.'

She took out a package, and slid it across the table to Mummy.

It was a swimming costume; exactly the same as the one that th young mother had been wearing. Mummy's eyes filled wi tears. She tried to say something, but stopped and took her hank out and dabbed her eyes. Then she said, 'Oh Muriel! Yo shouldn't have. You have no idea what you... what this means me.' She cried some more.

Muriel explained that the mother had looked so lovely in h costume, and seemed to be about the same height as Mumm which was quite tall, though her *friends* were considerab larger. When Muriel had run after her, it was to ask her whe she had got her costume from. She said that she had bought it i Gamages, so Muriel popped into the fashionwear departme while Mummy and I were choosing my coat.

I didn't worry about Mummy crying, because I knew that sh was full of emotion.

Muriel ordered our sorbets for dessert. Mummy said, 'I use to be able to swim the whole length underwater,, before I starte smoking.'

I said to her, 'I wish I had a word to describe how you looke when you were doing the breasts stroke.'

Muriel said, 'I know one. I was watching her when I was up o the diving board. I think the best word to use is *graceful*. An she was doing the *breast stroke.*'

'That's what I said.'

'No you didn't. What you said means something completel different.'

Mummy said, 'Muriel! That's enough! You can be quite rud sometimes. And fancy referring to your breasts as your *friends* It sounded like she was telling Muriel off, but she had a bi smile on her face.

riel smiled back and said, 'Well that's what they are. I've
'ays thought of them like that.'
mmy laughed and was about to say something, but looked at
and changed her mind. I knew that she had been about to say
nething about the size of her own chest.

I learn about divorce

Every Sunday, I saw Michelle and her family at Mass.
ually her little brother misbehaved, and had to be taken out by
dad. Michelle's dad had a very short haircut called a *crew-*
. We used to feel sorry for boys in our school who had crew-
s, because it usually meant that their parents didn't have
ugh money to pay a barber, so they cut their son's hair
mselves. Or perhaps they didn't care what their son looked
:, so they told the barber to cut his hair however he liked, or,
rst of all, the boy had head lice. I thought Michelle's dad was
y handsome, and that his crew-cut suited him. Michelle
eed with me when I told her that I liked her dad's hair. She
d she liked the prickly feeling she got when she ran her hands
:r his head.

chelle told me that her mum had once said that if Michelle's
l ever grew a beard, then she would divorce him. I had heard
word *divorce* before, but didn't know what it meant.
chelle said that it meant that a mum and dad didn't love each
er anymore, so they went to live in separate houses. She said
: the man and woman who owned the fish and chip shop had
divorced. The man had married another lady, who now
rked with him, serving the fish and chips. Michelle said the
v lady was very mean with the chips, and grumbled if you
ped yourself to the vinegar and used too much. She wondered
his was why the Catholics didn't like people to get divorced,
l wouldn't allow them to get married to someone else.

One Sunday, I saw Michelle and her family at Mass. Her
l had started to grow a beard. I prayed to God that He would
p Michelle's mum and dad from getting divorced. In school I
:ed Michelle about her dad's beard. She said that her mum had
:n joking about getting divorced, but she really did think that

beards were horrible. Her mum had told her dad that if he k
the beard, then there would be no *nookie* for him. I had ne
heard of *nookie* before.

Michelle said, 'You know, making babies.' She made a ci
with the fingers of her left hand and poked her right point
finger in and out of it. The horrible boys on the bus had m
that sign to me. I had an idea that Michelle was talking ab
being sexy. I told her I didn't understand what she meant.

She stuck her tongue out at me and said, 'Well if you d
know, then I ain't gunna tell yer.'

At that moment, I really hated Michelle, and didn't wan
be her friend anymore. For some reason I felt a sadness co
into me, like I had breathed in a big grey cloud. I thought
Peter, and realised how much I missed him. He would ne
have talked to me about nookie and being sexy, and if I dic
understand something, then he would always do his best
explain it to me..

I told Michelle that I was going to play with Glenn.

She said, 'I'm sorry, I'm sorry. I'll tell you all about
tomorrow.' I didn't want her to tell me all about it. I knew it v
about what men and women did in bed in the night, when t
made noises and touched each other.

In the afternoon, I felt tired and couldn't concentrate. M
told me off for not paying attention, and this made me wan
cry. Thinking about divorce and being sexy and making babi
was upsetting me. I wished that none of these things existed,
then I wouldn't have to know about them. I wanted to go hor
and stay in my room and never come out again.

I knew that I had to talk to Muriel.

When Mummy came to collect me, I was feeling very hot, a
my legs kept trembling.

Mummy was worried, but said, 'I think you've got the sa
thing as Muriel. She woke up this morning feeling terrible, a
she says she's got The Flu. She's been asleep in bed all day.'

Muriel and I are ill

By the time I got home, I felt so weak that I could hardly walk upstairs. Mummy gave me a drink of water and put me straight to bed. I must have fallen into a very deep sleep, because I had a nightmare about being in a huge lake. The sides of the lake were so steep, that I realised it would be impossible for me to get out on my own. I swam to the side, and Mummy tried to pull me out. But she slipped over, and I accidentally dragged her into the water. I knew where she had fallen in, but the water was completely black, so I couldn't see her. I dived down to the place where I thought she should have been, and thrashed around with my arms. I screamed and screamed, but I knew that Mummy had drowned.

This is the first time I had had this dream, but I have dreamed this, or variations of it, many times since.

Mummy came into my room and gave me a hug. I said, 'I don't want to go to school anymore, because Michelle is saying horrible things.'

She said, 'You must come into bed with us. That'll make you feel better.'

When I woke up in the morning, I was very surprised to see Muriel fast asleep next to me. Her hair was wet with sweat, and her cheeks were very pale. She was very hot, and smelled very sweaty. Mummy came in and quietly put me back in my own bed. She brought me some breakfast. I thought I felt better, but I felt sick as soon as I smelled the butter on the toast. I tried to sit up, but the room started to spin. Mummy said that she was going to telephone the doctor.

I slept for the rest of the morning. I felt a little better, but Mummy said that Muriel was feeling worse. I asked if I could see her, but Mummy said that she had moved Muriel into our spare bedroom, while the doctor came to visit. He arrived in the early afternoon. He went in to see Muriel, while Mummy waited with me. Mummy seemed very nervous, and wouldn't sit down. The doctor knocked on my door and examined me.

341

He told Mummy, 'These are two classic cases of influen[za]. Practically every other person in Rayners Park has it. All I c[an] suggest is that they have plenty of rest, and drink lots of fluids. Then he smiled at Mummy and said, 'Of course, a lady of yo[ur] background will be giving both these charming patients lots [of] chicken soup.'

He packed his bag, but kept talking. 'I know I'm not here [to] see you, Mrs Dunbar, but I had a look at your file before I car[ne] out. There are a lot of reports from The Glassman Clinic, a[nd] even a letter from Dr Gold. It's not every day that one receive[s a] letter from Britain's most eminent psychoanalyst. All the sig[ns] indicate that you have made excellent progress; and particula[rly] in the past few months. I had the chance to hear Dr Gold give [a] lecture once. When he had finished, a woman asked him if [he] thought that love was the best medicine. He repli[ed] "Absolutely!" '

Mummy smiled. The doctor said, 'His thoughts on women, a[nd] particularly, how can I put it?' He looked at me. 'His though[ts] about women in relationships… in relationships with oth[er] women, are very positive.'

Mummy said, 'Yes, thank you Doctor, we can talk downstairs.'

He said, 'No need for that. I'm just going. But please don't [let] your friend…'

Mummy interrupted him, 'You mean my lodger, n[y] companion…'

He interrupted her, 'Yes, yes, whatever you may wish to call he[r]. Please don't let her stay for one minute longer in that awful b[ed] you've put her in. It'll ruin her back in no time. Please put h[er] back where she belongs, and give both these two charmi[ng] patients lots of TLC. I can find my own way out.'

After the doctor left the room, Mummy sat down on my bed. S[he] was laughing to herself.

I asked her what *TLC* was. She said, 'Tender Loving Care,' a[nd] gave me a hug.

Mummy explains everything

The next day, I felt a lot better, but the doctor had told
Mummy that I should spend the rest of the week at home. This
was the best news, because I was still worried about Michelle.
Mummy had lit the fire in the front room, and we sat on the
settee together. She explained how babies are made. It sounded
horrible. I was quiet for a long time; looking at the fire, listening
to the wind, and watching the rain pouring down. Mummy had
explained all about what mummies and daddies do when they
love each other. She had said, 'I know it might sound a bit ugly,
but it really can be the loveliest thing for grown-ups to do.'

I had to ask, 'But what happens when a man tries to force
himself on you? Does it mean that the man tries to make you do
it when you don't want to?'

Mummy sighed, 'Yes. And that can be the ugliest, most horrible
thing in the world.'

Then I made a mistake. A very big mistake. I asked
Mummy, 'Are you and Muriel lesbians?'

Mummy looked like I had just slapped her very hard across the
face. I became very frightened, and tried to move away from her.
A big lump of burning coal fell out of the fire and onto the
hearth. Mummy jumped up, picked the coal up with the fire
tongs, and put it back on the fire. All the time that her back was
turned on me, I was imagining the expression on her face.

When she turned round, she looked sad. Then she tried to smile,
and took hold of both of my hands. Her hands were trembling
slightly. She asked me, 'Where did you hear that word? Who
said it to you?' She looked very worried.

I explained about Bernadette and Frances washing their breasts,
and how some of the girls in their class had called them lesbians,
and that Bernadette had told me that a lesbian was a lady who
loved another lady.

Mummy sighed again. She was still holding my hands. She said,
'It's true. I love Muriel very much. And you heard what the
doctor said; our love for each other has made me feel much
better. But please don't ever use that word again, when you are
talking about me or about Muriel. Because some people; some

343

grown-ups, just don't understand. I want you to promise me th
you will never use that word again. If people ask about Murie
you can say we are friends; which is perfectly true.'

I said I was sorry, and promised never to tell anyone th
Mummy and Muriel were lesbians. I couldn't understand wh
the problem was, but it worried me. I felt that the three of us ha
been inside a big bubble full of love and kindness, but someho
I had taken a great big pin and burst it.

Muriel got out of bed the next day and said that she fe
much better. I was certain that she and Mummy had had a lor
chat about being in love, but not being lesbians. I imagined th
somehow they had used a big piece of sticking plaster to mak
our bubble whole again.

The Iceberg, a pair of scissors, and God's Punishment

On Monday, our teacher was ill again, so Sister took o
class. She seemed to be cross with everybody, and kept bangin
her ruler on the desk, to make us be quiet. She told us the sto
of Noah's Ark. I had loved the story when I was little, and onc
spent several days in my room making a large model of the A
and the animals going in *two by two,* using bits of wood from t
garden and plasticine. I knew that there had been a big flood, b
had completely forgotten what had caused all the rain.

Sister destroyed the story for me, and made it ugly an
frightening. She wanted to tell us about Noah and The Floo
because at the weekend she had seen a film on TV called .
Night to Remember. It was a true story about a ship called *Th
Titanic.* It had hit an iceberg and sunk, and lots of people ha
drowned in the freezing cold water.

Vincent shouted out, 'We watched that film! It was horribl
There was an old man with a baby, and there wasn't enoug
room for them in the lifeboats, so they drowned. My mum crie
when she saw that.'

Sister didn't shout at Vincent for calling out. She seemed ver
pleased that he was talking about such a horrible thing. I put m
fingers in my ears, and tried not to listen to what Vincent an

344

ne other children were saying about the film. I tried to think
out what we had been doing on Sunday afternoon while this
rrible film was on the TV. Muriel and Mummy had gone to
d together and had a nice rest, while I thought about how I
uld paint pictures of Mummy swimming, and the lady feeding
r baby. I had started a painting of Muriel stroking Mummy's
re back.

I felt Sister tap me on my shoulder with her ruler. She said,
hilippa! What in Heaven's name are you doing?' She stood
hind me and carried on with the story. I was too frightened to
rn round and look at her. She told us that God had been very
gry with all the people on The Earth. He had made them as
rfect likenesses of Him, but they had done so many wicked
ings, that He decided to drown them all. That's why he told
oah that he was going to flood the whole of The Earth.

ystyna put her hand up, and asked a question that I had been
inking about: 'If God made a huge flood, and everybody was
owned, does that mean that all the children like us and babies
re drowned too? Surely the children and babies hadn't been
cked?'

ster explained that God's punishment could be terrible, but He
uld also show Great Mercy. I thought about Mummy when she
s a little girl, and the people who had wanted to kill her
cause she was Jewish.

ncent called out again, 'So why did God tell Noah to collect
o of each animal? Why not just one?'

ster tapped her ruler on my desk and said to Vincent, in a very
iet voice, 'That's enough, Vincent. If you shout out once more
rill be forced to punish you, and I won't show you any mercy.'
eryone looked terrified.

Sister said we had to draw two animals each, colour them in
th crayons, and then cut them out.

oked at Glenn. He looked at me and made a face that said,
h God, this is so boring!'

ster told me to draw two zebras. I was very pleased, because
se were my favourite animals at the time. Sister explained that

345

there were only 15 pairs of scissors, so we would have to sha
Then she sat at her desk and began marking our English books

At playtime, it was pouring with rain, so we had to stay
the class and continue with our drawing and cutting out, wh
Sister went downstairs to her office. Some children had alrea
finished drawing, and were busy cutting out. I was just beginn
my zebras, and for some reason looked over at the table wh
the scissors were. I saw Vincent put a pair of scissors in
pocket. When Sister came back in, Vincent asked if he could
to the toilet. I was sure that he was going to put the scissors
his bag.

All through the lesson, I tried to draw my zebras, but th
looked awful. While we were tidying up, Sister noticed that th
were only 14 pairs of scissors in the box. She made us all lo
for the missing scissors. I asked if I could go to the toilet. Si
looked at me suspiciously, but decided I could go. I went into
cloakroom and looked in Vincent's school bag. The sciss
were right at the bottom. I hid them up my sleeve and went ba
into class. Sister was telling the children to empty out th
pockets. She wasn't looking at me, so I bent down by
radiator, and very quickly slipped the scissors underneath it.
As I was straightening up, Sister said, 'Hurry up Philippa.'
I said, 'Sorry Sister.' I shouldn't have said anything, because
voice was out of control and shaking.
I looked at Vincent. He looked frightened; but so did all
other children.
Sister made us all sit down. She said she was convinced that
scissors had been stolen.
She said, 'I want the person who has stolen the scissors to o
up. I want them to have the courage to admit that they have do
the wrong thing. Whoever stole the scissors should stand
now.'
I looked straight ahead. I was certain that Vincent would sta
up, but I didn't dare look at him, because I was sure Sis
suspected me.
Nobody stood up.

Sister was tapping her ruler on her desk. She said, 'This is the tip of the iceberg. An iceberg has a small part sticking up above the water, but underneath there is a massive part that nobody can see. That's how ships full of innocent people crash into them. All the Innocent people in this class are suffering, because one person won't own up. Someone who can commit a sin like stealing, then doesn't own up, can go on to commit bigger sins. You can't trust them. They are *devious*.'

She stood there, looking at us, watching her terrible words sinking into us.

'But if they own up, then they might be punished; but everyone can see that they have made a mistake, and are honest enough to admit it. And remember, God sees everything, so you can't hide your sin from God. Now, is anyone going to own up?'

I looked at Vincent, out of the corner of my eye. I thought about him getting a beating on the legs from Sister, and then his father taking his belt off, and hitting Vincent on the bottom and back, until they were black and blue. I stood up. I could hear the children gasping. The children in front of me turned around and stared at me.

I said, 'Excuse me Sister, but I think they might have fallen down behind the radiator. I don't think anyone has searched there.'

Sister looked at me very closely. She asked me, 'Philippa, what do you mean when you say that the scissors *might have fallen*?'

I was too frightened to answer.

'Did you drop them there? Did you perhaps do that on purpose? Remember, you must tell the truth. If you tell a lie, the other children will know that you are like an iceberg. On the surface you look very nice, but underneath, the real you is dirty and horrible and dangerous.'

I couldn't speak. My legs felt wobbly and I tried to sit down.

I looked at Vincent. He was lifting his hand, as if he was going to tell Sister something. I imagined his back with the purple bruises. Sister said, 'So are you an iceberg? All clean and tidy on top, but the bit we can't see is full of sin?'

347

I closed my eyes. I heard myself say, 'Sister you are a bloo
bitch.'

There was another gasp from the children. Sister said, ve
quietly, 'I beg your pardon?'

I opened my eyes, and saw that Vincent had his hand up and w
shouting, 'Sister! Sister!' He was about to stand up.

I shouted at Sister, 'You are a fat shit! And a big bastard! And
slag! And you have a smelly cunt!'

I saw Sister rush towards me. She grabbed me by the coll
of my blouse, and pulled me to the front of the class. I heard h
say, 'How dare you use such foul language! How dare y
commit such sins!'

As she was saying this, I could feel her pulling down my tigh
and then she hit me several times very hard on my bottom a
the backs of my legs. I didn't cry out, and I didn't put my ha
out to try and stop her. I fell to the floor, but she pulled me
and kept on hitting and hitting.

I don't know exactly what happened next, but I rememb
Krystyna taking me to the office, and crying as we walked do
the stairs. I remember the look of shock on the secretary's fac
when Krystyna explained what had happened, and that Sist
said I had to stand in front of the painting of The Crucifixic
until Mummy came.

All the time I was standing there, I could hear children walki
past and whispering. Then I felt Mummy touching me. She kn
down in front of me and gently pushed my hair away from n
eyes. She said, 'Pippa, whatever is the matter? What h
happened?'

I couldn't speak. I just looked straight ahead.

We went into Sister's office. Sister was sitting behind h
desk. She pointed to the chair in front of her desk and said
Mummy, 'Sit down, Mrs Dunbar.'

Mummy said, 'It's Herman actually. My name is Herman, and
prefer to stand.' She held my hand. Mummy's hand was shakin

348

ister said, 'Your daughter has used the most vile language wards me, in the classroom. Obviously, she has been hysically punished for that.'

Iummy said, very quietly, 'You struck Pippa? You struck a hild?'

ister ignored those questions. She said to Mummy, 'I have no ea why she behaved in the way that she did. This type of ehaviour is quite unacceptable, but not entirely surprising, ven her home circumstances.'

Iummy said, 'How dare you strike my daughter. I've had nough of this Catholic nonsense. This is Pippa's last day here.'

Iummy opened the office door and, after we had walked rough it, shut it behind her, very firmly.

We went upstairs to get my coat and school bag. It was unchtime play, but it was still raining, so all the children were uside their classes, or talking in the cloakrooms. Krystyna saw s and went into the class to get Michelle, Glenn and Vincent. hey came running out, and Michelle started crying. I just ooked straight ahead. We walked past Sister's office. The door as open.

Iummy took me into the secretary's office. She said to the ecretary, 'Thank you for being so kind to Pippa while she has een here, but I shan't be allowing her to come back.'

he secretary said, 'Oh. I'm very sorry to hear that. I really am. ippa is such a lovely girl. Everyone makes mistakes.'

Iuriel was waiting for us in the street.

I can't speak

I don't remember how I got home, but I shall never forget us anding in the kitchen, while Mummy and Muriel helped me ke my tights and knickers off, so that they could see the amage that Sister had inflicted. She must have hit me with her are hands as well as the ruler, because my legs and bottom were overed in large red marks, and I had been bleeding. Muriel said ie couldn't believe how anyone could be so wicked. Mummy ng the doctor and explained what had happened, and he said at he would visit in the evening.

Mummy asked me to explain what had happened. I wanted to tell her. I wanted her to know that I wasn't a bad girl, but that I had just been trying to save Vincent. I wanted Mummy to tell me that I had made a mistake, but had been very brave for trying to save my friend from getting more terrible beatings.

But I couldn't speak. Every time I tried to think about what words and sentences to use, my heart started to beat very fast and my mind went blank. I was frightened, and I could see that Mummy and Muriel were frightened too. Mummy helped me put my clothes back on, and asked me if I would like a drink. I nodded my head.

She said, 'Good girl,' and brought me some milk. I tried to swallow it, but it went down the wrong way and I began choking. Mummy started to cry, and Muriel put me on her knee and gave me a hug.

I wanted to cry too, but no tears came out, and no sound either. Then I wet myself all over Muriel. I hadn't been to the toilet all morning. Muriel's skirt was completely soaked. She didn't say anything, but let out a sigh, and hugged me tighter. Mummy sat down at the table and put her head in her hands.

Then she stood up and said, 'I've had enough.'

She went into the hall and we heard her dialling a number. She said, 'This is Mrs Ruth Dunbar. I'm the wife of Mr Andrew Dunbar. Please put me through to Mister Shepherd. Yes, immediately. No, it can't wait. Yes, it's urgent. Then ask him to ring me as soon as he can. What is it about? It's about Mr Dunbar's daughter. There has been a serious incident, and Mr Shepherd needs to come to my home immediately.'

Mummy came back into the kitchen. She was shaking all over. I thought she was going to have a fit.

Muriel said to her, 'Ruth, what are you going to do?'

Mummy's voice was shaking, 'I'm not sure, but I want Shepherd to know exactly what's going on. I have to protect Pippa, and he has to help me do it.'

Muriel said, 'Well done Ruth. It's going to be difficult, but I'm sure you've done the right thing. By the way, we are both

ered in wee. Would you mind most awfully if we used your
hroom?'
mmy said, 'Muriel, thank goodness you are here.'

Muriel took me upstairs, and ran the water for the bath.
:re was a dark stain all over her skirt. She took it off and said,
ght, let's get in.' I wasn't sure what she meant. She said,
me on slowcoach, before the water gets cold.' She took all
clothes off and sat in the bath. I just stood, looking at her.
: said, 'What's wrong? You've seen me with nothing on lots
imes. Quick, jump in.'
ok my clothes off and got in the bath. Muriel was already
ing down. I stood in the bath, and she asked me to turn round,
she could look at the back of my legs.
: said, 'I'm going to kiss every single one of those cuts and
ises, and blow on them, to start to make you feel better.'
: told me to sit down very slowly in the water, because it
ght sting. It did.
n Muriel held me tight, between her legs, and said, 'Let's
ke you feel better.'

I think we were in the bath for a long time. We heard the
ne ring downstairs and Mummy talking, but we couldn't hear
at she was saying. When she had finished, she came upstairs
knocked on the bathroom door. She came in and sat on the
ol. She stroked my hair.
: said to me, 'Pippa, nobody's cross with you, but I'm furious
h Sister. Mr Shepherd is coming. Mr Shepherd is your
ldy's *agent*. He arranges lots of your daddy's business and
al affairs in this country. He also arranges for me to receive
ney every month; to pay for you, and where we live. Your
ldy and I are not divorced, but we are like divorced people.
fore I left Malaya, I agreed that your daddy should decide how
are educated. I haven't always liked the decisions that have
n made about where you go to school, but I have agreed to
m. But I can't agree to you going back to that awful school
r again. I'm going to tell Mr Shepherd that.'

351

She was quiet, and stroked my hair again. She said
Muriel, 'Muriel, I'm trying to be calm, for Pippa's sake
haven't discussed this with you. I know I should have, but th
hasn't been time. I've told Shepherd to contact Andrew, and
insist that he comes here.'

Muriel let go of me for a moment, then held me tight again.
said, 'Oh. And will he come? And what shall I do? Do you w
me to go away?'

Mummy said, 'How can you say such a thing? How can y
even think it? I want you to be here. They have to meet y
They have to understand what is happening, and what is best
Pippa.'

Even now, I don't understand why I reacted the way I did.
why I didn't react at all, I just sat perfectly still and didn't ma
a sound. Whenever I made a movement, it felt as if someone e
was moving. It felt like my head had been removed from
shoulders, and my body was moving of its own accord. The o
way I can explain it, is that somewhere inside me had be
switched off, to stop me from going completely wild a
exploding.

The bathroom was full of steam, and the tiles were covered
condensation. I saw my finger write *I'm sorry*.

Mummy burst into tears and said, 'Oh no Pippa, you have
done anything wrong. This all had to come out sometime. It's
who should be sorry. I'm the one who has done all the harm
you. I'm the one who should be beaten black and blue, not you

Mummy had completely lost control. Muriel stood up and
out of the bath and held Mummy tight. She said, 'Now don't
silly. I think you should get in the bath now.'

Mummy just stood there, crying.

Muriel started to take Mummy's blouse off. Mum
stopped her. Muriel laughed and said, 'Well honestly, are y
going to get in the bath or not?'

She wrapped a towel around herself and left the bathroo
Mummy undressed and got in with me. She held me tight, an
closed my eyes. I could feel myself floating back to when I v

352

ur years old in Northumberland, and had asked Mummy if we
uld have a bath together, and she had cried. Then I could feel
ne rushing past me, and we were in a swimming pool in
alaya. Mummy was talking in a funny language to someone
ho was in the pool with us. I could see a green snake moving
ar a chair where our clothes were. Then time rushed past
ain, and I was sucking Mummy's nipple and drinking her
vely milk. I could hear Mummy talking to me, but didn't
derstand what she was saying, because I was a tiny baby.

The phone rang. I heard Muriel's voice. She had left the
throom door open. She said, 'Hello? Yes, that's right. Muriel.
uriel Standish. Ruth is upstairs with Pippa. I'll just go and get
r. Oh, all right. Frankfurt. Yes. What happened? Well, it's best
Ruth tells you herself. Oh. Yes, I see. Well it seems that Pippa
d an argument with the nun in charge of the school. The nun
s beaten Pippa very badly. Very badly. Bruising all over her
ttom and the backs of her legs, and the skin is broken in three
aces. Sixteen bruises. Hello? Are you still there? Sorry, I
ought we had got cut off. I'd say that Pippa has gone into some
nd of shocked condition. She can't speak. Yes. The doctor is
ming this evening. Yes, it's just terrible. Ruth? Ruth is very
gry and upset. Thank you. I try my best. No, not at all.
oodbye.'

Mummy called out, 'Muriel, who was that? Was that
epherd? Was he ringing to say what time he is coming?'
uriel came upstairs and said, 'No. Mr Shepherd's not coming
day. That was your husband. He's in Frankfurt, and he's flying
London tomorrow morning. He wants to come here tomorrow
ternoon.'

I don't care anymore
After hearing that piece of news, I seemed to completely
ut down. I hadn't eaten anything since breakfast, and didn't
el at all hungry. Muriel made me a bowl of cereal, but I just sat
oking at it.

Mummy said to Muriel, 'I'm not going to let this go on. I'm gla
that Andrew is coming tomorrow. He has got to agree that t
Catholic religion is doing Pippa serious harm.'

In the evening, the doctor came and examined me. He sa
that the way I had been punished was a complete disgrace. Sist
had used considerable force; with her bare hands, and a ha
implement. He thought it might have been a ruler, but it cou
equally have been something else. He promised to write a repo
so that Mr Dunbar, and anyone in authority, would be in
doubt about the severity of my bruising.
After that, I went to bed. I just wanted to go to sleep, and forg
about everything. Mummy came to tuck me in. She told me
could sleep in their bed if I wanted to. Then she said, 'I suppo
you'd like to be with Ursula. We haven't heard you talking
her for a long time.'
That was true. Since Muriel had been with us, I didn't need
ask Ursula lots of questions. If I didn't understand something
just asked Muriel. Mummy said, 'You poor thing! Mummy
going to try and   make this all right. What a surprise that yo
daddy is coming to see you! I've been very angry with yo
father for a long time, but I'm not angry anymore. I promise I
do my best to be nice to him. He's a good man, really. I think v
didn't understand each other, and we didn't know what each
us needed. He can be very funny sometimes, and he loves a
I'm sure he'll love to see all of your pictures.'
She kissed me on the forehead, and said she would see me in t
morning.

As soon as Mummy left the room, Ursula came to me. H
hair had grown much longer, and she seemed older. She sat
my bed, and told me that she didn't mind that I hadn't needed
see her. She had been watching me all the time, and kne
everything that had happened. She had been talking to the oth
angels, and they thought that swearing at Sister wasn't a si
because I had done it for a very good reason. But the angels sa
I should have just pretended to faint. Then Sister would have ha

354

pick me up, and then she might have forgotten about the
upid scissors.
said I couldn't bear the thought of Sister picking me up, and
nyway, she would have known that I was pretending.
rsula said I was probably right. She told me to tell her what
as really upsetting me. I said I couldn't talk about it. She said
he already knew, but I must tell her, otherwise I might never be
ole to speak to anyone again, and that would be too awful.
he climbed into bed with me and held me tight and said, 'Will
ou tell me now?'

I told her all my worries. One of my biggest worries was
at if I stopped being a Catholic, then Ursula might stop coming
see me. She said that she would be with me always, even if I
d forget about her sometimes. She also told me not to tell my
addy that I didn't want to be a Catholic anymore.
hen I realised that I had no idea what Daddy looked like. I fell
sleep, imagining a man wearing brown trousers, and with the
me colour eyes as mine.
the middle of the night I woke up and went to sleep with
Mummy and Muriel.

I meet Daddy
I woke up a few hours later, and it was still dark. Mummy
ad rolled over and was squashing me. Muriel was fast asleep. I
imbed over Mummy and she said, in a sleepy voice, 'What
me is it?' and moved towards Muriel. I went back to my
edroom, and saw that Ursula was still fast asleep in my bed. I
ut on my dressing gown and slippers, and went downstairs. The
ove in the kitchen was still warm, and the cat lay stretched out
n the floor in front of it. Our neighbours had moved away
cently, and told us that we could keep him, because he seemed
prefer us to them. His name was Archibald, but I called him
rchie.

I stroked Archie, and he woke up and purred. I picked him
p and took him to the window. It was still dark outside, but I
uld see that there had been a very sharp frost. A bird started to

sing, but then went quiet again. I said to Archie, 'Maybe she
like Mummy, and has gone back to her nest to sleep with h
Muriel.'

Archie jumped out of my arms, and went back to the warmth
the stove.

The bird started singing again. Archie swished the tip of his tai
I felt my legs hurting. I touched my bottom. It still hurt. I thoug
of Muriel kissing my cuts and bruises, and blowing on them
make them feel better.

I went upstairs, and Ursula was awake. She said I should write
letter to Daddy, telling him what I was thinking.

At breakfast I managed to eat some Weetabix and a piece
toast. Muriel asked Mummy if she was worried about meetin
Daddy. Mummy said, 'Not really. I'm glad he's coming. I kno
what I'm going to say to him first of all, but after that I have r
idea.'

Muriel asked me to go with her into the front room, to light th
fire and listen to some records. She loved The Beatles, and san
along to *Can't Buy Me Love*. After that she helped me tidy m
bedroom, and sort through all my pictures.

She looked at one in particular and said, 'Are you sure you wa
your Daddy to see that one?'

I found a pencil and I wrote on the back of the painting, *This
my favourite painting. I love it more than any other picture
have ever done. When I look at it I feel warm inside and kno
that I will be safe.*

Muriel smiled and then frowned. She said, 'Let me take it dow
to Mummy, to see what she thinks.'

She pulled my ear and kissed me on the tip of my nose. She sai
'I really, really love you, Pippa.' Then she hurried out of th
room, with my picture in her hand.

At half past ten, Muriel took me for a walk to the doctor
surgery, to collect the report about my bottom and legs. At th
zebra crossing, a big shiny car with two men in it stopped, to l
us cross the road. After we left the doctor's, we went into th
greengrocer's. Muriel bought some bananas, and she gave m
one to eat in the street. Then we went into the newsagent, an

riel bought a bar of chocolate. She said it was for her and
mmy and me to share. I picked up a Flake and a bar of
axy.
riel said, 'Do you want to give them to your daddy?' I
ded my head.
n we had to pop into the chemist, because Muriel needed to
a few things. She whispered, 'I've just started my period.
lay of all days! My tummy always feels a bit funny on the
day, and I usually have a headache. So I'm going to buy
e towels and some aspirin.'
ent a bit red. Muriel said, 'Whoops! I didn't mean to make
feel embarrassed.'
I knew that she had said those things on purpose, to take my
d off the awful things that had happened, and to stop me
rrying about what was going to happen next. And perhaps she
trying to help me to talk. I wanted to tell Muriel that I loved
, but couldn't. I held her hand very tightly, all the way home.

As we reached our house we saw the big shiny car parked in
driveway. Mr Shepherd was sitting inside. He was reading a
vspaper with pink pages, and didn't notice us at all. It was
f past eleven and Daddy was early. That took me by surprise.
stopped in the porch. As usual, Muriel had forgotten her key.
crouched down in front of me. She said, 'How do you feel,
pa?'
an ordinary day, Muriel would have known exactly how I
s feeling inside; by looking at my face, and listening to my
ce, and watching how I moved. But since Sister had hit me,
body had become stiff, and my face was like a blank mask,
my voice had disappeared. I wasn't sure how I felt. I think I
s *nervous*. Muriel said, 'I feel very nervous. I don't know
at to say, or how to behave. I think I'll try and just be quiet.
at do you think, Pippa?'
oked in her lovely big blue eyes, and she looked in mine.
said, 'You're the loveliest girl in the whole world.
rything will be all right. I know it will. Have some fun,
ting to know your daddy. I don't even know what he looks
!'

She tidied my hair with her fingers, then kissed me on the tip my nose. Then she got up and gave the door knocker a very swing, and it made a very loud noise. Muriel said, 'Whoops.'
I turned round and saw Mr Shepherd look up from his p newspaper. Then he carried on reading. I wondered if he wo soon need to use our lavatory.

Mummy opened the door and said, 'Pippa, your dadd here. Quick! Come and meet him. He's having a cup of tea in front room.'
I saw a pair of very large shiny black shoes by the front door big light brown coat and a black hat were hanging on the c stand. Mummy said, 'Those are your daddy's shoes. He insis on taking them off.'
I heard a man cough, and I smelled cigarette smoke. Muriel s she was just going upstairs to the toilet, and to tidy herself u bit. Mummy kissed her, on the lips.

Mummy took my hand and led me into the front room stood by the door. A very tall old man was sitting in an armch by the fire. His hair wasn't just grey; it was almost complet white. He was wearing a very smart navy blue suit, with creamy-white shirt and a dark blue tie. His long legs w stretched out in front of him. He was wearing black socks. had a black moustache and black eyebrows. I could see that eyes were bright blue; just like mine.
Mummy stood next to me and said to the old man, 'Here you a Here's your daughter. Do you recognise her?'
He took a draw on his cigarette and blew the smoke in the then slowly stubbed his cigarette out in the ashtray. He stood and came towards me. He bent down as low as he could, a held out his hand for me to shake. I put my hand in his. He ha very large gold ring on one of the fingers on his right hand. he shook my hand he said, 'I'm yourr daddy. How do you do?'
I just looked at him.
He said, 'I expect yourr a wee bit shocked to see me after these yearrs. Do you rrememberr me at all?'
I just looked at him some more. I had forgotten that he was fr Scotland.

ldy said to him, 'Are you all right, waiting in the car? We
ld be quite some time.'

Shepherd said, 'Actually I do rather need to use the lavatory.
you think they would mind most awfully if I popped inside
a few moments?'

s made me smile. Daddy saw me and said, 'Good man,
pherd! You've managed to make my daughter smile!' I
led again.

Shepherd banged on the door with the door knocker.
mmy opened it. Her face was very red and she looked very
otional. Mr Shepherd said, 'Hello Mrs Dunbar. Would you
d most awfully if I used your lavatory?'

mmy smiled and said, 'Yes of course you can. And then
ne and have some lunch with us.'

said to Daddy, 'Please, Andrew, will you stay for lunch? We
en't got much, but we would all love you to stay as long as
sible, wouldn't we, Pippa?'

dded and put my hand in Daddy's again. Daddy said, 'I don't
it to put you to any inconvenience.'

mmy told him not to be so silly. She thought we would all
e a lot to talk about. She looked at me, and put her hand on
shoulder. 'And we want to make the most of you being here.
you can see, things have been very fraught here, and we all
d to calm ourselves down, and decide what we should do
t. Don't you agree?'

ldy said, 'Yes. Quite. Quite. But first of all, might I go with
pa and look at some of her pictures? You know how much I
e art, and have heard so much about her talents.'

mmy said, 'Yes of course. Pippa, take Daddy upstairs to your
m, while Muriel and I make the lunch.'

Daddy sat beside me on my bed, while he looked through
pictures. He still had his shoes on. He had brought his
efcase upstairs with him. He said, 'I love them. I absolutely
e them. But there are so many. It would take me days to look
hem all properly.'

looked at some of my drawings of Archie. He said, 'You've
lly captured his...his essence, and how he moves. You can

363

almost get a sense of what he's thinking. In this one, I imag[e]
he's thinking about his dinner!'

That's exactly what I had thought when I had drawn it.

Then he picked up some of my paintings of people with
clothes on. He looked closely at one of Ursula. I looked at
face, but I couldn't tell what he was thinking. He said, 'Wh[o's]
this wee lassie? Is she one of your school friends?'

I felt alarmed. I didn't want him to think that I painted
friends with nothing on. I shook my head. Daddy looked at
He could see that I was getting upset. He said, 'I'll tell you w[hat.]
You can write down what you'd like to say.'

He took a gold pen out of his jacket pocket. He took a noteb[ook]
out of his briefcase and handed it to me. He unscrewed the to[p of]
his pen and said, 'This is my favourite pen. Have a go at writ[ing]
with it.'

I wrote

> *The curfew tolls the knell of parting day,*
> *The lowing herd wind slowly o'er the lea*
> *The ploughman homeward plods his weary way,*
> *And leaves the world to darkness and to me.*

Daddy looked very surprised. He said, 'That's Gray's *El[egy*]
Written in a Country Churchyard. It's one of my favou[rite]
poems.'

I wrote, *My favourite teacher, Miss Dawson, wrote it on one [of]
my paintings. I think she really liked me.*

Then he looked at the painting of Ursula again.

I wrote, *That's Ursula. She's my Guardian Angel. I talk to [her]
in bed. She sometimes talks to the other angels and she tells [me]
what to do. I think Muriel is Mummy's Guardian Angel.*

Daddy said, 'Ah. That's very interesting.'

We both sat side by side, while he looked at more pictu[res.]
He looked up and saw a painting on my table. He said, 'W[hat]
about that one? Pass it to me.' It was the one that Muriel [had]
taken off me and put in Mummy's bedroom. I got up, then st[ood]

ll. Daddy said, 'Pass it to me. Do as you're told, there's a good
rl.'

gave it to him. He said, 'This is just like a painting by an artist
lled Degas. Pippa, you must tell me all about it.'

tood perfectly still.

e said, 'Tell me about it.'

at down next to him and looked straight ahead.

e said, 'Listen, Pippa, Daddy has come all this way to see you.
would be such a shame if I had to leave this house without
er hearing you speak.'

ooked straight ahead.

e said, "I know you can talk, but you are just choosing to be
ent. Now speak. Do as I say.'

He was frightening me. I closed my eyes. I thought of Miss
awson and her ring, and how she had been upset with us
cause we laughed at Krystyna, and how we had all wanted to
good for her, because we all loved her so much. I tried to
nagine her sitting next to me, and asking me about why I had
inted Mummy and Muriel with no clothes on, and Muriel
uching Mummy's shoulders and back with tenderness.

I took a deep breath and heard myself say, 'Lady Celia said
at when people have no clothes on, you can see them as they
ally are. You can see how they move. And you can see what
me and Life have done to them. You can know their story. I
dn't know what she meant by that. When Mummy and Muriel
ere getting changed at the swimming pool, they were being so
nd to each other. They were a little bit like children; like me
d Peter when we were up in his tree, or playing at the pump, or
st sitting quietly together. Mummy had just been holding a
by, and telling his mother about me when I was little. She had
lked about you in a very nice way.

'When I saw them like that, I knew that I would be safe. I
ought of Mummy being a little girl, and her mummy giving her
vay, because the German police would come to kill her. And I
ought about the neighbours stuffing her in an armchair on the
ck of a lorry, and driving her for days, and then her not

365

knowing what had happened to her mummy, and one day findi
out that she was dead, and perhaps she had been shot and h
body burned, and all her ashes going up a big chimney. But no
she has someone who strokes her shoulders and her back a
says, "That mole is getting bigger, and you really must get
looked at." And I thought about all that when I painted th
picture.'

Daddy crossed and uncrossed his long legs and touched h
moustache.
I kept talking. 'Sometimes Mummy gets very... I don't kno
what word to use, but it's just before she has her period. Mur
helps Mummy to calm down. Muriel makes Mummy laugh, a
they talk to each other a lot. Mummy listens to Muriel, a
thinks about what she says. I used to be frightened of aski
questions, so I never knew what was going on. Now Muriel
with us, I can ask all sorts of questions, and get some ve
interesting answers.   And Mummy doesn't drink whis
anymore, and she doesn't need to take medicine.

'I think that Mummy is ashamed of something. I thi
Muriel is worried about what you might think. They love ea
other. I like that, because it makes me feel happy. I think th
would be very upset if they knew that I have told you that. Bu
think everybody sees it. They can't hide it. But they are
lesbians. I know that. When Uncle Eric stayed here, he used
be in Mummy's bed, and they made rude sexy noises, and tri
to make a baby. But Mummy and Muriel just talk and laugh, a
go to sleep. I hear them both snoring. So that's why I know th
they are just two ladies who just love each other, but are
lesbians. That's all I can say.'
Daddy was very quiet. I looked in his face and he looked
mine.
He said, 'Thank you, Pippa. Thank you for talking to me, a
telling me all those important things. I understand now.'
I thought of the detective who kept saying the same thin
that he *understood.*

addy said, 'That's so interesting. It's a very beautiful painting. ut I'm a wee bit worried that I might forget what you have just id. Do you think you could do Daddy a wee favour and write at all down for me? Then Daddy will have something to member you by.'

looked in his face. He smiled at me and said, 'Go on. Don't orry about the spellings or what your handwriting looks like. ou can start with today's date. Do you know what today's date ?'

did. I smiled at him, and he showed me a fresh page in his tebook to write on.

e said, 'There's no need to write about Uncle Eric. Just about ummy and Muriel, because what you said was so lovely.'

While I was writing, he got up and looked out of the indow. Just as I finished, we heard Mummy calling, to tell us at lunch was ready. Daddy said, 'You go downstairs, while I ve one last look at these lovely pictures.'

went out of the room, but I didn't go downstairs straight away. stopped for a moment, and listened at the open door. I heard addy open his briefcase and take something out. Then I heard a ick and saw a flash of light. Then another click and another ish of light.

r Shepherd was talking on the telephone downstairs in the hall. e said, 'Yes, put it all in a taxi. To this address. Pay the driver advance if needs be.'

addy came out of my room. I almost jumped with fright. He id, 'Why Pippa, I thought I told you to go downstairs. Why dn't you do as you were told? I'm disappointed that you have en disobedient like that.'

Mummy had made some sandwiches and heated up some mato soup. She said, 'I'm sorry it's not very much, but we eren't expecting you until this afternoon.'

addy smiled and said, 'Don't worry, Ruth, I'm just delighted to here, and to meet Pippa, after all these years. I hope that we in see more of each other.' He smiled at me. He added, 'And I pe we will meet under happier circumstances.'

I had almost forgotten about my sore legs and bottom. Mumm
said, 'We can talk about that after lunch.'

Daddy said, 'I'm afraid that won't be possible, because I mu
rush into London, and then fly out again. I'm due in Sau
Arabia tomorrow. The Germans don't mind me cancellin
meetings, but in Saudi Arabia they expect me to be there
person, and on time.'

He looked at Mr Shepherd. Mr Shepherd stopped eating h
sandwich. He looked at Daddy and said, 'Saudi Arabia? Qui
quite.'

Mummy had a strange look on her face.

Daddy opened his briefcase and took out a large brow
envelope. He passed it to Mummy and said, 'I keep the origina
of these in a safe place in my London office. Mr Shepherd ha
some copies made for you. I thought they might bring back son
happy memories that you can share with Pippa.'

There was a photo of me as a baby. Another show
Mummy and daddy standing in front of a big tree. Daddy w
holding me. Mummy said, 'Ah, Andrew, you are so kind a
thoughtful. I'm afraid I lost all of my photos in one of o
moves.'

I knew that wasn't true, because once, when she was ill, I ha
seen her tearing them up and throwing them in the dustbin, alor
with some of my drawings of Daddy.

Mummy passed the photos to Muriel, and she said that the
looked lovely.

The third and fourth photographs made Mummy gasp a
put her hand to her mouth. They had both been taken in t
swimming pool. One was of Mummy holding me. I was abo
two or three years old. Mummy was crouched down in the wat
She was looking straight at the camera, and had a huge smil
Her shoulders were bare, and I could just see part of her brea
sticking out of the water; so it was obvious that she had
bathing costume on. I was completely naked. The fourth one w
of a Chinese-looking lady. She was in the pool too, and w
holding me. She was standing up and was naked as well.

mmy and Muriel looked at each other, but didn't say
thing.
ldy said, 'I found your camera after you left, and had the film
eloped.'
wasn't smiling.

Mummy asked Daddy, 'What happened to my friend?'
ldy said, 'You know that she was dismissed from our service.
I found her. I realised that... that a mistake had been made.
was from a poor family, and they relied on her to send them
ney. When she returned home, the family felt that she was a
grace, so they sent her away. But I tracked her down, and
ught her back to work for me, on one of my other plantations.
is a very clever and hard-working young woman, as you
w. She has a very responsible job in my organisation.'
mmy sighed, but Daddy ignored her. 'I suppose I felt guilty
ut the way she had been treated, so I have helped her family
ots of ways. I pay for her brother to go to university. You see,
tend to continue helping the family, and naturally your ex-
nd is very loyal to me. Her memories of the time she spent
h you are still very clear. I must get her to write them down
retime. To write down her testimony.'
smiled at Mummy as he said *testimony*. It was the sort of
le that someone might have when they are playing cards, and
y know that they have just won.

Mummy didn't say anything straight away. She just looked
he four photos. Eventually she said; 'It seems like such a long
e ago. I was another person then. So much has happened
:e.' Then she said something odd. It didn't sound friendly at
She said to Daddy, 'Andrew, what exactly do you want?'
ldy touched his moustache. 'What do I want? What do you
an, Ruth? I think it's best if you and I talk in private for a
e while.'
mmy looked straight into Daddy's eyes. She said, 'No. If
rthing is to be said, it should be said for everyone to hear;
luding Pippa. We don't have any secrets here.'

369

Daddy said, 'So I hear.' I didn't know what that meant. Th
was a hint of something in his voice that wasn't nice. No
would call it *sarcasm*.

Mummy said, 'I want to explain something. It's v
important to me. When I was a child, I was deeply, dee
traumatised. I didn't know it at the time. But Max has helped
to understand how I had forced all my awful experiences d
inside myself. I was very sick when I... when you made me co
to England. My mind was in turmoil. In Malaya I was a g
mother to Pippa, but we all know that afterwards I was ill,
unable to look after her properly. That's something that I m
live with for the rest of my life. I'm doing my best now. I th
you know that.'

She stopped talking. I was sure she was thinking v
carefully about what words to use next. She closed her eyes
took a deep breath. She opened her eyes and said, 'I'm not
same person I was when we met, and I'm not the same per
that you knew in Malaya. I understand myself much better n
I understand my true nature. I know who I am, and I know wh
am. And I'm glad of who I am and what I am. I don't feel sha
I don't feel guilty. I feel proud.'
I could feel her voice wobbling. I thought perhaps she would
say anything else, but she did: 'I love Pippa, and I'm very pr
of her. But the choices that have been made about her upbring
and education... that you made me agree to, have not b
successful, to say the least...'
Daddy interrupted her, 'Ruth.' He did not sound friendly at
He sounded like Mr Grigson. He sounded like Sister. 'Ruth,
know just how important my Catholic faith is to me; as is
standing in the Church...'
There was a very loud knock at the front door. My father said
Mr Shepherd, 'That'll be the taxi. Tell him to wait. I'll
shortly. I'll meet you at the office.'
Mr Shepherd left the room. A man said, 'Where do you want
to put this parcel?'
Mr Shepherd said, 'Oh, just put it down there will you?'

interrupted her and said, 'Well I really mustn't keep that poor
taxi driver waiting any longer.'

Muriel grabbed my hand and pulled me out into the hall. We
both stood by the front door, blocking it. My father came out of
the kitchen. He bent down to talk to me. 'A lot of important
things have been said. I think that we have said enough now,
don't you?'

I couldn't look at him. I saw the big parcel.

He put his finger on the side of his nose. I thought he was going
to tap it twice, as if to say, *Our little secret is safe*. But he
stopped, because he saw, and I saw, that Muriel was looking at
him. He scratched his ear and said, 'I have a feeling I've
forgotten something.'

He put his hand in the inside pocket of his jacket. 'Ah yes. My
pen. Never mind. If you find it, Pippa, you can keep it safe for
me, and give it to me the next time we meet.'

I ran upstairs and found his pen. Then I ran downstairs and put it
in his hand. He smiled and said, 'You don't want it? You don't
want to use it to write me another letter, or to write some more
about your paintings? It has been lovely meeting you. I'm sorry
that school is not working out as well as we had hoped, but I'm
sure we can all come to an agreement about what is best for you
in the future.'

He straightened up slowly, and took his coat and hat from
the coat stand. He put them on, very slowly. Muriel was still
standing in front of the door, blocking my father's exit. Mummy
was behind us, by the kitchen; I looked at her. She had her arms
folded.

My father put his hand on the front door latch. As he did so, his
hand pushed Muriel's shoulder. He didn't look at her. He didn't
bend down to look at me. He didn't touch me. He didn't give me
a kiss.

He said, to the front door, 'Goodbye Pippa.'

Then he turned his head and looked over his shoulder at
Mummy. He still had his hand on the door latch. He said to her,

'You know Ruth, you really should get that large mole on your back looked at.'

He opened the door, walked out, and closed the door behind him. I heard him say, 'Thank you for waiting. Central London. Baker Street.'

Mummy ran to the door, opened it and shouted, 'Andrew, wait!' But the taxi was just leaving.

I ran into the kitchen. I opened the back door. There was a dead bird on the step. Archie was sitting a few feet away. He looked at me and twitched the end of his tail. He had bitten the bird's head off. I slammed the door shut and hid under the kitchen table. I went right up into a corner and curled up into a ball.

I told myself that I deserved to be hit. I knew I was going to be hit. It was all my fault. Why did I take that picture out of Mummy's bedroom? Why did I speak, and tell him that they loved each other? Why did I write down that they loved each other? He had taken photos of my picture. He was going to destroy Mummy and Muriel. Muriel would have to go away, and Mummy and I would have to live on the streets, and sit in a shop doorway and beg for food.

I heard Mummy and Muriel come into the kitchen. Mummy said, 'Let's find Pippa. I think she's out in the garden.'

Muriel said, 'Perhaps we should leave her for a little while?'

Mummy said, 'No. I think she needs to know just how much we love her. She's probably terrified that she's done something wrong.'

Muriel said, 'Ruth, we will be all right, won't we? I mean, you and I.'

Mummy said, 'Of course. Nothing has changed.'

'And the three of us can still live together?'

'Of course. How can you doubt it?'

'I don't doubt it. It's just that life will be very different. We'll be quite poor; at least at the beginning.'

'I don't mind that. I can do anything as long as I know my daughter will be happy. And as long as we can find a decent school for her, with no more nuns.'

Muriel opened the door. She must have seen the dead bird.
shouted at Archie, 'Oh you naughty boy! We don't want
sents like that!' She shut the door. She said, 'I don't think
pa is out there.'

mmy said, 'I don't think so either.'

en I burped. It just came out. Mummy crouched down and
l to me, 'Come out of there, my little Pipsqueak.'

voice wouldn't work. I felt like Daddy had forced me to talk.
throat hurt. And I had said too much. I had said all the wrong
igs!

ept saying a sentence to myself, My mouth moved, but no
nd came out.

riel passed me a piece of paper and a pencil. I wrote down, *I
wed my daddy the painting of you and Muriel with nothing
* I passed the note to Mummy.

wrote something and passed me the paper. It said, *We know*.
en we passed the paper back and forth to each other, writing
ssages each time.

: *And he made me write a letter about you.*

mmy: *I'm sure he did. I imagine he put it in his briefcase.*

: *I wrote that you and Muriel love each other.*

mmy: *He knows that already.*

: *But I did tell him that you weren't lesbians.*

Mummy laughed at that. She didn't pass the paper back to
She said, 'I don't mind what Daddy knows. Do you mind,
riel?'

riel said she didn't mind. She didn't mind at all.

mmy asked her, 'Muriel, are you ashamed?'

. Not ashamed. I'm proud. I'm very proud of Pippa.'

hy?'

cause she's a big strong girl.'

you think Pippa will be all right ?'

ι yes.'

en Mummy said, 'Come on out Pippa. We're going to live in a
ce called Canada. Let's go and pack a little bag each.' I came
and Mummy hugged and kissed me.

We saw the big parcel in the hall. I had forgotten all ab
it. Mummy told me to open it. It was very heavy, and wrap
up in brown paper, and tied with rough string. Mummy sat on
bottom step of the stairs, watching Muriel help me. There wa
brown envelope tucked into the string on top of the parce
opened it. There was a black and white photograph of me, sitt
in Lady Celia's front room, wearing a white toga, and witl
laurel wreath on my head. I was holding a pencil and look
straight at the camera and smiling. On the back was written,
Pippa, love from Daddy.

Inside the parcel were boxes of paints, lots of different types
brushes, several pads of paper, a long pen with a metal nib, a
three small bottles of ink. There were four boxes of pastels of
different colours, and a book about how to use them.

Mummy said, 'You see. He's not a bad man. You must use th
lovely paints to paint a picture and send it to him.'

I whispered, 'What's Daddy's true nature?'

Mummy said, 'I think it's to work hard, and to be in control
other people, and to earn lots of money. He believes that he
doing that for the benefit of other people. He once told i
"When Andrew Dunbar works, lots of other people have w
too." '

I whispered, 'And what's my true nature?'

She smiled and said, 'That's for you to find out. That is w
being a grown-up is all about.'

She laughed and said to Muriel, 'I'm a grown-up. Muriel,
you a grown-up?'

Muriel sighed, and then laughed a very small laugh. She said
am now. But can we please hurry up and go to Canada?'

My voice came back. I said, 'Yes please, but would you m
awfully if first I used your lavatory?'

Mummy and Muriel laughed.

o   o   o   o   o   o   o   o   o   o   o   o

It's been pouring with rain for three days and nights now.
e been reading for three nights. I was so young then, but so
!

st Sunday was my day off. (Who wants a day off on a Sunday,
en everything is closed?) I had nothing else to do, so went for
long walk in the forest. Everything around me was soaking,
d all my clothes were beginning to get wet through. I stopped
d looked behind me.

at's when I had a terrifying waking nightmare. I was there, in
forest, with all the people who had ever loved me. German
ldiers with guns were ordering us to big a big hole. All of the
ldiers had grey uniforms, except one, who was dressed in
ack. I knew he was from the SS. One of the grey soldiers was
mplaining. He said to the soldier in black, 'This is stupid.
ey are digging on a slope. Soon all the soil will be washed
ay, and the corpses will be exposed.'

e SS soldier laughed and said, 'Who cares? We are invincible.
w go and argue amongst yourselves about who is going to
llect the gold teeth, after we've shot them all.'

en I was kneeling in front of the pit. Everyone else had been
ot, in the back of the head, and had fallen into the pit. I was
oking at their bodies. Someone was still moving. I think it was
uriel. I knew I was next. I wanted to be next. I wanted to be
ot, so my body could fall next to hers.

umped into the pit, to be next to Muriel. The soldiers laughed
me, and started arguing about who should shoot me. Then one
the soldiers slipped and fell in, and that gave me the chance to
n away, down the track. I heard gunshots.

I read once, in *All Quiet on the Western Front*, I think it
as, that if you hear a gunshot, and don't feel anything, then you
ven't been hit.

ran and ran. As I was running, I thought that perhaps the
ldiers were shooting at Muriel, to make sure that she was dead.
man saw me, and asked me if I was all right. That shook me
t of my nightmare. I said I was frightened. He asked me what I
as frightened of, and I said, 'Her. I'm frightened of Her.'

377

He said, 'Who's she? Come and talk to me about it.'

But I was frightened of him too, and ran away. As I ran, ⁣ school beret fell off, but I was too frightened to go back and ⁣ it.

I wish I didn't know so much about what happened in The Wa⁣ Now I can't shake off that terrible daytime nightmare. An⁣ going mad? Is it because I can't sleep?

I don't think I've changed very much over the last ten yea⁣ I still want someone to cuddle me all night long.

I've tried comforting myself, to help me to go to sleep, but⁣ doesn't work anymore. It's like that part of me is all dried up.

The real love of my life (I won't write their name; it still hu⁣ too much) gave me a postcard. It's precious to me, and I⁣ propped it up, so that it's the first thing I see when I wake ⁣ It's of Roy Lichtenstein's painting *Good Morning, Darling!* ⁣ so silly; the blonde girl, lying on her side, with her eyes wi⁣ open, looking at a photo in a frame. I imagine it's me, with ⁣ love behind me. We had comforted each other in the night, a⁣ fallen fast asleep. My love has just woken me up, because th⁣ can't bear me to be asleep any longer. And it's them who ⁣ saying those lovely words.

That's all I want. If I could just have that person behind n⁣ holding me tight all night long, then this nasty little carav⁣ would be a cosy love-nest, and I'd be as warm as toast, a⁣ sleeping like an angel.

Muriel would have understood that.

When I read what I wrote about Muriel, it makes me want ⁣ cry. But I'm not going to cry anymore. You mustn't cry he⁣ because it's a sign of weakness.

I was covered in mud and soaking wet, but I decided ⁣ hitch-hike into town. I had a funny feeling that the couple w⁣ gave me a lift knew who I was. I supposed that they were H⁣ friends. I found a café and ate some chips. The man in the ca⁣ looked at me strangely. I was filthy, after all. Then I went to t⁣

378

ema, just to keep warm, and watched *All the President's Men.* fell asleep almost straight away. It was dark when I left the ema. I walked to the outside of town and hitched back to the lage. When I got back to my caravan, someone had locked the or.

Lightning Source UK Ltd.
Milton Keynes UK
UKHW010831170821
388988UK00002B/98